"MINE EYES HAVE S

It started off with a deep bass, the men picking up the words, their voices echoing across the plains. Ramrods clattered in fouled muskets, cartridges were run home, pieces were raised, bayonets poised.

He clicked open his carbine, sliding a last round in, and cocked the hammer.

The breeze was blowing fair and clear, the standards fluttered in the wind.

There seemed to be a far-off place now. It wasn't here. No, it was Antietam again. The young terrified officer standing there, looking like a lost boy. He had watched him grow, grow to lead a regiment, an army, an entire world.

The son he never had, the son in fact that he now did have. That was enough to leave behind.

"He has loosed the fateful lightning . . ."

"God keep you, son."

The nargas sounded. . . .

TERRIBLE SWIFT SWORD

William R. Forstchen

A ROC BOOK

ROC
Published by the Penguin Group
Penguin Books USA Inc., 375 Hudson Street,
New York, New York 10014, U.S.A.
Penguin Books Ltd, 27 Wrights Lane,
London W8 5TZ, England
Penguin Books Australia Ltd, Ringwood,
Victoria, Australia
Penguin Books Canada Ltd, 10 Alcorn Avenue,
Toronto, Ontario, Canada M4V 3B2
Penguin Books (N.Z.) Ltd, 182–190 Wairau Road,
Auckland 10, New Zealand

Penguin Books Ltd, Registered Offices:
Harmondsworth, Middlesex, England

First published by Roc, an imprint of New American Library, a division of
Penguin Books USA Inc.

First Printing, February, 1992
10 9 8 7 6 5 4 3 2 1

 Roc is a trademark of New American Library,
a division of Penguin Books USA Inc.

Printed in the United States of America

For Eleanor Wood. It's wonderful to have the best agent in the business; it's even better when that agent is also a close and trusted friend.

For Joel Rosenberg, who has always been there as an adviser for so many tough questions both personal and professional.

And finally, for L. Sprague and Catherine de Camp, who inspired me so many years ago with their wondrous tales and more recently with their friendship, which I shall always cherish.

ACKNOWLEDGMENTS

A special thanks goes to Professor Dennis Showalter, who helped with many an obscure and difficult question regarding logistics. A general acknowlegment should go out as well to my professors and fellow graduate students with the history department at Purdue for their advice and encouragement. Finally, a long overdue acknowledgment to Dean Miller for all those lunchtime conversations that wove together the world of academia with the universe of science fiction and fantasy.

Prologue

"Ship oars."

Somehow it had all gone too easily this time. He waited expectantly, sniffing the air, as if one could actually catch the scent of the Merki on the wind. The air was damp with the sea. Coiling vapors rose around him in the darkness, the only sound the gentle lapping of the waves on the rocky shore.

Where were the cloud-flyers, and the patrolling galleys dogging their flanks?

It just wasn't right, and yet he was close, too close now to turn back.

Hamilcar Baca, exiled leader of the Cartha, leaned against the prow of his galley, nervously stroking his oily black beard, intently watching the darkness to the west.

"There it is," a rower whispered, pointing to the flash of light winking in the gloom. It disappeared, then flashed twice more.

"That's it," Hamilcar whispered. He nodded to the signalman beside him who, facing aft, unsheathed his lantern, flashing the all-clear to the flotilla of ships a league further out to sea.

"Take us in," Hamilcar whispered, feeling somewhat foolish for speaking softly.

If Merki were waiting, he thought, they would

know we are here, loud voices or not. He looked up at the double moons, one rising in the east, the other fat and gibbous on the western horizon. The sea was a crisscross of shadows highlighting the ships, which drifted ghostlike through the patches of fog.

The rowers dropped their blades, the muffled oars dipping into the light chop of the Inland Sea. The late-night mist swirled and eddied, glowing dimly with the moonlight and the reflected lights of the city of Cartha, half a dozen miles to the south. The fishing village ahead was dark, quiet.

It would be the largest rescue attempted so far, and the one most important to his heart. It was strange to come back to his own shore, a fugitive, slipping in and out to rescue a lucky few from the Merki pits.

Two years ago he had been king. To be certain, he knew the Merki were coming, but what concern was that in the end, for as a noble he and all those close to him were exempt. Certainly he had harbored dreams of rebellion—who hadn't?—especially when word came of the Yankees' decision to fight the Tugars. How he had coveted the few weapons they offered in trade, gazing upon them in the night, and wishing that somehow he could forge such things as well and cast the Merki out!

He shook his head sadly with the memory. Yet I sold my soul again he reflected, when the Namer of Time had arrived at the gates, bearing a warning not to resist.

He cursed the uncaringness of Baalk, who had blinded him thus, and in the end led him to this destruction. I became their tool, he thought bitterly, and in my cowardice lost everything. And now I skulk through the night, hoping against hope to save a precious few.

To his amazement Keane had stood by his promise, keeping none of them as prisoners, and offering a safe haven for any who would fight the Merki.

It was an offer he'd had to take. When the *Oqunquit* had gone down he had hesitated for a moment between swimming to the west bank and the Merki lines, or swimming to the east and capture. He had thanked Baalk a thousand times that he had gone east, for the Merki would surely have sent him to the pits for the defeat they had suffered.

Twice in the last forty days he had run down the Inland Sea, the first time leading six ships, which had brought back nearly five hundred refugees. The second time, with twelve ships, they had saved a thousand, but the damned cloud-flyers of the Merki had found them and sunk two of the galleys on the way back.

Yet in coming back both times he had proven something—that he was committed to the alliance—and now Keane had given him forty galleys and two gunboats to offer some form of protection. There was even a regiment of Suzdalian infantry with him, acting as rowers, but also armed with muskets, with four-pound guns mounted on swivels for use against the cloud-flyers. If Andrew had offered such an arrangement on the first trip he would have felt they were along as a guarantee of his return; now he saw it as the offer that it was, armed protection to help him get the families of some of his men out of Cartha.

They had not seen the cloud-flyers all the way down—the cold winds of autumn had most likely kept them in their sheds—and he could only pray that this time they would escape unscathed.

Two lanterns appeared on the shoreline, marking the area between which the galleys could safely approach and land. His hands felt damp, sweaty.

The feel of a musket was still unusual, the wood hard and ungiving compared to the leather-wrapped hilt of his blade. But a musket could kill a Merki at a hundred paces, a sword could not.

"Twelve feet."

Hamilcar looked over at the leadsman, and waited.

"Ten feet, eight feet."

The beach was visible at last, marked by a thin ripple of white from the low curling waves washing in from the sea.

"Up oars."

The boat lifted slightly, racing in on curling wave, scrapping over the gravelly beach.

Leaping over the side, musket held high over his head, Hamilcar waded in, men pushing ahead of him with weapons raised. It could still be a trap. All they needed was for one person to find out and to sell the information to the Merki in return for an exemption.

A low cry rose up from the beach, and he tensed. A woman appeared, running into the water, carrying a child under either arm. More and yet more appeared, and within seconds wild shouts of joy were shattering the darkness as hundreds swarmed down to the single boat.

"Hamilcar?"

The voice drifted down from the beach.

"Over here!"

A shadowy form emerged out of the darkness. A lantern was unhooded, shining into his eyes and blinding him.

"Thank Baalk!" the man cried, and in obeisance went down to his knees in the surf.

Hamilcar smiled as he pulled Elazar, his oldest friend from childhood, back to his feet. Elazar had been raised beside him from infancy—they had even been born on the same day. It was through him as well that he had learned discipline. For his little crimes of childhood it was Elazar that had been beaten, since it was forbidden to strike one of the royal line. He had learned forbearance soon enough: Actions that he would have risked if the punishment were to be his alone he had never dreamed of doing out of fear for his friend.

"Elazar, just what in the name of Baalk and all the gods is going on here?" Hamilcar roared, looking in amazement at the mass confusion of the mob that was pouring out of the village and into the surf.

"It got out of control!" the man cried, tugging at his graying beard, his eyes rolling in fear. "Word spread through the city of your coming back; thousands of people have been pouring into the countryside. It seems like the Merki are taking everyone for the pits. Tens of thousands of others are being driven to make yet more weapons of war. There is talk they will invade the Rus lands come the spring, and they are preparing."

"Damn all of it," Hamilcar growled. This time it really was out of control. Nearly twelve thousand of his men had been captured in the war against the Rus and Roum. Nearly all had elected to take Keane's offer of sanctuary. He had promised to get as many families as possible out from under the Merki rule. Several hundred men had volunteered to slip back into Cartha to round people up and get them down to the coast. The Inland Sea had turned into a battleground as a result. Individual ships foraying out, hitting the coast at nightfall and running back towards Suzdal the following morning burdened down with refugees.

Yet a slow but steady toll was being exacted as well. The Merki air machines would come floating in on the still air of dawn. If a ship was sighted by them it was as good as dead.

"If this many people found out, the Merki must know as well," Hamilcar said, looking nervously at the shouting crowd, which was now pouring down to the beach.

"We were smuggling people up here as planned," Elazar replied, "and then this afternoon it started—hundreds of people coming out of Cartha."

"The Merki?"

"No sign of them. But they are coming." And he nodded to a man standing behind him.

Hamilcar turned his attention to what appeared to be a Rus standing expectantly behind Elazar, the man looking vaguely familiar. His once blond hair had gone to streaks of gray. He was lean of build, obviously inured to harshness, yet his dress was not of a peasant but was made of rich cloth, the tunic even trimmed with threads of gold. The cut was vaguely like that of the traditional Rus tunic and crosshatched leggings, but the tunic was slit up either side to make it more comfortable for riding.

"Rus?" Hamilcar asked warily.

"Once, but long ago, a full circling gone," the man replied in the tongue of the Merki, the words sounding strange, guttural, and vaguely obscene coming from the lips of a human.

"A pet of the Merki shield-bearer Tamuka," Elazar said coldly. "He came here shortly before you arrived, saying that the Merki were coming."

"Before Shagara disappears," the Rus stated, nodding towards the gibbous moon to the west, "they will be here."

"Why are you telling us this?"

"I wish to return to my people. In exchange I brought you the warning of the Merki closing in, and some additional information as well."

"What information?" Hamilcar asked, looking over at Elazar.

"He wouldn't tell me," Elazar replied, looking at the Rus with contempt.

"I left him for you to decide," Elazar whispered in Carthinian. "Never trust one who had been with them for a circling as a pet—they will eat the flesh of their own people to survive. Most likely this bastard's eaten the leavings of the pits, the flesh of his own race. I heard they force them to do that."

Hamilcar looked at the Rus closely. The man stood before him, calmly staring straight back, his blue eyes wide. There was no fear.

"What information do you have, then?"

The Rus smiled.

"The Merki and the Bantag Qar Qarths will meet at the next moon feast to discuss peace. I know the details of what will be offered, and when they will attack, but will reveal that only to the one called Keane, after I am safely returned."

"Damn them all!" Hamilcar hissed, and he looked coldly at the pet.

"Well, did you eat flesh?" Hamilcar asked, clumsily forming the Merki words.

"I survived," the Rus replied, looking straight ahead as if offering no apology.

Hamilcar grunted with disdain.

"Your name."

"Yuri Yaroslavich, goldsmith of Suzdal." This time he spoke in Cartha, looking over at Elazar as if to indicate he had understood every word spoken.

The man said the words proudly, his Suzdalian accent returning in a clear tone.

"Go to the boat," Hamilcar said, his lips curling in disgust. "I'll take you back for your own people to judge."

The man bowed slightly, and headed into the water.

"He's too oily," Elazar said, loud enough for Yuri

to hear. The man ignored his words and kept on going into the surf. "Why would he leave the security of being a pet to throw in with us?"

"Patriotism," Hamilcar growled cynically.

"Unlikely. Cut his throat and throw him overboard. Would you trust someone who had eaten human flesh? I'd cut his heart out and jam it down his throat to choke on. It's what we've always done to pets who try to hide with us. They are únclean."

He looked over to where Yuri was pushing his way aboard Hamilcar's ship and spat on the ground.

"And you were the one with the soft heart."

"After what I've seen," Elazar whispered, "my heart is of stone."

"My family?"

Elazar nodded in the direction of a fishing shack. Pushing his way through the crowd, Hamilcar ran up the beach, while shouting for his staff to signal the other boats in.

He felt as if he were running against the tide, the swarm of people streaming down to the beach slowing his advance to a maddening crawl. Cursing and shoving, he edged his way through the mob.

"Drasila!"

The door of the shack was open, several of his old soldiers who had snuck back in to Cartha weeks before standing in front of the shack as guards. At his approach they bowed low and stepped back.

She seemed almost to be an illusion. When he had left for the campaign against the Roum and Rus, he had felt that somehow he would never see her again. Pushing his way through, he reached the door as she flung herself into his arms.

"I never dreamed of seeing you again!" she sobbed, pressing herself tightly against his breast. He let his musket drop to the ground.

He felt a tugging at his sleeve and, reaching down,

he swept Azruel up into his arms. The little boy squealed with delight, pulling at his father's beard and snuggling up against his broad chest.

"They said you were dead, but I didn't believe them!" Drasila whispered, her voice choking with tears.

"How did you escape?" Hamilcar asked, even as he anxiously looked back at the clamoring mob sweeping behind him toward the beach.

"It was Elazar. The day word came of the defeat he managed to sneak us out of the palace and into hiding. We just missed you the last time you were here. We almost didn't get out this time. The Merki have started the Choosing."

So the bastards were going to feed off Cartha flesh anyhow. He had expected it all along: The exemption for everyone he knew was conditional on defeating the Rus.

In a way he should be cursing Keane, Marcus, all of them, for if only they had submitted and been beaten none of this would now be happening. And yet he could not, for as Keane had said to him, if the situation had been reversed would he not have fought as well? The only real enemy was the Merki.

"My lord, we best get moving."

Hamilcar looked back at Elazar, who stood anxiously behind him.

"It got completely out of control this time—there were thousands of people on the road here. The Merki have to know."

Hamilcar nodded, and with Arzeul still in his arms he bent over, picking up his musket. With Drisila clinging to his side he started to press his way back through the crowd. He could sense a rising edge of panic to the mob.

"How many boats did you bring?" Elazar asked, keeping his voice low.

"Forty-one."

"It's not enough."

"I can see that," Hamilcar replied sharply. He tried to push his way through the crowd but saw that it was useless. Rank held no advantages here in the dark, as thousands pushed into the water, struggling to reach the boats that were now drifting in out of the darkness.

As each ship came in it was surrounded, people clinging to the sides, jamming up against the oars, threatening in more than one case to simply roll the galley over.

And then above the clamor of the mob he heard the sound which he dreaded the most, the high clarion call of a Merki nargas, war trumpet of the Horde.

A momentary hush came over the crowd, as if disbelieving that death had suddenly called out its warning.

The nargas sounded again, echoing across the beach, counterpointed by dozens more, sounding their call in a vast ring about the village.

"The Merki!" It was a shriek of terror, picked up in an instant by thousands of voices.

Helpless, Hamilcar felt as if he would be borne under by the crush, as by the thousands the panic-stricken crowd surged down to the water.

A ripple of explosions flashed in a vast ring. Seconds later the solid shot and exploding shell smashed into the mob, foaming the water and cutting bloody furrows through the crowds.

"Hamilcar!"

His ship was so maddeningly close, with Githra, the ship's captain, standing atop the prow, cupping his hands and screaming for his leader. The ship was less than a score of paces away, yet hundreds were packed between him and safety.

"Hang on to me!" Hamilcar screamed, as he felt Drisila's hand slipping from his. He tried to turn back to her. She looked at him, eyes wide with panic, and as if in a nightmare he felt his grasp upon her slip away.

"Save Azreul!" she screamed. An obese woman pushed between them, desperate to claw her way through. With his now free hand Hamilcar struck her, trying to push her quivering form aside. Her eyes mad with fear she clawed back, trying to fight past him to the water.

"Drisila!"

The mob surged, picking Hamilcar off his feet. The fat woman fell, shrieking in anguish. More and yet more tripped over her body, climbing over her and kicking her into the gravel.

Drisila was gone.

"Mama!" Azreul shrieked, trying to claw his way out of Hamilcar's arms. Hamilcar clutched the boy tightly, raising the child above the crush while Azreul wailed for her mother.

Above the mad confusion the nargas continued to cry out. The Merki artillery lifted its range, bursting shells over the water in their eagerness to cripple the ships, as if the people upon the beach were no longer worth the effort.

A ripple of shots snapped out from the ships—the Suzdalian musketmen firing over the heads of the crowd in a desperate bid to hold them back.

"Hamilcar!"

Githra was looking straight at him.

"We must get to the boat!" Elazar shouted, trying to push him forward.

"Drisila!" he roared, trying to fight his way back up the beach.

"My lord, get Azreul to the boat!" Elazar shouted. The survival of his only living child suddenly forced out all other thoughts. He turned aside, pushing back toward the ship, clawing his way through the mob. A contingent of sailors were over the side of the ship, waving their swords, trying to keep the crowd back, the water already pink from their efforts.

A shell detonated almost directly over the ship, snapping with a glowing brilliance, and as if by some divine guidance its breath cleared an opening in the crowd, as bodies dropped into the surf. Hamilcar leaped forward, holding Azreul over his head with both hands, the child screaming with terror.

The ring of sailors stepped past him and he held the child up to the side of the ship, Githra reaching down and sweeping the boy up on board. There was a dull snap of sound and, stunned, Hamilcar looked at the quivering arrow buried in the side of the ship. An instant later a sheet of feathered death rained down, rattling against the ship and striking dozens. Men tumbled back into the vessel, others over the railing and into the mob.

"Get on board!" Githra shouted.

Hamilcar turned away.

"Drisila!"

From the corner of his eye he saw the flat of Elazar's blade coming down.

"No!"

The blow slammed him up against the side of the ship.

"Get him aboard!" Elazar screamed.

Stunned, he struggled weakly, as he was half pushed and half dragged into the ship. A continual hail of arrows swept down, the barbed points acting as prods, driving the mob into an hysterical frenzy.

"Back oars!"

He tried to regain his feet, but stronger hands forced him back down, a coil of rope going over his shoulders. The world was a dizzy confusion, a blurred memory of a wide-eyed man hanging to the side of the ship, swordsmen screaming with an inner torment as they struck down their own people, wild shouts of panic, a severed hand clinging to the railing, and then ever so slowly the ship backing away, rolling low on the water.

And the nargas continued to cry out. Coming up to his knees he felt Elazar holding him tight, preventing him from standing. Several ships were trapped on the beach, one of them on its side, the oil from a lantern having spilled out, the bow of the vessel engulfed in flames that illuminated the nightmare. The beach seemed to be a shifting, writhing mass, as if it were a single living creature twisting and rolling in agony.

The closing ring of Merki was visible, dim shadow-figures towering in the streets of the village. He could imagine their gloating joy. After all, they were harvesting cattle, runaway cattle who would all be condemned to the slaughter pits. Those who had died tonight would be on their tables by morning.

Drisila . . .

Bristling with rage, he looked back at Elazar, who said nothing, his bearlike arms holding him down.

The rowers struggled at the oars, the men toward the bow powerless to move what with each blade jammed by desperate hangers-on. The cries of the thousands left behind rolled across the ocean like the mournful night-dream voices of the damned. A deeper boom snapped across the waters, the thunder of the heavy shot from the supporting ironclads rippling across the water. It was an impotent gesture.

Hundreds of flaming arrows arced through the air, adding their light to the madness. Merki cannon that had pushed down to either side of the village churned the water with shot. In the shadows he saw a galley riding low, and then ever so slowly roll over on its side, going down at the bow. Suzdalian rowers and the refugees on board spilled out into the surf.

Another galley appeared out of the darkness, swinging in close. Maybe Drisila is on another ship, he thought, even as the coldness within screamed at him not to dream. Few of the ships had even touched land, their captains holding back from the crush. As far as he could tell, his was the only one to get back out.

"Hamilcar?" The cry came from the closing ship.

"He's safe!" Githra shouted. "We run back for Suzdal!"

He wanted to protest, yet he knew that his voice would break with sobs, and so said nothing.

Azreul came up to his side, whimpering, and he gathered the child into his arms, crushing him tight against his chest as if he could blot out the memory his five-year-old mind would forever carry.

"Where's Mama?"

"She'll be with us later," he choked, looking over at Elazar, as if his old friend could somehow still work a miracle.

"She's a smart girl, young and strong," Elazar whispered. "I know her, she wouldn't stay with the mob. She'll most likely swim out and come back in to shore when it's safe."

Already the cries on the beach were growing more distant. Knowing what he would have to order, he looked up at Githra.

"We got a late start in, as is," Githra said softly. "We have to run—their air machines will be up before dawn, and there'll be no wind this morning. If we order any ships to swing back in they'll get mobbed by the people in the water, and the Merki guns will tear them apart."

Numbly he nodded, unable to voice the commands.

If peace was brewing between the Merki and Bantag he had to get word back to Keane, for this would change the balance against them even further. He saw Yuri sitting in the middle of the ship, eyes closed as if lost in serene thought. He was tempted to run the bastard through, so he looked away.

There is no hope left here, he realized, his heart tight, a bitter bile burning his throat.

When all of this was done the Cartha people would be but a memory, for whether the Merki won or lost would not matter for the Cartha people— they would be used in the war until all were dead. Even if he went back to them, his death offering would not change a thing. Keane was right in that: This would be a war to the finish between the Hordes and all humans on this world. But why did it have to be here? Could it not all have waited until after the Hordes had passed, letting some other people pay the price?

"Take us home," Hamilcar whispered.

Githra looked at him curiously, the single word sounding so strange. Hamilcar looked up at the man.

"To Suzdal."

Tayang, Qar Qarth of the Bantag Horde, leaned back upon his throne and smiled.

"There has not been a moment such as this since the forgotten grandsires of our grandsires met two hundred circlings ago, to divide between us our paths across the everlasting steppe."

Muzta, Qar Qarth of the tattered remnants of the Tugar Horde, sat in silence, looking over at the third Qar Qarth here this morning.

Jubadi gazed upon Tayang with barely concealed hatred.

"Yet you and I met less than two years before,"

Jubadi finally replied, as if each word tasted of bitterness, "and you violated the blood pledge of protection and tried to kill me."

"You knew what you were doing," Tayang retorted. "Your Vushka Umen slaughtered ten thousand of mine in reply. How do I know that they will not strike even now?"

"Each of us has an umen here," Muzta interjected. "Ten thousand of our finest. A circle, for three days' ride in every direction on this border between Merki and Bantag lands, is cleared of all living things— Tugar, Merki, Bantag, and even cattle. No one will kill another today."

Muzta looked from one to the other. Both had approached him, offering threats and promises, if only he would order his umen to swing over and aid in the destruction of the other.

He had been tempted, to be sure, but he knew as well what it would mean for all of them in the end. Even Jubadi realized that, or at least his shield-bearer Hulagar did. A curious idea, he thought. As a Tugar he had his advisor, old Qubata, but not even Qubata could exert such influence the way a shield-bearer of the Merki could. It was said that a shield-bearer strove not only to protect the life of his lord, but that if need be, for the sake of the clan, and if the Qar Qarth proved to be unworthy, he would *take it* as well.

Such a system seemed to be madness to him. What was a Qar Qarth, if not the ruler of all his clans with no one above him? For was it not said, "As Bugglaah ruled the choosing of death, so shall a Qar Qarth rule all who are living?"

Hulagar caught his look and held it for a brief moment. What did the shield-bearer think of all of this? But the look was inscrutable, as if he were gazing through him.

"And though you are the weakest," Tayang said quietly, breaking Muzta's thoughts, "here you are the strongest."

Muzta bristled inwardly. Yet again, another Qar Qarth was taunting him.

"If either of you had faced the Yankee weapons first, then it would be you who saw his horde destroyed, and now sat before the other two as a pauper."

Tayang laughed softly but Muzta could sense the wariness, for what he had said was in a way true. He had nothing left to lose. What could be taken from him now was nothing, therefore Jubadi and Tayang would never join together at this kurata, the meeting of Qarths, to slaughter him. For a brief moment it was he who held power over the other two. Yet if he should betray one or the other, their hordes were still numberless and would hunt what was left of his nearly defenseless people across the entire world until vengeance had been taken. The umen with him was barely all he could scrape together for this meeting—nearly all the rest were buried before the human city of Suzdal.

Jubadi held up his hand to Tayang, as if in warning.

"Don't laugh so loudly," he said softly. "Too many of our dead will not take your mirth so lightly."

"Tugar dead, Merki dead, what are they to me?" Tayang replied, but Muzta could see the quick upward glance of his eyes to the peak of the yurt, where malevolent spirits were said to enter through the smoke-hole.

"It will be Bantag dead soon enough," Jubadi said, "if we do not reach agreement."

"And that is a concern of yours?" Tayang retorted.

"It is a concern for all of us—Merki, Tugar, and Bantag."

Startled, Muzta looked over at Jubadi's entourage of clan Qarths, who sat beneath him in a circle around his throne of cattle bones. A Merki came to his feet, looking up at his Qar Qarth. He was slender of build, hair a shaggy brown, eyes dark and full of cold purpose and knowledge, more like those of a serpent than of a hunting tiger. His armor was simple: chain mail of black steel, the coverlet over it adorned with a white circle on black silk, trousers of browned leather faced with metal strips to protect his thighs. Over his shoulder was the round, over-sized bronze shield of his office.

There seemed to be a look of surprise in Jubadi's eyes, that one who served beneath him would dare to interject his thoughts at this moment when three Qar Qarths had come together. Jubadi looked down at him, as if weighing a decision, then nodded almost inperceptibly. The Merki stepped forward.

"I am Tamuka, shield-bearer of the royal heir, the Zan Qarth Vuka."

He had seen this one before. He could only hope that he had the strength to control Vuka, for if ever there was one who was not fit to be a Qar Qarth it was he. Muzta could see the wary look in Vuka's eyes as Tamuka strode to the middle of the yurt.

"Is your tongue so weak it cannot speak for itself?" Tayang asked, looking over at Jubadi.

"Perhaps I can form the words best for all of us," Tamuka said. "I am not Qar Qarth, concerned with my power and that of my horde. The three of you are guided by your *ka*, the spirit of the warrior, as is fitting for those who rule. But all of you here know that the shield-bearers of the Merki, those born to the White Clan, are guided by the *tu*, the *ka-tu* shaped by the inner spirit."

"I have heard of this," Tayang said, his voice betraying a hint of curiosity.

"Though to allow such as you to have influence would never happen with the Bantag," he added quickly, looking over at Muzta. "Nor the Tugar Hordes as well, I would assume."

"And perhaps if I had listened more to one whom I suspect was guided by the *ka-tu*," Muzta replied, "all that has happened would not have been, and it would be the cracked bones of the Yankees that bleached in the sun rather than that of the Tugars."

There were certain moments in one's life, he had come to learn, which are relived a thousand times; and each reliving is a torment, filled with a desire to somehow go back into time, to change an action or even a single word and thus prevent all the anguish that had come since. Two such moments had come in his life. One from so long ago, a moment in his inner life with a consort long gone, the other as Qar Qarth. Qubata had stood before him, counseling against a headlong attack against the Yankees; and he had ignored him. And Qubata was dead, as were nearly all who had charged into the battle that day.

"Listen to him," Muzta said. His voice carried such force that Tamuka turned, a glimmer of acknowledgment in his eyes.

Tayang looked over at Muzta and then let his gaze drop on Tamuka.

"Speak then, one who does not live by the *ka* spirit of the warrior."

Tamuka gave a nod of acknowledgment, ignoring the insult of not being called a warrior, and stepped into the ceremonial circle of gold cloth in the center of the yurt, the marking place where truth must be spoken.

"All of us have fought," he began softly, turning to look at the three gatherings of Qarths and Qar Qarths. "Bantag against Merki, Merki against Tugar, and before the great kurata which divided the world,

Tugar has fought even against the Bantag. I could recite the honors we have all gained, the grievances we all bear, the deaths across two hundred circlings we wish to revenge.

"These are the things which drive our spirits, which give us the thrill of the charge, the singing of the *ka* within as we ride against each other, chanting our songs of battle. It is the fullness of what it means to be one of the Hordes."

He smiled for a moment, as if recalling a pleasant memory.

"It is what makes us alive, for without a foe, how else may one measure oneself and one's *ka?*" All nodded in agreement, murmuring to themselves about the intelligence of his words.

"And now, at least for this moment, it is all meaningless."

Tayang stirred uncomfortably, but remained silent.

"Cattle have been the source of life. They have come through the tunnels of light, the portals our ancestor gods built which once gave them the power to walk between the stars. The working of it is a mystery we do not understand, something we have lost. The tunnels of light seem now to be a thing of their own will, pulling all through who are near them, opening and closing at different times and bringing to Valennia many strange things.

"It was a good thing our ancestors made—at least in the past it was a good thing. It brought the cattle to this world, many of the plants which have taken root, the animals of the woods and steppe, and it brought us the horse which set us free to ride the world."

"Yes, that at least is good," Tayang mumbled, and the entourage of the three Qar Qarths nodded in agreement, as if they had somehow been responsible for what he had said.

"The horse has given us freedom, has enabled us to own all of Valennia, riding forever eastward toward the rising sun. We who were once few, living in the fastness of the Barkth Nom, the mountains that are the roof of the world, became masters of wherever our mounts could ride.

"The cattle we bent to our will, for as we grew in numbers and started our everlasting ride we found some of them already here. And then more came, and yet more. It seems that whatever world they come from beyond the stars they must breed like carrion flies, and thus spill out of the Tunnel into this world.

"We have seen that they are the same and yet different—some of white skin, others brown, yet others black, their tongues different, their customs different as well. Our grandsires in their wisdom learned to place them about the entire world. The cattle built their cities, which they love to hide within. They brought with them yet other beasts to eat, and planted the fields. Their numbers grew, far faster than our own. Yet we learned something else as well. We learned that their flesh is good, and we came to harvest them along with the food that they prepared for our coming. And most importantly of all, they freed us yet more from labor, which is beneath the dignity of those who are of the Horde.

"They freed us so we could do that which is most worthy of all who are of the Horde. They freed us from labor, from want of food, so that we could war against each other and thus gain honor."

He paused for a moment, and saw the self-satisfied nods of agreement.

"We are fools."

"You dare to say that before me?" Tayang roared, coming to his feet.

Tamuka looked about the yurt.

"All of us—Tugar, Bantag, and yes, my own Merki—are fools!" Tamuka shouted, turning and facing each group with his hand extended, pointing accusingly.

"Is your dog mad?" Tayang snarled. "Silence him, Jubadi, or I'll do it myself!"

"For the moment at least, he speaks with my voice," Jubadi replied.

Tayang shifted uncomfortably, looking over to Muzta for support.

"Let him continue," Muzta whispered.

Tamuka looked up at Tayang. The old Qar Qarth cursed softly and then finally nodded.

"I am not speaking now as Merki," Tamuka said, turning to face Jubadi and bowing with an air of apology. "I speak as one of all the Hordes."

Muzta looked at Jubadi with surprise. He saw a sharp look of disdain cross the features of the Zan Qarth Vuka, and just as quickly disappear.

There is tension there between the two, Muzta realized; more than tension, almost a hatred. Tamuka did not seem to notice. He closed his eyes and looked up, as if his gaze could somehow pierce the golden covers of the yurt and reach into the night beyond.

"There is a distant wind, a memory, a soft calling of what we once were," he whispered. "It is like turning back to one's own youth, to a dream of what was, and what can never be again. It is a chant unto the sky of evening, the breeze sighing through the high grass of summer, the musty smell of the earth in the spring. It is riding alone at night, the great wheel lighting one's path, the endless sea of the steppe rolling on forever before our gaze. To awake before dawn, and to ride up to a high place, and to raise your voice in praise as the sun lifts into the sky, its light flashing across the winter snows, the world turned crimson with flashing fire . . .

"That is what we are."

His voice was low, filling the tent. It was as if he chanted the words, and Muzta closed his eyes and flowed away with the words, sharing the memories.

"It is the moment of the *ka*, when your gaze lifts up and behold, you are one of ten thousand, riding stirrup-to-stirrup, a vast line sweeping across the steppe, the war cries rising to the heavens, the thundering of the hooves; living or dying does not matter, all that exists is to be there in that moment. And you know that if you should live for five circlings, a hundred years, you will never forget the thrill of that charge.

"That is what we are."

He paused, and all were silent.

"These are the moments we have all shared, it is part of all of us, it is why I can say I speak not as Merki, but as one of all the Hordes.

"The cattle will destroy all of that forever. It shall never be the same again."

There was a grumbled response to his words. Muzta felt uncomfortable—he had been lulled by the chant, which now had changed to a cold voice of warning.

"They have given us the freedom to be such, and now they have the power to take it away.

"The cattle have changed. They have learned not only to think like us, but beyond us. They will destroy us and this world shall be theirs, if we do not change as well. We must end, at least for the moment, what we are, if we wish to save ourselves. Though you see it without honor, it is the cattle of the north who are the true enemies, what we do between each other is for now without meaning. If we do not settle this issue, in the end it will destroy us, and they, the lowly cattle, will inherit the world."

There was a low murmuring from the dozens of Qarths sitting beneath the feet of their leaders. Some had grasped the hidden meaning of his words, but only a few; the rest gazed at him in confusion or disdain.

"For a moment, I found I could listen," Tayang growled. "Now your words are like the buzzing of flies on offal."

Tamuka waited for the angry retorts to die away.

"My lord Jubadi is even now building weapons of war. Or should I say, we have cattle who are building them for us."

"Like your last folly, which they destroyed!" Tayang laughed.

"I was there and you were not, Tayang Qar Qarth," Tamuka retorted. "I saw what you have only heard. I know what you have not even yet to dream in your darkest nightmares.

"I saw cattle who fought with a discipline that rivals our own. I saw cattle who charged in to battle, shouting their hatred of us, willing to die, dreaming but to take but one of us with them.

"I remember a time when one of us alone could have ridden into a city of ten thousand of them and they would have submitted, baring their throats. Now I tell you that in the north they wait with their cannons, guns, ships, swords, their bare hands. If we kill ten of them to our one, still we will lose in the end. Because if their infection of hatred spreads east, south even unto the realm of the Bantag, you too will see the fields littered with the corpses of your warriors. For the seed of the cattle is strong, and they spread about our world by the millions.

"You say there is no honor to fight them. Listen well to my words, Tayang, all of you. Honor or not, you will be just as dead from their bullets, and they will laugh as they shovel you into the ground."

He lowered his voice.

"They will laugh as they shovel our entire race into its final grave."

Tayang shifted uncomfortably, taken aback and yet unable to respond, for he could see the look in the eyes of his Qarths, his clan leaders, who sat in silence, their attention fixed on Tamuka.

"Fighting these new cattle is like wrestling with the Ugrasla, the great serpents of your own forests. You grasp them, you think you have held them down, and then they slip through your hands and coil about you.

"We built the weapons of the cattle, or should I say that we had cattle build them for us, and it took us a year. The Yankees then built weapons as good in one tenth that time, and weapons that were even better.

"We build a weapon that can shoot flame and lead, killing a man at fifty paces, like the one you saw before this meeting. They then build one that can kill at two hundred, simply by changing the shape of the bullet and cutting grooves inside the barrel.

"We must learn to build these things on our own, with our own hands."

"You call for those with the *ka* to labor?" Tayang snarled. "Perhaps this thing inside you called the *tu* would be a spirit more willing to do such demeaning labor, but not a warrior."

And those in the yurt, all except Muzta, nodded in agreement with Tayang's words.

"We must free ourselves of cattle if we wish to remain free at all," Tamuka replied defiantly.

"To be slaves digging in the mountains for the black iron, to pour out our sweat by the forges, that is not freedom, that is the life of cattle," Jubadi said quietly, though obviously disturbed by Tamuka's words.

Tamuka paused, as if searching for the right words.

"We live without changing, they live in order to change."

"And you are telling us to change," Muzta said, filling the silence.

Tamuka nodded in reply.

"If we wish to survive we must make change a part of our lives, casting aside what was for what is."

"Forever?" Muzta asked.

"At least for now, at least until this thing is settled, but even then it will never be the same again."

"And why not?" Tayang interjected. "I still do not see it as a concern even for us."

"I laughed when I first heard of the discomfort of the Tugars," Jubadi said. "My laughter is silent now."

The Qarths of the Bantag Horde looked up to their lord, waiting for his reply.

"What is it that you want, then?" Tayang asked, "You who speak for the Qar Qarth of the Merki."

"Annihilate them all," Tamuka said coldly.

"Kill all the cattle?" Tayang replied in shock. "You are mad. They raise our food, they make all that we have. They fashion our clothes and armor, they forge our swords, fletch our arrows, and make our bows. They raise the grains, the lower forms of meat that we eat, and they are the noble food that fills our stomachs. If we follow your mad plan, then what are we to eat, Merki? Grass?"

"Do not slay them, and in twenty years, when we ride again to this region, it will be they who ensure that we will feed the grass."

Muzta sat back in silence. Until this moment he had thought that the problem that the Yankees had presented could be contained. That in the end, even if it took twenty years of riding yet again around the world, they would return and have their vengeance.

Yet what would they meet in twenty years? Tamuka now drew the picture in his mind with a clarity that he had once turned to Qubata for. He had seen the Yankee machine that moved upon the land while breathing smoke. He had thought it curious at the time. But with such a thing the Yankees could, in a day, cross a distance that would take a week by horse.

"This Yankee machine, this machine that moves on land . . ." Muzta said.

"They call it a 'train,' " Tamuka replied.

"Yes, a train. If we, all of us, continue our ride eastward, when we return in twenty years they will have built these machines to unite a hundred of their cities against us. That is why it is your concern as well, Tayang. Ignore it now, and when your son brings his horde back to this place, a cattle army as numberless as the stalks of grass upon the endless sea of green will be arrayed against you, their armies moving ten days of ride in one."

Tayang looked down from his throne at the one Muzta knew must be the heir.

"Then what do you want of us?" Tayang finally replied.

"Peace, so that the entire might of the Merki Horde can march against the Yankees in the spring."

Tayang laughed softly.

"And in return?"

"An end to their threat," Jubadi said forcefully.

Tayang laughed.

"Am I a fool? What of these new weapons? I have heard how Merki can even fly. What of that?"

"It is true," Jubadi said. "We can fly."

There was a murmur of disbelief from the clan Qarths surrounding Tayang.

"It is true," Muzta replied. "I have seen the sky-riders, machines made by the Merki that can fly."

"How?" Tayang asked, unable to contain his curiosity.

Tamuka looked back at Jubadi.

"One of the Yankee traitors knew the secret of making an invisible air that enables one to float."

"Wind from his backside, most likely," Tayang said, laughing coarsely.

Jubadi smiled.

"A deadly wind that explodes when fire touches it. It is trapped inside a vast tent sewn together into a bag, and when filled it floats away. Beneath the bag we took machines found in the barrows of ancestors from before the circling. The rotted wheels of the carts were removed, and blades that spin in the air were fashioned to push the floating tents of the light air from place to place."

"The burial carts that move without horses?" Tayang asked.

Jubadi nodded.

"You violated the graves of ancestors. It will be your curse," a voice from behind Tayang snarled.

Jubadi looked at the shaman, waiting for Tayang to discipline one who had not been invited to speak, but the Qar Qarth did nothing. Jubadi bristled at the insult.

"The curse has struck several," Tamuka interjected. "Their hair fell away, they vomited blood and died. But others have not been stricken, a sign that not all the ancestors are angered, that they are pleased that we use these things to break our common enemy."

Jubadi stared at the shaman, who made the gesture to ward away evil as he backed into the shadows.

"With these machines we may fly over the Rus, even to the Roum lands, to spy, to drop weapons that explode. Even now I make more of them and will not stop, for it is the one thing the Yankees have not forged."

"Yet . . ." Tamuka whispered softly, his voice not heard.

"The curse will be on you, not I," Tayang said, though it was obvious he was curious to see this strange wonder.

The shadows in the tent were growing darker, the red light streaming in from the western flap fading away. A high piercing call rose up from outside the yurt, the cry of the watchers, announcing the setting of the sun. All fell silent, the three Qar Qarths rising from their thrones to face west, the Qarths about their feet dropping to their knees in the same direction.

"O light of the world!" the watchers cried. "Journey now into the night lands of the everlasting sky. Bring unto our sires, and our sires' sires, the words of our praise. Shine thy face upon the land of the dead, and then return in thy glory yet again."

The last thin shaft of light shimmered on the horizon, spreading out into a broad band. There was a momentary flash of green and all cried aloud with joy, for it was a good sign, a portent of favor to all who saw it.

The green flash faded away, the voices of the three umens arrayed on the hills rising up in exaltation at the omen.

The three Qar Qarths turned away as the western flap was closed, and lit torches were brought into the yurt, pushing back the gloom. The circular brazier near the center, where Tamuka stood, was piled high with sweet-scented wood which filled the tent with its smoky perfume. Tamuka looked at it with pleasure. Those who rode the central steppes would go at times for months without seeing a wood fire, cooking with knotted grass, dried dung, or the branches of a thorny bush rich with an oil that caused an acrid, smoky flame.

Tayang, nodding with satisfaction as if he had somehow caused the omen, sat back down and looked over at Jubadi.

"You want peace, then?"

Jubadi nodded.

"You want me to give you peace, so you can take these cattle weapons, master them, and one day turn them against us."

Muzta could see the look of exasperation on Tamuka's face.

"Thinking like that will be the end of us all!" he shouted angrily. "It is the cattle who are the enemy. First it was the Rus, now the Roum, beyond them all the cattle throughout the world will hear of what has happened. Already the vermin who crawl before us, the wanderers, have spread the word of the rebellion a full season beyond our furthest outriders.

"There is only one answer left. Give the Merki peace, that they may turn their full strength against those led by the Yankees. If that is allowed, we shall slay them."

He hesitated for a moment, as if knowing the reaction to what he would say next.

"Then kill every last cattle upon this world. Cleanse ourselves of them. Only then can we return to what we were."

"Kill our own cattle!" Tayang roared, caught somewhere between rage and incredulous disbelief. "And who will feed us?"

"We will feed ourselves, as our grandsires did."

Tayang shook his head.

"And dig in the dirt! You are mad."

Muzta could see the looks of agreement on the faces of Tayang's followers.

"Shield-bearer, you no longer speak what I wish," Jubadi said quietly. "All I ask is peace to bring the Yankees to their knees, to make them again cattle or to slay them, nothing more."

"I speak as my *tu* demanded," Tamuka replied, not backing down.

"Then at least give Jubadi peace," Muzta interjected, before Jubadi and Tayang were diverted by Tamuka's words. "Let him exterminate all the cattle who have been infected by these new ways."

"And what of the weapons? You still have not answered that."

"When we defeated the Yor we destroyed their weapons," Jubadi said, "for our grandsires knew that the power of such things that could turn another to dust would end us all. We must do the same again. When they are defeated, we will destroy all vestiges of what they are."

Tamuka looked back at Jubadi.

"Cattle have come through the Tunnel since the beginning of time. They will continue. And what if they are even more dangerous than the Yankees?"

"That is not my concern for now," Jubadi replied sharply, the tone of his voice indicating that he would not tolerate such challenge from one who was the not his own shield-bearer, but merely one of his son's.

"The guarantees?" Tayang replied.

"Guarantees," Jubadi retorted, looking past Tamuka. "In the spring I wish to ride north with the new guns—forging, even as we speak, the new flying machines—and all my umens and end them once and for all. I will lose many warriors in this, but we have learned much. In the end we will defeat them. Perhaps I should be asking guarantees of you."

Tayang laughed and shook his head.

"What do I get for not striking you?"

"A third of all the guns we make this winter, and all the cattle of Cartha who know how to make such things once the cattle war is done," Muzta interjected, looking over at Jubadi. "Give him that."

"The Cartha are mine, the guns mine."

"There will be more than enough of the guns in the spring. Captured Rus, or even the Roum who have learned of these things, will replace whatever Cartha are traded away. When the Yankees are at last defeated, the two of you can agree then to destroy the weapons together, so that we may ride as we once did and fight with bow in hand."

The two Qarths looked at Muzta.

"Perhaps it is an idea to start with," Tayang said craftily.

"None of you have heard," Tamuka said, his voice filled with sadness.

The three Qar Qarths paused.

"Chances are we will defeat them, at least for now," Tamuka said, "but all of you still dream that the world will be as it was. You do not see that a war has started which will end only one of two ways. This world will either be a place of the Horde, or it will be of cattle, but never again will it be both. That is what the three of you should be speaking of today."

"My concern is to defeat the Yankees!" Jubadi roared. "Do you doubt that we can do that, shield-bearer?"

"No, my Qarth," Tamuka replied, "but just re-member this: They will try to change how things are done yet again. We will most likely bear them down, in a war that will bleed both of us white. We will fill our tables with their corpses, and even their leader Keane will be led before us. We shall make a scattering of bones of what were once their cities.

"It is just that we will never be the same afterwards. Remember that warning. The three of you will argue now for days, over whether it shall be three guns in ten, or four. Whether it shall be five hundred Cartha cattle or five thousand.

"We will leave here and none will trust the other. That is our greatest danger, not the cattle whom we will kill in the spring. Kill them all, my lords, kill every last one upon this world without mercy. Then we can enjoy the sport of killing each other again, and not before. If you do not do this, in the end it will be they who shall hunt us into the ground."

Without waiting to be dismissed Tamuka bowed low to the east and west, and with head held high, he walked out of the yurt.

There was a quiet stirring as each looked uncomfortably to the other. Muzta looked over at Jubadi. He could see the Qar Qarth of the Merki was disturbed, though whether it was in anger or agreement he could not tell.

"Did you say half of all guns?" Tayang said.

Muzta looked back and saw the smile lighting the features of the Qar Qarth of the Bantag.

Feigning indifference to Tayang's words, Muzta reached over to the tray by his side and took up a morsel of boiled cattle flesh and chewed slowly.

All was now clear to him: There would be a difficult path for the Tugars to weave between the three forces of Bantag, Merki, and cattle.

Tamuka was right at least in his prophecy of the war. Rivers of blood would flow come spring, as each maneuvered according to his own plan. Yet with the weapons being forged even now by the cattle slaves in Cartha, and with the new machines that could fly,

Jubadi would most likely win. The cattle were simply too few to stand against such strength.

Yet the trick was to survive. And as he ignored the haggling between the other two, a thin smile finally crossed his features.

"Bring him back in," Andrew said, without looking back at the door.

He opened up the stove and pushed another log into the fire. The first real chill of autumn was settling in, and outside a cold rain was slashing against the windowpane. The grandfather clock in the corner ticked softly, and he found a sense of threat in the sound: each second a click, measuring off the precious time. It was funny, he thought, how a clock sounds as it ticks away. The sound is barely noticed until one is alone. It is a reminder of mortality, of time passing, slipping through one's fingers, its voice loud, remorseless, unstoppable.

He looked back out the window. It was dark, nearly two in the morning, Kathleen and the baby asleep upstairs, the house silent except for the creaking of the wood as a gust of wind swept by outside, and the ticking of the clock.

He looked back at the clock.

How long do we have? he wondered. They will not come with winter—they don't have the weapons, there isn't enough food to support a horde three times the size of the Tugars, and there was their war with the Bantag that delayed them. No, it will be in the spring, when the grass is up, that they will come.

He drew the imaginary lines in his mind, not even needing to look at the map. The Potomac River a hundred miles to the southwest—he smiled at the name. They were fixing such names to all the places of their new world, as if to make it feel like the lost home of fading memory.

Always fight an enemy outside your own territory if possible, but beyond that the Neiper could never be held for long. The Merki could move upstream through the woods, following the river as it turned east. They'd be on our flank, cutting in east of Vazima. Rough terrain there, too rough for a rail line. Flank us, and fall into Rus from behind, and then the finish. No. Last time all we had to hold was Suzdal, now we have all the Rus, the alliance, the rail line to Roum. We can't hole up again—Suzdal can't hold everyone, they would starve us out if we even attempted to try.

No, it had to be the Potomac, even though Hans was against it. Hold them out there, out on the edge of the steppe. Build a line like Bobbie Lee did at Petersburg: trenches, earthen bastions, traps, and entanglements. Make it so strong that they'll bleed white against it. And then hold out till they finally get sick of it and leave.

Yet why am I unsure? he wondered.

There was a soft knock on the door to the parlor. "Come."

He heard him walk in, but waited a moment before turning. He could hear the soft breathing of the man, and there was a momentary chill, as if a fetid air lingered about him, the smell of the pits.

"You know everyone, including my own people, would be happy to see you driven out—or even better, receive the punishment of the outcast."

"I offer no apologies." The voice was cool. Suzdalian in accent to be sure, with the broad rolling vowels, but tinged with the guttural pronunciation of someone used to the language of the Hordes.

Andrew turned and looked at the man.

"To eat the flesh of another human . . ." Andrew whispered.

"It was that or die," Yuri replied. "Any who are

pets are forced to do it—it is their way of forever separating us from our own kind. I wanted to live."

Andrew tried to imagine how he would react if caught thus. There was the Donner Party, the men of the *Essex* who had gone so far as to draw lots as to who would be clubbed and eaten, the son of the captain being one of the flesh offerings. For this is my body . . . Blasphemy! He pushed the thought away.

The haunted lives the survivors must have led, the breaking of the most forbidden of taboos: Eat not the flesh of your own kind.

"It is easy to say, to think, in the comfort of this room, that you would not," Yuri said, the slightest of smiles crossing his pale features. "And then you see it, the moon feast, the victims led in struggling, the shrieks of agony, the convulsions of the dying, and the taunts of the Merki, the golden spoons flashing in the torch light. The eyes of the tortured victims going dark. Then they look at you, and they thrust the platter beneath your eyes.

" 'Eat,' they taunt," and he whispered the words in Merki, " 'eat, or you shall be next.' "

He looked into Andrew's eyes.

"I wanted to live. . . ." He paused. "I couldn't stand the terror in the eyes of the moon offerings. I could not imagine my own skull being thus ripped open while I was still alive. I could not face the horror of the ending, my own skull open, the shaman pouring the golden flask . . ."

His voice faded away, the slightest of tremors passing through him.

"And so I ate. . . ."

Andrew said nothing. There was a perverse sort of fascination in listening to this. The cool horror of gazing into something obscene and yet not turning away, being compelled by the fascination of the forbidden, the grotesque. While his wife and child slept above him he listened, as if Lazarus had come back from the gates of Hell to speak.

"The second time it was not as hard, for after all, when one is already damned, one cannot be damned even further for one's iniquities. And finally, I didn't even notice what was upon the plate, it was a part of my existence in hell. I was one of them. After a time, I no longer cared."

"So why did you leave?" Andrew asked.

"One never forgets the whispering of the waters of home, the smell of one's hearth, the voices of one's people, the laughter of children when one was a child. Yankee, you must know that—I have heard tell of your Maine."

The word stabbed through him. *Maine. Home.* The streets of Brunswick, the tight Yankee drawl of his friends and neighbors, the lazy mornings teaching a class in springtime, when the world was alive with the scent of apple blossoms, the calling of the loons on a summer lake in the woods near Waterville (that was magic on moonlit nights), the waters of Merrymeeting Bay filled with the geese of autumn, the surf crashing on a rocky shore. It flooded back into his heart.

He nodded, lowering his head for a moment, his heart heavy, throat tight.

"Even if you drive me out, even if I am condemned and killed, still I will have seen Suzdal one more time, that is enough."

"If that was the only concern," Andrew replied, "I would not even be speaking to you now."

"I realize that," Yuri said, his voice soft and controlled. "You can't decide the rest of me, the truth or lies of what is locked in up here," and he pointed to his head.

Andrew nodded.

Yuri looked around the room with frank curiosity, an inquisitiveness that Andrew found interesting. He looked over at the clock, and then questioningly back at Andrew.

"A machine for the measuring of time."

"So much has changed," Yuri said. "Twenty-one years ago I left here, to go to Cartha and trade in foolish trinkets of gold. When I departed Ivor was not yet boyar, my wife was still young and not yet dead, my city . . ."

He shook his head and looked about the room.

"Not yet changed by all you had done."

"My entire life, because I thought of a mere profit to be gained by going south, was shipwrecked on the eastern coast, and there taken by the Merki as they rode out from Cartha. Now, twenty-one years later, I am back."

He sighed, as if realizing the folly of dreams.

"You know that we have no one who has ridden with the Merki for a full circling," Andrew said, carefully watching Yuri's reactions, "no one who has seen them as you have."

"They usually kill their pets at three moments," Yuri replied, his voice distant. "All but the most cherished are destroyed when the sacred mountains of Barkth Nom are first sighted. Next, if there is the death of a Qar Qarth."

"And all but the most trusted when one's home land is again near," Andrew interjected.

Yuri nodded.

"Only the most trusted."

"Were you trusted?"

"I served Tamuka, shield-bearer to Zan Qarth Vuka, heir to Qar Qarth Jubadi va Ulga of the Merki Hordes," Yuri announced, and there was a note of pride in his voice. "I fashioned for him the gorget of gold that even now he wears, and the bindings of the sacred writings of names. I taught Tamuka, Shield-Bearer of the White Clan, the language of the Rus.

"Yes, I was trusted. I was shown with pride as speaker of a dozen tongues, master of the fashioning of precious gold; I was allowed to wear the gold collar of the pet of the shield-bearer," and he absently touched his neck, ringed by a faint line of calluses.

"There are some who say that you were sent here to mislead us, to spy, to learn what would be needed if this land was to be taken."

"I came with word of the meeting of the three Qar Qarths."

"We would have found out soon enough without your help."

Yuri laughed softly.

"Then kill me," he whispered. "I have seen my home again, though all turn their faces from me. My wife dead, my sons grown to manhood only to die in your wars."

He paused for a moment, looking straight at Andrew. He looked down at a gold ring on his finger and absently ran his thumb over it, then looked back up at Andrew with cold eyes.

How many parents look at me thus? Andrew suddenly wondered. Yuri's eyes cut into him, and he felt an uneasiness. This one had a power to him, a coolness and self-assurance that he could not quite grasp. How could one who had lived on the edge of the pits, had seen the horrors and lived thus as a slave, be so inwardly calm?

"I offer all I know, Andrew Lawrence Keane of Yankee Maine. If I betrayed my people the day I took their flesh, it is easy to betray those who made me thus."

The two were silent, the clock ticking, its voice again loud, filling the void.

Yuri looked over at it.

"The voice of time," he said with a chuckle. "A curious machine. You know, you don't have much time left, and when they come it will be like a storm out of hell."

Andrew nodded, still uncommitted.

"Believe me, Jubadi has spent countless hours learning of you. He has the traitor Hinsen, and those few Yankee sailors of the great ship who are still prisoners and have traded their honor for their lives. Jubadi spends much time creeping into your mind, you have no means of learning his."

Andrew looked up at the mention of Hinsen's name. It carried now as much dark meaning as the name Benedict Arnold, a name to be spit out with disgust. He was the only one who could have told them how to make hydrogen for their machines, and much more.

"Did you see Hinsen?"

Yuri nodded.

"Many times. Groveling before Jubadi, promising much, telling him all of your means of fighting, the formations used, the way you think, the way you lead."

"And the others?"

"Most of the Yankee sailors, the Suzdalian sailors, are dead, some refused to help, others tried to run. But there are still a handful who remain. There are the other sailors, the ones who spoke your language and were from the southern sea. They took one of your steam land machines back to Cartha, but when word came of your victory they slipped away."

He chuckled softly.

"They stole one of the iron ships that Cromwell was making but was not ready for the war. Several of the Suzdalian and a couple of the Yankee sailors went with them. They went south, and have not been heard from. Jubadi was furious."

He paused for a moment.

"He killed five thousand who lived along the waterfront as vengeance."

Too bad they didn't run north, Andrew thought. The engines in Cromwell's boats, though crudely made, were of a solid design. Again he cursed the man for holding back his knowledge when it was needed the most.

"Cromwell? What ever happened?"

"Moon feast. It was said he died well."

Andrew said nothing. Though a traitor, he could pity anyone doomed to such a fate. Even though driven against his will, Yuri was a traitor as well. He had to be totally loyal, elsewise they would have slain him years ago. Twenty years with them must have left their mark.

"We've had too many traitors," Andrew said softly, looking straight into Yuri's eyes.

"Use me, and I will tell you what they fear. I will tell you of Jubadi, of Vuka, of Shaga, and of Tamuka."

The names, rattled off, sounded dark and full of menace, and he suddenly realized just how little he really knew of his enemy. They were a faceless mass, a dark seething entity of dread, like the shadowy demons of the apocalypse. Yet he knew nothing of them—who they truly were, how they thought, and what they dreamed. This was the first voice out of that darkness that might tell him.

He knew as well that not one of the Rus he had spoken to this evening had said a word of trust for this man. A few remembered him from before his disappearance, a merchant despised even then. A man now with the scent of burned flesh on his lips.

A man who had betrayed his own kind to save his life, a life thus rendered worthless and without hope of redemption. The more humane demands were simply to drive him out, but all the Rus, even Kal, wanted the punishment for a runaway pet: cut his tongue out, jam it down his throat, and tie him to the city wall as he choked to death. It was the old punishment set down by the Tugars and Merki for a runaway, yet it also spoke to a dread of one who had lived so long with the hordes that he might now have become like them and turned traitor to his own race.

Again there was the silence, the clock ticking out the seconds, the minutes, and hours until the horde would return. Outside, the cold autumn rain sounded softer, different, and he looked out the window to see the first heavy flakes drifting down, freezing against the glass.

He looked back at Yuri.

"Sit down, Yuri Yaroslavich. We need to talk."

Chapter 1

"My dearest love, your precious daughter and I are thinking of you longingly."

He smiled at the memory of her letter. When he was still a professor at Bowdoin he would have scratched "longingly" out from any student's paper. But from Kathleen it was endearing.

Six weeks now, or was it seven? He could hardly recall the days since he had last sat before the fire, holding Maddie in his arms, Kathleen by his side, the fire crackling before them.

Longingly.

A gust of icy wind swept across the open steppe, driving needlelike slivers of frozen rain before it. Mumbling a curse, Colonel Andrew Lawrence Keane pulled his battered kepi down low over his eyes. Damn hats, they never were worth anything. Whatever fool back in the War Department had authorized them for the Union Army had never stood out in a driving rain, or marched beneath a blazing Virginia sun. He had never been a stickler over regulation uniforms, and most of the men from the 35th Maine had tossed the ridiculous cap aside at the first opportunity, adopting the broad-brimmed, high-crowned Hardee, which did a splendid job of keeping rain, snow, and sun off of one's face. But as the

51

commander of the regiment he had always complied with army regulations, even here. Old habits certainly die hard, he thought, with a sad shake of his head. Now he was Secretary of War and Vice-President of the Republic of Rus, and yet still he wore the old battered uniform of a colonel in the Union Army of the Potomac.

Did that proud army still march? he wondered, feeling a tug of nostalgia. It would be what year now back there . . . ? Funny, he didn't even think of it as home anymore. Home was here, the city of Suzdal, the Republic, and the world of Valennia.

Almost four years now, so it'd be late 1868. No, most likely all the boys had gone home by now, the war over. The long swaying columns of blue, the circling fields of campfires, the serpentine river of men flowing over the countryside had disappeared by now, the hundred thousand parts drifting back to their homes, to loved ones, except for the dead. Except for the survivors of the 35th Maine, exiled here, wherever here was.

He remembered a march a couple of days before Gettysburg, when a thunderstorm had rolled over the columns. The sky turned a dark black-green, illuminated by forked tongues of fire. He had paused atop a low ridge and looked back, the column snaking across the valley. With each electric blue flash it seemed as if twenty thousand muskets had picked up the light, reflecting back Thor's bolts of war, blinding the eyes with their brilliance. The rain had come, drowning the world in darkness, and yet they had marched on, shimmering in the flashes of light, an electric body of blue swaying toward their final destiny.

He could remember the sound of their voices, the songs drifting down the marching columns, the laughter floating with the evening air, the triumphant shout as they rushed to victory, the paeans rising to the heavens, the rattle of drums in the distance, the haunting call of the bugle hovering over all when night finally came. Where were they now? Where are *we*?

He looked up as he so often did, always thinking that they were somewhere out there, beyond the Great Wheel, obscured now by the driving storm. Was the old country safe? he wondered. Lincoln would be finishing up his term, and the memory of his old hero brought a sad smile. His second term would be ending soon, hopefully over a United States that was whole.

"The old country," that was how he thought of it now, the same way Hans spoke of Prussia, Pat of Ireland, Emil of Hungary. Yet this was different. He had transplanted something of America here—"the United States of Rus," they called it now. They were molding it into a memory of home. At least in the woods beyond Suzdal it did in a way feel like home, like Maine, especially in the winter when the vast forests were still and draped in a crystalline white mantle. He could let it all drop aside, at least in those rare moments when he would ride north into the woods to be alone. It was so much like the land he'd grown up on—the boulder-strewn woods, the towering pines, the sharpness of the icy wind.

God, how I miss Maine, he thought sadly. There was a time when he'd been nothing more than a professor of history at Bowdoin, in the quiet, tranquil backwaters of life, giving his lectures, reading in the library, walking the rocky beaches, and yet always dreaming of something beyond. That, he knew, was the lure of being a historian, the dreaming of what had been and the imagining that somehow, someday, one could play such a part. And when the bit part in the vast drama of the war had been offered he'd rushed to it, never realizing all that he'd be leaving behind. Winning his dream, he had lost a dream.

Of course, I never could have imagined *this*, he thought with a sad smile: the last trip aboard the *Oqunquit*, the awakening in this nightmare world. Funny, now he found himself dreaming that somehow it could all come back, that he might awake as if from a dream. But then, he reflected, I would lose everything—Kathleen, the baby, Emil, Pat, Hans, Kal, and the strange pulse of power that this world has given me—as if I alone were shaping the destiny of an entire people. But at least there, before I left, I knew what peace was.

Peace. He mulled over the word, letting it drift through his mind. Over two years of war against the rebs, and nearly twice that here. It was leaving its mark: Though he was just barely forty, his hair was flecked with gray, his face lined and creased. He thought of himself as he was, the day before Antietam, and he seemed now to have been a child then, before the "seeing of the elephant," as the veterans called a recruit's first battle. Could he ever have been so young?

Antietam, Fredericksburg, Gettysburg, he silently clicked off the names, Wilderness, Cold Harbor, Petersburg, the Peasant Rebellion, the First Tugar War, the Roum campaign, the naval battles before Suzdal, the incessant skirmishing of the winter campaign in the Shenandoah Hills, and now the next one, whatever its name would be—and in his gut he knew it was coming.

He turned his back to the rain and looked southward toward the vast open steppe, but there was hardly anything to be seen in the storm-swirled mists of early dawn. But he knew what it looked like, the vast open spaces that he found vaguely disturbing.

Was it because of the land, the endless, low, rolling hills that seemed to go on forever, so alien to one from New England? Or was it because of the threat that he knew waited out there, coiling up in its power, waiting for the weather to break and for the first grass of spring before it struck?

He knew they were coming, that was as undeniable as the rising of the bloodred sun. The intelligence that the bitter and near mad Hamilcar had returned with, from his raids down to Cartha, in a desperate bid to save at least some of his people, bore that out. The refugees coming back with him had told of the incessant preparations, the foundries turning out cannon and yet more cannon. Vast sheds were going up just on the other side of the Shenandoah Hills to house the flying machines. The Horde had wintered through at Cartha, nearly three quarter of a million of their people going into the pits as the Horde marshaled its strength, the umens maneuvering through the winter, practicing with their new weapons, freed from fighting against the Bantag, who even now were reported to be moving farther east.

The refugees also told of the feasting, of the hundreds of thousands who had been led to the slaughter pits. The age-old saying that "but two in ten would die for the tables of their masters" had long since lost any meaning, as if the Merki planned to devour all humans in their path.

They were coming, he realized, and this time it would be a fight to the death for one or the other, it would be a war of annihilation.

"You know, if Emil saw you out here like this, he'd die of apoplexy."

Andrew turned back into the driving rain and saw Hans Schuder standing behind him, a look of reproach in his eyes.

Andrew said nothing and turned away.

"How's the fever?" Hans asked, coming up to stand beside him.

"All right."

The mention of it made him realize just how sick he still felt. Despite Doctor Weiss's drive for sanitation, which had nearly eradicated the disease in Suzdal, typhoid was still a fact of life in army camps. He fought to suppress a shiver.

"Son, why don't you get back into your quarters where you belong? The train will be pulling in shortly, and you should be resting."

Andrew smiled sadly and looked over at his old mentor. Hans Schuder's dark eyes looked up at him through a face riven with deep-set lines, wreathed in a beard that had gone over to a bushy gray. Hans shifted uneasily, favoring the right leg a bit, the reminder of a rebel sniper before Cold Harbor. They both bore the souvenir of their profession, and for a brief moment he felt as if he could almost flex the fingers of his left hand. "The ghost limb," the old soldiers called it. Even though the arm was gone just above the elbow, there were times when it felt as if it was still there. He would absently reach out to touch the empty sleeve, half expecting that the long-lost limb, buried at Gettysburg, had somehow returned from the dust of another world.

He felt the compulsion but pushed it aside, little realizing that all those around him knew that when he was lost in thought his right hand would drift over to hold the rounded stump.

He looked back to Hans and smiled weakly.

Though Hans was commander of the Suzdalian army, like him the sergeant major still wore the insignia of his old rank on the threadbare blue jacket, hidden now under a cracked and aging poncho. Hans had been with him since the beginning, shepherding him along, teaching him the business of command and killing, and then stepping back to see the man he had created forge a new nation and offer a hope of liberation from the suzerainty of the hordes.

"I just needed some air, Hans," he finally said, breaking the silence. "I'll get back inside in a couple of minutes."

Hans sniffed the wind, like an old dog trying to pick up a scent.

"Backing around to southwest, it'll be rain soon, most likely warm up a lot by the end of the day."

"The last snow of the season, I expect," Andrew replied absently.

The storm had come on hard the afternoon before, catching everyone by surprise, burying the first pale green hints of spring and blanketing the world with a thick swirl of heavy wet snow. He wished it had gone on forever, covering everything in a blanket so deep that neither man nor horse could move. Every extra day gave them just that much more time to prepare. But it was already what he would have considered to be mid-April back in Maine. This storm would most likely be the last of it. Within the month the steppe would be knee-deep in grass. It was most likely green already on the other side of the Shenandoah Hills fifty miles to the south, which was the forward picket line, beyond which was the realm of the Merki.

The ice on the Potomac had broken two weeks ago. He could hear the river rushing by, thick and heavy with the muddy runoff of spring. A hundred yards down the slope the water was lapping at the edge of the forward rifle pits, rushing over the rocky bottom of the ford. He could imagine the position— heavens knows, he had spent enough months looking at it. This was the first ford, forty miles up from the sea, the river running broad and deep from here down to the sea.

Yet all that line had to be held as well, though thinly manned at the moment. The river was full of shoals, which made the maneuvering of ironclads impossible except at the mouth. Leave it empty and they could get across—there were reports they had built hundreds of lightweight boats which could be used for pontoon bridges. Forty miles of trenches and bastions had to be constructed along that sector straight down to the sea.

To his right, for another sixty-five miles up into the forest, there were a dozen more fords, each one faced with heavy fortifications, in places three lines deep. By midsummer, though, the situation would change, unless it poured every day, something that he had prayed for nearly every night. When the river dropped, becoming a muddy stream during the dry summer, the entire line nearly down to the sea could be crossed. But by then there would be three more corps ready for action, while at the same time the Horde would be forced to disperse across a wide area to feed their mounts when the summer grasses thinned out.

We'll still have the rails and they won't, he thought, as if seeking an inner reassurance; the rails are our only hope in this. He could draw the line in his mind, going out of Suzdal, up to the Neiper Ford, down the west shore of the river and leaving the woods after thirty miles at Wilderness Station and coming straight down to here. The line then forked, running parallel to the river down to the sea, and in the opposite direction running northwest along the river up to Bastion 110 set nearly ten miles back into the woods. At Bastion 100 another rail line ran straight back east along the edge of the woods for ten miles, and then turned up the broad trail, the path used by the Tugars all the way to the Neiper Ford. It was a vast circle of rail, over three hundred miles of it, hastily laid down during the fall and winter. A strategic gamble that had consumed over fifteen thousand tons of light ten-pound-to-the-foot rails.

And straight ahead were the Shenandoah Hills.

O Shenandoah, I long to see you.

Longingly.

The snow was most likely even heavier back home, back in Suzdal. He could imagine her by the fire, nursing Maddie—Madison—Madison Bridget O'Reilly Keane, a long name for fifteen pounds of squalling humanity, and the thought of it filled him with a cold aching pain. All he wanted was to lie down by the stove in the parlor, to take an entire day of nothingness, other than his daughter, Kathleen, and quiet solitude.

He started to shiver.

"Son, let's get back inside; the train will be coming in shortly."

Andrew looked over at Hans. He had gone for some time without calling him "son." It was funny, but it felt almost strange now. Hans was still the mentor, the father figure from the beginning. With Hans by his side he had carried the crushing responsibility of running first a regiment, and then an entire war effort. He felt far distant from the young professor of history who had gone, wide-eyed like a boy, to see a war. It was now nearly impossible to define himself as someone's son.

Hans smiled sadly.

"You know, I never had a son of my own. Married to the army too long, I guess."

Andrew nodded, saying nothing.

"I'm getting old, Andrew."

"We all are."

"No, it's beyond that. I'm not talking about the rheumatism, the eyes that don't see quite as sharply, the game leg. It's just that I'm tired. Now I know what they mean by 'old soldier.' "

He hesitated for a moment, looking off into the swirling mist.

"I've got a bad feeling about this one, son," he whispered.

Hans looked up at Andrew, as if startled by his own admission.

"It's just that no matter how hard we try, they keep coming at us. Each time they're stronger, smarter—it's like it will never end."

Andrew felt an inner shiver, beyond the cold, beyond the weakness of the typhoid. Hans had been the rock upon which he had built his own strength as a leader. And now the rock was shifting away.

Hans fell silent, as if embarrassed.

"Go on," Andrew said quietly, "I need to hear this."

"I haven't said a word for months, but I feel the need now, before the others come up for this final conference. You know I didn't care for this Potomac line idea."

"I'm sorry we disagreed," Andrew replied.

The debate had been bitter at times, when they had started planning for this war more than a year ago. The first goal was to build the rail line to Roum—in that they had been in full agreement. Without the link to Roum there was no chance they could stand against the Hordes. But Hans wanted to try to hold onto the Neiper, even though the terrain north of the first ford was a nightmare for the building of a rail line to provide support. They had spent endless nights, pouring over the rough maps their survey teams had worked up. There was no fallback if the Neiper failed, he had argued. The Potomac

Front is on the steppe, terrain for their cavalry, Hans had replied, a front of a hundred miles far too long for them to hold with strength. In the end he'd had to order it. Hans had cursed soundly, but then saluted and thrown himself into the task. This was the first time in months that the debate had cropped up again.

"We can't afford to lose even a single battle, while even if they lose the entire war they'll still be back for more," Hans finally replied, saying each word slowly, as if they carried an actual weight and form.

"We defeated the Tugars, and it damn near destroyed us. Then they send the Cartha and we win it by a hair's breadth. Now we face them again. How many did that Yuri say, forty umens? Four hundred thousand warriors armed, with over four hundred field pieces and maybe twenty thousand muskets. They're capable of flying, while we've yet to get a single powered ship off the ground.

"The first time it was against bows and lances and they damn near took us, the second time against ironclads, and now, with nearly three times the strength of the Tugars, artillery like ours, and those damn flying machines."

He shook his head and fell silent.

The flying machines. At least they wouldn't be up today. At last count there were over twenty of the things. One had been brought down, or rather something had caused its engine to stop. The machine had drifted far out into the steppe between Suzdal and Roum, and finally had crashed when the cigar-shaped bag of hydrogen that supported the engine and the engineers' compartment burst into flames. What they had been able to sift out of the wreckage was the most troubling revelation of the winter.

The first people to approach the scorched machine had fallen sick within hours and died within days. It was fortunate, Andrew realized, that Ferguson, the engineering genius who had done so much to save all of them, had not been nearby. He would have crawled over the wreckage to learn the mystery of their engine, which apparently could fly for days without fuel. Before he got there Emil had passed up a firm order to keep him back, and to have the machine buried. Half a dozen more had died in carrying out that order.

Just how they had obtained the mysterious engine was an enigma. It was obviously far in advance of anything they had managed to create. During the winter, when Ferguson and several others had come to his home for an evening visit, they had agreed that any topic related to the forthcoming war was forbidden for the night. It had been an evening of pleasant diversion, of speculation about the world and how it had come about. Ferguson had gone so far as to suggest that perhaps the tunnel of light was a machine, drawing a comparison to electricity traveling through telegraph wires. If his speculation was true, then who had built it?

If such things were hidden on this world, what else might the Merki have access to?

"Ferguson will get us in the air," Andrew said quietly.

"Whistling in the wind will work for the others," Hans replied, a note of irritation in his voice, "but I don't need the reassurance."

Andrew leaned against the side of the parapet, Hans joining him. Meditatively, he chewed slowly on a precious piece of tobacco and spat over the side.

"Just how the hell are we going to get out of this one?" Hans whispered, as if to himself.

"The flying machines?" Andrew said, realizing that this was but one small part of the issue. "Ferguson is working on this caloric engine idea; we'll be in the air within the month."

"I mean everything."

Andrew felt shaken. Hans had always been the one source of strength, the quiet reassurance standing in the background. Like the best of all possible mentors he had first taught and then at least stepped aside, though he was always there when you really needed him, if for nothing more than an approving nod.

Damn him, Andrew thought quietly, I need him now, and instead he needs me.

"We'll fight them here on the Potomac line. We've got the beginning of a line back at Wilderness Station, and then if need be on the Neiper River itself."

"They outnumber us at least six-to-one, Andrew, and they have the mobility of the horse. All of them are mounted, something we don't have."

"You heard John Mina's assessment," Andrew replied. "That's four hundred thousand horses that have to be fed, at least sixteen million pounds of grass a day. Their forage problem will be a nightmare. Damn them, if they had any sense they would have hit this winter, coming in on foot if need be, but at least in that they're predictable. The Horde lives by the horse."

"When they hit, it will be a hurricane," Hans said quietly. "Now I know how the rebs felt. No matter how many of us they killed, we kept on coming. We were one of the worst-led armies in history—McClellan, Burnside, Hooker—and yet we kept on coming."

"You're saying we're going to lose this one," Andrew replied, trying to hide the weakness in his voice.

Hans looked over at him and smiled wearily.

"This time be prepared for anything, son. Be prepared to lose here, at Wilderness, even Suzdal. Be prepared to go into the woods after everything is gone. All they need is to beat this army once, and we have no reserves. Oh, I know the Roum are drilling, but they've only had six months, and half of their divisions will be armed with smoothbores since we can't make the rifles fast enough."

"You really believe this, don't you?" Andrew asked quietly.

Hans, his features set hard, came closer to Andrew.

"You've got the touch of the gods on your forehead," Hans said, "a killing god who's never known defeat. Perhaps the taste of defeat is occasionally good for a man—too much victory leaves him weak in certain ways.

"Maybe it's how I trained you. I'm cautioning you that it won't be easy this time around. You'll have to think like you never have before, because if this army starts to unravel it will be you alone who can pull it back together. The Rus are exhausted from four years of war—they won't have the same wild-eyed fervor they did back the first time. I think the Merki will know that and play upon it. This one is going to be hell."

"And you're telling me that you've lost hope."

"I'm just far too tired of it all," Hans said, and as he did so Andrew for the first time truly realized that his friend was getting old. There was the slightest catch of frailty in the sergeant's voice. "You know, I thought that by now I'd have retired out. I was thinking of heading west, out to California—there was good land there—maybe marry and set up a business, a tavern or something."

Andrew laughed softly.

"You, a shopkeeper? You're a soldier, Hans; hell,

I imagine you've been a soldier since the beginning of history, and a hundred years from now you'll still be one. You're the eternal sergeant."

"I'm only human, Andrew."

"Somehow, those people back there"—and Andrew pointed behind him—"think differently, both of you and of me."

"That's the problem, Andrew, I'm not."

"And myself?"

"You can't afford to be anything other than what you are; that's what I trained you for, that's what fate cast you to be."

"Small comfort," Andrew whispered.

"It's not my job to comfort you anymore, you're beyond that. Let any frailty show in what's coming, and it'll all unravel. God help us, we're going to need that from you."

"And you, sergeant," Andrew whispered. Just who do I turn to now? he wondered, his insides feeling numb. Just where do I continue to find my strength?

"I'll try," Hans whispered. "I'll put on the bravado. I'll continue to knock their heads together when it's needed, I'll fight to my last breathe, but this time, Andrew, I'm starting to feel the cold chill of their coming for us and . . ." His voice drifted away into silence as he turned and looked back out across the parapet.

The thin shriek of a whistle, muffled by the storm, disturbed his thoughts, and he looked over at Hans.

"That should be them."

He looked back over at Hans. A bitter gust of wind came up, driving a cold thread of water down his back. It set him shivering.

"Damn it, son, I came out here to drag you back in before they arrived! There's going to be hell to pay now."

Hans reached over, and with a clumsily gruffness

threw his arm around Andrew's shoulder, turning him away from the trenches and back into the driving storm. A vent of steam came swirling out of the mist, filled with the damp smell of wood smoke. Like a ghostly shadow of a fire-breathing dragon stirring out of the past, the engine drifted into view, the bells ringing weakly against the voice of the storm. Just beyond the railroad siding Andrew could see the low silhouette of the blockhouse complex, which was serving as his field headquarters. It was an ill-lighted and smoke-filled place, and he steered instead for the single passenger car behind the engine. Beyond this was a row of flatcars, burdened down with twelve-pound field pieces fresh from the mills. Six flatcars, laden with twelve guns, their caissons and limbers, a weeks' worth of casting for Napoleons. Damn, there simply weren't enough guns.

Gaining the car, he looked it over with affection. It was the presidential car, covered with the usual Rus wood carvings, its side emblazoned with a Gilbert Stewart-like representation of the signing of the Constitution of Rus. He could pick himself out in the group, standing beside Kal, both of them slightly larger than life-size. Larger than life-size, that's what they want to believe in.

Gaining the steps to the car he climbed up, struggling to control the weakness in his legs. The door above him was flung open.

"Hans, what the hell are you doing, letting him run around like this?"

"Doctor Weiss, I'm quite capable of looking after myself, without Hans playing nursemaid."

"Like hell," Emil sniffed angrily, coming out onto the platform to help him aboard. "You're as pale as a ghost."

Emil pressed his hand to Andrew's forehead, and

clucking noisily he led Andrew into the car, while shooting a chilly stare of reproach at Hans.

The stuffy warmth of the room was a shock, and he felt the perspiration beading on his forehead. His hand shaking, he started to fumble with the buttons of his old and worn army overcoat.

"Let me give you a hand."

Andrew looked down as Kal—President Kalencka—stepped up to him, the crown of his stovepipe hat barely at eye level.

"One hand a piece for both of us; we should be able to manage this," Kal said cheerily, looking up into Andrew's eyes.

"I've got a packet of letters from Kathleen, the last one pressed into my hand not four hours ago," Kal said, as he dextrously worked the buttons loose, while Hans helped Andrew slide the rain-sodden wool jacket off.

Andrew looked around bleakly, and nodded his greetings to the group. Overhead, scurrying across the roof of the car, he heard the footsteps of the telegrapher, hooking into the line, followed seconds later by the rattle-tap of the telegraph key in the small office in the forward part of the car, tapping out the connect signal, reestablishing communications for this small group, the architects of human resistance against the unmeasurable might of the Hordes.

"You've lost weight, Andrew."

"Well, you certainly haven't put much back on yourself, you thick-headed Irishman," Andrew replied, forcing a smile.

Pat O'Donald came up, grasping Andrew's hand. They both looked at each other appraisingly. Pat's recovery from the stomach wound had taken far longer than expected, a process not helped by his sneaking out whenever possible to violate Emil's injunction against vodka. There was a standing order to every tavern keeper in Suzdal to refuse service, an order that had resulted in at least one bar's being broken up by an explosion of Pat's less-than-pleasant temper when denied strong drink.

"You had us worried, me bucko," Pat said, helping Andrew over to the conference table in the forward end of the car. "That damn doctor"—he looked over at Emil—"wouldn't allow a one of us to come see you."

"Quarantine serves two purposes," Emil replied defensively, "to keep the disease from spreading, and to protect the patient from fumble-fingered visitors pawing at him and breathing their drink-laden breath in his presence."

Pat mumbled a good-natured curse in Emil's direction and went around the table to settle back into his seat.

Andrew looked around at the rest of the smiling group.

"John, how's the family?"

"Well sir, first baby on the way."

John Mina said the words matter-of-factly, the way he always did when talking of anything beyond his work as Secretary of Commerce and Industry, the logistical genius behind the organization of an industrial state to support a modern army.

"Dimitri, how are things in Roum?"

The old soldier, chief of staff to Vincent Hawthorne's Army of the Roum Alliance, came stiffly to attention even as Andrew motioned for him to relax.

"As well as can be expected, sir," he replied, his voice a little too loud.

Pat chuckled and looked over at the gray-haired Rus, who had volunteered as a private in Hawthorne's original company and had risen alongside the young Quaker to prominence.

"You're sounding like an artillery man, Dimitri—a bit deaf and loud-voiced."

Dimitri smiled and said nothing. Beside Dimitri was Julius of the Graca, a former slave of Marcus's household and now Consul of the Plebian Council. Andrew smiled at the man, who looked around a bit self-consciously. It was good politics of Marcus to send this man as a liaison. Far too much needed to be done in Roum to spare either him or Vincent, and the sight of a former slave representing Roum was heartening. The bicameral government of Roum—a senate for the patricians and a house for the plebs —was less than satisfying to the radical republican elements of Roum and Rus, but Vincent's plan, Andrew realized, was the best one for a quick transition to wartime emergency status while setting the groundwork for what would come later—if they ever pulled through this. Vincent had argued that the economic revolution of industrialism would soon render the patrician class all but obsolete, in much the same way that the House of Lords had atrophied in England. Though Julius was still a complete novice, lacking the far more cunning skill of Kal, he would learn soon enough. But for the duration of the present military emergency it was obvious that Kal and Marcus would have near dictatorial powers, with Andrew acknowledged as being above them in all things military.

He had noticed a curious thing that his men had created. He had always refused to promote himself, feeling it to be a foolish bit of vainglory, while Hans, Pat, Vincent, and more than forty others had been elevated to brigadier general or above by his orders. Yet he was still a colonel. But of late they had worked around that behind his back. There were lieutenant colonels to be sure, but, if promoted to regiment command, Hans kept the man's rank the same until he moved up to brigade command and earned his first star as a brigadier. There was but one colonel now in all of Valennia. So the title of colonel, like it or not, had been changed to the highest rank.

Andrew looked over at Bullfinch, sporting an eye patch like a pirate of old. The boy had recovered completely from his terrible wounding in the battle of Saint Gregory, as the great encounter between the two fleets was now known, referring to the local name for the point off of which the two fleets had clashed. He had to admit that, horrible though the wound was, it had made the boyish lieutenant into an almost rakish-looking character, who had his hands more than full with the Rus girls who seemed to be forever following the young admiral of the fleet. We damn near all seem to have earned a wound or two in our profession, Andrew thought dryly.

Next to him was father Casmar, prelate and supreme court justice, wrapped in simple black robes without adornment and nodding a smile.

"Your health is improving?"

"Thank you, father, I'm feeling better."

"When word came of your illness," Kal said approvingly, "Father offered a high mass everyday for your recovery."

"Your prayers carried their strength to me," Andrew replied openly.

"To be honest it was a prayer for all of us, for without you, my dear friend, we would truly be lost."

Andrew did not reply, unable as always to say anything in response to such a statement.

In the far corner of the room Andrew saw Chuck Ferguson, with Jack Petracci by his side. The young engineer, the driving force behind so many of the technological innovations, was as bright-eyed as always, as if ready to spring yet more miracles upon them. He thought back to young Chuck as he had been in the early days of the war, the old war with the Army of the Potomac. He had felt the man to be the least likely of good soldiers. More often than not he was on sick call, recovering from yet another bout with one of the myriad of camp illnesses. When not in the hospital he had struggled along on the march, and by the end of the day, more often than not, sergeant Barry or one of the others was carrying his musket. And yet he had doggedly refused to quit. More than once Andrew had offered him a place in the rear with a quartermaster unit, and Chuck had always replied indignantly that he would do his part. Thank God he had stayed and survived, Andrew thought, as he smiled at the soldier who, since coming to this world, had not fired a shot in anger, but had done more than perhaps all of them put together to save them from the feasting pits of the enemy.

Lastly there was Hamilcar, who seemed almost to be standing in the shadows. Kal and Hans had objected loudly to his being present, but Andrew had insisted. Only seven months ago this man had been an enemy who had come close to defeating them. And yet now he might be one of the keys to winning. Nearly forty thousand Cartha had been relocated to Suzdal, settling down along the coast on the frontier between the Republic and Roum. Their raids back to their homeland, to rescue their people, were a constant harassment of the enemy and a valuable source of information. He wanted Hamilcar to fully realize that his people were being accepted into the alliance, that technically Cartha was now considered an allied city under enemy occupation. Of course if Marcus had come it would have been impossible, so deep was the enmity between Roum and her former enemy. Though Hamilcar's hatred of the Merki was now evident, Andrew knew for certain that the man's grasp of Rus was rudimentary at best, and he would not be around after this initial session, when maps and other secret information were laid out on the table.

"Gentlemen, we've got a long couple of days ahead of us," Andrew said quietly, "so let's get started."

He nodded appreciatively to the young steward who came out of the tiny galley next to the telegraph office, bearing a trayload of heavy earthenware mugs, filled with the traditional Rus brew of dark fragrant tea. The steward looked over at Emil, who gave an approving nod, before setting a mug down before Andrew.

"Off that damn broth, at last," Andrew said with a sigh.

"Just be careful," Emil replied. "Not too much. And be sure to eat something with it."

Andrew felt no need to argue with the doctor, as a second steward deposited a wooden tray of dark bread, liberally spread with a thick coating of fresh cheese. It was a rare treat for the Rus, since the first war had killed off most of their livestock, which after three years were just starting to get their numbers back up. Kal always made it a point of spreading a table that was no better than what the common working families of Rus enjoyed, and more than once Andrew had found nothing more than bread and butter that bordered on being rancid on his plate.

"It keeps us from becoming boyars," Kal would remind them. It was also damn good politics, Andrew realized as well.

Andrew wrapped his hand around the mug, letting the warmth seep in, and, raising it to his lips, took a sip, a smile of contentment crossing his features. It was the first tea he had tasted in nearly a month. This had been his second bout with typhoid, and this time he had half believed it was going to kill him.

He took another long sip, the tea jarring his senses awake. Setting the mug down, he looked around the table.

"John, why don't you start with an overview of things."

John Mina pulled open a folder and looked up at the group. The papers in his hand were never really necessary, for the facts and figures danced through his mind without ceasing.

"Production is slowing somewhat. It's what we talked about before. Morale is down. It's been nearly three years nonstop, and two major wars with a third on the way. Our illness rate was up, for starters."

"To be expected in the winter," Emil said almost defensively, "and still a whole hell of a lot less than if we hadn't put in clean water and sewers."

"No one's doubting your efforts, doctor," Kal said gently. "We couldn't have accomplished what we have without your work."

"I was just pointing out a fact," John replied. "Nothing more, doctor."

Emil said nothing, but Andrew could see that his old friend somehow took disease as a personal affront.

"For artillery we have three hundred and ten light four-pound guns, a hundred and twenty twelve-pound Napoleons, and twelve guns of the new ten-pound Parrott-rifled pieces, firing percussion shells.

"For the navy and coast defense we've got forty-two of the seventy-five-pound carronades, twenty long seventy-five-pounders, the captured pieces from Cromwell's fleet, and fifty of the swivel-mounted four-pounders for the galleys.

"We've mounted sixty of the four-pounders and a dozen Napoleons on carriages with high elevation to use against the balloons; in a pinch we could remount them for ground work.

"We're turning out just under two hundred Springfield-type rifles a day, and another two hundred smoothbores of the old flintlock variety on the old assembly line in Rus. The Roum works are just starting up a couple dozen smoothbores a day, and two four-pounders a week. That should really pick up in the next month."

"Totals?"

"Just under twenty thousand percussion rifles firing our old .58-caliber minié balls, another forty thousand flintlocks converted to .69-caliber minié ball rifles, and thirty thousand flintlock smoothbores. If we hadn't lost nearly eight thousand guns in the naval battles we'd be in a lot better shape."

"It's not bad," Andrew said. "Enough for sixteen divisions, five and a third corps, along with garrison troops and home guard militia."

"Still, that will only leave us ten divisions for this front," Andrew replied. "We need to keep a full corp of three divisions stationed in Roum, in case they hit from that direction, and a corp in reserve in Suzdal to move either east or west. That's sixty thousand men for a hundred miles of front. They'll still outnumber us nearly six to one out here."

"Another month will give us another corp," John replied.

"Barely trained," Hans interjected, and he looked over at Dimitri.

"We have nearly forty thousand men in training," Dimitri said. "Not more than ten thousand have weapons at the moment—the field batteries are practicing with logs mounted on wagons. It'll be at least two months before the 7th Corps can be sent up."

"They won't give us the time—we heard the reports from Hamilcar," Andrew said, nodding over to the Cartha commander, who, though he had learned some Rus, turned inquisitively to his translator at the mention of his name.

"Within the month," Hamilcar said haltingly in Rus, "when horses can eat grass here. They will ride immediately after the next moon feast; the Moon of New Grass Riding, they call it."

At the mention of the moon feast the group fell quiet, each now knowing the details as told by Yuri to Andrew. Andrew looked over at Hamilcar. Perhaps fifty thousand of his people would die that night.

"They have the damn air machines to keep tabs on us, and we don't," Pat said, a note of bitterness in his voice.

"We'll get to that later," Andrew said, aware that Chuck and Jack had been taking far more than their fair share of criticism on that score.

They had grown complacent, expecting to have the technical edge on their opponents, and the fact that the enemy had been able to launch balloons that could not only fly, but could travel at will in any direction, had left all of them in a state of shock.

Throughout the winter, whenever the weather was good and the wind was down, Merki air machines, ugly cigar-shaped vessels, had roamed the sky at will, keeping watch on the building of the fortifications and repeatedly bombing Suzdal. The first attack, only a day after the victory over the *Oqunquit* had made a shambles of the powder mill, and the repeated air assaults, though more of a nuisance than a serious threat, had wrought a stunning impact on Rus morale, the former peasants looking at the Merki machines with dread. Two raids had reached even as far as Roum, bombing the navy yard and setting a long string of precious boxcars on fire with a rain of small projectiles that burned rather than exploded.

Andrew leaned back in his chair and looked at the map of the Potomac front spread out on the table.

"What's the situation in your department?" Andrew asked, looking back over to John.

"Rations are the easy part—thank god, harvest last fall was better than expected. Bob Fletcher has been working miracles as quartermaster for the armies. We've got one hundreds' days worth of salted beef, pork, and even that damned whale meat the Roum like so much, stockpiled for the army. There's enough hardtack for a year. Throughout Rus supplies are good right through to harvest time.

"As long as we stay near a rail line we're in fairly good transport shape. As of this morning, we have sixty-eight locomotives and just under seven hundred cars. We can move two corps from here to Roum and back without much delay. Our reserve corp on this front has all trains ready, and transport for the other two corp can be moved up quickly. Our copper wire supply is good, so is the zinc for hydrogen, and lead is up—we've taking to rewrapping the iron ball cartridges we were forced to produce last fall, and replacing them with lead rounds.

"Replacement timbers for all major bridges are in place, and we've made up a number of precut sections for emergency repairs on the lines.

"Shortages are still plaguing us in cast iron and steel. Rails are damn near still warm when they're getting laid, precision tools, especially for building up an arms center in Roum, are scarce, the men to make them even scarcer. Saltpeter is still the bottleneck for powder; we've turned over every manure pit and outhouse in Rus. If it wasn't for Roum we'd be finished.

"Is there any way to up production on our muskets?" Hans asked, bringing the conversation back to its original starting point.

John shook his head.

"We were starting a works in Roum—it might get up to maybe seventy-five a day by the end of the month. Remember that just before the Tugar War we were only doing a hundred a day. The trouble is that we've had three years to train our workers here, but we're starting from scratch with the Roum. It's the old problem: We could detail more men from Rus to go out to Roum to train these people, but it hurts our production here, while it will take months to up the lose and come out on the positive side."

"Can we spare some more people from our own factories?" Kal asked.

"We've already sent two hundred to train the Roum," John replied. "Take any more out, and production here will slide even further."

Andrew looked over at Kal, who sat back quietly, absently fingering a button on his jacket, a habit he had whenever he was making a decision.

"Send another fifty," Kal said quietly, raising his hand to stop any objection from John.

Julius, listening to Dimitri's translation, nodded his thanks. It was part of the alliance game, Andrew realized; they'd lose a couple of hundred weapons a week on this end, but hopefully gain it back on the other side.

"Can we take the men out of the specialized weapons areas?" John asked. He looked over at Chuck, who immediately stirred, as if ready to spring to the defense of what was another of his pet projects.

"They might seem like a waste now," Chuck said angrily, "but it's through things like that that we might get an edge."

"What progress have you to show?" Andrew asked quietly.

"I've got half a dozen of them running at the moment. General Hawthorne suggested that we make some Whitworth sniper guns. Those are already under construction. The first one finished two days ago. I brought one along if you'd like to see it."

Andrew nodded his acquiescence without comment.

Chuck stepped over to a gun cabinet set against the wall and opened it, pulling out a long leather case. Almost lovingly, Ferguson laid the case on the table, opened the top, and drew the weapon out.

There was a whistle of approval from Pat, and Hans stirred out of his chair to come over for a closer look.

"We didn't have any type of original to go on," Chuck said, almost apologetically.

"Superb piece of work," Hans whispered, extending his hand and then looking over to Chuck, who gave a smiling nod of agreement.

Hans picked the long-barreled weapon up.

"Damned heavy."

"Just over twenty-five pounds," Chuck replied.

"The gun's nearly five and a half feet long, the barrel forged out of our best steel. It's got a hexagonal bore to it."

"A what?" Kal asked, looking at the gun with a certain nervous curiosity.

Chuck motioned for the gun, which Hans surrendered reluctantly. He laid the gun back down on the table, the barrel pointing down the table for Kal to see.

"The inside of the barrel is not round, it's six-sided."

Going back to the gun case, he pulled out a finely crafted, oversized cartridge box of black leather. Opening it up, he broke a paper seal and pulled out a single bullet, shaped like a long bolt, blunt at both ends, six-sided, the sides set at a very slight angle to the long axis of the shot.

"This was the hard part of the job. We had to cut the barrel perfectly, six sides, with a tight rotation, just over a revolution and a half down its length. The bullet, forty-five caliber and over an inch and a half long, had to be cast the same way, fitting to nearly a thousandth of an inch. It's the finest precision job we've ever done."

"Fifty skilled workers for four months to turn out just this first gun," John sniffed coldly.

"We've learned a hell of a lot in the making," Chuck replied defensively. "This taught fifty workers to become precision craftsmen and toolmakers, unlike anyone we've trained so far."

"A lot of good it'll do in the next sixty days," John retorted.

"What's the range?" Andrew asked quietly.

"We've yet to train anyone to really handle it well," Chuck replied.

He pointed at the telescope mounted down the entire length of the barrel.

"This still needs adjusting—laying the silk threads in for the crosshairs has been a devil of a job. I've worked up a sighting gauge to help a man judge distance, then we've got to teach him how to adjust for wind and even for whether it's a humid day or not. It'll take time before this beauty gets matched to someone who really knows how to use it."

"Back in our old war," Hans said, "I heard of a sniper dropping a reb general at a mile with one of those things."

"Old Uncle John Sedjwick, 6th Corps commander, got hit in the head at eight hundred yards by a reb sniper using one of those," Pat said, looking at the gun with approval.

"That'll be a hell of lot of good against a charging Horde, when it takes five minutes to load the damn thing back up," John replied. "Boring out a hexagonal barrel is a bloody waste of men and time."

Andrew looked over at John.

"I told him to give it a try six months ago," Andrew said quietly. "Not everything pans out, but it's still worth the gamble."

"Do you want to continue with it?" John asked.

Andrew looked at the weapon for a long moment.

"How many do you have on the line?"

"This was a custom job, sir—no line yet. Just two more finished with this one, but they're not as good."

"Hold on to them for right now," he said quietly. "You did a good job, but if one of your well-trained people can train fifty Roumans to turn out muskets, it's going to help a lot more. That's where we'll get the people to send to Marcus."

Chuck said nothing, as if wanting to save his points for later arguments.

"What else do you have for me in your report?" Andrew asked, knowing there'd have to be a surprise someplace or it wouldn't be a typical effort by Chuck.

"We're finished making the molds from Sergeant Schuder's Sharp's carbine, and the machines to mill them. In another three months I could start turning out a small run of breech-loading carbines based upon the model."

"And what else?"

"We've got a hundred revolvers a month coming out for our officers—they're almost as good as our own Colts. Good God, sir, I'm jumping patents like mad out here!" He chuckled to himself.

"Tell him about those damn Gatlings," John snapped.

"Gatlings?" Andrew asked, raising a quizzical gaze at Chuck, who looked over angrily at John.

"Mr. Ferguson, I don't recall this in any of our conversations."

"I wanted to, sir, but you kept saying to stick to the basics, and John over here wouldn't let me get a word in edgewise any time I wanted to bring it up."

"I am your immediate superior," John replied sharply, and immediately Andrew could see that there had been some bad blood between the two regarding this issue. When they had first started the building of their army, a regiment at a time, contact had been a lot closer and far more intimate. But now the numbers had increased beyond their wildest dreams of three years ago. Well over a hundred and fifty regiments had been mobilized, with another sixty planned over the next two months, as Roum manpower finished training and came on to line units. The system was becoming far too complex for him to ever keep an eye on everything.

"Go on and explain it, Chuck," Andrew finally said quietly, looking over at John to still any complaint.

"Well, sir, I think it's a hell of an idea," Chuck said enthusiastically. "Now, I've never seen one of them, I don't think any of us has, but this damn crazy dentist out in Indiana had made the darn things, and I remember how General Butler even brought a couple to use during the Petersburg campaign. So I started to do some sketching. It's a simple enough weapon. Six barrels that are rotated by a crankshaft, just like a giant revolver. Each barrel has it's own breech, and as it turns the breech opens and receives a round from an ammunition hopper. The individual barrel and breech continue to turn, and as they do so the bullet slides into place, the breech plug closing behind it. A cam snaps off the firing pin when the barrel is at the bottom, and then as it rotates back up the breech slides open and the spent cartridge is ejected. Hand-cranked, it can put out a couple of hundred rounds a minute."

Chuck looked around the small room and was met with silence. Andrew found himself intrigued by the idea—it was something he had heard about, but never really considered.

"We've got an ammunition shortage as is—it's just a hundred and fifty rounds per man. We can burn that up in two major engagements and then we'll be out," John interjected. "We lost a hell of a lot of our stocks in last summer's campaign, a lot more when the powder mill was bombed, and you're talking about one machine burning up in ten minutes the volley power of an entire brigade."

"It's concentrated firepower," Chuck replied.

"Tell him the rest," John said sharply.

Chuck hesitated.

"Go on, Mr. Ferguson. You know I've backed you in damn near everything else."

"Well, I started to thinking, sir."

"You always do," Pat said with a smile, which sent a ripple of appreciative laughter around the table.

Chuck smiled in acknowledgment.

"Steam-powered, sir, it's a natural. Take the gun up to eight or nine barrels to stand the heat of rapid fire, hook the crank to a steam engine, and I could rip it up to a couple of thousand rounds a minute. I was thinking about it in terms of the enemy balloons. Sure we fired on them, we even put a cannon shot through one, but it was still able to get back home. With a steam-powered Gatling gun, we could tear that thing apart in a matter of seconds. Against a Horde charge it's tear them to shreds at six hundred yards."

Andrew looked back at John, who was shaking his head in disagreement.

"Pipe dreams," John replied. "I'd love to believe this one, Ferguson, but you failed to mention that you're talking about copper cartridge, rim-fired ammunition. We've got all our silver nitrate and fulminate of mercury going into percussion caps for the Springfield rifles and revolver ammunition. You're talking about hundreds of thousands of rounds of the stuff, and the horde will be at us in less than thirty days. You want to divert hundreds of workers into a project that won't even see light till the end of this year at earliest. You've got a lot of highly skilled people needed elsewheres."

"At least let me try?"

"We don't have time, Chuck," Andrew said reluctantly.

He saw a flicker of anger on Chuck's part that was directed at John. But there was no getting around the current crisis: A thousand guns now would be worth far more than all the Gatling guns in the world a year hence.

"We could field an army of a quarter of a million men if we only had the weapons."

"And we don't," he said quietly, looking out the window, where the storm had gone over completely to rain.

"It's closed, Chuck," Andrew said softly. "But do you have anything else?"

"Just the rocket idea, but John's not too wild about that one either."

"He's only doing his job, Chuck," Kal said soothingly. "We're running a race, and General Mina is responsible for logistical support. If I don't have the supplies that we need, especially weapons, it'll be his neck—it'll be all our necks. You've worked a lot of miracles, and after we win this one I'll look for some more. Now tell me of this rocket thing."

"It's just that I started thinking. We know they're making artillery, and lots of it. We'll have somewhere around four hundred guns when this war gets started; if anything, the problem is not the guns but getting enough horses to move them and their ammunition limbers. A battery of six of the four-pound guns needs eighteen horses, a battery of twelve-pound Napoleons or the new three-inch rifles needs over one hundred horses—that's where the big shortage is. Rockets could give us an edge."

"They're terrible things," Pat interjected. "Back early in the war some of the boys from the 24th New York Battery were given 'em. They had a devil of a time: The damn things couldn't hit the broad side of a barn, and every once in a while the demon things would turn around and come straight back at our own lines."

"I know that," Chuck responded hurriedly. "But we won't be shooting at a barn, it'll be the entire damn Horde. I was figuring we'd make them about three feet long and six inches in diameter. They'll weigh out at around twenty pounds each; with a ten-pound exploding spherical-case round, it should have a range of nearly three thousand yards.

"The advantage is tremendous when it comes to weight. A Napoleon with its limber weighs over a ton. We could load one hundred rockets on to a wagon for the same weight. Fire that into an umen and you're bound to hit something."

"And the ones that come back?" Pat asked.

"We duck," Chuck said quietly.

Pat shook his head. Andrew looked over at his artillery chief, deferring to him for a decision.

"Easy to say, but you've never had one come back at you."

Chuck bristled slightly.

"I was in the charge at Fredericksburg and Cold Harbor, sir," he said quietly, "I know what it's like to face enemy artillery fire. Even if one in ten come back at us, the other ninety per cent will play hell with the enemy."

"You know, laddie, you might have something," Pat said reluctantly.

Chuck looked expectantly at Andrew.

"Have you tried any yet?" Hans asked.

Chuck nodded.

"And?"

"Well, sir, it kind of got away from us."

"Blew up an outhouse five hundred yards behind us—a beautiful shot," Jack Petracci interjected.

"Thanks for the help, Jack," Chuck mumbled quietly.

Andrew shook his head, laughing softly.

"Go ahead then, see what you can come up with. But I want something that can at least hit the broad side of a barn—and the one you're aiming at."

"That's fifteen pounds of powder per shot," John replied. "That's worth seven Napoleon rounds."

"I think we can spare a couple of hundred pounds for starters," Andrew said. "Concentrate on that, keep the revolvers coming, but the carbines, sniper guns, and Gatling guns are on hold."

"Now, to the airships?" Kal asked.

Andrew nodded in agreement. Chuck cleared his throat nervously.

"We've built three large sheds in the forest north of Roum to house them. So far the Merki haven't flown near that area. If they catch us on the ground at this stage, one torch dropped from the air will finish us. We've got three bags done, and another four under way in Roum. It's still the engine."

"What about theirs?" Kal asked.

Chuck shook his head.

"It's buried where it fell."

"And you haven't gone poking around?" Andrew asked.

"I'm curious, but not that crazy," Chuck said quietly.

"There had to be some poison in it," Emil interjected. "We got that one report that several of the Merki who had been flying that ship earlier have died horribly, their hair falling out first. Those two Merki that crawled away from the wreck were vomiting blood, and everyone of our people who went up to the machine after it crashed got sick, with six of them now dead. Same as the Merki—hair falling out, vomiting blood. The poor fellows that buried it, some of them are still in the hospital, or in their graves."

"The damned thing is in the ground, and let it stay there!" Father Casmar said sharply. "It's a cursed devil tool."

"I'll not argue that one," Chuck replied.

It was just lucky, Andrew realized, that the ship had come down far out in the countryside, and that the effects of whatever was inside had become known before Ferguson had gotten to it—though the deaths of the peasants were tragic nevertheless. Emil had theorized that it might be some sort of arsenic poisoning, explaining the hair falling out and the vomiting, but why would arsenic be locked up inside a machine that without any visible source of fuel could power the Merki balloons about the sky? The power they utilized was tremendous, and coming out of an engine that reportedly could be lifted by one person.

"How soon will we be flying?"

Chuck looked over at Jack, as if searching for support.

"I'm not sure, it all depends on the engine. Weight is everything."

"Maybe you should have stuck to a proven design," Andrew asked.

"Sir, we never would have gotten anything effective into the air. A steam engine weighs a hell of a lot, and not just the engine but the water and coal along with it. A caloric engine is the way. Ericsson built one nearly thirty years ago. Rather than water it runs on superheated air—that cuts a lot of weight right there. We've figured out how to boil the oil we found out in the Caprium province and convert it into a form of coal oil—I think it's like kerosene. It'll weigh a fraction of the coal and with as much power locked up; it's a hell of a fuel."

"And the last two engines exploded," John replied wryly.

"Look, John, just whose side are you on?" Chuck snapped peevishly.

"I'm the one allocating the resources and labor!" John retorted heatedly. "You've got at last count over a dozen projects going, God knows you've most likely got more hidden away I'm not even aware of, and it's tying up thousands of workers. I need the basics: guns, guns, and more guns, and the ammunition to feed them!"

"Do you want powered aerosteamers, or don't you?" Chuck snapped, looking straight at Andrew.

The tension was rippling through all of them, the unrelenting stress of repairing the damage from the naval war and preparing for the next attack. Just the replacing of the lost locomotives and the damaged rail line had set them back two months. It was wearing them all down.

"We need something to counter the Merki machines," Kal replied soothingly.

"It's got to be caloric," Chuck announced, as if the

debate were closed, "otherwise we'll have to make balloons twice as big just to lift one man and a machine. It'll be too damn big, and with so little power it'll barely move. In fact, it'll be downright dangerous in anything other than a dead calm."

"Lift is the key thing," Jack Petracci said quietly, speaking up at last. "My last balloon, the one we lost in the Tugar War, could raise just over two hundred and sixty pounds on a cold day. Ferguson and I did a little experimenting and found that gravity here is about eighty-five percent of home's, so we have a little advantage there.

"We've floated two aerosteamers so far, neither one with engines. On a cold day, with the engine running, we figure the lift is nearly eight hundred pounds, enough for an engineer to steer it, another engineer to run the engine, drop some small bombs, or operate a telegraph if tethered."

"How fast will it go, and what's the range?" Hans asked.

Chuck shrugged his shoulders.

"It'll be a mystery to me until we actually fly one. This is a whole new field for all of us. I did change one part of the design, which I think will help."

"And that is?" John asked.

"We'll still use the hydrogen for lift, in two bags, one forward and the other aft. But in the middle I'm putting another bag hooked into the exhaust smokestack of the engine. We start the engine, the hot air goes into the bag and up we go. Cut the engine and back down. We've got the hot air already, so why not use it?"

John looked over to Jack for a response.

"It's dangerous," Jack said quietly. "If a spark ever gets into the bag and starts a fire, it's good-bye."

"The kerosene isn't like coal or wood, it'll be spark-free," Chuck said. "We've heard the Merki are having problems getting up and down, and more often than not they're venting a lot of gas, forcing them to keep refilling the bags after every flight. We'll have some leakage, to be sure, but nothing gets vented unless it's an emergency. Once we seal up our bags and inflate them, they'll stay that way."

"We'll have to trust your judgment on this," Andrew replied.

"You mean *I* will," Jack interjected, trying to force a smile. "I'm the damn test engineer for the thing."

"Just make sure it stays that way, Chuck," Andrew said forcefully. He knew Ferguson had a penchant for being the first one to play with his new toys, but this entire venture was far too risky to hazard the world's best inventor and engineer.

Chuck gave an almost wistful smile, but he knew better than to argue. His own staff of young aspiring engineers had received strict orders from Andrew to protect their precious leader, an action that Ferguson bridled against but knew there was no hope of resisting.

"To other things now," Andrew said, looking over to Hans.

"The fortification lines are almost complete," Hans said, rising from his seat to point out the positions outlined on the map.

"From the Inland Sea to the Great Forest we've laid out a hundred and ten miles of fortifications along the banks of the Potomac. In sections around the fords the lines are three deep. An outer line halfway down the bluffs, then the main line atop the bluffs, and then a reserve line to the rear protecting our rail tracks.

"Granted, in some areas it's a bit thin, especially where sections of the river, at least through the end of the spring flood, will be impassable. But every mile there's an earthen fort which can be held as a strong point. The ones facing the fords are bigger, usually holding a couple of batteries, projecting bastions, and interlocking fire fields. If they should come that way, the Potomac will turn red."

"*If*," Kal said emphatically. "What is your current assessment?"

Hans leaned back and looked over to Andrew.

"From the mouth of the Inland Sea, up to a good forty miles inland, is safe. The flood plain is two miles wide for a good part of that. It means they'll have to cross open ground, and cross the river under fire the entire time from the bluffs, which we command."

"The threat from the sea?"

"Our spy reports"—he looked over emphatically at Hamilcar—"indicate that we'll have the edge at sea. If they try and do an end run, our fleet will be there to meet them."

"But their air power," John said sharply.

"That's why we need our own aerosteamers," Hans replied, looking over at Chuck. "Their bombing of land targets is more a nuisance then anything else, but they are taking a toll of galleys and they'll know where we are, and we won't. They'll be able to see how we've positioned our troops, have maps made of our fortifications, and when they hit they'll know far more of us than we do of them."

Hans walked down the length of the table and stabbed the northwest flank with his stubby finger, tracing the line where the fortifications went into the forest for ten miles to finally end atop a steep-sided ridge, the line then turning back east at a right angle for several miles.

"They'll come against us up here."

"That's where our fortifications are strongest," Andrew said, almost as if to reassure himself. "The entire section is reinforced with log blockhouses, ditched and faced with abatis as well."

"Yet *this* is where they'll hit," Hans said emphatically. "We have to have a flank somewhere, and that's where the blow will land."

"Into the forest?" Kal interjected, "Hans, we've been going over this since last fall. It would mean the Merki would have to backtrack in an arc of several hundred miles. The woods are pathless, except for our own line of fortifications. That flank is secure."

"A flank is still a flank," Hans replied. "We've built these defenses almost too well. But we had to. We're nearly a hundred miles out into the steppe down here. If they break through anywhere along our front, their mobility would destroy us. So we fortified to the teeth, and now they'll go for the flank. If they take it, two days of hard riding would get them up to the ford where we first met the Tugars, and from there they're bound to jump the Neiper further up river."

"You still want us to abandon our forward position and fight on the Neiper, don't you?" Pat asked.

"Our gunboats can hold the line up to the ford," Hans said. "Beyond that we can hold the river line with two corps for fifty miles into the forest beyond."

"It's fighting on our home territory," Andrew said quietly. "Lose anywhere, and the enemy is inside our land. If they flank Suzdal, we'll be cut off from Roum and the rest of our country."

"We might be fighting that way anyhow," Hans replied, his voice full of warning.

"The amount of rail construction we've done down here, if the same effort had been applied to running a line along the Neiper for a hundred miles north of the ford, we'd be secure."

"We went over that a year and a half ago," John

replied sharply. "That terrain is murderous for rail construction, nothing but hills and marshy gullies. It's a wilderness, worse than the one in Virginia. The Merki will get tangled in it if they ever get that far.

"And besides," he added quietly, "what's done is done."

Andrew felt the old sense of exhaustion seeping in. Since the end of the naval war every moment had been consumed with preparing for this next conflict. He had decided over two years ago that their defense against the Merki, if they should move against Rus, would be a forward one, attempting to block the enemy before he got anywhere near home territory. All of his thinking had been predicated upon this basic principle of avoiding war on one's own land at all cost. Hans had been in full agreement at the beginning, but starting in midwinter he had begun to grow cautious, and now he was finally coming down on the other side.

Andrew knew that the typhoid had sapped his strength, leaving him feeling weak psychologically as well as physically. But beyond that was the deep-seated fear that had been gnawing at him all along, that no matter how much they did, the Merki, now armed with modern weapons, would be too much for them, and that everything attempted would in the end result in ruin.

"What you're saying here is that we can't hold them on this front," Andrew said quietly.

Hans looked around the room and nodded.

"Then where the hell *will* we hold them?" Pat asked. "If they gain the Neiper, sooner or later they'll flank us above the ford and jump between us and the Roum, wilderness or not, no matter what John says."

He looked over at Julius, who was intently listening to the debate, nodding in understanding as a translator explained the rapid-fire conversation.

"We must stand together," Julius said. "It is like our facies: one stick alone and we are broken, three united and we will stand."

"Suppose they don't strike here at all, but move on Roum instead?" Kal asked rhetorically, knowing that that question had been debated endlessly and was still up in the air.

"Difficult. If they send everything, we could always move against Cartha and liberate what is left," Andrew replied. "Beyond that it'll double their distance of march, and we'll still be in their rear. Going through us and then on to Roum is the direct route, otherwise it'll be a campaign of over fifteen hundred miles.

"Sherman did it on foot," Andrew continued. "But we've already laid that plan to rest. From what we've heard the Merki are afraid to give us another year, so the campaign will come straight at us."

"Our patrols down through the narrows in front of Cartha, show they have moved at best one umen, maybe two, across the channel," Hamilcar said through his translator.

"Give me another year," Chuck interjected, "and they'll regret it."

Andrew nodded and smiled. What he wouldn't give for another year, or another five years. But then it was always that way, there was never enough time.

"We can expect at least some sort of feign run up the east side of the Inland Sea towards Roum. Fifth corps will stay in Roum, while the 4th is positioned in Rus as our strategic reserve. When 6th and 7th Corps under Vincent are fully mobilized in Roum, we'll shift them as need be. Undoubtedly they'll feign in that direction at the very least, but I want to focus on what we do here. For the last six months we've invested all our strength in fortifying this line."

Andrew looked back at Hans.

"I'm merely saying it as I see it," he replied sharply. "And I'm telling you that when they hit, they'll come at us with everything. They're under time pressure, just as we are. That Horde is huge— it's a vast eating machine of horses and of Merki— and if they stop they'll starve to death. John, what's the quartering ability of horses for this type of land?"

"Well, as near as we can figure," John said quietly, "it comes out to something like twenty-five acres to support one horse for a year on grassland. Now that's for year-round, mind you. In late spring you could most likely graze twenty of them on an acre for a day or two, but you'd need a good two weeks or more before you could use that again. So, doing some rough figuring, the settled area of Rus is about the size of Maine, about thirty thousand square miles or so. It could barely see the Merki through a sea-son—and that's just for the horses, mind you, as to what they eat." He fell quiet.

"The Tugar Horde was a third their size," Hans said quietly, "and starvation was getting to them as well by the time the siege ended, and there was a hell of a lot of Rus territory where they controlled the harvest. Jubadi is no fool, we've seen that already. He knows he'll have to strike and break us before summer even sets in, and he needs to get all the way to Roum before fall and break them as well, otherwise he's finished.

"That's why I'm worried. I hate it when I'm fight-ing an enemy who might be every bit as desperate as I am, or more so. The rebs showed us that: Those bastards were kicked into the ground, and they still kept coming back for more."

"We can't forget that we are desperate," Hans said quietly, "but never forget that Jubadi knows us—Muzta and the Tugars did not. He's desperate, and he'll not make the same mistakes."

Andrew sat back in his chair, looking around the room, which was quiet except for the clattering of the telegraph key in the next room.

Too much had gone into their bid to fight it out here. To pull up now would shatter months of careful planning, and perhaps shatter the morale of the Rus as well, who were faced with the prospect of fighting a third war in as many years on their own territory. If the position here failed, Merki siege guns would be on the Neiper within the week, ready to reduce Suzdal. He would have to hazard the fight on the Potomac line, and yet as he looked at his old mentor he had a gut-coiling sense that the old man was right. No matter what they did, chances were they would lose.

"We fight it out here as planned," Andrew said quietly.

Hans looked at him and nodded, a sad smile lighting his features, as if a sentence had been pronounced that he had known all along was inevitable.

"Deployment will stand as before," Andrew said, and he could see a sigh of relief from John, who had based months of logistical planning on the Potomac defense. Pat shifted noisily in his chair.

" 'Chief of Artillery' sounds mighty grand," Pat sniffed, "but bejesus, Andrew, that sticks me back in Suzdal with the reserves."

"I need you back there, Pat. We've got Schneid commanding 1st Corps as our front line reserve, Barry in command of 2nd here on our left flank, and Tim Kindred commanding the 3rd Corps on the right flank. They're all old 35th men. Alexi Alexandrovich is in command of the 4th, back as mobile reserve. He's good, but I want you to keep an eye on him nevertheless. As Chief of Artillery you'll still hold higher rank. Fifth corps is under Marcus and back in Roum, and when 6th comes on line under Hawthorne in Roum it'll go wherever the action is, chances are to move under you."

"We've got two full battalions, twelve batteries assigned to each corps," Hans interjected, "with six battalions, over a hundred and fifty guns in reserve, under your direct command. What the hell more could an artilleryman ask for?"

"To be at the front where the action will be," Pat complained.

"The front may be in your lap soon enough," Hans said quietly.

"Mr. Bullfinch, what's the latest from you?" Andrew asked, finally breaking the uneasy spell.

The young admiral brightened.

"Fifteen ironclads, ten mounting two guns, the other five with four guns, ready for action, sir, along with over a hundred galleys."

"And the *Oqunquit*?"

His bright features dimmed.

"She might serve as a floating battery, sir, but it'll be months before you see her under steam again. Getting her side blown in and then rolling over made a mess out of her. We're still working on the boilers, but without Cromwell, or his old engineers, I'll have to admit they're damn near a mystery to me."

"Chuck?" Andrew asked hopefully.

"Complex pieces of machinery, sir. I'd have to spend some time on them, both of the boilers were cracked when we brought her back up. There's a lot inside that ship we just don't have the tools for yet."

"Do what you can, Mr. Bullfinch," Andrew said quietly.

Andrew sighed as he looked over at Emil.

"Making chloroform as fast as I can. Andrew, on the conservative side a full-blown war with those beasts will create thirty or forty thousand casualties. We're low on silk—all of it had gone into the balloons. John's given priority to high-grade steel for instruments, but the best instruments in the world are useless in the hands of a bumbler. I've got to train a couple of hundred surgeons and a thousand nurses. Your Kathleen has the nurses' school well organized, and she's teaching the first batch of Roum surgeons herself. The trouble is, I had maybe twenty good people trained in field surgery by the end of the Tugar War. There's only so much I can do with books and lectures, but those men and women will have to learn the theory and test it out for the first time in the field.

"There's only one way to teach amputation, and that's to do it. Amputations around here are precious few in peacetime, just several a month."

"Thanks to you," Casmar interjected. "That carbolic acid spray, and your sterilizing, have cut infections to a fraction of before. The dead flesh, your gangrene, is not near as common now."

Emil nodded a thanks, his pride showing. Kathleen had kept him abreast of the doctor's work, rendering a revolution to the Rus he had never thought possible. Emil's lectures in the surgery school were filled with his new theories: Boil all instruments and bandages, wash in diluted carbolic acid between each examination or procedure, work to clean out the wound and spray yet more carbolic acid.

Though resources were stretched beyond the limit, Andrew had agreed to a drastic increase in medical assistants. Back in the old war against the rebels Emil had been the only surgeon, with one assistant for a regiment of five hundred men. He was demanding that the number of surgeons be doubled, and that three assistants serve with each unit. A special train of fifteen cars for moving wounded had been constructed, over John's near hysterical protests. Fully equipped hospitals were already in place in Suzdal, Novrod, Kev, and Roum, with tentage for a field hospital for three thousand men. Yet like everything else, this, Andrew realized, though an improvement over the old, was still not enough as far as Emil was concerned.

"Most of my people will perform their first operation in the field, where there'll be fifty others waiting for treatment. Damn it, there's no way for me to know who will be good at it and which ones will throw up and pass out the first time they see a boy brought in with his guts hanging out."

He shook his head.

"God help those poor boys who get taken into them first. . . ."

Andrew could see that the thought troubled the old doctor, who shuddered at the sight of dirty hands and had gained a reputation in the Army of the Potomac as a crank, with his constant ravings about asepsis surgery and his mentor Simmelweiss.

"We've all got to do what we can," Andrew said, leaning back in his chair and nodding a thanks as an orderly poured another cup of hot tea.

It was going to be a long day, a very long day. Each point would have to be gone over in detail. A meeting with all corps and division commanders for the Potomac front would be next, and after that the entire hundred-and-ten-mile line would be visited over the next two days for yet another survey.

He looked over at Hans. The old sergeant was lost in thought, staring out the window, which was washed with the rain now driving in from the west. A gust of wind howled outside, forcing a draft of smoke back down the stove chimney. For some reason which he found troubling, the smell of the wet smoke reminded him of that endless night with Suzdal in flames, and that last desperate charge across the square.

He tried to push the thought aside, remembering the letter from Kathleen.

Longingly . . .

But the memory of her would not form. No, there was the fire, and then the darkness of a river of corpses, the air thick with the smell of damp smoke and death.

Why did I think of that now? he wondered, and the thought filled him with a cold, lingering dread of what was to come.

Chapter 2

Shaduka rode low in the evening sky, its ruddy glow drifting in and out behind the high, drifting clouds, which for a moment were silhouetted like spirits caught in an ethereal glow. But then, after all, it was the Night of Spirits.

His rhythmic breathing slowed, and again he was aware of the incessant drumming that echoed from ten thousand circling fires. He let his gaze drop from the quiet contemplation, the Shadta, the trance-walking, to Shaduka. From the high prominence, the camping place of the Golden Blood, ruling clan of the Merki Horde, he looked across the endless steppe to the west. To the far horizon, and for five days' ride beyond, the vast assemblage was spread, the low flickering of the horse-dung fires sending smoky coils, like rising ghosts, into the evening sky. And that was but a small part of their power, but ten of the sixteen clans of the Merki Horde, spread out across the vast lands of the Cartha, eating their fill, fattening their horses on the early spring grass, coiling in their strength for the campaign to come.

He turned his head, looking southeast. The dark low walls of Cartha lined the shore of the Inland Sea. For two seasons he had been encamped here and he shuddered inwardly with disgust, escaping it only to fight last season against the Rus cattle, and then to attend the meeting of the three Qar Qarths. Beyond that he had barely known a moment alone, the joy of a swift mount beneath him, the wind blowing in his face. Instead he had been trapped in their stinking buildings, choked with cattle sweat, smoke, and the blazing fires of the foundries. There was not a secret of them he did not now understand. The places of cattle were fit but for a wintering season, a place to gather one's offerings. Indeed they had corrupted his people, forcing them to remain thus in one place.

"Pak thu Barkth Nom, gasc yarg, gasc verg taff Ulma Karzorm. [From the place of our fathers, come, light, come, guardian of the night Ulma Karzorm.]"

Smiling, Tamuka rocked back and forth, turning his gaze to the east as the high singsong chant of Sarg, eldest of the shaman spirit walkers, called out the prayer of greeting to Ulma Karzorm, second light of the midnight sky. The chant echoed down the slope of the grass-covered hill, picked up and echoed yet again by the spirit walkers of the clans and then of the tribes, hundreds of voices rolling across the endless steppe.

A red glow shimmered on the horizon, spreading outward in a dark flat line, rippling across the waters of the Inland Sea. Though places of water were vaguely disquieting, a moon-rise over water still held him with its beauty; it reminded him of Barkth Nom, the lights of the night sky reflecting off the glacial walls.

The band of light expanded outward, and the chanting of Sarg was washed out by the commingling of a million voices, roaring like a storm across the steppe, the cry of exultation at the rising of the second light in its bloodred fullness. Yet he did not join in.

"Gasc yarg, gasc verg taff!"

The storm of voices soared to the heavens, tearing into his soul as if they were brands of fire. As if wretched from the very womb of the world, in a bloody birth of fire, Ulma Karzorm broke free from the horizon, its red orb rising, shimmering. His breath felt as if caught and slowing, ever slowing into one final drawn-out sigh that would stretch into eternity.

The night cry of the Horde thundered about him, yet it was but a whisper. The soul of Ulma Karzorm filled him with her bloody vision, the sky turning to liquid flame, rising higher and yet higher.

The banishing of the darkness, and he smiled at the thought. If there was to be a banishing it would be through blood, a bathing of the world in a sea of blood. The still waters of the sea appeared to him to be like an ocean of that rich-smelling liquid. He knew that the ancestors were somehow speaking unto him as the vision formed. But whose blood?

A deep thunder punctuated the drifting cries of the horde, rippling across the steppe with a steady cadence, stabbing the night with tongues of hot white explosions. Startled, he looked down, and in the plain before the city he saw the flashes string toward him. A thunderclap snapped from the top of the hill behind him, the concussion fluttering the hair at the nape of his neck. The artillery of the Horde fired in greeting to the rising of the moons of the month of Cagarv, the traditional day of stirring to ride again for another season.

Their thunder bothered him. The contemplation and fasting, the chanting of the shamans, the first cry for Shaduka, and then the great exultation for the appearance of Ulma Karzorm, these were the traditions of the Horde. But now they had even taken the guns of the cattle into that tradition, as if the voices of the Merki crying to the spirits of their ancestors were not enough, that the thundermakers had to be used as well to evoke their attention.

Tamuka, shield bearer, snorted with disgust. He stirred, looking about. Hulagar, shield-bearer to the Qar Qarth Jubadi, was looking at him, and nodded as if in understanding.

"The contemplation was disturbed," Hulagar sighed.

Tamuka did not reply.

"Come, they will start without us," Hulagar said, and with a creaking of joints and leather armor the shield-bearer stood up, offering his hand to Tamuka, who rose to join him, the two hoisting the oval bronze aegis of their exalted offices, swinging the shields into the harness over their right arms' shoulders.

"It was a moment of wonder, nevertheless," Hulagar said, looking toward the twin moons and then to the soaring fires across the open steppe beyond the cattle city of Cartha.

To the far horizon the fires now glowed. Once before, while spirit-walking, he had soared above the encampment and gazed down upon it as if from a great height, seeing, as the spirit ancestors would see, the power of the Merki filling the vastness with their light.

"I hope our fathers' fathers look down upon such a moment when again the horde stirs next spring to begin its ride," Hulagar whispered.

"They shall," Tamuka said, his voice distant.

Hulagar looked over at Tamuka and smiled, his fangs glistening in the moonlight.

"It is unseemly for the two shield-bearers of the royal blood to be late," Hulagar said, and putting an affectionate hand on Tamuka's shoulder the two started up the hill.

The scent of the fresh green grass and flowers rose up with every step, cutting through the cool night air. In the moonlight the carpet of white petals of the etor, the wild flowers of spring that came after the first blooms of lavender and yellow, had been turned to deep red by the light.

The scent could not fail to evoke memories of the yearly stirrings gone by when, coming out of winter, the Horde had moved at last. The foaling season ended, the yurts were raised back onto their horse-drawn platforms, and as one the horde embarked eastward yet once more, the warriors spreading out in search of wild game, or swinging either north or south, toward Tugar or Bantag depending upon whom war would be waged against that year.

The great cry had died away, replaced by the sing-song calling of the chant-makers, the incantations of the shamen, and the shouts of delight for what was to come. There were the other voices as well—over fifty thousand it would be this night—for each circle of yurts would have several and already he could hear their cries.

Reaching the crest of the hill, the great yurt of the Qar Qarth was before him, its golden cloth illuminated by a hundred torches, the inside a sea of light as bright as day, shouts of laughter echoing from within. The entrance awning was raised high, on poles encrusted with gold and precious gems that twinkled like stars. Encircling the tent were the guards of the one hundred, the elite chosen of the Vushka Hush, first umen of the Horde, their ceremonial armor of silver flickering in the torchlight, nocked bows riding upon their backs, scimitars drawn, points resting upon the ground.

Passing through the circle of guards they were

closely watched, but none spoke. For the hundred who were vouchsafed with the highest honor of guarding the Qar Qarth made a sacrifice to attend as they did upon their ruler: Their tongues were drawn out, since they stood present even at his most secret of conversations.

The two fires before the entrance into the vast yurt blazed wildly. Pausing, Tamuka bowed first to the west, and then to the other three quarters, before passing between the flames and on into the tent.

"Ah, I thought we would have to wait."

"I am honored that you would contemplate such a consideration," Hulagar replied, bowing low to the raised dais upon which Jubadi sat, with Muzta, Qar Qarth of the Tugars, to his right, and the heir Vuka to his left.

"Join me," Jubadi announced, "both of you."

Tamuka hid his pleasure before the circle of clan chieftains who gazed at him with envy, and he knew as well with a touch of fear. His opening speech at the meeting of the three Qar Qarths had opened the way for the agreement of peace between Bantag and Merki, ending a war of over ten years that had come close to crippling the horde. It had given them the breathing space needed for what was next contemplated.

Stepping unto the dais, Tamuka moved to the side of the circular table around which Jubadi, Muzta, and Vuka sat. Hulagar moved to the left of Jubadi, settling down onto the ground by his side. For a moment he hesitated, then he seated himself beside Vuka, the Zan Qarth whom he was sworn to aid and protect.

"I chose the fare myself," Vuka said, looking over at Tamuka with a disarming grin that Tamuka returned.

"Then we shall fare well," Tamuka replied smoothly.

Since the day of the defeat before the cattle city of Suzdal he had stood by this one's side, fulfilling his obligation as shield-bearer; but it did not mean that he had to like the heir, or even more importantly to respect him as one worthy of his rank. In his heart he knew that Vuka had murdered his brother, and by the killing of the only other blood descendant of Jubadi had thus kept himself from the execution that should have been just his reward.

If it had not been for Vuka they would have taken the cattle city of Roum, yet beyond even that fault it was obvious that Vuka was not fit to lead the Horde. He vacillated between insane audacity in a moment of passion and acts that could be interpreted as cowardice in his moments of contemplation. Yet Jubadi now refused to see this, interpreting foolhardiness for bravery, and deceitfulness in the shrewdness required of a Qar Qarth. Jubadi could not see that the direct heir, the one legitimate son acceptable to the clans, was guilty of fratricide committed to save himself, though the rumors were whispered in all the tents. Hulagar, as befitted a shield-bearer to the Qar Qarth, had spoken of this suspicion, and had nearly paid with his life. If the injunction which made the person of the shield-bearer sacred had not been in place, Hulagar would have lost his head before the accusation had even been half spoken.

A terrified shriek of anguish filled the tent, and, looking up, Tamuka saw their meal coming in, dragged along by two of the tongueless ones, Sarg Qarth, eldest of the shamen behind them. This one was male, well built, with the dark tanned skin of the Cartha. The human screamed in terror—most of them usually did—and Tamuka viewed the display with disgust, while many of the clan Qarths laughed gruffly, hurling taunts. Servants came out from behind the dais, opening the table up like a scissors that was hinged only on one end. The cattle was pushed forward, his guards how grabbing hold of his arms and legs, lifting the writhing form into the air. Sarg Qarth came up to the side of the table and, bowing low, directed the guards as they pushed the cattle's head into the clamp. This was tightened down, holding him firmly in the center of the table, and closed back so that only the head was above the board while the rest was pinned beneath.

The cattle struggled and shrieked, trying to turn its head, but the clamp was tight. Its arms and legs underneath thrashed and kicked.

"He'll bruise his flesh," Vuka said, shaking his head, and the clan chieftains laughed appreciatively.

Other offerings were brought in to the lower tables, so that the tent was filled with wild shrieks of terror. Tamuka looked at them with a vague sense of disgust. The least they could do would be to sing a death chant, to take this with some dignity, rather than to beg so pitifully. It only aroused in him a sense of loathing, a desire to be done with it and get on to the main course.

Sarg Qarth, as eldest of the shamen, now set to work. The other shamans stood beside the lower tables, waiting for this most important of auguries, which would apply to the entire horde, to be performed.

The curved blade flicked out from his belt and he held it before the cattle's eyes, at the sight of which the cattle shrieked even louder. It was good sign— he did not weep or, worst yet, swoon—and all took this with barks of approval. With a deft single motion the scalp was cut across the forehead, above the ears and around to the back of the head, straight down to the bone, and there were more grunts of approval for Sarg's skill. To nick an ear would mean the hearing of bad news, the accidental gouging of an eye would mean to behold an evil sight, if it fainted evil would arrive without warning, which of course would apply to all of the Horde.

Sarg leaned over the head, which was tossing back and forth violently, watching the pattern of blood fall.

"It is to the north," Sarg announced, and there was an expectant pause, for all knew that was the direction they would ride. But whose blood was being foretold?

Now came the most delicate part of the ceremony. Sarg Qarth reached into the long slender pouch by his side and drew out the curved saw. Though rivers of blood were running into the cattle's eyes he could still see the blade and knew what it meant. A howling shriek of pleading rose from his lips.

"It will be theirs," Sarg announced, and more than one of the clan chieftains leaned back, raising a roar of triumph.

There was now an expectant hush as Sarg mumbled his incantations, passing the saw around the cattle's head in a circular motion. With the lightning action of a striking serpent Sarg grabbed hold of the cattle's head with his left hand and, leaning over, cut into the bone above its right ear—a difficult maneuver which Tamuka could not help but admire. The cross-over cut was an act of bravado that only the most accomplished would attempt, especially for this, the most important of divinations. If he should fail in cutting correctly the auguries would be bad, and there was silence, except for the rasping of the blade and the hysterical screams.

Sarg's arms knotted with the effort. Several strokes, pink foamed bone spraying out, then he shifted further back, cutting again, working his way around. The cries of the cattle suddenly grew weaker and there was a murmuring. After all, many of them did faint at this point, for they were only cattle, but it would be bad if this one should suddenly die, ending the ceremony before the final auguries had been obtained. Not once did his saw break through into the brain, but always stopped just at the edge.

The cutting continued, and the table was soon covered with a circle of bone chips and pink splattered foam. Sarg cast the saw aside and ran his fingers up underneath the cut scalp, refusing to lower himself by taking direct hold of the skull. For after all, only the youngest of shamans removed the skull in such a manner, still not sure that they had cut through all the way around and thus wanting a firmer grip when they pulled. On rare occasions a shaman would pull upward and only the scalp would come away. Though the augury was bad, Tamuka remembered seeing it and finding the entire thing to be vastly amusing: the humiliated shaman holding nothing but a bloody hunk of hair while the cattle appeared to be wearing a white cap. Such a mistake had been performed on the Yankee Cromwell, who had said nothing throughout, his eyes wide with some inner madness that had rattled the shaman as he'd performed his duties.

But for Sarg such things were unheard of. It seemed to require no effort at all as he raised his hands up, the top of the skull separating away with a barely audible pop. Barks of appreciation filled the yurt, counterpointed only by the wails of terror from the other cattle, who were clamped into their tables in such a way that they could behold what was in store for them.

A gurgling groan escaped the cattle's lips and he

was still. Sarg looked down upon him as if insulted, and leaning over he lightly slapped the cattle's cheeks, setting the skull down before his eyes, which came back into focus wide with terror.

The brain was still sheathed with a gray fibrous layer. Cutting at the back Sarg peeled the layer up, as if removing the skin from an overripe fruit, to reveal the gray convoluted folds beneath, a gush of light-colored water running down the side of the cattle's head.

Sarg peered at the convolutions of the brian, the arteries pulsing, chanting softly, and after a long moment looked up at Jubadi.

"There are many rivers to cross, some pulsing with red blood, others with blue. I see fires of yellow and dark hidden paths."

He drew closer and then pointed.

"There! It floats above the coils of the brain, a white fleck, like the great ships that float on air. I see many of them, moving some to the east, others from the west. I see fire coming up to them. The blue, the color of the Yankee, is spreading over the gray field of death."

He looked up at Jubadi.

"It will be victory."

Wild shouts greeted his words. Tamuka joined in, even though in his heart he found doubt that the future could be thus foretold. For except in the rarest of moments, the divinations all sounded the same. But there was no feeling of kinship between those who walked as he did with the mysteries of their tu and those who read the brains of the cattle. The readers viewed the shield-bearers as rivals, while those of the white clan felt that though there was much that was truth in the shaman ways, there were truths revealed to the white that the divinators would never have revealed unto them.

Sarg then drew a long needle out of his pouch and held it above the convoluted mass of gray. Mumbling a quiet chant he slipped the needle in. The cattle's teeth started to chatter, strange words escaping its lips. The needle was withdrawn and inserted again. This time the legs started to kick, and then the arms. With an case almost bordering on arrogance Sarg performed the Ujta Eag, the Spirit Dancing, his demonstration of how to snatch the animal spirit of the cattle and have it perform to his will. As he slipped the needle in, his whispered commands were acted out by the cattle. The yurt was silent, even the other cattle watched in silent horror, at the demonstration of the skill of a master divinator.

As Sarg turned to look back at the chieftains he revealed a smile of inner satisfaction at a task well done, as the assembly pounded the tables with their fists, more than one of them obviously nervous at the unnatural powers thus demonstrated. Sarg nodded to Jubadi and, kneeling down by the side of the table, placed his ear to the cattle's mouth.

Jubadi, standing up, leaned over the table, taking up a golden spoon which sliced into the cattle's brain where the forehead used to be. The cattle groaned, its legs kicking spasmodically. Jubadi chewed softly on the repast and then scooped again, and yet again, going deeper in. The cattle's teeth started to chatter, a gurgling hiss escaping its lips. The spoon went deeper, cutting in. Jubadi nodded to his comrades around the table. Tamuka lifted the golden spoon set before him, and leaning over he carefully scooped up a mouthful, careful not to dig down below the level of the cut. The brain was warm, melting in his mouth after a few chews. He scooped up some more, his spoon clicking against the others, grunts of approval echoing around him, the chieftains and their retinue at the lower tables watching in silence, more than one with moistened mouth eager for their own meal to begin. Sarg watched them, smiling, listening to the murmuring pleas of the cattle drifting away as his mind was devoured, its eyes going wide in panic as vision disappeared, as the essence of his thoughts and soul were consumed.

The shaman's hand shot out, directing them to stop. Assistants came forward, unsnapping the table and levering it back.

Sarg took hold of the cattle's hands and drew him up to his feet.

The yurt was quiet as Sarg came around behind the cattle, the fingers of his right hand going into the cavity of the skull. The cattle started to shudder, its now sightless eyes rolling, a trickle of drool running down its chin. With a ghostlike shuffle it stepped forward.

Even the other cattle were silent, eyes wide with horror at the spectacle of the shaman leading the walking corpse.

"So shall all the cattle be led by our Qar Qarth!" Sarg announced, and there were barks of approval at his words, and also for the fearful power he now displayed in leading one whose mind had already been consumed. The cattle was led to the center of the yurt and stopped, Sarg holding it up from behind as it swayed, mindless, a breathing corpse.

A young shaman came forward and, bowing low, presented Sarg with a golden flask and a flickering taper. The shaman poured the contents into the open skull and with eyes raised to the heavens called upon the ancestors in the ancient tongue of his order. He touched the flaming taper to the skull.

Screams of terror escaped the other cattle as a coiling tongue of fire rose up from the open skull, as if the cattle were wearing a towering crown of blue and yellow flames wreathed in oily smoke. With a grin of satisfaction Sarg stepped back, the cattle motionless, flames licking up from his open head, his sightless eyes rolling, convulsions trembling through his body. Tamuka felt a shiver of fear no matter how many times he witnessed the ritual—there was something ghastly about a mind, even a cattle mind, being thus consumed inside a flaming skull while it was still alive.

The oily flames flickered, exuding a dark cloud. As if his legs had turned to jelly the cattle finally started to sag, Sarg looking about the yurt with satisfaction that his sacrifice had remained standing for so long. The cooking of the brain inside the open skull continued, even as acolytes grabbed the still trembling body and dragged it back to the table. The cattle was hauled onto the table, and even as the flames continued to flicker Jubadi reached in with his spoon and scooped out the cooked delicacy, nodding with approval while Sarg placed his car to the cattle's lips in case there were any final words. Vuka, with a usual show of bravado, took up a hunk that was still flaming and swallowed it, the chieftains shouting their approval.

Curious, Tamuka held the dying cattle's sightless gaze, looking into its dark eyes as it returned to the soulless dust. He watched without emotion as the eyes slowly rolled back in their sockets and the clenched jaw went slack. Sarg stood back up, a quizzical look on his features.

"Did he say anything?" Jubadi asked, nervously.

"He said two would die; he said it in our own tongue," Sarg whispered.

Jubadi looked around the table and at the clan chieftains.

"It is bad; it is of your own table," someone whispered.

"Two will die," Hulagar replied. "Rus, and the Roum—who else could it be?"

Tamuka could see a look of relief cross Sarg's features, replaced in an instant by hatred that he had been saved by one of the white clan. Yet he nodded in agreement.

"Victory will be complete, as the auguries say," Sarg announced, as if he had divinated it himself.

The tension slipped away into cries of lust for battle. With a wave of his hand, Sarg indicated that the other shamans could begin the rituals at each of the lower tables now that the most important one to decide the fate of the entire horde was completed. Criers went out of the tent, their voices rising, announcing to the waiting Horde the augury of good fortune. A thunder of voices echoed across the plains.

Shrieks of pain and terror filled the tent as the other shamans set to their work, while Tamuka leaned over, scooping out a large spoonful of his favorite food. The cooked brain was neither too firm nor too watery, dissolving after several seconds of chewing, and the five at the head table quickly scooped the cranial cavity clean, their spoons clinking against each other as they jokingly raced to empty out the last drops of gray pink slush. Vuka, unable to contain himself, finished by running his fingers on the inside and then licking them.

The smell of meat filled his nostrils, and he looked up to see dozens of servants come into the tent bearing platters heavy with roasted limbs, trays overflowing with cracked bones, marrow oozing out, pies of liver and kidney covered with a golden crust, long links of sausages fried to a dark brown, and heavy cauldrons of blood soup and delicate sweetmeats covered with dark sugar.

Servants unclasped the table and dragged the

corpse out, wiping the floor beneath him before scattering fresh-scented grass and flowers down and then clamping the table shut again. Within seconds the eating board seemed to groan under the weight of the meal spread out before them. Reaching for a long section of leg bone, Tamuka grunted with delight as he broke it open with his teeth and then used the marrow as a dip for the heavy, grease-coated sausages. There was little to talk of—one did not waste breath on speaking when a long day of fasting was being broken at last.

Chant-singers stood in the dark corners of the vast yurt singing of the noble lineage of the Merki, starting with Puka Taug Qarth, the father ancestor who had first led his people through the portal of light, and then of the countless begetting of generations afterward, their song accompanied by the low, hair-raising groan of the single-string strummer, the strident sounding of the nargas, the great war horn, and the incessant rolling of the chant drums. The cries of the last of the offerings finally drifted away, the open skull flickering with fire. The members of its table looked about with pride, for to have the last crier was a good thing, while those of the yellow clan looked downcast, for their offering had expired before the skull even had been lifted. Low curses were hurled as the shaman slinked out of the tent to hide his shame. Following the older form of the ritual, the table with the last to die had the now empty skull filled with oil and reignited to provide a lurid light for the feast, the body underneath the table a source of raw meat which could be sliced off during the course of the meal.

More servants came in, bearing great platters of thinly sliced meat, drawn from the bodies that had been alive but moments before, the raw flesh of the Moon Offering. With a ceremonial flourish Jubadi held a sliver aloft and then cast it into the smoking brazier set at the foot of dais, an offering to the ancestors.

Leaning back, Tamuka scooped up a handful of the raw flesh, nodded with pleasure at the full-grained texture of the meat, and dipped it into the marrow. He ate the repast with relish. Tankards of fermented horse and cattle milk were brought in and set down, the clan leaders exclaiming noisily over the rich brew, tossing their heads back to drain the draughts in a single long gulp, their voices rising, barking, laughing, shouting ribald taunts to each other.

Caldrons of hot blood, freshly drained, were set at each table, the warriors eagerly shoving at each other, dipping in their now empty tankards, more than one of them grabbing hold of the iron bucket, snatching it away from his rivals and tipping it up, the hot sticky foam running down their faces, splashing off the leather armor. Howls of protest greeted the strongest, and it was good that nothing more than cutting knives was allowed, or there would have been more blood, Horde blood, splashing.

Jubadi, as was his right, took the bucket without a struggle and drained off but half, and in a show of diplomacy offered the rest to Muzta who took the drink, finishing it in silence.

The frenzy of eating slowed and long sonorous belches echoed about the tent, acolytes of the shamans interpreting each as to the portents revealed, the warriors nodding approvingly since all were promised more horses, and offspring. The number of kills was not discussed, for after all it was cattle they were facing this year, and there was no honor, no raising of stature in the hunting of game, no matter how skillful or deadly their foes now were.

At last the sight of another kidney pie, browned

sausage link, or finely broiled rib was enough to turn his stomach, and Tamuka leaned back from the table with a groan. There was some slight dishonor in being the first to finish, but as a shield-bearer he felt no need to worry about such trivialities. He saw a quick look from Vuka, a thin smile lighting the Zan Qarth's features, as if Tamuka had revealed some weakness. With a noisy display Vuka took up an entire leg bone and cracked it open with his teeth. Raising it up on end he sucked the marrow out, tossing the empty husk over his shoulder.

Fresh tankards of fermented milk were brought it, and taking the offered drink Tamuka merely sipped at the contents, letting the feeling of content-ment settle in.

"We eat well at the table of our Qar Qarth! Ten circlings of life to our Qar Qarth Jubadi!" Gorn, chieftain of the clan of the three red horses cried, leaping atop his table and raising his tankard in salute. A mighty shout echoed up from the tent to be picked up by the wives, concubines, and children who had gathered outside the yurt. The cry echoed down from the hill, sweeping out to the vast encamp-ment, hundreds of thousands of voices calling out the name of Jubadi.

Tamuka felt a cold shudder run through him at the voicing of such power, a mighty cry that shook even against the gates of the everlasting heavens.

Jubadi stood up, holding his arms out, his features alight with the effects of drink and of the power, and stepped up unto the feasting table. Chieftains of the clans stood, shouldering past each other, clamoring up unto the dais. Tamuka drew back.

Grabbing hold of the table they hoisted it up, plat-ters of meat sliding off, with Jubadi standing in the middle. Warriors, who in their own right com-manded umens of ten thousand now fought with each other for the honor of bearing their Qar Qarth. Table raised high, they carried him out of the yurt, through the high flaps, raised so that Jubadi did not have to lower his head to anyone or thing.

As he emerged from the tent the shouting across the vast plain rose up into a wild deafening thunder, a screaming chant.

"Qar Qarth, Qar Qarth, Qar Qarth!"

Tamuka looked over at Hulagar, whose voice was added to the thunder, and then behind him to Vuka, who stood in silence, tankard in hand, a look of lust in his eyes for the power thus displayed. And in his heart Tamuka felt the power as well, and struggle though he did with all the teaching of his clan, he felt it holding him with a desire stronger even than when Yuva the courtesan came into his tent for pleasure.

Startled at what he was feeling, Tamuka saw that Vuka was staring at him with a cold grin, as if the Zan Qarth had suddenly read the thoughts of the shield-bearer rather than the other way around.

He looked away.

Noisily the chieftains brought Jubadi back into the tent. His features flushed, Jubadi looked down at Hulagar and smiled.

"That is our power, that is the power of the Hordes!" Jubadi barked, and not waiting for the table to be lowered he leaped down to the dais.

"The cattle of the north, the Rus, the Roum will feed us until our bellies burst, until the grease pours out of our mouths when we turn our faces to the sun!"

Hulagar nodded, saying nothing.

And how many of ours will rot in the sun? Tamuka wondered. The plan was good—he had helped in the shaping of it, something unheard of for a shield-bearer—yet even Jubadi had now come to admit his worth, knowing as he did of the ways of cattle war.

"Let not one of them be left alive, let us scorch the world of them," Tamuka said quietly, and his words caused Jubadi to turn.

Hulagar looked over at him, shaking his head as if in warning. Jubadi still wanted to believe that when their power had been cast down the cattle would again return to being docile slaves, ready to fashion what was needed, ready to offer their flesh for the tables of the Hordes, which could then continue their never-ending ride, to pursue undisturbed the hunt and the sport of war against their own kind.

"You have drunk too deeply, shield-bearer, to my son," Jubadi snarled, his voice heavy with menace. "We fight as I have directed, and we shall win as I have directed. When they are defeated they will be subjugated, but to slaughter all would destroy forever our way of life. Thus I have commanded, thus shall it be."

Tamuka bowed low, cursing inwardly at his folly for having spoken out of turn but guided by some inner voice which he could not deny, and which as shield-bearer he was expected to voice.

"I have drunk deeply," Tamuka replied, "but the voice within is not touched by drink."

Jubadi looked at him coldly.

"I shall retire," Tamuka said, holding his head low and backing down from the dais.

Turning at the entry to the tent he stepped out into the cool air, breathing deeply.

"Tomorrow we ride!" Jubadi roared, breaking the tension, and the exulting shouts of the chieftains drowned out the silence.

Tamuka walked between the fires of cleansing, bowing low to the four corners of the world.

Though he had withdrawn with honor it was obvious to those who stood outside that he had spoken words out of turn, for he was but shield-bearer to the Zan Qarth and not invulnerable to censor as was Hulagar. The vast assemblage outside the tent offered the half-bow that was befitting his rank, but none spoke to him. He was, after all, of the shield-bearers and thus held in superstitious awe, but it was obvious as well that he was not quite in favor at the moment.

At times of the Moon Feast the trading of words of anger was all too common. Dozens of the Horde would be dead before the night was finished as long simmering passions, inflamed by the surfeit of food and strong drink, finally exploded. Come the aching heads of morning, such arguments, more often than not, would be put aside or forgiven, but when it came to the anger of the Qar Qarth it was wise to avoid one in disfavor until his fate was decided.

Passing through the ring of the silent ones he walked into the darkness, back up the slope to where he had watched the rising of the moons. The hoarse cries of laughter, the rising songs of the chants, drifted out to him. Looking back down on the vast plain, the steppe was awash with light to the far horizon, the ceremonial bonfires to greet the rising of Ulma Karzorm now serving as the roasting pits of cattle, their speared bodies turning on the spits.

He could feel the coiling power of his people, the Horde that for hundreds of generations had ridden the world, rejoicing as they had down through the ages at the moon feasting of the spring grass, the marking of the time of the ride. There was but one moment that surpassed this, the day of the first moon feast before Barkth Nom, when all of the peoples gathered together at the foot of the mountain standing as one host, torches in hand, chanting the songs of praise onto the ancestors who dwelled on high, singing words of strength to the yet unnamed males who on that night would ascend the mountain for the first time. He shivered inwardly at the memory of it: gaining the high place and looking back at the ocean of light below, each torch marking a soul, the combined light as bright as day, their voices rising like thunder to the high places.

He sensed that power now, looking out across the steppe. Tomorrow twenty-five umens, two of them Tugar, would turn northwest, followed three days later by seven more who would ride straight north through the hills. Two umens were already across the narrows, having crossed over during the last month, and would move to harass the Roum. The remaining five would stand as a reserve, kept back in case the Bantag decided after all to double back on their march and harry them from the rear.

It would work, it had to work, for there was no alternative. If the march north and east was blocked but for a season, starvation would be staring at them by autumn. For that matter there was always the chance that the Bantag would shift north after all, cutting in front of their march a year further on. They had to break through, smashing all the way to Roum by fall, and then quickly move eastward for two seasons' march by the year afterward.

"His anger will cool, shield-bearer, it was merely the power of the drink."

Tamuka whirled around, nervous that someone had been able to approach him without being heard.

"It is a curious rank, your shield-bearer," Muzta Qar Qarth said, coming up to stand by Tamuka's side, a thin smile lighting his features at having caught him unaware.

Tamuka said nothing but bowed low, even though this was the Qar Qarth of the disgraced Tugar Horde.

"As I look back upon the things that were, I see a use for such as you, though if one had told me five seasons back that I would have need of someone who could speak to me, and I would be forced to listen, I would have laughed."

Muzta shook his head, looking down at his boots, kicking them absently through the grass.

"I did have one such as you—a warrior, though." He paused, a sad smile lighting his graying face.

"Qubata," he whispered. "He tried to tell me in the end, but I would not hear."

"His name was known even in our yurts," Tamuka said politely.

"From the moment he first heard of these Yankees, some inner voice seemed to warn him of what they might do. He tried to tell me of that . . ." he said, his voice trailing off, "but I would not listen . . ."

Tamuka said nothing.

"If I had heeded his words then, the Horde of the Tugars would still live in its power."

"And his words were?"

"I think in the end he believed that we should simply leave them, to go elsewhere, to make our strength stronger and wait for another day. To come perhaps even to an agreement."

"To make peace? That is what the hero of Orki counseled?" Tamuka asked, a note of sarcasm in his voice.

"Yes, the planner of victory at Orki," Muzta said, looking over at the shield-bearer.

"I was there," Tamuka replied. "Not old enough to draw a bow, but I was there."

"Your sire?"

"Killed in the stand of Qarth Barg, commander of the Yushin Umen."

"The Yushin, they fought well," Muzta replied.

"Not one of them lived, Tugar," Tamuka said, his voice cold. "I remember the calling of their death songs as they held the pass of Orki, drowned beneath your river of arrows. Ah yes, Qar Qarth, I still remember that moment."

"You still hate us for that," Muzta said, "though it was you who saved the council of the three Qar Qarths. And yet now I hear hatred in your voice."

"I hate the cattle more," Tamuka said. "My sire, all of the Yushin Umen now ride the everlasting sky. They died well, though I can hate you for that. But those who died against cattle? How will they ride, how will they sing of their death? First the cattle corrupted us, and now they slay us."

"How many Merki have they slain so far?" Muzta asked. "Five hundred, a thousand at most in last autumn's campaign and during this winter. I lost seventeen umens, a hundred and seventy thousand of my warriors. If anyone has the right to hate them, it is I."

Muzta paused, his features impassive as he looked at Tamuka.

"Though I forget, of course, the cattle also slew all the other heirs."

Tamuka looked into Muzta's eyes. Did he suspect? Were the quiet rumors about Vuka known even in the Tugar camp?

"I do not sense the hatred you should have for them," Tamuka said, deciding to shift the topic away from the death of the Zan Qarth's brothers.

"Oh, I hate them. I had promised myself long before that there would be a day when Keane would be my guest for the moon feast."

"But?"

Muzta shook his head and smiled.

"He is as good as any commander of the Orkons or of your Vushka Hush. That was my biggest mistake. I underestimated him and those who followed him. For after all, I had said to myself, they are only cattle. You saw that yourself, in that fiasco of last year: in less than forty days they built a fleet to match ours, they deceived you and your cattle Cromwell when victory was actually in your hands. Keane outfought my own Qubata, and do not forget that it was Qubata who once outfought you and your entire horde, though we stood outnumbered two to one."

"Why are you telling me this?" Tamuka asked. "I am but the shield-bearer to the Zen Qarth. Speak these words to Jubadi, to his commanders of the umens and to the commanders of ten umens."

Muzta smiled.

"Would they listen to a Tugar, to the leader of a people in disgrace for having lost to cattle?"

Muzta shook his head, laughing softly as he looked up to the great wheel that stood high in the night sky.

"There are times I still cannot believe it, that I lead my people thus to disaster, that I am now reduced to leading but two umens under the banner of your people, begging thus for a scrap of protection while the yurts of my clans are fifteen hundred miles away, defenseless, and hostage for our behavior."

Muzta stepped away from Tamuka, his gaze sweeping the vast assemblage, which resounded with the shouts of celebration, the cries of dying cattle, the song chants of the singers, the deep rumbling strength of the Merki Horde.

"They'll change you the way they changed us," Muzta said coldly. "When I was born into the yurt of my father the bow was placed in my hand—the first thing I grasped before clutching at the teat of my mother. When my one surviving son sires his firstborn, what shall be placed in his hand?

"Shall it be the tools of the cattle, the weapons they force upon us, the shrouds of the ships that fly the air, the hammer that beats at the forge, the rails of iron that their fire-breathing dragons ride upon?

"All these things the cattle force us to take if we are to survive," Muzta said quietly.

"That is why I say we must kill them all," Tamuka replied sharply, an edge of hard passion in his voice. "In order to save what we are, in the end we will have to destroy them. We will have to learn all that they know, smash them down, and then destroy any memory of cattle and their devices. Only then may we again wander the steppe as is our right."

Muzta shook his head, laughing.

"And who will feed us? We ride fat and bloated, we arrive at their cities in the autumn knowing that all that we shall need will be provided by them. And when they are gone?"

"We will again be the Hordes, with this world wiped clean. We will learn new ways, without the vermin of cattle who threaten to destroy us. We will learn to create our own food. There will never be peace between us. Jubadi is wrong to believe that we can simply defeat them here and then all will be as it was."

Angry with himself for having voiced a direct opposition to his Qar Qarth in the presence of one outside the Merki, he turned away with an angry growl.

"If I mentioned that you spoke these words to me," Muzta said quietly, "you would die. For if one of my trusted advisors did such to me I would cut him down with my own blade."

"Then do it," Tamuka snapped, not bothering to look back.

"It is safe with me, shield-bearer," Muzta whispered.

Tamuka knew he should offer thanks, for after all the Qar Qarth of another horde at this moment held his life in his hands.

"And your Zan Qarth Vuka, would he ever listen to your words?"

Tamuka looked back.

"Do not expect to bribe me with my life, Tugar." Muzta smiled.

"There is no intent. Your life is yours, I have no desire to hold it."

Tamuka nodded finally.

"Is your Zan Qarth ready to lead if Jubadi should fall now?" Muzta asked quietly, as if speaking to himself. "You might believe your Jubadi to be wrong when it comes to the question of how to manage the cattle when the war is won. But neither you nor I may deny that he is a worthy warrior. Overconfident, yes, against these Yankees, but capable. But your Zan Qarth?"

Vuka as Qar Qarth? It was what he had trained a lifetime for, picked above all others to stand at the side of the next leader of the Horde. Vuka was useless. He would rush in headlong, the same as he did in the streets of Roum, the same as this Tugar did. There would be no such art as Jubadi was using.

And he was the murderer of his own flesh, of that he was certain.

"He will be ready," Tamuka replied, his voice cold.

"But of course." And Muzta smiled, his teeth glistening red in the moonlight.

"I must return to the tents of my warriors," Muzta said. "It will be a long ride tomorrow."

Tamuka bowed low as the Qar Qarth turned, his

cattle-hide cloak rustling in the night air, sending up a swirling scent of flowers and fresh spring grass.

A light mist was starting to rise, casting a ghostly shadow as Muzta disappeared into the night.

Drawing yet farther away from the great yurt of Jubadi, Tamuka drifted into the night, the mist rising up out of the ground and embracing him with chilly hands.

Settling down on the ground he stretched out, letting the fog wrap around him. It glowed faintly from the twin moons drifting opaquely through the night sky.

His breath started to come in short staccato bursts, faster and yet faster, a continual motion of drawing in and rapid exhaling. A gradual tingling started at his finger tips, coiling up through his arms, knotting into his chest, and then ever so gently his gaze lost its focus. His breath came at longer and yet longer intervals, until it seemed as if he were already dead.

He could feel his *tu*, the spirit of the shield-bearer, stirring within, ready to leap forth, to rise into the night sky, to seek the voices of the ancestors, and he followed it outward, so that the vast and rolling steppes seemed to race beneath his soul.

Faces drifted before him, his sire laughing with the joy of battle in his fiery eyes, and he felt that joy. And there was Yourga, his master of the hidden paths, whispering to him to turn away from his *ka*, the spirit of the warrior, and to delve instead into the soul of *tu*, that of the shield-bearer.

Do not be driven by the *ka*, let it pass beyond your heart, beyond your soul, be Merki and yet be not, be warrior and yet be guide to the warrior *ka*, the spirit of the Horde, for it is thus that all of us shall survive.

And even as he wandered he chanted the hidden words of the *tu*, but the *ka* called. A host galloped past, warrior souls racing across the midnight sky, hearing the voices of those who still rode upon the endless sea of grass. He could see them as well, the vast spread of the Horde, on this the eve of spring riding and of war.

Spirits raced past him, through him, riding the everlasting ride of the everlasting sky. And yet he could see others moving closer and yet closer, moving in, spreading outward, hedging about them.

The spirit-riders turned, drawing back, their shouts of triumph stilled.

Cattle stood upon the horizon, waiting, cold gleams of hate in their eyes.

Could they come thus even here? Tamuka wondered. In the end would cattle cross even through the gates of fire to the very realms of the everlasting sky?

Yet surely it could be so. For when Merki cast down Tugar upon the grassy sea below, then was it not so that, in the everlasting sky above, Merki would then drive Tugar? How else could it be, for were not all things but reflections of others, the victory granted in one place strengthening the spirits above? The strength of the spirits in turn giving power to the *ka* of those below?

The spirit-riders turned, gazing upon him as if he were somehow responsible for this abomination. The voice of his father, of all the Yushin Umen who had died in glory, as noble as any might wish, all of them were silent, their gazes intent upon the northern horizon.

He thought for a moment of his pet, wondering, knowing. That alone was his design, known by no other. That had been a masterful bending, a training without the cattle pet even being aware, sending him forth yet inwardly knowing what he would do. At least in that was the hidden plan within the plan.

His *ka* now realized all which would have to be done, even as the spirit of the shield-bearer, the very power which allowed him thus to travel without form, to learn the inner knowledges, rebelled. And he watched in silence as Yourga, the master of the white clan, master of all who had trained beneath him as shield-bearers, wept.

Yuri stirred uncomfortably in his sleep. Again the dream, the nightmare returning. Half-awake for a moment, his composure dropped and the tears filled his eyes, clouding the light of the moon showing through the window of his room. It was called his home, yet it was a prison nevertheless. Still, it was a place where he was safe from those who would kill him out of hand, the outcast, the flesh-eater, the pet, the one despised. They allowed him a semblance of freedom, yet there were always the guards, passing the lazy days in a village far beyond Novrod, where none knew him. Yet always they were with him, watching him.

Keane. He was almost awake as the thought formed. Keane must know why he was here. Keane had sent him here, saying it was to protect him, to keep him alive. Alive for what?

He blinked the tears away. Keane knew, Tamuka knew as well; he could feel their voices inside of him. Both were playing out some mystery, and he was in the middle. Were his actions now his own, or was he the illusion of someone else's designs?

Tomorrow would be like the day before. Like all the days before, except for those rare moments when, late in the evening, he would be taken to one of their machines that rode on iron rails, to visit Keane and talk. And then he would be brought back here, alone. He wanted for nothing. Yet he wanted for everything.

He closed his eyes, sleep drifting back gently, softly. Again, as consciousness fell away, the inner calling stirred through his dreams.

Chapter 3

Choking with laughter, Andrew wiped the tears from his eyes.

"But soft, what light through yonder window breaks? It is the east, and Juliet, bejesus, is the sun."

Pat, engaged in a dramatic piece of overacting, delivered the lines in his thickest brogue, convulsing the Yankees in the audience with gales of laughter. As he stumbled through several of his lines the audience cheered him on, prompting him when needed.

"O Romeo, Romeo, wherefore art thou Romeo?"

Bob Fletcher appeared on the balcony, dressed as a Rus peasant girl, wearing a horsehair wig that came down to his knees. The Rus and Yankee audience exploded with laughter and Bob gave a cheerful wave, blowing kisses, while Pat, with one knee bent, looking up imploringly, hands clasped together.

Romeo and Juliet was a favorite with the Rus, and though the words were being delivered in English, so conversant were they with the famed scene that more than one shouted the words in unison in their own tongue.

Reaching the climax of the scene, Pat scrambled up a conveniently placed ladder to plant the legendary kiss. He closed his eyes, leaning forward, and

131

Bob turned around, presented his more than ample backside, and the scene blacked out.

The theater was rocked with hysterical laughter.

"Mixing Chaucer with Shakespeare," Kathleen said, holding her sides.

"Thank God Pat and a couple of other boys had copies of Shakespeare in their gear," Emil said, between gasps of laughter.

The earthier humor certainly would not have played to a mixed audience back home, even though outrageous parodies of Shakespeare were all the rage there, but the Rus obviously loved it, calling for several encores before the next act appeared.

The next scene was far more serious, a vignette from *Macbeth* played by several Rus actors, the main character now portrayed as a mad boyar, the audience sitting spellbound at his death scene, applauding wildly when his body was dragged off. Macbeth, played by the young Gregory, who had survived his now legendary ride to deliver the news of Andrew's planned return from Roum, appeared for a curtain call.

"That boy could be another Edwin Booth someday," Kathleen said approvingly. "Did you ever see him play?"

"At the Astor in New York," Emil replied, "though I preferred his father as King Lear."

"Papa loved the Booths," Kathleen said, her voice suddenly filled with nostalgia.

"I didn't care for the youngest," Emil said, "too full of himself; a bit too much madness in that one's eyes."

"Maybe you have to be a bit mad to be an actor," Andrew said quietly.

A troupe of jugglers appeared on stage, the audience cheering them on at first but booing loudly, and with obvious relish, when the act did not progress beyond the simplest of routines. When one of them missed a throw, hitting his partner on the head with a club and knocking the man over, the audience broke into wild cheers of delight, the crestfallen team retreating to a barrage of heckles.

Several patriotic tableaux were next, starting with the signing of the Constitution of Rus, then the driving of the rail spike completing the MFL & S line to Roum, which drew a rowdy cheer from the railroad workers. Then came the killing of the traitorous senator Mikhail, his staged appearance drawing curses and hisses from the audience. Mikhail was shown groveling in cowardly fashion, a Merki standard behind him to clearly identify his loyalties, the Rus soldiers looking at him with exaggerated gestures of contempt. The staged tableau broke the traditional frozen form by the single action of a gun firing. Mikhail fell over and the audience broke into cheers. The final presentation was the triumph of the Rus over the Tugars, based upon a highly popular illustration in *Gates' Illustrated Weekly* paper. Part of the stage was filled with soldiers looking heroically off to a far horizon, the rest of it piled high with Tugar bodies. The staging even included a wind machine off in the wings, a propeller powered by hand crank which allowed the flags to flutter. The audience broke into a spontaneous rendition of "The Battle Cry of Freedom," sung in Rus, climaxed with wild cheering as the tableau team broke their rigid poses to accept the ovation.

The next act came out—a Rus choir singing several of their traditional love songs—and the entire audience joining in with enthusiasm. The love songs finished, the group started a round of songs brought to this world by the Yankees, and the audience sang along, a fair number of them weeping openly, especially when "All Quiet Along the Potomac" started.

It jarred Andrew back for a moment, for the song had cropped up again during the winter, a strange ironic pull from the old world. It was followed in turn by "When This Cruel War Is Over."

The two songs worked their old effect, with many of the veterans around him, including Emil and Kal, unashamedly wiping away their tears.

Andrew sat in the shadows of the presidential box, his hand in Kathleen's. She had always denounced such ballads as syrupy sentiment, but he could feel her hand pressing tightly into his.

> Weeping sad and lonely,
> Hopes and fears how vain,
> Yet praying, when this cruel war is over,
> Praying that we meet again.

He tried not to look over at her, but he couldn't help himself as the chorus, singing in the deep Rus bass, picked up the final refrain. They said nothing, just looking at each other in the shadows. She had once said that she would never marry him, that she could not bear the anguish of another love going off to war like her first fiancé, never to return. Yet she had reached out again.

It was thirteen days since the twin full moons. They must be coming by now. It could be tonight that his brief visit home would finish—definitely before the end of the week.

"I love you," he finally whispered, the only words he could bring himself to say.

She leaned her head on his shoulder, pressing his hand in tight between her breasts.

"You must come back," she said, her voice barely

audible as the chorus continued. "I couldn't bear life without you."

He said nothing, not wanting her to hear the choking of his voice.

As the song ended most of the audience was silent, a few clapping weakly.

The theater darkened and Gregory appeared alone on the stage, dressed in the blue uniform of a union colonel, his left sleeve pinned up. Andrew looked around uncomfortably. Kathleen squeezed his hand and, feeling embarrassed, Andrew leaned back in his chair so that no one outside the box could see him.

Behind Gregory there was a flash of smoke, then flames appeared and behind the flames a backlit curtain was filled with the shadows of men marching. A nargas sounded, sending a chill down Andrew's spine, its strident call filling the hall, many in the audience shouting, some in anger, others in discomfort and fear. There was a rattle of simulated musketry, a deep kettledrum booming like cannon fire, bugles in the orchestra sounding the charge.

It was all quite effective, as good as anything he had ever seen on the stage, and Andrew felt strangely moved. The effects died away as if the battle were still being fought in the distance, the flames licking up behind Gregory.

"Once more into the breach, dear friends, once more!" he began, his voice low, melodious, and filled with power.

Andrew felt a deep stirring as the young Rus officer continued to recite from *Henry V.*

> But when the blast of war blows in our ears,
> Then imitate the action of the tiger;
> Stiffen the sinews, summon up the blood,
> Disguise fair Nature with hard-favour'd rage;

The boy's voice increased in pitch, rising to be heard as the rattle of musketry grew louder, the flames rose higher:

"And you, good yeomen,
Whose limbs were made in Rus, show us here
The mettle of your pasture: let us swear
That you are worth your breeding, which I
    doubt not:
For there is none of you so mean and base
That hath not noble lustre in your eyes.
I see you stand like grey-hounds in the slips,
Straining upon the start. the game's afoot:
Follow your spirit; and upon this charge,
Cry, "Kesus and Perm for Rus, our Republic,
    and mankind!"

There was a moment of silence, and then as if a dam had burst the audience was on its feet, roaring its approval. Gregory turned to face the presidential box and, coming to attention, he saluted, not dropping his hand.

"Go on," Emil prompted, urging Andrew to stand up.

With tears in his eyes Andrew came to his feet, his knees feeling weak. He came to attention and saluted Gregory, and then turning to face the audience saluted them as well. The ovation rose to a sustained thunder.

It seemed as if a lone voice called out the words at first, to be joined within seconds by all those in the hall: "Mine eyes have seen the glory. . . ."

Andrew joined in, his voice barely a whisper. He felt an arm go around his waist. Looking over her head he saw Kal standing beside her, his features drawn and solemn, hat over his heart.

The song died away, followed by yet another ovation. Andrew bowed his thanks to the audience and to all the actors who had come out on stage to join in "The Battle Hymn of the Republic" and left the box, stepping out a side exit of the hall to avoid the crowd.

It was a warm spring night and he breathed deeply, enjoying the fresh air after the smoke-filled stuffiness of the music hall. The crowd pouring out the front exits started up the hill toward the village green of the Yankee settlement, where an outdoor ball was still in progress, the faint strains of the music drifting along the street.

"The men have been planning that one for weeks," Pat said, coming out the backstage exit and wiping the greasepaint off of his face with a dirty handkerchief.

Andrew nodded his appreciation, still unable to reply. Kal and Emil stood beside him with approving grins.

"Rather embarrassing," Andrew finally whispered.

"Well, the boy was your orderly before he became a hero with a Congressional Medal of Merit, and an actor to boot. He remembered your saying how much you loved *Henry V*, and he wanted to do it."

Gregory came out the back door, still dressed in the blue uniform of a colonel of the 35th. Seeing Andrew, he nervously came to attention and saluted.

"I hope you liked it, sir."

Andrew stepped forward and patted Gregory on the shoulder.

"Embarrassed the hell out of me, but I loved it. Thank you."

The boy grinned with delight.

"How's that chest wound, son?" Emil asked.

"Fit as can be, sir. I just got my orders to report back."

Andrew smiled.

"Assistant Chief of Staff for Hans Schuder is a tough job, Gregory. You'll do all the real work and get none of the glory."

"Actually, sir, I was hoping for a field command," Gregory said.

"Take it easy for a while, son. You did your part last time—it's a miracle you lived."

"Your horse Mercury saw me through it, sir; all I did was ride along."

Andrew nodded.

"Give yourself a little more time to heal, get some experience with Hans, and we'll see about a field assignment in a couple of months."

"Thank you, sir!" The boy grinned with delight.

He backed away, saluted again, and then dashed off to where a girl, dressed in a simple peasant dress, waited in the shadows.

Andrew grinned as the two disappeared, arms around each other, the boy talking with animated excitement.

"Shall we go back to our place for some tea?" Kathleen asked. She paused for a moment to look over at Pat, who stood before them, looking rather ridiculous with streaks of makeup smeared into his red beard. Bob Fletcher stood behind him, still in a dress, grinning over his performance.

"And maybe a bit of the cruel," she whispered in a lilting voice, while giving Pat a conspiratorial wink.

"Now, Kathleen?" Emil interjected.

"Good heavens, Emil, too much abstinence might kill the poor suffering man."

" 'Tis true," Pat groaned. "I need a fortifier after the humiliations I suffered on the stage."

"Well, you volunteered for it," Emil replied. "Chief of Artillery behaving such."

"All in good fun," Kal said approvingly. "It shows

none of us are too caught by our titles. Anyhow, a touch of the cruel, as you say, sounds most welcome."

The party stepped around to the front of the theater, exchanging pleasantries with the last of the crowd who had lingered to offer their best wishes and congratulations on the performance.

The theater was something new to the Rus, who before the arrival of the Yankees were more used to the occasional novelty acts and troupes of singers in the great square during market days, or to morality plays, usually of a somber nature, performed on the steps of the cathedral.

The love of Shakespeare, and parodies of him, of minstrel-styled shows, melodramas of the most overwrought kind with such titles as *Her Love Betrayed, or the Boyar and the Peasant Girl*, all interspersed with some of the more traditional Rus singing, was yet another touch of Yankee culture, translated and blended into Rus society. Two privates from the 44th New York, one of whom had briefly worked with a Traveling Tom show, had formed the theater group, obtaining backing to build a five hundred seat auditorium which was filled nearly every night.

Rivals had already opened a second theater near the end of last year on the north side of town, scrounging up leftover lumber and opening with a successful thirty-night run of *The Merchant of Venice*, translated into Rus and retitled *The Boyar of Novrod*, with Shylock recast as a former boyar. Though John had complained about the disappearance of some necessary resources and the waste of time spent on the theater, Andrew had wholeheartedly approved of the venture, suspecting that if anything it was John's Methodist sensibilities that were far more offended. He had agreed with John, though, that for now *Julius Caesar* would have to be censored for diplomatic reasons, as far as Marcus and the Roum were concerned.

Leaving the theater the group walked up the hill, following the last of the crowd. Andrew looked heavenward, soaking in the lingering warmth and enjoying the stars overhead. For an entire day he had managed to forget the pressure. There was really not much more he could do. The army was in place, the pickets fifty miles forward in the passes. This evening represented one final brief moment away, the first time home since the typhoid bout. The group laughed gaily about Pat's performance, the artilleryman joining in the fun with several rude comments about Bob.

They walked toward the village green, drifting through the shadows. Many of the homes facing the square were still lit. In the center of the square, under the octagonal band shell, the band was playing a quadrille and couples swayed in the shadows. There had been a review and open-air ball for the men of the 35th and 44th and their ladies, which had continued even while the theater performance had gone on. Couples passed them in the shadows, with soft voices whispering, some in Rus, a few in Latin or Carthinian, others in English, some in a blending of all four.

The band struck up a quickstep and the couples, many not sure of the steps, laughed and danced about the shell, their shadows flickering in the torchlight.

Andrew stopped to watch them.

"Gentlemen, the house is open," Kathleen said quietly, "Pat, you know where the vodka's hidden."

"And be quiet," Kal interjected, "or my Ludmilla will come storming down on the lot of you for waking the baby."

Pat bowed a thank-you to Kathleen, and the small

group who had fallen in with them crossed the green, weaving their way through the dancers.

"Reminds me of '64," Kathleen said, watching the dancers with a wistful smile.

"How's that?" Andrew asked.

"Second Army Corps held a ball on Washington's Birthday. It was a poignant, wonderful night, all the fine young officers and their ladies. They danced the night away, a final night of romance."

She paused.

"And three months later there was the Wilderness."

"Let's not think about it now," Andrew whispered.

She looked up at him and smiled.

"No, let's not."

He extended his hand, and she drifted into his embrace as the music shifted back to a waltz.

He had always felt clumsy when dancing, and yet for this moment they seemed to flow together, drifting across the green with all the young soldiers, the old veterans, the smiling girls shining with love, the wives with tears in their eyes. All seemed to know, yet all were caught, at least for that moment, in the dream that time would stand still for them, that the dance would go on, the music lingering forever. That this moment would become the reality, that the dream would hold off the darkness approaching from the south, at least until dawn. The couples swayed through the shadows and the band played on, its gentle sound drifting up to the stars.

Kal stood alone, watching them, holding his hat, head bowed as if in prayer, the grass beneath his feet damp with tears.

The dream had a soft, gentle quality to it, as if it floated on a breeze-wafted cloud. The field was green, the rich intensity of green that came only in the warmth of high spring, when every breath was ladened with the scent of life. It seemed to stretch on forever, a floating sea of green, the high stalks of grass wavering, shifting their color as the shadows of clouds drifted past like whitecaps flowing across a windswept ocean.

Somehow she felt aware that, after all, it was a dream. Curious, it wasn't here. No, this wasn't Valennia, it was back in the other world, back on Earth. She felt herself young, a girl again, fifteen. That's where she had seen this, out in Illinois, her father engineering the building of the rail line to Galena, the prairie a vast ocean marching to the far horizon.

If she but turned around he would be behind her, smiling his sad, distant smile. She could smell his tobacco, the faint scent of his afternoon brandy.

God, it was so beautiful, so unlike the stuffy closeness of Boston.

Is this a dream? It had to be. Daddy was dead, fifteen years was half a lifetime ago, but it all felt so real at this moment.

Why am I doing this, why am I dreaming this?

"Beautiful, is it not, Kathy darlin'."

She felt a cold shiver—it was Daddy's voice, and tears instantly clouded her vision.

"It's a dream," she whispered.

"Is it?" He laughed softly.

Now she remembered. This was her spot, the low knoll that she had found after Mama had died. It was where she was buried, just outside of town. She'd come here everyday to sit by her grave, to talk to her, to look out across the endless prairie, to find some comfort—and now she was back.

"I'm scared, Dado." Even as she spoke she heard her voice as that of a young girl, slipping into a touch of the brogue she had worked so hard to press out.

"You have every right to be scared," he whispered.

She felt the gentle touch of a hand on her cheek, and she started to tremble.

"You're dead." She choked on the words.

"Not really, not for my Kathy darlin'. Nothing can part that cord, here or there. I'm always with you, Kathy my angel."

Without looking back she reached behind, and felt his hand touch hers.

The wind swept past, sighing, the high grass rustling, golden flowers filling the air with cool scent.

"You're crying."

The voice was gentle, different, as if from another land.

She felt the hand squeeze lightly and then, as if made of gossamer, the fabric of her dreams unraveled.

A soft ticking echoed. Insistent voices rushed in. A distant boom rattled, window panes shaking.

With a start she sat up, and there was a single arm around her shoulders. Another boom snapped, followed by two more, closer. There were the scents of wool, horse, and leather, and a voice whispered in her ear, "It's all right, darling, just another air attack on the factories."

A high, insistent cry now brought her fully awake. Andrew was sitting on the bed, his arm around her, rocking her back and forth. He was home, he had been since yesterday. There was the dance last night, they had danced the night away, and then afterwards . . . That's why she was sleeping now, in late morning. It had been such a long, wonderful night, the first time in nearly two months.

The cry was now a drawn-out yell for attention, and through her tears she saw Maddie sitting up on the bed beside her, scared by the bombing and the artillery fire sending up a reply, arms outstretched to be held. They must have fallen asleep together after Andrew had left.

The dream? She knew there had been a dream, but it was already fading even as she tried to cling to it. Reaching out, she pulled Maddie into her lap, so that all three of them were together.

Andrew wrinkled his nose slightly.

"I think our angel needs a change," he said quietly.

"You mean it's time for me to change her," she replied teasingly, even as she loosened her gown to allow the child to nurse, an action that elicited an immediate sigh of contentment and silence.

"We'll take care of it later," Andrew said, shifting closer and cradling the two in his lap.

Even as she continued to nurse Maddie reached up and clasped one of her father's golden uniform buttons in her hand, round eyes shifting from Kathy to him.

The booming continued, and just on the edge of hearing one could make out the low insistent humming of the airships, as they started to swing back over the city. Nervously, Kathleen looked toward the window, but Andrew reassured her.

"Eight of them, this time. Don't worry, they're after the mills and the rail bridge."

He kissed her lightly on the forehead and she snuggled back into his lap, cradling Maddie in her arms.

"Still early in the morning?" she sighed.

"Only nine."

She had a half-memory of his leaving before dawn, tucking Maddie in alongside of her, promising to be back by dark.

Tense, she looked up into his eyes.

"I'm going back up to the front in an hour."

She didn't want to ask, there had been the promise

of three days. She didn't want to believe any of it, that it would never happen, that the darkness would turn away and disappear, far out into the flowing steppes.

"It's started," Andrew whispered.

"You're getting better at it, sir."

Chuck Ferguson grimaced, knowing that the locomotive engineer's compliment was a lie. Somehow he had never quite mastered the technique of playing out a song on the steam whistle. The engineer took hold of the cord, and with the skill of a virtuoso tapped out the opening bars of "Dixie." Chuck smiled at the obvious delight the old Novrodian experienced at showing off his ability. It was a strange little incongruity, but the unofficial anthem of the rebellion was far catchier and easier to play than the "Battle Hymn." Each of the engineers had his own signature tune; the pious a hymn, the ribald an obscene ditty, the patriotic one of the war songs carried over by the Yankees. Mina had long since given up his argument about each playing of a tune wasting x amount of steam, which equaled so many hundreds of cords of wood a year.

The pounding clatter of the tracks changed in tone and, stepping to the side of the cab, Chuck leaned out. The border marker signifying the entry into Roum territory shot past, and they were on the trestle. Most people found the crossing of the Sangros to be somewhat unnerving, the four-hundred-foot-long trestle shuddering beneath them as the engine and cars behind it thundered across. But he gloried in it.

The damn thing was a wonder—six hundred miles of track between Roum and Suzdal, six major rivers, dozens of smaller tributaries, the fifteen-hundred-foot ridge of the White Hills beyond Kev, and the long, undulating roll of the open steppes beyond that, all the way here to Hispania on the western border of the Roum. All of it by his design.

It was as if God had given him a vast world to play with, to let his imagination build whatever it desired. Granted, it was all bent to the war effort, ever since that terrible day when the Tugar Namer of Time had arrived before the gates of old Fort Lincoln, revealing to all of them the dark truth of what this world represented.

He had given them the machines to beat them, and by damn he would do it again. But beyond that he could not contain the inner joy the power given unto him had provided. Bill Webster had created the financial system and beginnings of capitalism, Gates his paper and books, Fletcher the food supply, and Mina ran all of them as chief of logistics, but, damn it, *he* had the machines.

"Someday we'll run this railroad clean around the world," Chuck announced, looking back at the engineer.

"I heard there's mountains east of here so tall they reach to the stars," the Novrodian said quietly.

"You'll see 'em. By god, we'll blast a tunnel right through them."

"Tunnel?"

Chuck smiled and shook his head, then slapped the engineer on the back.

"A hole under the ground!" We won't go *over* the mountains, we'll go *under* them!"

The engineer looked at him with an incredulous gaze.

"Trust me," Vincent laughed. "Someday you'll point this train eastward, and a couple of months later come back straight into Suzdal. We'll ring the world with iron and call it our own."

"If we beat the Merki," the engineer said quietly.

"We'll beat 'em, I'll see to that," Vincent responded.

The fireman stepped past Vincent, swinging open the iron door into the boiler, heaving another log in, and slamming the door shut.

The hollow clattering of the trestle faded away, to be replaced by ten more solid rumbles of hard ground. The engineer eased back on the throttle, giving three quick blows to the whistle to signal the brakemen to their stations atop the swaying cars. Reached forward, and with a quick jerk of the wrist, he started the bells to clanging with the rhythmic harmony so beloved by the Rus. Even in the cab of the engine there were the little artistic touches—the handle of the throttle cast like a bear's head, the woodwork adorned with curlicues of the woodman's chisel, the three bells tuned to sound in pleasant concord.

The engineer pulled the throttle back, nodding to the fireman to tap the brake. Leaning out the side of the cabin, Ferguson saw Hispania station straight ahead, the mudbrick and limestone walls of the ancient city on the rise beyond. An entire new town had sprung up beyond the wall in the last year. It had started with rough cabins to house the labor gangs for the bridge and rail line. It was followed by machine sheds, sidings, warehouses, and a round-house, all of which were surrounded by a rough earthen fort thrown up during the brief Roum campaign and now strengthened as a major fallback point on the line if Roum should ever be threatened again. A line ran up north from the city, using one of the original two-and-a-half-foot engines from the first days of the MFL & S railroad, converted to the new three-and-a-half-foot gauge. The line ran past the silver mines, and from there on into the vast north woods, a dozen miles beyond to where a powder mill and Chuck's work station were now located, safely removed from the prying eyes of the Merki air machines.

With bells ringing, the engine drifted into the station. It was aswarm with activity. Smiling, Chuck nodded a farewell to the engineer and fireman and clamored down the side of the locomotive. The engineer treated them to a quick rendition of "Dixie," and the voice of the stationmaster announcing their arrival was drowned out by the song.

The station was a touch of Rus in an alien land, but no one could mistake that they were in Roum. The laborers at the water tank and wood yard wore the tunics of Roum freemen, freemen who but last summer had still been slaves.

The sign swaying from the side of the station, in Rus, English, and Latin, announced that the line had entered the territory of the state of Ruom and that all local laws were to be obeyed.

A stone pillar was set in the middle of the platform before the rough board station. The pillar was shaped to look like a bundle of faeces, atop which was the eagle, or what passed for an eagle on this world, which to Chuck seemed more like a fat turkey vulture with blue feathers.

The voices were a cacophony of Latin, mingled with shouts of Rus. Vents of steam shot out from the engine, driving the spectators back, and the engine shuddered to a halt.

Leaping down from the cab, backpack over his shoulder, Chuck waded into the crowd. At least it smelled better, he realized, and he found himself scratching, longing for a good Roum bath. Perhaps that would be one habit the Rus might learn to good use.

"Vincent!"

Smiling, Vincent saw Jack Petracci wading through the crowd, a bevy of aides pushing in behind him.

After the conference Jack had returned, while he had stayed on in Suzdal for another week to inspect some of the changes in the factories and troubleshoot a host of problems. He'd left the city with a major migraine headache as a result.

Back to the real work, Chuck thought with a smile. The thunder of the engine, the talking of shop with the engineer, had served to clear his head. Out on the steppe he had opened the machine up to what he figured was damn near forty. If the track bed had been better than the emergency rush job of last year, he could have gone even faster. The headache was gone, washed out by the pounding pistons, the hissing steam, and the wind in his face.

From out of the first car he saw the plebeian consul Julius alighting, the workers cheering at the sight of him. The diminutive, dark-eyed man smiled nervously, and his smile broadened with delight as a young woman with black, waist-length hair pushed through the crowd and leaped into his arms.

"The old boy doesn't have the style of Kal," Jack said in English. "Kal would come off with a quick joke and some pressing of the flesh, kiss a couple of babies, and then go down to the water tank and want to pitch in."

"He'll do for starters, but it's Marcus running the show," Vincent replied absently, unable to take his eyes from the lithe body of the woman who now stood by Julius's side, her arm around his waist. "These people will learn some good Yankee politicking soon enough."

Julius, seeing Chuck, motioned for him to come over. Snapping to attention, Chuck saluted.

"A wonderful machine," Julius announced.

"Thank you, sir."

"I understand the need for secrecy, but would it

be possible for myself and my daughter to see what is inside the great building?"

Jack cleared his throat nervously. The workers involved in the project lived as virtual prisoners in barracks inside a separate stockade. Chuck realized there was a certain foolishness to it—the shed could contain only one thing, and what that was was an open secret, but only those people, and the workers at the powder mill, were allowed to pass beyond the silver mine on the spur line going north.

"Your train will be leaving in ten minutes, sir," Jack replied a bit too hurriedly.

"Daughter, sir?" Chuck asked.

Julius smiled at the look in the young man's eyes.

"Olivia, good sir," she whispered quietly, a smile broadening her features.

"I think it would be all right," Chuck replied nervously, and then looked over to the schedule board.

"There'll be another train into Roum in eight hours. You can run up with us, and take the afternoon train back down here to the station."

Jack sighed, but said nothing.

The girl smiled at him with delight, and he pointed to where the diminutive engine known as "The Old Waterville," the second engine ever made on this world, waited for its passengers. She was dwarfed by the *Malady* class engines running the main line from Suzdal to Roum, which could haul five times her weight at well over twice her speed. The "Waterville," her gilded letters on the cab slightly tarnished with age, held a certain nostalgic appeal for him as he walked up to her.

She seemed like nothing more than an oversized steam kettle with a tiny cab on her back, the wheels jutting out too far from the conversion from two-foot to three-and-a-half-foot gauge. She seemed more like a toy now, yet he felt a fondness for her, as if three years since she was built represented a gulf into a far less complicated age. After riding at the helm of the *Malady*, the heaviest of the MFL & S's engines, it was strange to be back to where it all had started.

The engineer, checking a bearing, turned around and saluted at Chuck's approach.

"How's she running?"

"A bit wheezy, sir, cylinders will need repacking soon, but she's still got some of her old heart." With a gloved hand he affectionately patted the side of her boiler.

Chuck looked over at the clock tower next to the station. The *Malady* let go with a long blast of her whistle, and with tolling bell started out of the station. Late passengers ran out of the station, some with a handful of bread or a bag of dried fruit, and raced down the platform to leap on board.

The *Malady* was no sooner out of the station heading on to Roum than the train waiting on the siding, pulled by the *City of Hispania*, let go with a long blast. The switchmaster looked up at the telegrapher, who leaned out of his office and hoisted up a green ball, the signal that the road west was cleared to Orono station and the Penobscot crossing a hundred miles up the line.

The switchmaster opened the way, and the engineer, leaning out of the cab, waved a salute. The engine started forward, pulling a string of fifteen boxcars packed with enough hard bread and salt-pork rations to feed the army in the field for several days.

Chuck watched with a swelling of pride. Andrew might be providing the leadership and vision to help them win this war and ensure the survival of the Republic, but without railroads they wouldn't stand a ghost of a chance against the Horde. It would be railroads that would win or lose this venture, more than any other factor.

He had heard more than one railroad man say that if the war against the rebs had started ten years earlier the Confederacy most likely would have won, that it would have been impossible to conquer a country bigger than all of Europe without rail lines to move and supply the armies. Well, the same stood true here: The alliance, supplies, and the mobility against horse-mounted warriors could be matched only by steam.

The train started across the Sangros, her whistle playing out the "Hymn to Kesus."

"Petrov Petrovich at the throttle," the *Waterville*'s engineer announced. "He's getting good at that tune."

The engineer looked back at the clock.

"Time to leave, sir."

Chuck smiled, feeling tempted to climb up into the cab. But there was something he had suddenly found a bit more interesting than the engine, so he went back to the single passenger car, mounted behind four hopper cars loaded down with sulphur for the powder mill.

Chuck could see his dozen odd aides chomping at the bit to get his attention, ready to deluge him with hours' worth of technical questions, but for the moment his attention was focused on Olivia as he helped her into the narrow passenger car.

The *Waterville* started up, its boilers sounding like an angry tea kettle compared to the deep throaty roar of the *Malady*. The train started out of its siding, clicking through an intersection leading into the roundhouse, where several engines were being overhauled.

The light ten-pound rails of the spur line rode up and down over the landscape with no attempt at grading. The earthen walls surrounding the warehouses and rail yard drifted by to the left, the ground around the fortification a mad warren of deadfalls. Originally he had wanted to put the shed inside the warehouse area, but the danger of it, and the need for some form of security, had forced him to agree with Keane that it would have to be built far beyond the town.

The bone-jarring ride carried them northward, out beyond the old cultivated fields that had supplied Hispania, past the outlying plantations of the wealthy, and onward until the distant forest seemed to be marching down out of the high hills. The high grassland started to give way to hills clumped with towering pines, which filled the air with a fresh brisk scent that Chuck found all so reminiscent of home. The track swung in along the high bluffs, looking down on the Sangros River, and the noise of its passage stirred up a flock of noisy ducks. By the thousands they took flight, and he watched them with amusement and a sense of envy as well.

Farther up the river, a long raft of logs was slowly making its way downstream to the sawmills at Hispania, the river men waving as the engine rattled past.

Another turn in the line dropped the train down into a narrow valley, across a rickety trestle, and then up a long slope covered with ancient trees. They were into the forest.

The world seemed to change in an instant—the air was cooler, damp, rich with the smells of spring, the dark gloom a welcomed change from the glare of the open steppe. Rus, just north of Suzdal, was like this, and so was Maine. He loved the open steppe, where the twin rails went straight for a hundred miles, the lines vanishing into one like the single-point perspectives he had learned to draw in school, but this felt far more like home.

The train pulled its way upward into the hills, passing occasional open stretches of fields and scatterings of trees, but ever so gradually it felt as if the forest were closing in, growing thicker and darker. The going was slow, for the track had been laid down at times in tight turns, to weave past a rough stretch of ground or stands of trees too thick to be cut down and instead simply bypassed.

Chuck kept looking over at Olivia, who cheerfully returned his somewhat longing gaze, but he found himself unable to think of anything to say. Now, if she'd only ask a question about the train, or one of his projects, but she sat across from him as if expecting the man to make the first move. So he kept a nervous silence while his staff chafed, not feeling comfortable discussing technical questions in front of a stranger, even if he were the plebeian consul. He spent long minutes in silence, looking out the open window as the forest drifted past. He'd sneak a look back at her, then gaze out the window again.

The long rise completed, the train passed a vast open area piled high with thousands of cut timbers. Julius looked at them with curiosity.

"All the bridges on the line have duplicates hidden right here," Chuck explained. "If raiders should burn a bridge, the way they did the Kennebec crossing last summer, we can move these timbers down and in a couple of days have the bridge up again—we're not going to be caught like last time. The lumber is pre-cut, numbered, and just needs to be fit in place."

"Who thought of this?" Olivia asked.

He wanted to lie, but couldn't.

"Hermann Haupt, back on the old world. Raiders kept burning our bridges, but it was said he could build them back faster than the rebs could light matches."

"Matches?"

Chuck fumbled in his pocket and pulled a lucifer out. Several of his staff looked slightly horrified.

"Don't worry, I was going to dump them out before we got there," he said quickly.

He struck the match into a flame, and Olivia looked at him as if the match, far more than the very train she was riding on, were a miracle.

The engine started to slow, and dropping down the side of a boulder-strewn slope it slid to a stop.

"All out!" Chuck announced, standing up and banging his head on the low ceiling. With an embarrassed curse he got out of the car and extended a hand to Olivia. She took it and held on for several seconds after alighting.

A track followed off from the switching into the woods, weaving its way around trees too large to be dropped, while the engine and its five cars were poised to continue straight ahead once the passengers were off.

"No engines up to where we're going today—too dangerous what with the sparks," Chuck announced.

"But the powder mill. It goes up to there, why not to the sheds?" Julius asked, pointing straight up the line.

"The powder mills are safe. We're just being cautious today since the wind is up slightly from where the track runs straight into the shed," Chuck replied, surprised for a second that Julius knew about the other secret hidden up here.

After the Merki air attack of the previous summer, Mina had pointed out that to rebuild anywhere in Rus would have been to reinvite attack on one of their most crucial and vulnerable industries. There was another logic as well, since the sulphur and, far more importantly, the saltpeter resources of Roum were virgin territory. So the mill had quietly been constructed out here, while a fake plant, which had been repeatedly attacked, had been constructed near Novrod.

Leading the way, Chuck moved alongside the track. Olivia let her hand slip away, but kept by his side. The track made a sharp turn to the left after a hundred yards through the heavy forest, and coming around the bend Chuck came up short, a child-like grin of delight brightening his features.

The balloon shed, constructed of rough-cut boards and nearly forty feet high and over a hundred and fifty in length, stood before him in the clearing. A second and third one stood behind it, with a fourth already under construction on the far side of the stump-littered field beyond. Floating in the middle of the first shed his latest weapon hovered, as if ready to take wing at any moment.

Jack looked over at him and smiled.

"We finished the inflation two days ago. So far there don't seem to be any major leaks. It's just a question of waiting for the engine to be mounted, and we're ready to fly."

"The engine?"

"We were waiting for you to start the test run."

Chuck nodded absently as he walked forward, all else forgotten. The doors of the hanger were wide open, the louvers above the shed also propped open to allow any errant wisps of the dangerously explosive gas a way out.

"And this will fly?" Olivia asked.

"Of course. If those damn beasts can do it, so can we. Just give us a little time, and we'll push them out of the air."

As if approaching an altar, Chuck walked into the

rough-board hanger, the long, sausage-shaped balloon hovering above him.

"Any problems with inflation?"

"One of the wooden interior support struts in the aft part of the rear bag shifted, cutting through the fabric, but we got it fixed," Jack replied.

Chuck nodded. He had argued that rather than simply be a loose bag of gas, the aerosteamer— as he was already calling it—should have a rigid interior structure onto which the double layer of silk would be stitched. The Merki balloons lacked this feature, relying on internal pressure to stay rigid, and he had noticed their tendency to wobble and bulge in flight.

The frame was of nothing more than thin strips of a bamboo-like wood, lashed together into a long, basketlike frame, but it thus required a lot more lift. Still, the balloon looked far more solid. Walking down the length of the shed, Chuck stopped in the middle of the balloon and peered up into a round hole cut directly above him. The inside of the balloon was lost in darkness, but he could imagine the vast frame rising above him. All that was needed now was to install the engine underneath the hole. The exhaust heat would go straight up, providing the necessary lift and the control for maneuvering. The gas bags of hydrogen fore and aft would provide the rest of the buoyancy. It still made him extremely nervous to be hooking a steam engine to a hydrogen balloon, but there was no other alternative. He had heard about helium gas, but how in the world it was to be found, captured, and processed was totally beyond him. If it hadn't been for Jack's past experiences with the circus, and his knowledge of how to bathe zinc shavings with sulfuric acid to make hydrogen, no one on this world would now be flying. He could remember Hinsen's hanging around while Jack had been working on the project, and could only surmise that the traitor had given the secret to the Merki. The hatred that thought triggered disturbed him, and he pushed it aside. For him this war was not about hatred. It was a question of outthinking a foe.

Walking down the rest of the length of the shed, he pointed out the details of the balloon to Julius, knowing that Olivia was soaking it all in.

"The engine is the final stage," Chuck said, and leaving the rear of the hanger he led the group across the stump-littered field. In the distance a busy crew of workers was swarming over the latest hanger going up. Trees dropped in the clearing were going straight into the steam-powered sawmill, which was safely operating downwind from the field.

In the center of the clearing half a dozen four-pounders were set, the barrels now mounted on yokes that would allow the weapons to be swung up to a vertical position, their crews coming to their feet as the group passed. Similar emplacements were going up around all the key industrial sites in Rus and Roum. A number of hits had been scored on the Merki ships, but except for the one crash they had yet to bring the enemy down. He paused for a moment to look up at the high watchtower. On a clear day they could see all the way to Roum, seventy miles away. Only the week before a Merki ship had hit the city and then ventured northward, as if to scout, but had then turned back just south of Hispania. It had been a near thing. One firebomb on the hangers would have destroyed an entire winter's work.

The doors of the log cabin work shed were open, revealing an interior lit by kerosene lamps, and Chuck led the group in. A team of Rus mechanics gave him a cheery greeting as he went through the crowd, patting men on the back, firing off questions and quips. With obvious pride he walked up to the small engine resting on a workbench in the middle of the room. The air was heavy with a thick, oily smell, which Chuck seemed to breathe in with relish.

"It's powered by coal oil," he announced, looking over at Julius, who shook his head in confusion.

"From the oil that bubbles out of the ground at Caprium and Brundisia. We boil the oil, and get a fluid out of it that burns hotly." He nodded to a barrel off to one side of the shed, and to the lamps hanging overhead.

"Weight is everything for the aerosteamer. The oil holds a lot more energy than coal, and more importantly, it burns clean. We don't have to worry about any sparks. The exhaust from the engine will fill the middle portion of the bag. When we want to go up we close the top vent, when we want to drop we simply open it up. Now the engine was the tough part. . . ." He went into his subject with relish, not even realizing that Julius and Olivia were smiling politely, barely able to understand his Latin and totally lost as to the subject.

"A regular steam engine just weighs too much, and beyond that it needs water, lots of it. So I figured we'd go with a caloric engine. John Ericsson back home built the first one about thirty years ago."

He looked at Julius closely.

"John Ericsson?" Chuck asked. He said the name as if invoking the name of Cincinnatus. "He was the fellow who built ironclad ships."

Julius nodded politely, and Chuck smiled.

"Well anyhow, rather than using steam for power, he used superheated hot air to drive the pistons."

Chuck went over to the engine on the table and lightly patted the boiler, which was already heated up.

"Hot air rushes into the pistons, and as it expands

it cools, with a jet of hot air coming in on the other side to drive them back. The pistons start cranking the drive shaft, which then turns this."

He stepped behind the machine and pointed to a wooden blade propeller, nearly a dozen feet across with four vanes.

Chuck looked over at Jack, and his smile did little to ease a growing tension.

"Ready for another try?"

Jack nodded.

"Feyodor, the fit on pistons?"

"Rebored to a thousandth-of-an-inch tolerance. Overall weight for the machine is down to just under five hundred pounds," the young machinist, several years Chuck's junior, replied in a voice of authority. Chuck patted him on the back. The boy first had been trained as a toolmaker, when they had begun the mass production of muskets. But Chuck soon realized he had that rare innate ability of the born craftsman, and he raised him to be the chief mechanic for this most demanding project so far. His only problem was that Feyodor had an identical twin, Theodor, blessed with the same skills, and it was ofttimes impossible to tell the two apart.

"Then let's start her up."

Going over to the throttle he tentatively grabbed hold, hesitated for a second, and then nodded over to Feyodor.

"It's your toy," Chuck announced, after what was obviously a bit of an inner struggle.

Grinning, Feyodor stepped forward and grabbed hold of the throttle, then opened it up a notch.

Nothing happened.

Puzzled, Chuck opened the boiler, peered through the glass door, and reached over to open up the fuel supply. The small smokestack shimmered with heat.

With a gentle sigh the twin cylinders moved ever so imperceptibly.

Feyodor looked over at Chuck, who nodded in agreement as the young mechanic clicked the throttle back another notch. The stroke of one of the pistons reached out to its maximum as the other pulled in, and the machine seemed to hang there.

Chuck reached out to grab hold of the small flywheel attached to the drive shaft and spin it. With a hissing chug the cylinder went through the rest of its stroke, returned, extended, and returned, the propeller cranking over slowly on the end of the shaft with a soft, whistling sigh.

Smiling, Feyodor clicked the throttle back further, and the machine set into a slow, steady, hissing hum.

"Let's move it to the measuring table!" Chuck shouted.

Assistants rushed up, grabbing hold of the corners of the iron sheet that the machine was bolted down on. Picking it up and holding it high overhead so that the propeller wouldn't strike the ground while it was still slowly cranking, they carried it farther back into the shed, placing it down on another table that was covered with grease.

Chuck went around to the end of the table closest to the whirling propeller. Ducking low, he hooked a restraining cable to the side of the engine and another to a spring-driven scale.

"Everyone else out of the building!"

Jack came up to Chuck's side and grabbed hold of him by the arm. "Then you're going out, too. Keane gave explicit orders that you were never to be in any dangerous position."

Chuck shook his head.

"God damn it," he laughed, "I outrank everyone in this room! Now get out!"

"I'm staying," Jack announced, and the other assistants and workers nodded in agreement.

"All right then, we all stay!" Chuck shouted, nodding for Feyodor to open the throttle up.

The propeller, which had been windmilling over with a soft steady *thump*, started to shift into a blur, Feyodor's clothing whipping out around him. The hissing of the hot-air engine rose in tone to a demonic shriek, shimmers of heat rising off it, the forced-air exhaust puffing and filling the room with the oily smell of burned kerosene.

The hum of the propeller rose to a trembling roar, and with a shout of exaltation Chuck pointed to the engine as it started to slide forward, restrained only by the cable attached to the scale.

"Over a hundred pounds of push, and climbing! Give it all she's got, Feyodor!"

The Russian pushed the throttle full over, and the workshop was filled with the howl of the engine and propeller.

"Over three hundred and going up! By damn, we've got it!"

Chuck stepped back from his position between the propeller and the engine and started over to where Julius and Olivia stood wide-eyed, backed up against the wall.

"It's loose!"

Chuck turned and stood in numbed astonishment as the engine seemed to leap free from the workbench, driven forward by the thrust of the whirling propeller. It all happened far too fast for him to react, as the propeller hit the edge of the workbench and disintegrated, filling the room with a howling tornado of splinters. Something knocked him behind the knees and he was down on the ground.

Shouts of panic echoed, and a coal oil lamp, hit by part of a propeller, smashed, exploding in flames.

The mad cacophony of noise gradually died away, to be replaced by the shouts of workers rushing in from the outside carrying buckets of sand. The engine, now over on its side, was still chugging away, a machine gone berserk that simply refused to quit. A river of flame poured out from its upended fuel tank.

Chuck felt light-headed. A warm trickle was running down into his eyes, and he was unsure of how he had wound up on the ground.

"You're bleeding!"

He looked down to his legs and saw Olivia clinging to his knees, realizing that it was the girl who had reacted while he had stood dumbstruck, knocking him down just as the propeller had exploded.

She crawled up beside him, wiping the blood from his eyes. He started to sit up, but she forced him back down with a strength he found surprising. An excited crowd was gathering around him, while the engine continued to howl away and others fought to put out the flames. Feyodor, coming back to his feet, snapped the throttle down and the machine wheezed to a halt, the hot metal ticking.

"It works, damn me, it really works!" Jack shouted, kneeling down by Chuck's side.

Grinning, Chuck looked up at him.

"That was a three-hundred-pound spring scale!" Chuck replied excitedly. "It just snapped the damn thing and took off, pushing the whole contraption right off the table!"

"It's enough. We'll be flying with that thing," Jack announced.

"We've got extra propellers. Let's rig a new one on, and see how long the darn thing can run."

"It almost killed you, and you want to start it up again!" Olivia said angrily, a flash of anger showing at this boyish enthusiasm. It was a miracle no one had been killed.

He looked up into her eyes and suddenly felt rather weak, after all.

The gaze held for a long moment until, from the corner of his eye, he saw a young boy from the telegraph office standing in the smoke-filled room, breathing hard, a scrap of paper in his hand. The boy's features were pale, his lip trembling.

Somehow there was no need to be told what the message said.

"We better get back to work," Chuck said quietly, the childlike joy of the moment before, the lingering look of Olivia, now forgotten.

"No, damn it! You've got to come in *high*, you bloody idiot!"

Vincent Hawthorne turned as the sergeant's voice boomed across the drill field. The words were in a barely understandable Latin, but he had come to learn that, no matter what era it was, or upon whatever world, a sergeant enraged at a bumbling recruit would always sound the same.

The Rus sergeant snatched the musket away from the trembling recruit, snapping the weapon down so that the blade was poised at his stomach.

"Have you ever seen a Tugar?" the sergeant roared.

"On the crosses."

Vincent winced inwardly. After the long winter and early spring the Merki corpses were now nothing more than raven-pecked remnants of sinew and bone, though still wafting with the faint odor of death. The skull of one showed the cracked holes of the six rounds he had pumped into it. Marcus had left them there as a reminder, though in his heart Vincent felt that the gaping white jaws were still echoing with a taunt, reminding him of what he had become.

"Well, damn my bloody eyes!" the sergeant snarled. "I've seen them alive"—he started to lapse back into Rus—"coming at us in the thousands, bellowing their war cries."

He paused for a moment to point dramatically to the ugly scar that had turned his features into a perpetual grimace, mouth split open far too wide, half a dozen teeth missing.

"I was with the bloody damned 5th Suzdal, got this at the Battle of the Pass I did, so, damn my eyes, I know what I'm talkin' about!"

He turned a malevolent gaze on the company.

"They'll come at you like a wall, a mountain, unstoppable except for this!" he cried, and he held the bayonet point up.

The recruits had not understood a word he'd said, but none dared to challenge him.

"Come in too low," he shouted, thrusting the bayonet in toward a recruit, who jumped back, "and you'll go right under their balls.

"Remember, they're eight, nine feet high. Look out for the downward strike of their sword. But they're a bit slower than us, so wait for that stroke. Dodge the strike, and before he can recover come in low and then thrust upwards, up high. Stab high"—he shifted back into a thick Latin—"up into their belly, which will be staring you in the face!"

"Then twist,"—he rotated the bayonet—"and withdraw!"—he yanked the gun back.

"Now again!"

He threw the musket back at the recruit, who looked humiliated and red-faced, as if ready to burst into tears.

"Perm and Kesus help him," Dimitri said softly.

"The weak ones will die," Vincent replied coldly.

"I just hope they don't drag us all down in their dying."

Somewhat startled, Dimitri looked over at Vincent as he nudged his mount into a slow canter, continuing across the drill field, moving in the direction of an entire brigade that was lined up practicing. Vincent sat erect in the saddle. He had finally learned to keep a good seat on the huge horse, though he still looked almost childlike from behind: narrow shoulders, five and a half feet in height, and not much above a hundred pounds.

It was a fair, cool morning, with a promise of true warmth by afternoon, a faint breeze picking up out of the west, rolling in from the open steppe. A whistle cut through the air, causing Vincent to turn in his saddle and look back over his shoulder to watch another train, pulling up out of the siding located just south of the city walls.

At the sight of his drawn features, Dimitri realized there was nothing childlike about the twenty-two-year-old general anymore, or if there was, it was deeply hidden. His once gentle face was cold, set with a hard stare, his gray-blue eyes distant, as if chiseled from ice. He had allowed a thin narrow beard to grow (more of a goatee that was trimmed to a point), matched by the tracing of a mustache. He no longer wore the old regulation kepi of the 35th, having replaced it with what he called a "hardee hat": wide brimmed and black, with a high crown. The hat shaded his features, giving him a distant air. Affixed to its center were two gold stars, matching the stars on the shoulder of his dark blue officer's jacket, trimmed with a double row of gold buttons. After taking command of the 5th, he had switched to the loose high-collared white tunic and canvas trousers of the Rus infantry. But that was gone now. He was the general of two corps in training, and he had the look of a professional killer in his eyes. He had changed.

"Twenty-third Roum," Dimitri said quietly, turning in his saddle to look at the train, "moving up to join 4th Corps reserve at Suzdal."

Vincent nodded absently. Five hundred good troops for the crucible of the Potomac front.

Vincent cursed silently, looking over at Dimitri, as if somehow the old Rus general were to blame.

"Just how the hell am I to form up two new corps, when the Colonel keeps bleeding off trained regiments as fast as I can turn them out?"

There had been a flurry of angry telegrams over the detachment of the 23rd and 25th to augment a full division of Roum troops at the front.

"You've got sixty-two other regiments in training," Dimitri reminded him, "plus the other thirty regiments of Marcus's corps."

"And less than a third of mine have weapons, and Marcus's are still ten percent under."

He shook his head, watching the train straining under its burden.

"At least the Roum have manpower to give; we're at the bottom of the barrel otherwise."

Thank God for the Roum, Vincent thought, as the train slowly gained headway up the long slope.

The manpower reserves they'd offered were finally starting to kick in. By midsummer, if we survive that long, he mused, the Roum army will outnumber the Rus, and then keep right on growing. His own 6th and 7th Corps would field twelve brigades in six divisions. Thirty-two thousand men, just under the total strength of the original Rus army that had met the Tugars.

The current Rus army fielded nearly a hundred and twenty regiments, with an average strength of five hundred, and over fifty batteries of artillery.

Every available man from sixteen to forty-five who didn't have a skill needed in industry was under arms at the front. Two of the four divisions in Suzdal were manning the factories, with a fifth detached division working on the rail lines or in the other factories. The Roum troops were forming up another division for the 4th corps, so it would have at least a standard combat size of three field divisions with a total of thirty regiments. All those not fit to serve were in the fields and factories, ready to be called as militia. It was as bad as the Confederacy—there simply wasn't anyone left. Without the Roum, the war would already be lost.

Andrew had already discussed with him the long-term political implications of that, if indeed there was a future. With the Roums having a three-to-one population advantage, the alliance had to be kept firmly intact, otherwise there could come a day when the forces of Roum might again pick up the habits of their distant ancestors and march out on the road of conquest.

But for right now the quality of Roum troops was marginal compared to the Rus who had fought through two wars, and had experience over four years of tutelage with the men of the 35th and 44th. Those who had survived were veterans.

If anything, it was Roum resources, he felt, that would decide the survival of the Republic even more than the men. Back beyond the tracks, out in the river Tiber, the new harbor area was swarming with activity. A coastal lighter had just tied in, laden down with several hundred tons of refined sulphur, all of it destined for the powder mill hidden above Hispania or for the balloon works, for conversion into the sulfuric acid which, when combined with zinc, would create hydrogen gas.

Several galleys were out in the river, practicing

rapid turns. In the one brief sea war fought since their arrival, galleys had been proven to be far too vulnerable to a good short-range musket volley, but they still served their purpose of harrying the Cartha coast, gathering intelligence, and picking up the thousands of refugees.

Other ships were tied in, bearing foodstuffs, hogs and cattle still on the hoof, cordage from the vast hemp fields that rose up out on the far eastern marches, silk for the balloons taken from every noble's wardrobe, and traded for even into the southeastward lands of Khata, soon to be overrun by the Bantag.

Coal had been discovered below Capra to the south, and dirty colliers moved the precious rock up the coast, where along the east bank of the river a coking plant was converting the stone for use in the new blast furnace.

Beyond the furnace was the copper and wire-works, spinning out the desperately needed strands to fill the insatiable need for yet more telegraph lines and the millions of percussion caps required for muskets and shells. Next to that stood a tanning yard for accoutrements: belts, cartridge boxes, shoes, saddles, harnesses, right down to the patches that held the flints for the old muskets still in circulation. In Hispania, back up the line, mercury was being processed for the fuses and percussion caps, and a reserve rail maintenance shed had gone up, complete with all the tools required for the repair and overhaul of locomotives and rolling stock. In Cilcia, the fine sands along the beaches had been found to be superb for the making of field glasses, and next to that a bottle-making plant had quickly risen. The containers would be filled with wine from the presses, and preserved fruits and condensed milk to be used for the sick and wounded.

Inland, at Brindisia and Caprium, the oil wells were turning out several barrels of refined coal oil a day to power the airships, plus other products such as lubricant for the locomotives and the dangerously explosive benzene.

The locomotive drifted past, following the path laid out along the Appia Way, climbing slowly up over the last series of hills and then gaining speed as it clicked its way northwestward toward Hispania, then on to the Republic of Rus beyond.

Vincent looked at the forlorn souls sitting in the boxcars and hunched down atop supplies lashed to the flatcars. They looked smart enough, uniformed in white calf-length trousers and hobnailed sandals, with leather thongs crosshatching up to the knee. Their tunics, patterned on the Union Army sack coat, were dyed a dark tan—almost like Confederate butternut, Vincent thought—and their felt hats were broadbrimmed and the same color as the tunics. Some of the officers still sported the uniform of the old legion that had long since been disbanded, their burnished breastplates and crested helmets standing out as a strange incongruity for a modern army. Some of the men were wearing packs, but the majority were burdened down with the ubiquitous horse-collar blanket roll slung over the left shoulder, adding to their appearance as rebel troops. The regiment was one of the few Roum units armed with Springfield rifles, a fact which made him curse inwardly. It'd been hell getting the best weapons, and now they were being pulled out of his hands.

Unlike the Rus, they would not be fighting on their home soil, with an enemy at the gate. These men were traveling to a distant land over six hundred miles away. Though all the Roum knew what would happen to them if Rus should fall, still he wondered how well these men would fight when the time came and the first Merki charge came screaming in.

A memory flashed into his head for a moment: He was again holding the pass while the rest of the army retreated, a wall of Tugars on foot advancing at the run, chanting their deep guttural cries, the nargas shrieking, drums rolling, human skull and horse-tail standards held high. Blades flashing in the mist and smoke, the thunder of their advance like an approaching storm.

He looked back at a line of recruits, practicing to form into regimental square, and sergeants, some of them Roum but most of them Rus, bellowing out commands. The sun was out, breaking through the spring morning mist—a fine gentle day, in such contrast to the dark thoughts that clouded his soul.

They looked good enough, for men who had been at it for several months. How would they react when death was racing down at two hundred yards a minute?

"Did we ever look like that?" Dimitri asked, as if reading Vincent's thoughts.

Dimitri smiled softly. "Most of us couldn't tell our left from our right back when the old 5th was first formed. So you tied hay to one foot, and straw to the other. Hayfoot, strawfoot, that's how you drilled us."

"It's hard to remember now," Vincent said quietly.

"And your own Yankees, did they ever look like that?" Dimitri said, looking over at Vincent like a father who, all so quietly, was seeking to reassure a nervous son.

Vincent let a thin smile crack his features. God, how long ago had it been? The time before was actually starting to blur a bit. Yes, he must have looked like that once, a scared child, unsteady with a musket, not even sure if he could shoot, let alone stab someone.

The first killing? Novrod, the guard on the wall when he escaped. Funny, they were allies now, part of the same Republic.

The riot in the square was next, then the wars and blowing the dam. Fifty thousand had he killed with that? Maybe seventy or eighty. The morning after you could walk across the Neiper on Tugar corpses, the river was so thickly choked. The stench of death had hung in the air for weeks, and the banks of the river were still littered with skeletons.

"No, Dimitri," he whispered. "I can't remember ever looking like that."

"But you were. Perhaps even the Colonel himself looked like that once, a scared recruit on the point of tears."

Hard to imagine, Keane a new recruit, a lieutenant. The 35th once a mob of frightened, excited boys going to see the elephant for the first time, many of them wetting their pants when the first bullet whistled past.

"They'll learn when the time comes. The same way you did, the same way we did."

"Let's hope so, Dimitri; if they don't it'll be all our asses in the fire. The rebs at least took prisoners. One mistake with the Merki, and all of us are dead— all of us. . . ."

His voice trailed off, a cold, distant look in his eyes. He nudged his mount forward, passing the regiment in square, snapping off salutes to the waiting officers, who came to rigid attention at his passing. Dimitri and the rest of his staff trotted behind him. Riding down the length of the field, he drew up before the brigade practicing large-unit tactics for the first time. Some of the faces were familiar. There was even an old hand from the 35th, a brigade commander now. Behind him fluttered a triangular flag, red with a white cross, for the 1st Brigade, of the 2nd Division.

It was a touch from the old Army of the Potomac, corps badges. The Greek cross for the new-formed 6th, and he looked over his shoulder at his own guidon-bearer proudly holding the square gold cross flag on a dark blue field, marking the presence of the corps commander.

Strange that it would be the cross for my unit, he thought, and he had a flashing memory of the dead Merki hanging in the forum. But the men of the 35th, remembering the old ways, had insisted upon their new army's carrying the same emblems of old.

"Strayter, good to see you."

Roger Strayter gave a friendly salute in reply. There had been a little getting use to for Roger. He had been an old hand in the 35th, having served with the regiment since Antietam, a deep furrow in his cheek a souvenir from Fredericksburg. They had known each other vaguely back in Vassalboro, Maine, and Roger had been something of a village roustabout, ready for a good prank. He doubted if Roger even remembered once chasing him down the street, threatening to thrash the "little Quaker boy." He wasn't going to remind him.

Roger had proven his mettle as a regimental commander and was now doing it again as a brigadier, but Vincent could sense the faintest touch of resentment in this towering six-foot giant with broad shoulders taking orders from a diminutive warrior who barely weighed in at a hundred and twenty.

"First day of brigade drill, isn't it?" Vincent asked.

Roger nodded, looking slightly nervous.

"Well, don't let me stop you then."

Roger turned away to face his regimental officers.

"Again! And god damn it, Alexi, your boys have got the furthest to run, so keep them in line!"

The men saluted and raced back to their command.

Vincent looked appraisingly at the long line. Three regiments were to the front in line, stretching across nearly four hundred yards, behind them two more regiments in column. The sight gave him a sharp thrill—at least the three regiments in front had muskets, which glistened in the morning sun. A wall of steel and flesh.

"Brigade!" the command echoed down the line. "By the right in line"—he paused for a second— "wheel!"

The man farthest to the right stayed anchored, the men to the far left breaking into a double-time run. Like a vast door on a hinge the line started to turn, swinging across an arc nearly a quarter of a mile across. The pivot continued and Vincent turned his horse about, riding in front and looking over his shoulder. He watched with a cold, appraising eye.

A gap started to open between the 2nd and 3rd regiments, curses echoing across the field as staff officers raced about, trying to swing the hole closed. The gap widened, with the men at the edge of it trailing behind. The line started to curve and ripple like a taut string going slack. Over the commands echoed the thunder of feet, the rattling of accoutrements, the hoarse cries of officers. The 3rd Regiment started to lose all cohesion, turning into an inverted V. Vincent looked over at Roger, who was scarlet with anger. The two regiments to the rear, in column of company front, at least held together, the deep blocks turning sharply.

At last the wheel was complete, stragglers were filtering back into the ranks, and all eyes were on Vincent, as if waiting for judgment.

With Roger in tow he cantered over to the 3rd

Regiment, where a Roum commander waited for the explosion.

"It could be better," Vincent said, his voice carrying over the line.

The commander said nothing.

"A damn sight better!" Vincent snapped. "This is a goddamned parade field, and you can't even hold your regiment together! If a Merki charge should swing into the army's flank, god help us if you're on the end of the line and we're forced to refuse our flank. It won't be a parade ground, it'll be dust, smoke, and men dying, and you're going to have to do it perfectly or we're all dead. You bastards won't last five minutes in a fight."

Angrily he jerked his horse around and rode off, Dimitri by his side. He rode in silence for some minutes and then finally looked at Dimitri.

"Well go on, say it."

"What should I say?"

"That I've never lost my temper before, that I've always won through quiet explanation and example—I know what you're thinking."

"You said it yourself, my general."

"I want them to be ready to kill Merki, to kill all those damned bastards."

He fell silent, cursing inwardly. Kill them all, that's what I want.

"I can't stand the thought of those men fumbling, losing, making a mistake that could cost us."

"Shouting at them is one way of doing it," Dimitri replied. "But I do remember, when you were my captain, you led far better the other way."

Vincent wheeled in his saddle. He knew the old man was right. Something was giving way inside—he had somehow lost the gentleness that had once been there in such abundance. He had lost it pumping rounds into a tortured figure on a cross, and loving the sense of power it gave him. God help me, he thought, will I ever get it back?

Or is there even a God to hear me?

He said nothing, riding on in silence with Dimitri lost in thought riding by his side.

Barely acknowledging the salutes of the various units that he rode past, he seemed to be floating in another world, a dark world of fire and war, his crisp uniform a mantle for this new embodiment of Mars.

From out of the west gate of the city a cavalcade of horsemen emerged, riding hard. In the van Dimitri immediately recognized Marcus. The standard of the patrician consul, an eagle on a field of purple, fluttered behind him.

Vincent reined in his mount, a twitch of excitement trembling across his cheek—something that Dimitri had noticed was becoming increasingly common.

Marcus, his features grim, pulled up beside Vincent.

"It's started—ten umens reported so far, moving towards the center of the Potomac front."

"God damn," Vincent mumbled, edging his horse around to look back to where the brigade was again practicing a wheel.

"Another three months before we're ready, and I'm stuck out here."

"The front to the south of us?" Vincent asked quietly.

"Still the same, nothing."

Vincent nodded almost imperceptibly.

"They'll come straight on. They've got those damn airships and we don't. They'll know what we're up to, and we won't know a goddamn thing.

"Damn them!" He slapped his thigh with a balled fist.

"Anything else?"

Marcus shook his head.

"We stay here, get ready, and wait as planned."

Vincent said nothing, but cursed inwardly. He had not wanted this assignment, but Andrew and Kal had forced it on him anyway. At least Tanya and the three children were safe here, six hundred miles from the front. No, he had not wanted this at all. Whatever was left of his soul had warned him against it, had counseled him to ask to be relieved of command, to work for his father-in-law at a desk job and contribute that way.

But that counsel was barely listened to, and everyday he had stared at the body on the cross, the body he had so joyfully killed. Everyday now he rode across this drill field, shaping his corps. He was a major general in command, of the same rank as the men he had once read about in *Harpers' Weekly*: Hancock, Sedjwick, Pap Thomas of Chickamauga, little Phil Sheridan. He smiled inwardly, knowing that he had even taken on some of Sheridan's outward trappings. *Gates' Weekly Illustrated* had run a woodcut picture of him on its front page when his promotion had been announced, and he had taken a secret delight in the image, right down to the Sheridan-like beard. And he knew he had taken on something else as well: the unrelenting desire to unleash a killing machine against the Merki.

And now the action was starting, and he was stuck six hundred miles away. He looked back to the west, as if he could somehow hear the guns.

"We'll be in it soon enough," he whispered.

Dimitri felt an inward shudder at his commander's voice, for it was the whisper of a lover eager for an embrace with death.

Chapter 4

"Magnificent!"

Jubadi Qar Qarth reined his mount in, turning in the saddle to look back at Hulagar.

The shield-bearer of the Merki Qar Qarth could but nod in agreement, for in spite of what his *tu* might direct, the *ka* spirit of the warrior could not help but be stirred.

Seen from atop the pass, the vast plains rolling northward were lit by the afternoon sun, the knee-high grass rich with the full bloom of spring. But it was not the beauty of the steppe that held him.

Moving in vast squares of black, ten regiments of a thousand each, the disciplined ranks of the Baki Hush Umen moved forward, debouching out of the high pass of the mountains, rolling forward like an unstoppable wave. Grinning with delight, Jubadi tossed the long-seeing tube over to Hulagar. Uncapping the bronze covers, Hulagar extended the tube to its full length. It felt almost toylike, but then, after all, it had been fashioned by the Yankee cattle, captured the previous fall, and presented to the Qar Qarth as a present.

Holding it to his eye, Hulagar scanned the vast plain. A block of a thousand had spread out to the right flank, extending out the skirmish line to cover

TERRIBLE SWIFT SWORD 179

the front of a dozen miles over to the next pass. Far
to the right flank, barely visible on the horizon, were
yet two more umens, and he knew that beyond them
were yet two more clearing the pass right down to
the sea.

Seven full umens advancing across a front of sixty
miles—and that was but a fraction of their power.
With joyful shouts a battery of guns came rumbling
past, their crews lashing the horses as they crested
over the final rise. Hulagar looked at them appraisingly. The carriages were roughly made, far heavier
than ones fashioned by the cattle, but then, he tried
to reason, we have limitless horses and they do not.

Far out forward, like bloated beetles hovering on
the breeze, the airships floated, riding forward of
the advance, scouting into the cattle lines, looking
for any threat of surprise. At first he had not
believed the machines would prove of any use, but
now he knew differently. They had become the eyes
of eagles, and their crews had even decorated them
as such, painting winged outlines on the bottom of
the gas bags and large eyes at the front. Even now
thousands of cattle were laboring just beyond the
other side of the hills to build new sheds for the air
weapons.

Scanning to the left, the steppe rolled on undisturbed, except for a loose open order of skirmishers,
riding like tiny dots across the sea of green. Lowering the telescope, he passed the instrument over
to Vuka, who grunted with excitement.

"One good push and we might even break through
here!" the Zan Qarth announced, his teeth flashing
in a grimace of pleasure.

"The last thing we want," Jubadi said softly. "And
besides, they know we are coming here. This is the
butt of the head; it is the horn that counts."

He pointed to the toppled watchtower atop the

ridge, looking down on the pass, and then to the long line of poles that marched in an arrow-straight line due north back to the cattle position fifty miles away. The poles were bare of the precious wire, proof that they had had enough time in their retreat to bring the copper back. That device was still a mystery. He had hoped to capture one of the wire-talkers intact so that the pets who worked with Hinsen and the other Yankee crewmen from the *Oqunquit*, who had been left behind on the campaign of last year, might decipher its secret.

Thirty-odd Yankee and Suzdal sailors and their families were still back in Cartha. Some of them had proven resistant to helping out, but after witnessing a moon feast most of them had proven willing enough. For cattle they lived in luxury: the best of foods, women of their choosing, all that they might wish for. The cattle sailors under the one called Jamie had been far more wily, disappearing after they had delivered the Yankee machine that rides on iron rails. They were of no account, and could be hunted down once this war was over.

Perhaps for Hinsen, and those who worked with him, he would even honor his promise to spare them if they continued to help in the making of weapons. At least the one called Hinsen had proven invaluable, giving them the secret of the flaming air that made the ships rise to the sky. He was a good pet.

Vuka, his mount restless, edged over to Hulagar and motioned for the far-seeing tube, which Hulagar handed over.

"When the time comes for our full weight, only then will we attack," Jubadi said, looking back at his son. "Remember that. If your enemy is fixed in one place then prepare your trap well, do it with cunning, and strike with the weight of a mountain and not before."

Vuka reluctantly lowered the tube to look over at his father.

Jubadi pointed off to the west.

"Our riders will take the passes from this side, leading the Yankees to believe the strength of our blow is coming through here and that the left is of no importance. They will cut the observation posts in these hills off from behind, preventing him from seeing what is moving on the other side. Forward from here he'll see the standards of twenty-five umens, when in fact there are only eight. Only then will we attack where we want, for now we must keep them busy; our right wing will be more than enough for that.

"We are not needed here. The Yankees were not so foolish to offer resistance in the mountains, as I had hoped. Now let us go to where it will be decided." Nudging his mount into a canter, Jubadi Qar Qarth turned and rode down out of the high hills, moving toward the northwest behind his advancing cloud of skirmishers.

"Remember what Bobbie Lee once said?"

Andrew lowered his field glasses and looked over at Hans, who was leaning against the side of the high watchtower, chewing meditatively on a plug of tobacco and keeping his hands busy by whittling with a pen knife on a frayed stick.

"It's good war is so terrible, else we would grow too fond of it," Hans replied quietly.

Andrew sighed, passing the glasses over to Hans and readjusting his spectacles, which he had pushed up onto his forehead.

"Funny, he was saying it about us when we went in at Fredericksburg. It must of been a grand sight for him."

"He wasn't stuck where we were. I remember it as

Hell," Hans replied, taking the glasses and adjusting the focus. He then scanned the vast columns moving down toward the opposite bank of the Potomac.

The Merki maneuvered with a cold precision that filled him with admiration, coming forward in a vast checkerboard pattern, blocks of a hundred by ten deep, all mounted, each block riding horses of the same color, the umens screened a mile forward by skirmishers riding in open order.

Behind the columns of warriors, limbered batteries, spread out in open order, came inexorably forward.

"Once more into the breach," Andrew whispered.

He leaned over the side of the tower and looked down at the ground nearly a hundred feet below. For as far as he could see to either side, the entrenchments, earthen forts, and redoubts were lined with men, shouting excitedly and pointing out across the broad open river.

The telegraph key behind him started to clatter and he turned to watch as the boy copied the information down, tore off the sheet, and handed it over.

"From Barney down on the coast. Reports standards of four umens."

Hans grunted an acknowledgment and continued to scan the enemy line.

"But still nothing from the right," he said. "We've had them in sight since dawn and the left wing of their advance ends right here, less than halfway up our line. But their skirmishers are moving down the entire length of the Shenandoahs, screening straight back to the west."

"And?" Andrew queried.

"It's too pat. You know that as well as I do."

"Hans, it's over fifty miles of open prairie between here and the Shenandoah Hills. You can't hide a damn thing on them. We've counted fifteen umen standards so far, so it looks like it's coming straight in here."

"Could be an advance in echelon, refusing their left. I just wish I had one of them damned air machines," Hans snapped, nodding to where two Merki ships were ranging far behind to the rear of their position, and staying up high enough to keep out of the range of ground fire.

Andrew said nothing. Shading his eyes, he looked back out toward the enemy line.

"Getting across the river is going to be hell," Andrew said. "We've got thirty guns trained on this ford."

Hans nodded.

"They're coming straight in at our strongest point, and they know it."

Andrew watched the vast wave as it continued its advance. Suddenly the slow steady advance of the vast checkerboard formation quickened to a trot.

"By Jesus, I think they're going to charge!" O'Donald hissed, puffing hard. He had stuck his head up through the hatchway onto the platform, and was slowly climbing up to join them.

Andrew looked back over at Pat.

"What the hell are you doing here?"

"Came down to check on a reserve battery moving up," Pat said sheepishly, realizing that his excuse for coming up to the front was a slim one at best.

Andrew gave him a sharp look of angry reproach, then looked back at the Merki line.

"One damn hit on this tower and our entire command is gone," he said coldly.

A puff of smoke from across the river interrupted his thoughts. Long seconds passed until a faint concussion washed over the river. A geyser of water shot up in the middle of the turbulent water, and the shot skipped lazily on, slamming into the high mud bank.

Gunners in the battery down below looked up at Andrew expectantly.

"Let's get back down. I think the show is about to start."

This was the part he hated, but there was really no other way around the situation. Going to the side of the platform, he stepped into a small wooden cage. He then waved to the men below, who unhitched the rope from its stays and, running it through a windlass, quickly lowered Andrew back down to the ground. At the same time Hans and Pat made their way down the ladder. It was a convenience Mina had rigged up for Andrew, but he still felt rather foolish being hoisted up and down the watchtower like a sack of grain.

Running over to the side of the earthen battlement, he climbed up onto the top of the rampart and raised his field glasses. They were less than a mile away now, the undulating wall of horse warriors coming forward at a steady pace, horsetail standards to the fore, a strong skirmish line riding in advance a half-mile ahead. An advance line of scouts, who sat motionless on the far bank of the river a quarter-mile away, suddenly stirred to action, leaping up to stand atop their saddles, half a dozen of them raising red standards up high and waving them.

"They're marking the position of the ford," Andrew announced, unable to keep the admiration out of his voice at this display of cold professionalism.

The column of warriors started to shift so that three regiments of the checkerboard formation closed the space between them, presenting a front three hundred riders across.

Andrew could sense that all eyes were upon him. He looked over at the brigade commander in charge of the redoubts facing the ford and nodded without comment.

Within seconds the high clarion call of dozens of bugles cut the air. All along the earthen ramparts riflemen sprang to their positions, resting the barrels of their weapons along the wall. Gun commanders stepped behind their pieces, sighting them yet one more time, though they had practiced here for months in anticipation of this first moment.

Distant horns echoed and a faint drumming could now be heard, like the rumble of an approaching storm on the summer horizon. The line of skirmishers hit the opposite bank of the river, sliding down the muddy slope, their mounts neighing and kicking as they splashed into the still icy river.

"Hold your fire!"

The command echoed up and down the line. The men are following the drill so far, Andrew thought—no sense wasting good shot on a couple of hundred of the enemy when in another minute thousands would be in range.

The skirmishers pressed into the river across a broad front, those beyond the limits of the ford quickly sinking and turning their mounts about to struggle back to shore. The skirmishers within the half-mile front of the ford pressed in, raising red flag-tipped lances up high, marking the path of the advance.

"Damn aerosteamers!" O'Donald announced, and Andrew turned to look over his shoulder to where O'Donald was pointing.

Three of the ships were coming down out of the north.

"Observation," Hans replied, not even bothering to turn back. "See our defenses in action."

The thunder was growing louder, washing across the river in waves. He could easily pick out individual riders now with his field glasses, and the sight of them sent a chill down his spine. The riders sat tall, bows in hand, burnished helmets glistening, human skull standards marking the lines. The commanders rode forward with scimitars raised, flickering in the red light of the afternoon sun. It was like the old time again, and suddenly Andrew's knees started to feel weak. God, it was starting all over again.

The first rank hit the edge of the river bank and went over the side, funneling in between the red pennant markers.

A scattering of shots echoed along the line, and angrily Andrew looked up as a sergeant ran along the battlement cursing at the top of his lungs. But the discipline held: The men waited, the few who had fired looking sheepishly about while they furtively reloaded.

The first line surged into the water, followed seconds later by another and yet another. Like small boats plowing into a sea the horses breasted the waters, churning the river into foam, slowing in their advance and yet still pushing on.

"Coming straight damn in!" O'Donald chuckled, rubbing his hands with glee. Stepping away from Andrew, he went over to the nearest gun and shouldered the sergeant aside. He grabbed the lanyard and leaned over for a second to check the aim. Satisfied, he stood back up.

The advance reached into mid-river, the water rising up over the stirrups of the riders, who silently urged their mounts on. An eerie silence settled over the field, neither side giving voice, the only sound the neighing and splashing of the horses.

A dozen ranks were now in the water, well over several thousand riders, and still they surged onward. The mounts were starting to rise back out of the river, some in water only as deep as their forehocks.

Andrew suddenly realized that he had been holding his breath, unable to exhale, the tension building to the exploding point.

The brigade commander leaped atop the rampart and raised his arm up, holding an oversized pistol to the heavens.

The first horse reached the opposite bank not fifty yards below them, struggling to gain a footing on the greasy slope.

A dull thump snapped through the air and the brigade commander leaped back down, the flare shell rising up over the ford.

Across a front a quarter mile long it seemed as if the very earth had exploded, as twenty-five hundred rifles and thirty field pieces fired almost simultaneously.

The river lifted up in a blinding spray of foam. Screaming horses rose heavenward, bodies tumbled over, ranks disintegrated as the hailstorm of iron and lead slashed into flesh and bone.

In an instant the muddy river took on a pinkish hue, the slaughtered shrieking in pain, the rumble of the shattering volley echoing across the river.

There was a strange moment of near silence along the line, as all paused to look at what they had accomplished by the simple pulling of a trigger, the yanking of a lanyard. Excited commands suddenly echoed out, and the clattering of thousands of ramrods slamming charges home rattled along the breastworks, as officers and noncoms excitedly urged the men on. Gun crews leaped to their pieces, swabbed out the bores, and pulled the sponges out. Loaders stepped up with powder charges and double tins of canister. There was the metallic clang of the rounds being shoved home, the sight of rammers leaping aside, the sound of gun commanders shouting for the crews to stand clear.

Individual shots started to ring out in a staccato punctuation. The best-trained fired first, followed seconds later by the growing roar of hundreds of weapons discharging nearly simultaneously.

O'Donald, shouting a joyful curse, yelled for his crew to stand clear, and with an emphatic pull jerked the lanyard of the Napoleon, sending a spray of nearly two hundred canister balls into the disintegrating ranks.

"Cease fire," Andrew said quietly, looking over at the brigade commander who nodded in agreement. The command was picked up and echoed down the line by bugle call. A desultory fire continued for a brief interval, O'Donald getting off one of the last shots after raising the elevation of his piece to spray the far bank with canister.

As the smoke lifted, a wild cheer rose up from the line. The ford was jammed with bodies, already spreading out, tumbling over in the current, and floating downstream in a swirl of muddy water and blood.

"Hundreds, we must of killed hundreds of the filthy buggers!" Pat exulted, coming back to stand by Andrew's side. The far bank was swarming with the survivors, who struggled out of the water, dragging their wounded with them.

"Why cease fire now?" Pat asked. "It's still canister range out there."

"Save the ammunition," Hans replied. "Save it for when we'll really need it."

"Hell, we smashed the bastards up right good!" O'Donald shouted, and his cheery cries were echoed by the thousands who lined the tops of the ramparts, as they shouted their defiant taunts at the enemy.

A distant whistling cut through the air and, looking up, Andrew saw a black dot dropping away from the belly of one of the aerosteamers, followed seconds later by two more dropped from the other ships.

The concussion of an explosion washed over the line. Looking to his right, Andrew saw three snaps of flame rising heavenward a couple of hundred yards away. The second bomb hit closer, tearing out a section of battlement and lifting a gun into the air. The third seemed to hover straight overhead, growing larger, its ugly scream rising in pitch, to pass over the fortress and explode along the muddy bank of the river, sending a torrent of mud erupting half a hundred feet into the air. The Merki aerosteamers turned about to run back to the south.

"Damn pains in the bloody ass," O'Donald sniffed. "It ain't a decent way of fighting."

Andrew turned and looked over at Hans, who had not even bothered to watch the bombing. His attention was still fixed on the other side of the river.

"They know damn well better than to have done that. The Tugars did it at the Battle of the Ford, and we choked the river with their bodies."

Andrew nodded in agreement. If anything, they had just proven this position to be completely unassailable. Not a single rider who had come within fifty yards of the north shore had lived to tell of the experience.

The riders on the opposite bank were drawing back, some shaking their fists in anger at the taunting jeers that still echoed along the line. All along the broad southern plain the advancing lines had halted just beyond the range of artillery, the riders sitting motionless. The sheer mass of numbers was stunning to behold as rank after rank drew up, standards marking formations, a vast pale of dust rolling across the plains.

Andrew nodded to Hans and Pat, then turned away and climbed down off the rampart. Waving his aides and staff aside, he stalked across the narrow confines of the earthen fort and out the sally port to the rear. Crossing the killing ground between the main line and the reserve position, he followed the trail through the series of entanglements until he'd gained the sally port into the next line. There the reserve troops who were standing atop the wall to watch the action cheered him as he approached.

Lost in thought, he barely acknowledged the shouts as he crossed through the second line to the log huts that served as his headquarters complex. Reaching the log cabin that served as his field headquarters, he went inside, his two friends following. He motioned for the telegrapher and other staff people to leave, then shut the door behind them.

"Of course we'll proclaim it a great victory, but it was the most asinine thing I've seen!" he snarled, collapsing into a chair.

Hans, going over to a side cabinet and pulling it open, produced a bottle of vodka and several glasses. Andrew waved him off, but Pat, grinning and ignoring Andrew's warning gaze, took the offered drink.

"Now, don't be doctorin' me, Andrew darlin'," Pat sniffed. "The hole in the belly is long since healed."

He grimaced slightly as the first shot went down, and then a cheery smile lit his eyes. Hans, after pouring a second drink for himself, sat down on the table opposite Andrew's chair.

"*Now* will you believe me?" Hans asked, his tired eyes fixed on Andrew.

"Fifteen umens, maybe twenty-five positioned here," Andrew replied.

"Leaving maybe twenty-five elsewheres."

"No sign of them on the right flank," Pat interjected. "This is as far up as they've come."

"And their pickets are pushing up the north slope of the Shenandoahs right now. By tomorrow night they'll be a hundred miles to the northwest, far beyond our flank.

"We still have a watch post hidden in the woods all the way out to the right," Andrew replied. "If they come that way you'll have more than a day's warning. We can shift our reserve divisions up to you in under six hours."

Hans was silent.

Andrew sat back and looked at Hans with a weary smile.

"I have three corps, forty-five thousand men, to cover over a hundred miles of front. You've got a full corps on your end already, Hans. If trouble brews on your side, we can move Pat's corps over your way."

Pat looked up from his drink.

"That'll strip the capital naked," Pat said quietly. "I thought we'd decided to keep that reserve in case of the worst."

"It might *be* the worst," Hans replied. "But damn it, Andrew, you know better than that. Always reinforce victory, but never commit a single man to a defeat. If we lose the right flank, by Gott don't send Pat up. You'll need his men to hold the Neiper."

"So you want me to leave one corps, fifteen thousand men, to cover nearly a hundred miles of front, and put two corps on the far right?"

Hans nodded.

"You could have repulsed that last attack with five hundred men—one regiment, not an entire brigade. What they did was just a demonstration; they knew they couldn't get across, but they wanted us to think that they damn well intend to try."

Andrew sat in silence, staring at his old mentor's drawn features.

There just wasn't enough; nowhere was there enough. He had found a damn near impregnable position—at least as long as the river was up until the beginning of summer—but the line was so damn long he simply didn't have enough to cover it all. Something in his guts was telling him that Hans was right, to risk it all and put his strength on the right. He had half a dozen ironclads holding the river's mouth, so there was no possible way for the Merki to bring up boats to ferry their warriors across.

Yet he still had to picket the long stretches of front that extended for miles, for to leave them entirely naked was to court disaster. All the Merki needed to do was to get several hundred to swim across at night against an unguarded point, and within hours they could open a breech, throwing a pontoon bridge across to secure the position.

He had calculated and recalculated this problem for months. They had to hold here, or enemy artillery would be lining the Neiper.

"It stands," Andrew said quietly, looking straight into Hans's eyes. He suddenly felt a cold chill, as if somehow he had set off down a path from which there could no longer be any retreat.

Hans forced a smile.

"It's a tough decision either way, son," he said softly.

"Is it the right one?" Andrew whispered.

Hans cocked his head slightly, a frown crossing his features.

"And what did I tell you when you were the young captain?"

"Not so young anymore," Andrew reminded him.

"Make your decision and then live by it," Hans said, the hint of a fatherly tone in his voice.

"You made the best one you could. If it had been me instead of you, I might have made the same."

He hesitated for a moment, then poured another drink. Hans looked over at Pat, who in an uncharacteristic display of abstinence put his hand over his glass.

Hans shrugged good-naturedly and tossed the shot down. Standing, he went over to the corner of the room and hoisted up his Sharps carbine, which in spite of his general's rank was still his weapon of choice.

"I best be going back up the line to my position."

A flurry of shots echoed up from outside, then just as quickly died away.

"Never forget it, Andrew Lawrence Keane. Win or lose this one, but never doubt that you can command. Even if we should lose out here, if afterwards you ever doubt yourself, then, *Mein Gott*, you and everyone that follows you will die. I'd never forgive you for that when we meet in the next world."

Andrew came to his feet, suddenly filled with the desire to embrace his old friend, but he decided against such an outward show of emotion.

There was so much that he wanted to say, but a look from Hans stilled his voice. Nothing needed to be said; nearly eight years of serving together had taught each the finest nuances of the other, the slightest gesture conveying far more than words could ever gather and express.

"Take care, Hans."

"I'll see you after it's all over," Hans said. He turned in the doorway and started out.

"After it's over, you old Dutchman, the drinks are on me!" Pat shouted, his voice a bit too loud.

Hans looked back, a thin smile lighting his graying features. He shot a stream of tobacco juice against the side of the cabin.

"You'll do well, son," he said, his voice barely heard, and then he was gone.

*   *   *

"Colonel Keane."

Groaning, Andrew opened his eyes. A young orderly stood over his bed, holding a kerosene lamp in one hand.

"What is it?" Instantly he was awake, sitting up from his cot.

"Barney wants you, sir."

"Trouble?"

"You better come see, sir," the boy said, a touch of nervousness in his voice.

Standing up, he tugged at his rumpled uniform, motioning for the orderly to help him on with an overcoat.

The cabin was chilly, the fire in the stove having flickered down. A couple of the staff officers were sitting at the long map table, heads resting on their arms and snoring lightly.

Andrew went over and nudged one with his boot.

The boy stirred, then with a muffled curse sat straight up.

"Sorry, sir, dozed off."

"Obviously," Andrew said quietly.

Andrew looked over at the clock in the far corner of the room. Just before five; dawn in an hour and a half. The line should be standing, too, in another half-hour.

Going out of the cabin, he looked about. Shaduka was near to setting, its face casting a dull red glare along the battlements.

"Where's Barney?"

"At his command post," the orderly replied, pointing the way.

The early air was sharp, mingled with the scent of an army encampment: the usual smells of sweat, horses, badly cooked food, human waste, raw earth. The scent of home, Andrew thought.

The ground was damp with dew. Overhead the Great Wheel stood out dramatically in the high western sky, its fainter stars washed out by the moon but dramatic nevertheless.

Gaining the sally port he entered the fort, crossing the narrow parade ground and climbing the steps up to the battlement. Barney was leaning against the wall, but came to attention at Andrew's approach. Pat, who had yet to return to Suzdal, looked over at Andrew and nodded.

"Sorry to bother you, sir," Barney said nervously, "but I wanted you to hear this."

Andrew wanted to comment that the man could have called his division commander first, and then from there their old sergeant, Barry, who was now a corps commander, and so on up the chain of command, but he stopped himself from going into a petulant rage. Sometimes chains of command were a certain path to disaster.

"What is it?" Andrew asked, pulling the high collar of his jacket up to keep out the chill.

"Barney's right, Andrew," Pat said. "Just listen for a moment."

Andrew cocked his head, leaning over the battlement, the men around him hushed.

There was a faint, steady rumbling, the sound of hammering, and a murmur of voices, barely audible above the rippling tumble of the river as it flowed over the rocky ford.

"It started around midnight, sir. There've been several shots and once we heard a scream; it sounded human, sir. It's been giving me and the boys quite a stir all night."

Andrew looked over to the east. The sky was starting to modulate into the first indigo hues of dawn, but it was still deep night.

"Have the men stand to."

Within seconds the call to arms had sounded down the length of the line and echoed off into the distance. It was impossible to hear the noise from the other bank anymore, as men, grumbling and shouting, came to their posts to join the forces that had been tensely manning the line since midnight. He had been told that Merki tradition, like Tugar, was to abstain from night action, but the Tugars had finally broken that custom with near disastrous results in the Battle before the Pass.

The minutes seemed to drag out. An orderly came up with a hot mug of tea and a slab of cheese-coated bread. Andrew sipped the scalding brew leaning against the rampart, watching as the faint light started to rise like a curtain. The second moon rose to the southeast, its crescent now a couple of days from new.

The middle of the river was in hazy view. Wisps of fog drifted down with the current, the banks shrouded with hovering mists. The far bank was still shadowy, but it was obvious that somehow it had changed. Dim forms were visible, moving in and out of the mists. He raised his field glasses but the light was still too dim, the fog blocking the view.

Cursing quietly, he drained off the rest of the mug and motioned for the orderly to bring another cup for Barney and himself.

The sky to the east continued to brighten, turning scarlet. A lone nargas sounded from the far bank, followed seconds later by a rising thunder of drums and horns. Shadowy forms stirred, and then a low, bone-chilling howl echoed from the southern shore. A dissonant chant, rising and falling, the words indistinguishable but ever growing in volume.

"Prayer to the sun?" Andrew speculated. The professor in him was suddenly curious. Mohammedans prayed at dawn—was it the same here?

The chant continued to rise and fall, reaching a crescendo that coincided with a thin shaft of red light slicing across the steppe as the dull red orb of the sun broke the horizon.

The fog took on the appearance of pink foamy candy, obscuring the far bank, swirling and shifting. The full disk of the sun was at last above the horizon, its heat already radiating.

"A warm day coming up," Barney said.

"It'll burn this fog off quick."

Andrew trained his glasses back on the opposite shore. The fog shifted for a moment. Hundreds were on the far shore, indistinct forms shifting.

"People?" Barney whispered.

Andrew looked over at him.

"Your eyes are better than mine," Andrew replied, never quite sure if he saw better with his spectacles on or off when he was using a telescope or the field glasses.

"I think they're people," Barney said coldly.

"Don't shoot!"

The command from a high-voiced sergeant pulled Andrew's attention around.

Half a dozen men and women came splashing out of the mist, wading thigh-deep into the ford, waving their arms, their distant cries barely heard.

"What the hell?" Barney whispered.

The six continued into the river, running with the terrible, nightmarish slow motion of those wading through water. Andrew grabbed the field glasses back.

The water sprayed up around them, followed a couple of seconds later by the rattle of musketry. Four of them pitched over, thrashing and kicking. Andrew watched through his glasses, their features barely distinguishable, but he could sense the terror in their faces.

Another one tripped over, a long shaft sticking out of her back, and then the last went down, barely a quarter of the way into the river. Several Merki emerged from the mist, racing into the water and grabbing the nearest bodies.

A flurry of musket fire ripped down the line, the water around the three Merki splashing from rounds striking. One of the Merki spun around, grabbing its shoulder, and a defiant cheer rose up from the Rus. Two others continued in, scooping up the four bodies, one of which still struggled weakly.

"Breakfast," Pat said angrily.

The two retreated into the thinning mist, dragging their victims. Men continued to fire, and in annoyance Andrew looked back down the line as officers shouted for the men to save ammunition.

"It's starting to lift," an orderly whispered, his voice taut with excitement.

As if a curtain were being pulled back from a stage, the fog swirled into thinning wisps of smoke. Andrew felt his stomach tighten, and with clenched jaw he stood in silence. A growing murmur of curses rose up around him.

On the far bank, across the entire width of the ford, a heavy line of breastworks had gone up during the night, and in the ever-brightening light hundreds of shovels and picks could be seen, flicking up over the side of the earthen walls for a second, dirt flying and then disappearing again.

Yet that was not the sight that disturbed him. They could dig all they wanted to on the other side—it really wouldn't make any difference, unless it was the Rus who wished to attack.

"The bloody bastards," Barney snarled, and Andrew nodded in silent agreement.

A broad mole, the beginning of an earthen dam, was already stretching out into the river, the ends of it protected by a heavy wooden wall, which even as he watched was pushed forward another couple of feet. The mole was aswarm with workers, hundreds of them, carrying wicker baskets on their shoulders. When they reached the end of the mole they dumped the rocks and dirt over the top of the barricade and then returned.

The workers were human—Carthas.

Sickened, Andrew looked at the men around him who were gazing at him, awaiting his pronouncement.

He called for a telescope, then waited as an aide brought one up. He extended the instrument and laid it down on the rampart wall, then crouched down for a better view than the field glasses could provide. Along the embankment dozens of Merki guards stood, bows and muskets poised, with half a dozen field pieces trained on the ever-growing dam, ready to pick off anyone who hesitated. Even as he watched a man threw his basket aside and leaped into the river at a run. He had barely made it into the water before he tumbled over. Guards appeared from behind heavy wooden barricades spaced along the mole, cracking whips, driving their chattel back to their task.

Raising the telescope slightly, he saw a long serpentine line of men and women stretching up over the embankment, weaving their way out to a low hill, a fair portion of which had already been carved out. They swarmed like thousands of ants.

"How far out would you say it is?" Andrew asked, not taking his eye from the telescope.

"A good thirty yards or more," Barney said quietly.

"Further up the river, sir," an aide said. Turning the telescope, Andrew pointed the instrument to the spot where the officer had pointed.

A couple of hundred yards above the ford another

embankment had gone up along the bank of the river. Behind it Andrew could barely make out what appeared to be a long boom of logs, as well as several roughly made boats, each one with several boulders inside.

He stood back up and leaned against the parapet, trying to gather his thoughts.

"You say you first heard something around midnight?"

Barney nodded.

"It's two hundred and fifty yards across," Andrew said. "Thirty yards in six hours—maybe eight."

"They could get halfway across by tomorrow morning."

"The tighter they squeeze the river, the faster the current," Pat interjected. "They'll hit a point where as fast as they dump it in, it'll just get swept away."

"That's what the log booms and boats are for," Andrew said, pointing further up the river.

"Christ, it must of taken a hell of a lot of work to drag them things right over the mountains and down here."

"They've got the manpower," Barney said coldly.

"Get the mole out as far as it'll go, then push all of that into the river. Sink the boats across the rest of the opening, and create a log jam behind it."

"They'll be able to cross right downstream, getting below our heavy belt of fortifications," Barney said nervously. "If the dam holds for a couple of days, the entire front right down to the sea will be unmasked."

"God damn it!" Andrew snapped, picking his field glasses back up for another look.

"A simple plan, except for one thing," Pat said quietly.

Andrew lowered his glasses and looked over at the artillery man.

"You'll have to kill them."

Pat reached into his pocket and pulled out a plug of tobacco, then proffered it.

Nodding, Andrew bit off a small chew, the biting sting of the chew setting his already rapid heartbeat to racing.

He raised his glasses again to look back at the mole and the endless, bedraggled chain of slaves working upon it.

"They're Cartha," Andrew said. "They're prisoners of those devils."

"They're working for the enemy," Pat replied. "It's us or them, now."

Andrew looked at Barney, who stood expectantly, his features pale.

"Mr. Barney."

"Sir?"

"Order the batteries to open fire; first round canister, then switch to case and solid."

The gunners standing alongside their weapons looked over at Andrew.

"Do it!" Andrew shouted. "If we don't, the Merki will be in our lines!"

The battery officers stepped up to their pieces and shouted commands with quavering voices.

The first gun kicked back. Andrew raised his glasses. The water before the mole sprayed into a foam. More guns started in. Bodies started to collapse, and the sound of high, piercing screams rent the air.

Panic broke out along the mole, the prisoners dropping their baskets and turning to run.

A snap of fire erupted from the battlement along the far bank, sweeping down dozens who were now caught between two fires.

"God damn their black souls!" Pat cried, pounding the rampart with clenched fists.

Bodies carpeted the mole. Andrew watched in silence, praying that it was finished, but in his heart he knew it was not. Merki appeared from behind their protective barriers, their arms working up and down, whips lashing out. The panic subsided and gradually the work resumed, the tortured victims running down the length of the mole, dropping the contents of their baskets and then running back. A burst of several shells bracketed the mole, tumbling a knot of men over and sending a lone Merki down. There was a moment of hesitation and then another Merki appeared, cracking his whip, driving the prisoners back to their task.

But those who had emptied their baskets and started to run back to shelter were not yet done with. A Merki appeared, then crouched low against the shelling and pointed back. The prisoners stopped and, reaching down, began to pick up the fallen bodies, dragging them back. Yet more dropped, and yet more appeared. A life for a single basket of rock and dirt.

Along the enemy rampart human bodies now started to appear—Merki standing up for a moment to hold up corpses, waving them tauntingly. One held a limp form up, while another sliced out with his scimitar, hacking an arm free and waving it aloft.

"The bloody bastards!" Pat snarled. "We're giving them their rations!"

Unable to contain his rage, Pat grabbed a rifle from a soldier nearby, shouldered the weapon, drew careful aim, and fired. The Merki with the arm suddenly ducked down.

"My eye isn't as good as it used to be."

Andrew turned away from the methodical carnage and looked over at Barney.

"Pass the word down. Batteries to keep up a slow, deliberate fire; it'll slow them down. Detail out some of our best sharpshooters and have them go for the guards. Otherwise, no one else is to shoot."

"What about night?" Barney asked.

"We can rig up the guns with marker sticks, so they can be aimed in the dark," Pat replied. "By the time they get halfway out the range will be nearly point blank for canister, and it'll be hell out there."

Tossing the telescope to an aide, Andrew turned away from the battlement and stalked back to his headquarters.

"Gently . . . That's it, a bit more to the left now!" Trembling with excitement, Chuck Ferguson stepped back from the shed, watching intently as the crew, hanging on to the side cables, walked the aerosteamer out of its hanger. The engineers' cabin, a simple wicker-basket affair, was strapped underneath and riding on a wheeled carriage.

Already he could see one major error in his plans. In the future he'd have to figure out a way to make the sheds rest on a giant turntable, so the hanger could be turned directly into the wind. There was only the slightest of breezes this morning, but it was enough to force the crew to struggle to keep the precious silken sides from scraping, and possibly tearing on the side of the hanger.

The midsection of the aerosteamer emerged, with Jack walking anxiously alongside the engineers' cabin and Feyodor behind him, making sure the propeller didn't touch the ground. As the tail end of the balloon emerged, Chuck motioned for the crew to let it windmill around. The tail porpoised for a moment, then stabilized.

For the first time, he now had the chance to look at the entire aerosteamer by the light of day. He stepped back. The lines appeared symmetrical, but it was hard to tell for sure. The frame seemed taut enough, but figuring stresses on it was somewhat beyond him. He hated to admit it, but this project was definitely going to be trial and error. The only problem was, an error would most likely prove to be fatal for whoever was aboard.

"All right, Feyodor, crank her up!"

The mechanic waved an acknowledgment, and leaning over into the small boiler he lit the pilot light. Everyone held their breath as the Suzdalian struck a match, even though Jack had assured the crew that since hydrogen was lighter than air, if there were any leaks the gas would go straight up and not down.

Chuck waited patiently for the boiler to heat up, stepping around to the side to check the middle bag, which would soon be filled with hot air. The silk sides hung loose, and then ever so imperceptibly started to flutter and grow taut, stretching out from the frame.

"It's starting to get lighter!" Jack shouted.

Chuck looked once more to the high watchtower. The pennant atop it was barely fluttering. When Chuck had caught the watchman's attention, the man waved down that all was clear, not a Merki ship anywhere in sight.

Turning, Chuck ran up to Jack's side.

Jack grinned and stepped over to the wooden frame that held the engine. Mounting directly behind the wicker engineers' chairs, he grabbed hold of the side and pushed down. Releasing his hand, the aerostemer floated back up again.

"The balance is working out perfectly. It's just starting to get positive buoyancy. Just another couple of minutes, and we're ready."

Chuck looked into Jack's eyes.

"Scared?"

Jack tried to force a smile.

"So scared I'm glad I shit first before coming out here," he whispered in English.

"Let's just check the controls one more time," Chuck announced. Going over to the chief engineer's chair, he climbed in, and the aerosteamer sank back down on the wheels beneath the engine. Grabbing hold of a wooden lever with his right hand, he pushed it to the left and right, then looked over his shoulder to watch the rudder action. With his right hand he pulled another lever back and forth, then nodded in approval.

"The up-and-down rudder, left-and-right, are just fine. Now get in here, Jack."

Petracci climbed into the forward seat, while Chuck climbed into the one facing aft, toward the engine. Feyodor eyed him suspiciously.

"Just running through things one more time," Chuck said cheerfully. He reached over and checked to see that the fuel was full on, then grabbed hold of the throttle and cranked it down two notches. Ever so slowly the cylinders started to crank over, helped along at first by a quick push to the flywheel.

Still leaning out of his open chair, Chuck looked straight up to where the exhaust stack rose up into the bag overhead. There was a good four feet of clearance around the stack, and he could see the wavy shimmer of heat soaring upward. Pulling down on a heavy red cord he saw blue sky appear directly overhead on the top side of the bag, and yanking down on the black rope with his other hand the aperture closed.

"All set!" Chuck announced.

Jack leaned out of his chair and looked down to the ground just a couple of feet below.

"We're starting to get lift."

"Feyodor, give me that bottle of vodka."

The mechanic reached into his tunic and pulled the bottle out, passing it up.

Leaning out of the cab, Chuck swung it down against the bottom frame of the engine.

"I christen thee the *Flying Cloud!*" he roared, laughing with delight at having named his creation after a McKay clipper ship.

"Now cast off fore and aft! Jack, give her full up-rudder!"

"Colonel Ferguson, it's against orders!" Feyodor shouted.

"Hang the goddamn orders, I'm taking her up!"

Before Feyodor could stop him, he pulled the throttle wide open.

The gently turning blades shifted in seconds into a blur, the clearing echoing with their hum, which was counterpointed by the excited shouts of the crew. The hundreds of men and women who had worked months for this moment cheered wildly as the nose of the *Flying Cloud* started to pitch up.

The first seconds were pure exhilaration, but they quickly turned into pure terror as Chuck realized that the aerosteamer, though rising at the nose from the thrust of the engine, was at the same time dropping at the tail.

"Down rudder, Jack!"

Petracci, looking over his shoulder, his eyes wide with fear, slammed the rudder forward. A shudder passed through the ship and the nose started to come back down, the tail rising heavenward. At the same time the ship was gaining forward speed, moving across the narrow clearing hacked into the forest.

"Left rudder!"

"God damn it, *I'm* the aerosteamer engineer!" Jack shouted, "I know what the hell I'm doing!"

The nose reached the horizontal position and

started to pitch down again, while at the same time the ship started to turn. Jack pulled the up-rudder back, but for long seconds the nose continued its forward pitch. Finally it slowed, hesitated, and then started back up, the only thing saving them being the fact that the ship was rising up vertically from the hot air, and was now almost twenty feet off the ground.

"It takes time to react!" Chuck shouted, trying to be heard above the roar of the engine and propeller. "Push it down again before you want it to level out."

Jack nodded, even as the ship continued its swing around the clearing, and started to aim straight back toward the fifty-foot-high hanger.

"Shit!"

The nose of the aerosteamer continued to climb, pointing higher and yet higher into the air, and Chuck suddenly realized he had forgotten something else. If he ever got back he'd have to install belts for the chairs, to keep from falling out. Letting go of the throttle he hung onto the side of the wicker chair, looking over his shoulder at the rapidly approaching hanger. The ship continued to climb, propeller humming, the crowd below now silent, looking up gap-mouthed as the aerosteamer seemed to skim straight up the pitched roof of the building and then continue on into the sky. A wild cheer erupted.

The high, towering trees beyond started to drop downward, and still they climbed, the nose seemingly pointing straight up. Ever so gradually, Jack eased the up-rudder forward so that the tail rose up and the nose dropped back down. The clearing fell astern.

Jack looked back over his shoulder at Chuck, who was staring at him, unable to speak.

"Just took a little getting used to," he said, his eyes still wide with terror.

Chuck reached into his jacket, pulled out a small flask, and passed it over.

Jack took a long pull and smiled weakly.

"You know I hate ballooning," he whispered.

"Well, you're the only poor bastard on our side that knows how," Chuck replied, trying to keep the shaking out of his voice.

He took the flask back and drained off the rest of the vodka, then settled back for a moment to let the racing of his heart drop away. And for the first time he looked around.

It was wondrous.

Already he could see as far as Hispania, and a toylike train crossing the Sangros River beyond it. The air was crisp and sharp, and the red sun hung just above the eastern horizon. The dividing line between the steppe and the forest marched off to either side, the fur-clad hills giving way to the vast sweep of open grasslands, the low folds of ground still buried in deep shadows.

A distant cry came up from below, and looking straight down Chuck saw the powder mill, hundreds of workers pouring out, pointing up excitedly, shouting with joy that at last their side was in the air as well.

"How high?" Chuck shouted.

"Five, maybe six hundred feet."

"Keep pointing her north into the wind."

Jack nodded, gingerly working the controls. The ship continued to porpoise and swing from side to side for some minutes, until Jack gradually learned that the slightest correction would get him where he wanted to go.

Working the red-and-black rope, Chuck kept an

eye on the ground, gauging the rate of rise and fall, while Jack kept the nose steady on the horizon.

"We got two ways of climbing and dropping!" Chuck shouted. "I think we can beat those bastards to hell, in that category at least."

The engine continued to chatter along, though all the time he had an eye on it. They had once run it for six hours straight without a hitch, but if it should fail now he wondered if they could stay aloft long enough to drift out over the steppe before landing.

The air was decidedly cooler, made even more so by the steady rush of wind around them. Yet another thing he had not planned for, and as he started to shiver he cursed himself for being so shortsighted.

A slight buffet ran through the ship, and Chuck felt his stomach tighten.

"Wind's picking up slightly," Jack announced, and Chuck could see a slightly green look on the face of his engineer.

"Feeling all right?"

Jack swallowed hard but said nothing.

"Well, maybe we ought to swing back in."

A visible look of relief crossed Jack's features, and with significantly more skill than he had displayed only a half hour before he maneuvered the ship into a gentle turn.

"We're way too high!" Jack shouted. "Maybe two thousand feet or more."

Amazed, Chuck spared the time for another look around.

It was godlike. On the southern horizon he could see the shimmering band of the inland sea, over seventy miles away, and far out over the steppe the distant smudge of two engines pulling their long trains westward. A vast flock of birds, heading north with the advancing spring, winged by, making the wide diversion around the lumbering creature that had risen to join them. Chuck laughed with childlike delight.

"A little more drop!" Jack shouted.

Berating himself for having lost sight of his task, Chuck pulled the red cord full open, leaning out of his chair to look straight up into the hot air bag and the hole of blue at the top.

The nose started to drop slightly, and with power still on Jack eased the ship into a dive, the wind picking up. Chuck looked back over Jack's shoulder and saw the clearing, which at first seemed impossibly small for such a big ship to land in, swarming with antlike creatures.

"I think we're going down a little too fast!" Chuck shouted, and before Jack could even respond he'd pulled the vent shut. But the ship continued to drop.

Jack started to ease the nose back up, yet the downward drop continued. With growing panic, Chuck realized that he must have spilled out nearly all the hot air left, and it would take several long minutes for it to build back up again.

"Bring it up!"

The ship continued to drop, even as the nose rose high and yet higher.

Chuck leaned out of his chair to peer over Jack's shoulder.

His friend's hands were white-knuckled on the controls, in a death grip, and his eyes were wide with fear.

The nose continued to rise, reaching horizontal and then pitching upward. The edge of the forest raced up, shooting past the nose. Chuck felt as if his heart were about to burst as he looked aft and saw the high-tipped trees spearing upward, then brushing astern by not half a dozen feet.

The ground continued to come up, and the nose

continued to climb. The tail settled, and then with a lurch the ship slowed, the propeller pointing skyward, the hot air bulging the bag back out. Ever so gently the tail continued downward, coming to hover not half a dozen feet off the ground, crews racing to grab hold of the dangling tow lines.

"Kill the engine!" Jack shouted.

Chuck reached over and slammed the throttle shut even as Jack pushed the up-rudder forward. With tail now restrained by several dozen men, the nose started to come ever so slowly down. Dangling cables hanging from the sides of the ship were snagged, and with a barely perceptible bump the aerosteamer settled back to the ground.

"I think we need a little practice," Chuck whispered.

"It was nothing," Jack replied, stepping down from the ship to admiring cheers from the workers. He looked around with a weak smile, acknowledging their admiration, then promptly leaned forward and vomited.

Legs rubbery, Chuck climbed out of his chair and looked a bit sheepishly at Feyodor, who stood in silent rage at having been cheated out of the maiden flight.

"Mass production of aerosteamers, and training of engineers, starts today," Chuck announced.

Even as the crowd cheered Chuck felt his knees go weak, and he sank down to the ground.

He had done it, he had flown like a bird, and the trembling passed. Looking up at the ship, he silently analyzed what they had done right, and even more importantly what they had done wrong.

Let the heat control altitude, the propeller speed. Hover up till clear, slowly drop back down to land. It was that simple.

He looked over at Feyodor and smiled.

"Go get a couple of leather belts."

Feyodor looked at him coldly.

"Damn it all, man, go get the belts! I don't want you falling out of your chair! We're going back up in ten minutes."

A grin of delight creased Feyodor's face and he raced off.

Jack looked over at him weakly.

"Get your legs back, Jack. I'll be back in a half hour and then it's your turn again."

"I should have kept my mouth shut about hydrogen," Jack groaned. "No one would have been the wiser, and I'd be safe on the ground."

"Hell, you're the master aero-engineer," Chuck retorted. "If Andrew was to hear I flew he'd skin me alive, so you'd better get used to it. You'll be in battle with these soon enough. You're the lucky one."

Jack tried to force a weak smile, but he knew that he was certainly not cut out to be a hero of the air.

It had almost been too easy. They had waited in the forest for nearly a month, having long since abandoned their mounts, moving stealthily through the woods, finding the places where the wire ran as they had been told they would by those who rode in the sky.

Once the wire had been found, all that was needed was to wait until a cloud-flyer passed overhead flying a blue pennant, and that would be the signal to move at night.

They surprised the small outpost with almost shocking ease. The slaughter had been sharp and quick, the meal afterward a welcome reward after endless days of living without fire on tedious and dull rations of curded milk and dried flesh.

The clicking machine chattered into life without

warning, and the Tuger turned, wiped his mouth with his sleeve, and motioned for the wide-eyed captive to do his task.

"I have learned the clicking words too," the Tugar growled in barely understandable Rus. "Answer wrongly, and you'll end like this." Laughing gruffly, he held up the broiled leg of a cattle.

The wide-eyed prisoner, captured at the Kennebec station in last year's war, nodded weakly. There had been a time when he thought he might resist, that in a brief flash of signal he might send the warning, telling the army that the watch station on the far right flank was in enemy hands. Now he could only look blankly into the leering grin of the Tugar, his hands trembling.

He tapped out the signal for "all clear," and with a heart knotted in anguish he leaned back, sobbing softly while the Tugars around him laughed.

"Fist seemed strange."

The messenger looked over at the telegrapher, stifling a yawn.

"How so?"

"Didn't seem like Eugene."

"It's late, Stanislav, he's tired," the messenger said, stirring and pulling the pot of tea off the stove, motioning to ask whether the operator wanted his cup refilled.

Stanislav held his tin cup out, and with his drink refilled he leaned back in his chair.

"Seemed like someone else."

"Who?"

"Can't remember now," Stanislav said, blowing on the edge of the cup to cool it down.

"Think you should signal back?"

Stanislav sat for a moment, looking at the dark

rafters of the ceiling, listening to the gentle ticking of the clock.

"Care for some honey in your tea?"

Stanislav looked over at the messenger, who was reaching into his haversack and producing a small earthen jar.

"Haven't had any in months."

The boy poured some into Stanislav's tea, and the telegrapher smiled his thanks.

He put his feet up on the desk as he sipped his tea, then drowsily listened to the ticking of the clock. Ever so gradually he nodded into sleep.

Chapter 5

In the early morning light Tamuka rode up to the encampment, marked by a flickering fire. Cresting a small rise, he looked back to the west. For as far as the eye could see the steppe was covered with the vast column—twenty-five umens, a quarter of a million warriors, the advance a half-mile wide and over twenty miles deep, the thunder of their passage like a storm as they splashed through the shallows of a broad, low stream.

Vuka, grinning with enthusiasm, leaped from his saddle, going up to join his father, who was leaning against a tree, watching the host in its passage.

Tamuka, bowing his acknowledgment, went over to join Hulagar.

"Going well?" Tamuka asked, taking off his helmet to run his hands through his mane.

"The raid hit as planned. It appears that we got this far undetected."

"They've surprised us before," Tamuka said cautiously.

Hulagar nodded.

"I think though we just might have them this time," the shield-bearer of the Qar Qarth replied. "Their river defense is well built up to where the river forks. They built along the branch that turns north. They only have watch posts out on this branch a day's ride further out."

Tamuka nodded and reached around to his hip, where he found and uncorked a water bottle. He took a long swallow, wiping his lips with the back of his sleeve.

"The Vushka Hush?"

"In position."

Tamuka looked over to where Jubadi sat, squatting on the ground over a map laid out before him.

Tamuka gave thanks inwardly that Jubadi had not agreed to the Zan Qarth's request to go with the Vushka. The Vushka, accompanied by a regiment of Tugars, had ridden more than two hundred miles farther to the west, departing ten days before the main column. Leaving their mounts, they had entered the forest four days ago, following a trail in the wilderness that had been blazed out in secret during the winter. It was an undignified act for one of the blood to go into battle on foot and the eleven thousand warriors had marched at a killing pace. But once the flank had been turned, their mounts would be brought up.

Hulagar went over to join his Qar Qarth, Tamuka following. Jubadi looked up, nodding a greeting to Tamuka, and he felt himself breathe easier. They had not spoken since the moon feast, and this was the first sign that whatever displeasure had been felt had dissipated. Tamuka saw Muzta standing to one side, and the Qar Qarth of the Tugars motioned for him to come over.

"I hear your warriors did well," Tamuka said politely, after bowing low.

Muzta chuckled lowly.

"Of course. The great forest might be strange to you, but it is the northern border of our realm."

Tamuka nodded in agreement. He found the

looming woods to be dark and disquieting, as if carrying a vague threat in their sinister stillness. They seemed to hem in the world, and he looked into them with displeasure.

"My path-chanters can tell you every hill, every river crossing, every mountain pass, across this entire world for an entire circling, but a quarter-mile into those woods is a mystery. It is only here, and at Kyhmer on the other side of the world, that we must ride into them to avoid the seas."

Muzta paused, looking out across the steppe. Three winters back he had ridden this same land, coming forward at the head of his umens, ready to sweep up the Rus in what he thought would be a war of not more than a day—a minor diversion or sport. Only Qubata had thought differently; and now Qubata was dead.

What a world of change! Shading his eyes against the morning sun, he looked eastward. On the far horizon he could barely discern the sausage-like blur of a cloud-flyer, hovering in the sky, marking the outer line of skirmishers, pushed far forward to mask the advance. A battery of six guns clattered past, their crews lashing the sweating mounts, with a fresh team trotting alongside, ready to be hooked in if a horse should collapse and be consigned to the master of food.

Two horses a day, to feed a regiment of a thousand. Now they were slaughtering their own mounts to keep the army alive, until the hoped for hordes of prisoners had been garnered in.

How it had all changed! He kept his features fixed, revealing nothing.

"Still thinking of doom?" Muzta asked quietly.

Tamuka looked over at the Tugar and said nothing.

A clattering tapped through the glade, and Tamuka turned to where a circle of Tugars stood next to a wire-talking machine. A cattle sat on the ground, looking around in wide-eyed terror.

One of the Tugars said something to Rus, prodding the cattle with his boot. The cattle looked over at Tamuka for a moment, and he could sense the hatred boiling up.

Their gaze locked but for a second, and then the cattle placed his hand on the machine, the key starting to click a message back.

An instant later the cattle's head was on the ground, its legs kicking spasmodically.

"He betrayed us!" a Tugar snarled. "He sent the word 'trap.'"

Jubadi looked up from the map.

"Can you fix it?" he snapped.

Hesitantly the Tugar knelt down by the body, placing his fist on the key. He tapped out a message and waited.

There was no response. He looked back at Jubadi nervously.

"They must know," he whispered.

Cursing, Jubadi came to his feet.

"We can't wait. Signal the Vushka to attack. We move!"

A signaler, standing next to Jubadi, rushed out of the glade, shouting orders. Within seconds a mounted warrior held up a high pole, atop which was a bright red flag a dozen feet square, slashed with a white strip. Several miles to the east another flag shot up, and beyond that another, and then yet another. The command of Qar Qarth was racing eastward through the forest, to where the Vushka, long-concealed, waited for their orders to go in.

"So what do you think?" Andrew asked.

The hooded form drew closer, the thin trace of a smile on his features.

"It is as I expected. Remember, I suggested this might be their method," Yuri replied.

Andrew nodded almost imperceptibly.

"It's good to be out in the open again," Yuri said, "to smell the wind of the steppe, the scent of the blooming Kargak."

Andrew looked at the man. *Kargak* must be a Merki word. He didn't ask. This man was as much Merki as he was human.

"What you call protection is for me hell," Yuri said.

Andrew did not reply. Yuri was an outcast from his own people. He had ridden with the Merki, and even though it had been as a captive, he had been one of them nevertheless. He was an eater of human flesh, an untouchable.

He struggled with his own revulsion. He liked to think that if he were a prisoner he would die rather than submit. But the spark of life was strong. He tried not to think of the possibility.

Two days after Yuri had returned someone tried to stab him. Since then he had lived comfortably out in the countryside, but guarded and confined.

And now Andrew needed him.

"The steppe—it's home now, isn't it?"

"Twenty years, Keane. I've ridden around the entire world. I have seen Barkth Nom, the roof of the world, snow-clad, lightning dancing between its peaks. I have seen the vast plains of the Ur, where one rides for twenty days and the world is as flat as if it were spread out upon a table.

"When the Horde crossed up over the hills of Constan I stood atop the highest peak, and as far as the eye could see I gazed upon them in their multitude. I have ridden in grass so high that it crested above my head—an ocean of green wavering in the breeze, dotted with the heads of a hundred thousand warriors. I have seen the twisting storms, the green flashes of sunset, the world encased in ice, and fields of Kargak so red that the world seemed to be a carpet of scarlet.

"I've seen more than you who live in one place can imagine. I have lived like a Merki."

"And you found it to your liking," Andrew said.

Yuri smiled again.

"If not for certain requirements for survival, who could not love it? Keane, every day that you awake you know what you will see when you step out your door. Days into months into years, always the same. I have forgotten more than you will ever see."

"And you have seen the feasts."

Yuri looked straight into his eyes.

"Yes, I have seen the feasts."

Andrew looked into his eyes. What had they really seen? As usual, Yuri's expression was emotionless, and Andrew had a flash memory of the contraband, the runaway slaves coming through the lines. They had had that same expression. The blank stare, not showing emotion in the presence of a white man, a man who could control them. That is how this one survived as a pet, a slave. He had conquered all feelings, all hates, all loves, standing with blank eyes to the horrors, remembering instead only the moments that had struck some inner chord of his heart. Yet nearly all the contraband held a deep and abiding hatred for their masters. Nearly all. There were some who, in that strange perverse relationship of slave and master, had come to love their owners.

He looked closely at Yuri. Was he one of those, after twenty years still loyal to those who ate the flesh of his fellow humans? Was he a plant, as Hans and Kal believed? Or was he now some poor tormented soul, cursed by his sins to be outcast from both the worlds he had known?

"There are times when you loathe me," Yuri said with a smile.

Andrew did not reply.

"I understand. Most of the time I loathe myself as well."

Andrew looked away from him, back toward the enemy lines.

"Tell me what will happen," he finally said, breaking the uncomfortable silence.

"Do you see that standard, the red pole with the cross tree?"

"Almost like a cross," Andrew said, swinging his field glasses toward where Yuri pointed.

"It's the standard of the Qar Qarth Jubadi. Twenty horsetails hang from the pole, one for each of the sub-clans of the Merki Horde. That means he is there."

Andrew nodded.

"Or at least, it means that he wants you to think he is there."

Andrew looked over at Yuri, noticing from the corner of his eye his own guidon-bearer, holding the standard of blue cloth with the eagle of a colonel's rank emblazoned on it. The standard hung limp, and he suddenly wondered if letting his own people know his position had been such a good idea after all.

"What can we expect next?"

"Even when he is fighting a losing war," Yuri said, "the craftiness of Jubadi is legendary amongst his people. When he is not present they affectionately call him 'Vag Oge,' 'the Wily Fox.' I told you how two years ago he trapped the elite umen of the Bantag and annihilated it."

Andrew nodded.

"That's his style—he likes to be at the front. If it wasn't for his shield-bearer, he most likely would have been killed by now."

"Shield-bearer?"

Yuri chuckled.

" 'Pak qar numradg,' is more the term."

"What is it?"

"The Merki are ruled by Jubadi, the Qarth of Qarths, or Qar Qarth, leader of the Qarths or clans. The shield-bearer, a curious combination. He is part bodyguard, thus he carries the bronze shield and rides by his side in battle. But he is also part shaman and part advisor. He is the only one capable of speaking to Jubadi without fear. If the Qar Qarth proves to be completely incompetent he can even remove him."

"Kill him?"

Yuri nodded. "Curious. So he is as powerful as the Qar Qarth—in a way, more powerful."

"Not exactly. They believe that the few who are shield-bearers are ruled by a different inner spirit, what they call the *tu*. It renders them incapable of being a true warrior."

"Why?"

"Because they are trained to think, to reason, to guide, and never to act directly, all their energy being devoted to the guidance of their Qarth."

"The intellectual advisor, thus unfit for war," Andrew said, chuckling softly.

"I wonder what they would think of a college professor of history running a war," he whispered in English.

He looked over at Yuri.

"Tell me what Jubadi will do."

"The unexpected. You see that already, with the use of those poor bastards out there." He pointed to the mole, which even as they spoke was being swept by fire from the first line of fortifications.

"They know that will shatter you, killing your own, that it might even crack your loose alliance with Hamilcar. They are forcing you to waste your ammunition, knowing that at the same time you're helping to slaughter their rations for them."

As if to add weight to his statement, a battery of four-pounders fired a salvo, and a second later the opposite bank seemed to explode in a shower of spray and mud as the canister rounds slammed in.

"As I've told you before, his favorite field maneuver is 'the horns.' Both flanks ride far out while the center butts into the enemy and holds them; then the horns close in."

"Hard to do here," Andrew said.

"Remember, though, that the Merki are bound by tradition. Their world, at least as they see it, is one of unchanging change. It is the everlasting ride to the sun. Behind them, the endless generations of the ancestors, as it was, and as it shall be. Tradition, and the symbols of that tradition, are all."

A shell fired from the opposite bank hummed overhead, tracing a slow, lazy arc at extreme range, detonating a hundred yards away. Yuri flinched, looking slightly embarrassed as Andrew remained still.

"Not used to it," Yuri said sheepishly.

"No one ever really is. You just learn when you really need to duck."

"A terrible way to make war."

"The only way to defeat them," Andrew replied sharply. "You were talking about tradition. To use artillery must stick in their throat."

"They hate it," Yuri said with a chuckle. "Last year they thought they'd just use humans for the dirty work. Now they have to soil their own hands, and it's degrading. War to them is the bow, the lance, the scimitar, fighting against those of equal caste. Honor is even more the goal of war than conquest. That was the hardest thing for them, to fight a war against cattle."

The way he said the word "cattle" bothered Andrew—he seemed almost to spit it out, as if it were distasteful.

"Jubadi would like to think that when you are defeated, he can smash the weapons, the same way they did against the Yor more than a hundred circlings ago."

"The Yor?"

"Their chant-singers tell of a small group, shaped not even like us or the Merki. Their weapons shot light that melted all who tried to stand against them. Thousands died killing the few, and when it was done the weapons were cast into the sea."

"Where?"

"Beyond Constan," Yuri said.

Andrew nodded and said nothing.

"Will they attack with their strength here?" he finally said.

Yuri smiled.

"You are asking me to guess. I was just a pet. I know not their plans, and it has been months since I escaped."

"You know how they think. You're the only man who has ridden with them for a circling and come back to tell us."

He looked over intently at Yuri. What he had started to consider for this man he had yet to discuss. The idea had started to vaguely form from the moment they had first met. He suspected why Yuri was here, the game within the game. He let the thought drop, focusing on the more immediate concern.

"What will they do?"

"What you don't expect."

"The flank, like General Schuder said?"

"If they can build that mole, the river will drop for miles. They might come straight across anyhow."

He pointed to the aerosteamer hovering above the front, like a malevolent hawk watching its prey. Its nose was pointed into the northerly breeze, the twin eyes and beak painted on the front giving it a cold, evil look.

"With that, they know exactly where your troops are."

Andrew nodded, saying nothing but cursing inwardly that their own efforts were going so slowly. Yuri had told him the first night how they had raided an ancient burial vault of their ancestors and uncovered the strange machines that now powered the enemy ships. The Yor, the burial vaults . . . what else was hidden on those endless steppes?

"Where will they hit? 'Mus kala bugth Merki, org du pukark calingarn Bugghaal.' "

"Enlighten me," Andrew said.

" 'Like the wind is the passing of the Merki, the goddess of death will roam where they have been.' "

"You're saying we will lose," Andrew said coldly.

"Keane, no matter how well you've planned, they have planned as well, I can assure you. It might be here, it might be far to your right, but they will come. Remember as well that the Tugars ride with them."

"Strange, isn't it?" Andrew replied.

"Muzta is in Hell. Humiliated, his umens dead, dragged like a beggar before Jubadi and offered a crumb from the feasting table. But he has told them all. They have learned from his mistakes, and are ready."

Andrew raised his glasses and looked back toward

the south bank, where another long line of fresh prisoners was being run up to the mole, the first of them already dropping from the smattering of rifle fire.

"You're a small comfort," Andrew replied sadly, watching the relentless slaughter on the opposite shore.

"I didn't come here to be a comfort. You didn't send for me to fill that task."

Andrew looked over at him, as he spoke again.

"You suspect you might lose, don't you?"

Andrew didn't reply.

"I came to tell you how to win even in your defeat."

Hans cursed silently, struggling to control his temper.

"You mean you suspected something last night and did nothing?"

Stanislav nodded weakly.

"And then today this word 'trap' came through."

"There was something afterwards, but it was clumsy, a slow fist: 'Nothing to report.' But I'm positive it wasn't our regular operator."

Hans looked over at Kindred, commander of 3rd Corps.

"Reports of skirmishers skirting the woods fifteen miles west of here," Tim said. "Our mounted pickets have been pulling back since yesterday."

Hans pulled on his rough beard, his eyes squinting shut.

"Maybe a skirmish party of Merki found the position," Tim said.

"It was well hidden," Hans objected.

He had learned long years ago, out on the prairie against the Comanche, to trust his gut instincts.

"Send a telegram down to Colonel Keane. Inform him that I suspect a move to my right."

The humming of an airship rose in pitch, but he ignored it while Kindred went over to the doorway to look out.

"It's flying a red pennant with a white stripe," Kindred said quietly. "That wasn't there before."

Hans raced to the doorway, shouldering past Tim and out into the enclosed parade ground of the bastion.

"Kindred, sound the alert!"

Climbing up to the bastion wall, Hans looked straight up to the aerosteamer riding high several thousand feet above the ground, the pennant fluttering down from the cab.

There seemed to be a strange silence hanging in the air, and then from the north, like a distant storm, a rolling boom of thunder came drifting down.

Hans ran over to where his command train waited, its engine venting a slow plume of steam.

"Get me up to Bastion 110!" he shouted, his staff running behind him, climbing aboard as the engine started northward.

Andrew had to control his rage, his guilt. They were doomed anyhow, and perhaps this was the greater mercy. But it didn't help.

The Potomac was a spreading carpet of the dead. Dawn had revealed the mole nearly halfway across, despite the horrendous slaughter of Cartha prisoners. Even if every yard of advance was purchased by a hundred dead the mole still advanced, the Merki gorged in the process by the surfeit of food.

A steady patter of musket fire rippled along the line, dropping more and yet more. An increasing number were attempting to break away and run, but with the narrowing of the river in half the current was running far stronger. The few who made it into the river were dropped by their Merki tormentors.

Three had managed to escape during the night, two of them tragically killed as they were shot dead by nervous guards as they attempted to gain the ramparts. The lone survivor reported that the Merki had brought up tens of thousands of slaves, boasting that if need be they'd build the mole with their corpses.

"Message from General Schuder, sir."

Andrew took the paper, gazed at it for a moment, then crumpled it up and stuck it in his pocket.

"What is it?" Schneid asked.

"You know, Rick, we're going to have one hell of a fight here by dawn tomorrow," Andrew said coldly, nodding out to the mole. "I'm going to want our artillery reserve from your corps positioned here by sundown."

"What did Hans have to say?"

"We've been flanked," Andrew said quietly. "A full umen, perhaps. A rising dust cloud is reported to be coming in off the steppe from the west as well."

"And?"

Andrew looked over at his young corps commander.

"If I released you to move your divisions up to Hans, and it turned out to be a feint, we might be unmasked here. If it is the real attack up there, and this is the feint, and I don't move you now, we'll lose the entire flank by tomorrow morning and this line as well."

A Napoleon kicked back next to him, sending out a spray of canister that swept a dozen bodies off the mole. From the opposite bank a score of guns fired a volley, iron shot snarling overhead, plumes of dirt and rock kicking up from the side of the parapet in a deadly hail, showering Andrew in dust.

From overhead a Merki airship went into a dive, its engine humming louder and louder. Andrew looked up for a second. A battery of four-pounders mounted in swinging yokes was pointed up, the guns firing. The airship started to level out, a black dot breaking clear. The bomb winged down, smashing into the next battery position seconds later. It exploded with an earth-rocking report, a gun carriage tumbling into the air. A jeering yell went up from the Merki side of the river as the ship turned, running back to the south with the tail wind coming out of the north.

"The reserves are waiting to be moved," Rick said. "I've got twenty trains full of them back up the line."

Andrew nodded, fingering the crumpled telegram in his pocket. Sixty miles, up to Hans at Bastion 100. An hour to get the trains moving, two hours up, two hours to unload and deploy. It had been practiced a dozen times. He looked back across the river. On the far bank, just beyond artillery range, at least five umens were drawn up in battle order. Upstream thousands were gathered around the log booms, rafts, and rock-filled boats. If the northwest wing was not the real attack, he'd have to turn the entire corps around, load them up and run them back down here. Sixteen hours of travel, exhausting them for a defense here and a possible long day of fighting tomorrow.

His worst nightmare was already unfolding, and they'd been fighting for only two days. If he started running back and forth with each crisis, committing his precious reserves when the threat might only be a feint, he'd be finished.

"For right now you're staying put," Andrew said slowly, looking over at Rick.

"What about Hans?"

Andrew nodded, and looked over at an orderly.

"Is Pat back in Suzdal yet?"

"Message came in that he was at Reserve Corps Headquarters, waiting for orders."

"Good. Get this message to General O'Donald in Suzdal. Move one division of Roum troops out of Suzdal, and run them straight out to cover the flank of General Schuder's position along the Potomac line."

The orderly scribbled down the message, which Andrew initialed. He ran off.

Andrew knew he was breaking the plan to keep O'Donald as the fallback reserve if disaster struck here.

"There simply aren't enough men," Andrew said quietly. "We're out on a limb."

He was starting to think that no matter where they held—here, on the Neiper—there would never be enough.

He looked up at the darkening sky, and as he did so the first chilled drop of rain struck his glasses.

"Jesus, here they come!"

Field glasses barely penetrating the gloom, Hans looked northward. It was like an inexorable wall of flesh and steel, coming forward at a run, the Merki's deep-throated growls thundering above the staccato roar of musketry and booming cannon.

Bastions number 110 and 109, the two positions on the flank of the line, had disappeared, swarmed under by the sudden and brutal assault. One moment the woods had been silent, and then within minutes the walls of the earth forts had been carpeted with dead and wounded Merki, the interior of the forts a shambles as the attack swarmed over them and kept on going. The line was starting to roll up, like a collapsing deck of cards.

The advancing wave was rolling into number 108,

hitting it from the west, north, and east. The secondary line, a half mile back from the fort, was going under as well from the end-on attack.

He felt a moment of pity for the men in the fort—they would all be dead in another couple of minutes, but they were buying time, precious time.

Hans walked out of the bastion and nodded to Charlie Ingrao, artillery commander for the corps reserve guns of six batteries.

The pieces were lined up nearly hub to hub, facing north. To their right an entire brigade was formed up, nearly twenty-five hundred men across a front of four hundred yards, positioned in the clearing cut through the woods for the now flanked fortifications. It was all that he had—stripping out everything from Bastion 100 at the edge of the woods, back to number 80, piling them aboard several reserve trains and racing them up to form here, leaving but a skeleton of just half a brigade behind.

"One-oh-eight is going down," Ingrao said quietly, pointing to the fort. A half-mile away the regimental flag of the Novrodian Regiment in the bastion fluttered down from the pole. Tiny forms appeared on the south side of the bastion, sliding down the ramparts and then breaking into a run, towering forms appearing behind them, bodies tumbling over.

Across the broad, open front, covered with scattered clumps of trees, the Merki umen continued on, advancing at a steady pace.

Hans swung up on his mount, slinging his carbine into its scabbard, his staff mounting as well. The command guidon drifted up alongside of him. He looked over at the tow-headed Rus boy carrying it.

"Scared, son?"

The boy gulped and shook his head.

"Well, I sure the hell am," Hans whispered.

"Gregory!"

"Here, sir." The young staff officer edged his mount in alongside of Hans.

"Get down to the far right of the line, and keep it anchored on the far side of the clearing. Now move it!"

He reached over and slapped the rump of the boy's horse. Grinning as he saluted, Gregory galloped off.

Hans again focused his attention forward.

The Merki advance halted for a moment, and he scanned the enemy line. They were shaking their columns out, forming into an attack front several ranks deep.

Ingrao, walking amongst his batteries, turned to judge the range.

"Batteries, load case shot. Four-second fuses, range eight hundred yards!"

A distant chanting started, an eerie, minor-keyed cry. It rose and fell, sending a shiver down Hans' spine. The warriors swayed back and forth and the chant grew in volume, counterpointed by the rhythmic stamping of their feet, which rumbled across the field.

"Batteries, fire!"

Twenty-four guns kicked back, and seconds later a scattering of shell bursts blossomed above the enemy line, bodies dropping.

The chant rose ever higher in volume.

"Reload case shot, same fuses!"

Four horse-mounted warriors appeared before the enemy line and stood tall in their stirrups, the leader raising his scimitar, the blade flashing. The three riders behind him lifted red standards in the air, and then held them out parallel to the ground.

As if guided by a single hand, the Merki battle front started forward.

"Batteries, fire!"

More bodies went down.

"Reload case shot, three-second fuses!"

The thunder of the chant started to resolve into a single word.

"Vushka, Vushka!"

Hans felt his throat tighten. Cartha intelligence had spoken of the "Vushka Hush," the elite guard of the Merki Horde. Was that what he was facing now?

"Batteries, fire!"

The standard-bearers raised their pennants, waving them in a circle, and then held them back out at a forty-five-degree angle. The advancing line broke into a slow run.

"Reload! Case shot, two-second fuses!"

"Vushka, Vushka!"

Hans pulled out a plug of tobacco and bit off a chew. His jaw working furiously, he offered the plug to Charlie, who took a bite and tossed it back up to the sergeant major.

"Batteries, fire!"

Gaping rents opened in the enemy line, but were quickly filled as the enemy formation dressed to the right.

"Professionals," Charlie snapped, looking up at Hans. "They know what they're doing, as good as reb infantry. These ain't no Tugars."

The standard-bearers stood up tall in their saddles, holding the pennants aloft, swinging them in a circle and then lifting them vertically.

"Vushka Hush da gu Merki!"

The Merki line broke into a running charge yet held in a perfectly straight line, still moving in step, each stride taking up five yards. The thunder of their advance was like the roaring of the ocean breaking on a rock-bound shore.

"Batteries, load with canister!"

Hans nudged his horse, moving down the line.

"Steady, boys, hold steady!"

The batteries kicked off tin loads of canister, two thousand iron balls cycling down range, dirt flying up, bodies tumbling over, hoarse screams cutting the air.

"Batteries, independent fire at will with canister!"

"Get ready!"

Twenty-five hundred rifles were raised up to the poised position.

"Vushka, Vushka!"

Hans looked over at the guidon-bearer. The boy was staring straight at the advancing charge, eyes wide with terror, his lips moving in silent prayer.

Hans leaned over, shooting a spray of juice to the ground. He unslung his carbine, then cocked back the hammer.

"Set range at three hundred yards!"

The long line of the infantry levered their rear sights up.

"Take aim!"

There was the reassuring sound of hands slapping barrels, the rattle of equipment, burnished steel barrels flickering in the drizzle as they raised up, and then lowered, bayonet-tipped weapons pointed straight down-range.

"First rank only!"

"Vushka!"

"Fire!"

A sheet of fire and smoke exploded out. The enemy line staggered, dozens falling, and without hesitation continued in at a run.

Ramrods snaked out and arms rose rhythmically, slamming cartridges home.

"Second rank, fire!"

Another volley ripped down the line, more bodies falling.

"Range, two hundred yards."

Hans watched in silence. The storm was advancing, and it seemed unstoppable. He could sense the growing fear, the tension coiling.

"First rank, fire!"

The Merki line staggered, as if it had hit a wall. The batteries to his left continued to thump out their deadly loads, canister tearing up swaths of dirt, smashing into bodies. The line slowed and then picked up, continuing on.

"Aim low, boys!" Hans shouted, unable to contain himself, the old instinct of the sergeant major coming back. He saw a boy in the line with sights still set at three hundred yards, and he wanted to unsaddle and go up and grab the gun away.

"I'm a general, goddammit," he mumbled to himself.

The charge pushed in.

"Vushka, Vushka!"

"Second rank, fire!"

This one, at one hundred yards, cut in with devastating effect, rippling the line, each body going down in a tangle with the warrior behind, alongside. Hundreds dropped.

"Independent fire at will!"

Miraculously, the Vushka commander and one of his pennant-bearers was still up, galloping down the line, waving his sword, the pennant dipping, pointing straight back at the Vushka line.

The charge stopped, and Hans watched in silence as thousands of bows were raised.

A steady patter of rifle fire increased to a crescendo, Merki dropping. Stirring, Hans drew a bead on the Vushka commander and squeezed the trigger of his carbine. The commander's horse reared up, nearly going over, and then collapsed.

"Eyes are getting bad," Hans growled, as he cocked open his Sharps and slid another round in.

The sky suddenly turned dark, followed an instant later by a whistling hail of bolts. Men collapsed, staggering backward from the impact. High shrieks rent the air; in an instant it seemed as if a forest of four-foot bolts had sprung up from the ground by the thousands.

Another cloud rose up, rising far higher, this one emerging from behind the charging line.

A second rank behind the first, Hans realized; they've got one hell of a lot more than I thought.

The cloud appeared to hover in midair, then came roaring down. The aim had been slightly long, and the majority of bolts struck forty or more yards behind.

At seventy-five yards the deadly firefight was traded out. The smoke eddied upward in coiling spirals, the enemy was all but invisible, the field guns kicked back and tore up the turf. Wounded horses screamed, cannoneers cut the tormented beasts from the traces of cassions, a continual stream of wounded poured to the rear.

Another shower of death rose up from the rear, hovering and then racing down, this time bracketing the volley line. Heavy bolts pinned men to the ground.

Hans rode up and down the line, gauging his strength, watching the men. These were veteran regiments, formed in the first Tugar War, armed with the newest Springfield rifles. Their pride showed— they were unwilling to break, knowing that to run now was certain death.

Holes were opening in the line. File-closers strung the double rank into a single row at points, while junior officers on the flank of each of the five regiments made sure that a dangerous gap didn't open between two units.

Light four-pound guns, two to each regiment, thumped away, their charges sounding almost tinny compared to the deep-throated roar of the twelve-pound Napoleons.

The fire forward suddenly died away. Standing tall in his stirrups, Hans looked forward through the smoke. A ragged cheer started to go up, and as the smoke dissipated he saw the enemy falling back, leaving a straight line of dead piled up not fifty yards away.

"General Schuder!"

Hans turned to see a courier galloping up from the rear, riding over toward Ingrao's batteries.

Hans looked around and saw that his guidon was missing. On the ground nearby the young boy lay spread-eagled, a four-foot arrow driven through his chest, the standard still clutched in his hands.

Hans motioned to one of his aides to get the messenger.

"Here they come again!"

From out of the retreating line a second formation started to surge forward at a run.

"Vushka, Vushka!"

"Prepare for volley! Fire at one hundred yards! First rank, present!"

The messenger came galloping over.

"From General Kindred, sir," the messenger shouted, reining his mount in alongside Hans.

He felt his heart knotting, a brief flutter. Again the shooting pain, but he forced it away. "Not now, don't trouble me now," he whispered to himself.

"The Merki, the Horde, sir, coming along the edge of the woods!"

"How many?"

The boy looked at him wide-eyed.

Hans saw that he was clutching a sheet of paper, and he grabbed it.

" 'Hans. A solid block of Merki, miles deep, advancing in from the west, along the edge of the woods. Looks like entire Horde. Will hit within the hour, near Bastion 90. Doubt if we can hold. Kindred.' "

"Fire!"

His mount shied from the explosion. He looked back at the advancing line. This time they were coming straight on, scimitars raised, bows slung over their shoulders.

"Independent fire at will!"

It was going to be hand-to-hand. The volley had torn gaping holes but the Merki pressed on, leaping over the casualties. Their formation started to disintegrate as the bravest, and fleetest, surged forward, swords flashing.

"Load double canister!"

Hans looked back up the line. *Murphy*.

"Where's Murphy?"

"Dead, sir." An orderly pointed to where the division commander lay on the ground, several of his staff kneeling around him.

Hans spurred his mount around, galloping back toward the massed battery.

"Ingrao."

The short, soft-spoken artilleryman looked up.

"Fire when they're on top of us!" Ingrao roared, then ran up to Hans's side.

"You're in command here, Charlie. Murphy's dead. Send a courier down to Gregory, tell him to take control of the division," Hans shouted. "You've got to hold, but get ready to pull out if ordered!"

Without bothering to return a salute he started to wheel his mount around, then looked back.

The wall came crashing in. The battery fired at

less than ten yards, the charge in front of the guns disintegrating. Merki bodies, heads, limbs, were lifted into the air, the few survivors staggering forward, gunners raising revolvers and firing at point-blank range.

A loud, thudding crash of steel on steel, and steel on flesh, snapped down the line of infantry, which in places staggered and broke clean open. Many of the first wave of Merki were rushing in without slowing, impaling themselves on poised bayonets, their weight crashing down the defenders. Those following them leapt in, swords flashing.

"Guidon!"

"Here, sir."

Another boy had filled the place of the last. He had not known the other, and the body was nameless now.

"Follow me, boy!" He kicked his mount into a gallop and raced across the field, back to where his command train waited on the siding.

"As planned," Vuka announced, laughing with triumph as he reined his mount in and signaled for a servant to bring a fresh horse up for the charge into battle.

Tamuka reined in beside him, pushing his helmet back to wipe the sweat from his brow. Another servant of the Zan Qarth tossed over a water sack and, raising it, Tamuka washed the dryness from his mouth.

Uncasing one of the precious far-seeing glasses, Tamuka scanned the enemy position on the other side of the stream. The battlements looked nearly defenseless, exactly as the airship hovering above the cattle line had announced. The ship was gone now, driven back southward by the rising storm rolling in from the north. A near thing—a couple of hours difference, and the signal might not have gotten through to the Vushka. The ancestors were watching, holding the weather back, and he mumbled a silent prayer of thanks.

The cattle had fallen for the bait, swinging north to engage the Vushka. It would take some loses getting across, to be certain, but the line was as thin as a rotting eggshell. One strong push and they would crash through, able then to wheel to the south and slice into the rear of the enemy fortress line.

The vast line of the advancing Horde, which had been moving in a long column, started to shake out into formation, ready to present a front a full umen across for the charge, sweeping in two miles' wide, the column of umens behind them coming forward to exploit the breach.

Tamuka tossed the water sack over to Vuka, who was astride his fresh mount. The Zan Qarth leaned back, water cascading down his throat and running down his armor.

Tamuka said nothing. Water was life, the gift of Narg to give life to the world. Even if a river was but a mile away it was improper to waste it.

Vuka unsheathed his blade. He made a quick turn of his mount, then bowed to the west in salute to his sires, beckoning them to witness what he would accomplish.

Tamuka felt a ripple of disdain. Was the brother he had murdered looking down now, cursing him? Was Vuka so ruthless, so blind, that he did not even care, feeling no guilt, no fear for what he had done?

Their gaze held for a second.

"What troubles you, shield-bearer?"

There was the slightest hint of taunting challenge in Vuka's voice. More than one of the companions turned from their excited chatter to listen.

Tamuka smiled.

"I am ready to ride at your side, my lord, my shield, my life, your protection," Tamuka answered, no trace of sarcasm betraying his contempt.

He could remember how Vuka had watched him fearfully after the fiasco in Roum, terrified that the shield-bearer had become Incataga, the messenger of death from the Qar Qarth to remove one not fit to rule. But now he was safe, the only surviving son of the blood, the only one to inherit.

"Then let us wet our blades," Vuka laughed, flicking his scimitar about. The tip of it whistled before Tamuka's eyes, but the shield-bearer remained motionless, refusing to blanch.

"The orders of the Qar Qarth were that the Kavhag Umen was to advance under the leadership of their Qarth, not under you," Tamuka said softly.

Vuka reined his mount in sharply, looking around at his companions.

"The blood should not be risked for the stray bullet of a cattle lurking in a pit; such death would be of little glory."

"And to linger here is of even less glory," Vuka snapped.

"His words, my lord, not mine. Even the Qar Qarth will not be in the van. This is but the opening move—there will be many battles to come. It would be a shame to miss them because a cattle shot you before the war had even started."

Vuka turned his mount away from Tamuka.

Regiment after regiment of the Kavhag Umen galloped past, wheeling to the southeast, falling in on the right, extending the line outward. Messengers on lathered mounts raced back and forth, signal poles tied to their backs, the flags fluttering above them, signifying who they were sent from and who they sought. Those bearing the gold flag of the Qar

Qarth rode sleek white mounts, the fastest of horses bred for their beauty and speed.

Red pennant-bearers positioned themselves in front of the Kavhag, broad red flags on long poles resting on the ground. Youths and old warriors with graying manes moved along the lines, bringing up strings of fresh remounts or moving away from the front, taking exhausted horses out into the open steppe to the south to be pastured and rested after the grueling forced ride that had started the evening before.

Tamuka took all of it in: the vast organization, the precision of the movements, the planning of months coming to fruition at last, right down to the number of arrows in each warrior's quiver and the whet stone in his carrying bag. Again he felt the stirring of the *ka*, the warrior spirit, seep into his soul as the steppe thundered with the power of the Merki Horde. Even against soulless cattle there was a glory to this vast panorama of primal strength.

Raising the field glasses he focused them on a rise in the ground a mile or more away. Jubadi sat atop the hill, the silent ones surrounding the position. Dozens of aides, messengers, commanders of umens, shamans, the sounders of the nargas, the rollers of the drums, and companions of friendship were positioned around him, the focus of power.

Vuka had deliberately chosen to range off on his own at this moment. He knew why, for to be in the presence of the Qar Qarth was to still be second. He could see Muzta standing behind Jubadi, the accursed leader joined by but a few, their two umens far to the rear. The breaking of the cattle line, the first victory, would not be theirs to boast of.

Tamuka shifted in his saddle, leather armor creaking, the bronze aegis of his office riding heavy upon his back. This was no place now for the *tu*, the spirit of the bearer, to speak, this was the place of passion. He struggled for the control of feelings to return.

"Merki Gor Rivah Macr!" (Who rides thus of the Merki?)

The lone chanter raised the call and the long line stirred, warriors coming erect in their saddles.

As one they raised their voices.

"Navhag vug darg!" (We are of the Navhag!)

The announcing of clan started on the lowest bass, rumbling like the throaty growl of the nargas. The rhythm of the chant having been established, other voices started to weave in the counterpoint, voices sliding high.

The chanters raised the question again, and the umen roared their response. The slow tempo gradually rose in speed, question and answer came faster and yet faster. Drummers, with huge cattle-hide kettle drums slung across their horses' backs, rolled out a steady beat, timed to that of a pulsing heart. Nargas, the horn-blowers, mounted as well, raised their fifteen-foot-long trumpets into the air, sounding a strident, dissonant note that grated through the air. Tamuka felt his hackles stand on edge, his pulse matched that of the drums, which ever so imperceptibly were picking up the beat.

Totem-holders positioned themselves forward of each regiment. Smoking pots shaped from cattle skulls coiled with blue-green clouds, as incense rose up on the breeze to awaken any of the ancestors who still might be slumbering.

A golden pennant topped by a red flag rose up from the position occupied by Jubadi. All along the front of the Navhag red flags were raised.

"Navhag, Navhag, Navhag!"

The red pennants dropped, held out sideways, the bearers twirling the colors in tight circles. Ten thousand scimitars flashed out and were held aloft, as if a curtain of burnished steel had materialized by magic.

The Navhag advanced, their mounts at the walk, chanting their clan name. Drummers kept the tempo up, horns trumpeted, totem-bearers trailed clouds of smoke.

Vuka swung his mount around, unsheathed his blade, and held it up.

"Let us take blood!" Vuka roared, spurring his mount forward.

Cursing silently, Tamuka pulled the bronze shield off his back while raking his spurs in. The horse leaped forward. And even as he cursed the insane bravado of his appointed charge, he gave an inner thanks for the release and the prospect of killing cattle.

Hans looked around at his aides, who stood gathered by the side of the command car.

"You've got your orders—now move!"

The dozen couriers galloped off.

"Here they come," Kindred announced.

Hans looked westward. The lowering sun, showing momentarily through a break in the storm clouds, forced him to squint his eyes half-shut.

The vast line was starting forward.

He looked down the line.

Two goddamned regiments, to cover a front of over six miles. One more brigade, and he could have held.

Wheezing, Tim leaned over the withers of his horse, coughing hard, his breath coming in short gasps.

"Goddamn asthma . . . It would hit at a time like this," Tim gasped.

"We better get going," Hans said sharply. "There's not much more we can do here."

Tim unsnapped his holster and drew out a revolver, half cocking the weapon and spinning the cylinder to check the load.

"Think I'll stay a while," Tim gasped.

"You're a corps commander," Hans snarled peevishly. "This isn't the time for heroics."

"I've just ordered a thousand boys to stay here, you know," Tim replied, "and I know not one of them will live through this."

He started to cough again.

"Damn spring grasses . . . Always said they'd kill me."

He looked over to Hans and extended his hand. "Navhag!"

Hans looked up. The line had moved into a canter as they'd hit the broad shallows of the Potomac, which here was little more than a stream. The single battery of four-pounders on the front kicked into action, while individual soldiers ventured their first shots at long range.

"I've decided to make my stand here," Tim said. "Take care, sergeant. I think we're all going to have to choose our place to stand, and I guess I'm just plain tired of fighting."

Hans grasped Tim's hand, holding it tight.

The few staff officers and the guidon-bearer behind Tim looked about nervously, knowing what this decision meant for them, but they remained silent.

Tim pulled free. Leaning over, he slapped the side of the engine, as he wheeled his mount to start back toward the front.

"Now get the hell out and save my corps!"

Hans watched as Tim cantered down the slope, moving straight toward the advancing Merki.

The engineer, who had been standing to one side, looked up at Hans.

"Get us back up the line to Bastion 100," Hans growled, trying to conceal the tightness in his voice.

The engineer saluted and ran back to his cab. Seconds later the train lurched forward, moving back north again to where Ingrao was still holding against the Vushka. Once this position here fell the line was finished—everyone north of Bastion 100, over two divisions, would be cut off from the rest of the army farther south. The Potomac line was finished.

He raised his carbine and fired off a round—a childlike action, he knew, as were the tears of humiliation and rage.

"We can expect them to hit come night," Andrew said, looking around at his staff. "I want fifty guns raking that crossing once the sun goes down, and then keep it up till dawn."

"That's going to come out to nearly ten thousand rounds fired by dawn," Yevgeni, the corps artillery commander interjected. "It's going to dig into our reserves, and the war is only three days' old."

"The Merki will be stuffed on the leavings," a young aide said coldly, standing up for a moment to look over the battlement wall.

The officer staggered backward, turned limply, and collapsed without a word. Andrew looked over at the dead soldier, who but seconds before had been trading a ribald comment with his friends. The casualties were becoming a slow yet maddening wastage, as the Merki guns across the river kept up a steady spray of canister and shrapnel.

Andrew looked away as the body was dragged off.

"You need some rest, sir," an aide ventured.

Andrew nodded woodenly. He had been up since

dawn of the day before. In another couple of hours it would be dark. He had to get some rest.

Without comment Andrew turned away from the battlement. He left the bastion and walked back to his headquarters, oblivious to the shells bursting overhead.

The tolling of a bell signaled a train pulling in behind the protection of the secondary line. The puffs of steam and smoke were shilhouetted behind the battlement walls.

A Merki airship, struggling against the increasing wind and lowering clouds, was turning about after attempting to hit the engine. With the strong tail wind it raced overhead, running back to the protection of its hanger somewhere beyond the Shenandoah Hills.

Andrew stepped into his headquarters and went over to his cot. He stretched out with a groan.

"Andrew?"

Startled, he sat up. Kathleen stood in the shadows. She came forward, a worried smile creasing her features.

"Just what the hell are you doing here?" he snapped.

"A fine welcome," she retorted, sitting down by his side. Her hands brushed against his cheeks, then pushed back a shock of pale blond hair, streaked with gray, from his forehead.

He leaned over, kissing her lightly. A sharp thunderclap, followed seconds later by the rattle of shrapnel raining against the outside of the hut, made him stiffen.

"I came down on the hospital train as the doctor in charge," she said softly. "Emil sent me along."

"Damn foolish of him," Andrew replied. "There is something known as a war going on out here."

"I can take care of myself."

"And Maddie?"

"She's with Ludmillia for the day."

Andrew relented, knowing it was useless to argue with her about the proper place of a woman in time of war. Such niceties might have applied back home, but this was now a nation at war for its very survival. Everyone was at equal risk, and who was he to attempt to order his wife to hide?

"It's going hard," she asked.

He nodded woodenly.

"I never anticipated this dam. It was so obvious, and we never planned for it. God help me, I've seen most likely ten thousand Cartha die out there. The river is running red with their blood. The Merki have slaughtered thousands more who've tried to escape. We're burning tons of ammunition to kill our own kind."

His voice trailed off. He was already feeling used up by what he was witnessing.

In the next room he heard the telegraph key start to chatter, and she could feel him stiffen.

Wearily he came to his feet.

She looked at him warily. He was different—his reactions seemed wooden, strained, and it wasn't just from the lack of sleep. She remembered him from the Tugar War, sensing defeat yet raging his defiance to the end, and in the process dragging all of them to a victory. This time there was something different, and looking into his eyes she finally saw it for what it was: He was afraid.

The telegrapher came bursting out of the next room, ashen-faced.

"It's Hans," Andrew said, his voice barely a whisper.

The telegrapher held the message up, adjusting his spectacles, his voice shaking.

"Message from General Schuder. The front has

been broken from Bastions 85 to 90. Estimate over twenty umens in the attack. Recommend abandoning entire Potomac line. Need trains to get two divisions out from Bastion 100. Expect road back to Suzdal to be cut by dawn."

Stunned, Andrew turned away, waving the messenger of doom out of the room.

Wide-eyed, Andrew looked back at Kathleen.

"My God," he whispered. "They've beaten us in just three days."

She sat in silence.

"A year of planning to fight it out here, to hold them back, and they slice through us, just as Hans had feared, and I couldn't see."

He walked over to the map table, tracing the extent of the breakthrough with his finger, shaking his head dumbly.

He slammed the table with his fist.

"God damn all of it!" She heard the quaver in his voice.

Kathleen stood up and came around to the opposite side of the table.

"If they've already broken you," she said, her voice edged with coldness, "then I might as well go back to Suzdal, smother Maddie, and then cut my own throat."

Startled, he looked up at her.

"Like it or not, it rests on you, Andrew Keane."

"I planned a disaster out here. I walked right into where they wanted us to be, believing we could hold them beyond our border. But we never had enough. We were too thin, and I should have seen it. Those damn aerosteamers could watch us like hawks, they knew everything and we knew nothing. I should have—"

"You should have and didn't," Kathleen snapped sharply.

He looked at her coldly.

"We did the best we could for right now, but it's not over yet," Kathleen stated, her voice a bit softer.

He tried to force a smile.

"You know," he whispered sadly, "I'm not afraid of dying, Kathleen. It might almost seem a release."

He looked away from her, the cabin shaking from a rapid volley of artillery.

"It's living through this, having to do all of it again and yet again, seemingly forever. God, I'm sick to death of it. I lost today. Thousands of boys who trusted me are dead, will be dead before tomorrow."

"The war has only started," she said softly. "A lot more will die even if we do win. But we will certainly lose, Andrew, if you fail yourself now."

She stepped around the table and took his hand, with a surprising gentleness after her flash of anger.

"I've got to get back to accompany the wounded out. It's up to you for the rest, my love."

She looked into his eyes for a moment as if searching, wondering at what had changed, what had been lost. She remembered the first time she had seen him, asleep in the wardroom of the *Oqunquit*, his frail, thin body stretched out, the boyish features filled with pain even as he slept. He had already been pushing the edge even then, three long years of war had done that. Would this war finish it?

She had sworn to herself that she'd never marry a soldier, not after losing her fiancé at Bull Run. "My dearest Kathleen," the letter had started, "if your loving eyes should read these words, then it means we shall never see each other again."

That had almost killed her, and yet in the end she had come to love this gentle, strong, and now frightened man. She loved him even more because of that fear, born out of the terrible burden he had carried for far too long, dreaming freedom for an entire world. Somehow she had to pour her soul into him now, to brace the strength that was starting to break apart like fractured glass.

"Even if we both should die in this," she whispered, "there will still be Maddie. Where will she be if you lose?"

He seemed to flinch at the mention of her name.

"Hug her for me," Andrew said. Kissing Kathleen lightly on the lips he stepped back, his right hand fumbling to straighten his uniform. She forced a smile. Again the fear, never knowing if any good-bye might be the last.

He gave a nervous nod and turned away as she left the cabin, ashamed that she might see the tears forming in his eyes. He stood alone for long minutes, knowing that just outside dozens were waiting to receive his orders.

The closest friend he had ever known was fighting for his life, for the life of all of them, not sixty miles away. He went back to the map, tracing out the lines. They had talked about this through endless evenings of "what if's," the thinking up of disasters and what to do if they should come to pass. But in all their original plans he had believed that they could stop the initial attack and that it would be into summer, when the river had dropped to a trickle, before they would be forced to withdraw to the line that would be built during the springtime at the edge of the forest. Hold until late summer, and the Horde would have to retreat or starve.

By dawn the rail line back to Suzdal from the north would most likely be sliced, and he could assume that most of the umens would drive straight in to the east and then wheel to the south to link up with the forces across from him.

Masterful.

Hans ran the risk of getting cut off, a fair portion

of his corps going down with him, some of the best troops in the army.

He gazed at the map knowing what had already been agreed upon. Knowing that the most basic of principles was to always reinforce victory, and never reinforce defeat. He felt his stomach tighten, as if Hans were standing next to him, his hawklike gaze fixed, telling him what would have to be done.

He walked back to the telegrapher's office, the six coded words given the telegrapher staring up at Andrew even as he tapped out the message.

Andrew walked out of the cabin to where his staff was waiting.

"He has sounded forth the trumpet," Andrew said quietly.

"My god, we're pulling out?" an aide cried.

Andrew nodded.

"More than half of his corps has been cut off. By tomorrow the Merki will attack this position from the rear. I've sent the orders for the reserve trains to move down here tonight to evacuate the army across the Neiper."

"What about General Schuder?"

"He's on his own now," Andrew said quietly. "If we try to save him the entire army will perish out on this steppe. We'll try and run some trains down from Suzdal on the northern line to Bastion 100, and get him out before they cut the line."

"Kesus and Perm help him," an aide whispered.

"Kesus help all of us in the days to come," Andrew said.

Forgive me, Hans, he whispered to himself, as he went back into the cabin and closed the door.

Chapter 6

"He has sounded forth the trumpet."

John Mina looked over at Pat.

"Which shall never call retreat," Pat said softly.

Kal shifted nervously in his chair, looking over at the situation map on the wall.

"How could we lose the Potomac line so quickly?" Kal asked sadly. He stood up, his one hand patting down the wrinkles of his long black jacket.

"It was a risk," Pat replied almost defensively. "Lee held nearly the same length of line in '64, with about the same numbers."

"Three hundred miles of rail, a hundred miles of fortifications, all of it lost," John whispered, shaking his head in disbelief.

The telegraph key continued to chatter in the next room. An orderly brought in the latest tear sheets, and Pat read them silently before passing them over.

"Are we ready for this?" Kal finally asked, looking over at John.

"Thirty engines and rolling stock are in reserve behind the lines, to move the troops and artillery back. Fortunately we decided to keep our main depot here in Suzdal. It'll mean losing whatever direct supplies are at the front, nothing else."

"But for the rest of our plans?" John shook his head.

"We gambled on the Potomac, figuring we'd have another two months at least to build the secondary line at Wilderness Station, and even heavier fortifications along the upper reaches of the Neiper. We were counting on having at least two more corps of infantry, another twenty batteries of guns, by early July for the final showdown."

He paused for a moment, leaning back in his chair as if calculating out a textbook problem.

"We might lose all of Hans's corps," Pat said quietly, looking at the reports coming in from the beleaguered third corps headquarters. "The penetration is five miles deep already—nothing to stop them except darkness."

Pat rose up out of his chair. Leaning over the table, he adjusted the wick of the kerosene lamp and looked over at Kal.

"If we lose all of Kindred's men, I don't think we'll stop them," Pat said quietly. "That's one-third of all our veterans."

"We might lose even if we do save them," John said coldly. "The Merki apparently have taken precious few loses. We had to trade casualties at ten-to-one to come out ahead. I doubt if we'll even see two-to-one. They'll hit the Neiper almost intact."

"What the hell are you two saying?" Kal snapped angrily. "All of us have gotten too damned confident of always winning. We lost this one, but it's only the first battle of the war."

Pat looked down at Kal and smiled.

"Assuming the best, can we hold the Neiper line?" Kal asked, looking over at Pat.

Pat pulled on his whiskers, frowning.

"That trick of building the dam . . . We never figured on it, and by me hairy ass we should have."

"They'll pull the same trick on the upper reaches of the Neiper. They got a hundred miles of river. They can probe, find an unprotected spot, and lash through. Once across . . ." He fell silent.

"How long?" Kal asked sharply.

"If they move up the Cartha prisoners, give 'em a week to march them a hundred and thirty odd miles," John replied.

"Then we have a week to figure something out," Kal snapped.

"I better get going," Mina said, coming to his feet. "It's going to be chaos on the Neiper River bridge, and we've got rolling stock to sort."

Picking up a sheaf of papers and stuffing them into his haversack, he walked out of the room.

Pat picked up his hat and started for the door.

"Where can I find you?" Kal asked.

Pat smiled.

"I'm going up to the front; somebody's got to get Hans out."

"Andrew expects you to be here."

Pat laughed good-naturedly and slammed the door shut behind him.

"Why are we stopping?" Tamuka snarled.

Against his own instincts he hunkered down in the saddle as a bolt of lightning snapped overhead.

He struggled to control his own fear, hearing the screams of whatever unfortunates had been struck. The thunder roared past. There was another bolt, flashing against the shield of his companion, showing hot and clear on the burnished surface.

Hulagar reached out, patting his fellow shield-bearer on the elbow.

"Because of that!" he shouted, as another boom of thunder rolled across the steppe.

"It's too dark, the rain, and we need rest. Rest my

young friend, your *ka* is boiling with blood-desire. Rest, the victory has been good today."

Tamuka shrugged Hulagar's hand off, ashamed at his momentary lapse into fear. Yet even for the Qar Qarth it was acceptable to show fear when the torches of Worg snapped down from the heavens, for after all it was the fire of a god. Turning his mount around toward where Jubadi sat, barely visible in the light of a sputtering torch, he started to urge his mount forward. Hulagar reached out and grabbed the mount's reins, and Tamuka looked over at him angrily.

"Don't!" Hulagar hissed. "It is not your place. You press yourself forward too hard."

"We have them! You saw them run, you saw the slaughter when the line broke!"

"Yes," Hulagar said softly, "and I saw you in the van. I saw you cut down the fleeing cattle, joy in your eyes. Is that a shield-bearer?"

His voice was heavy with reproach, and Tamuka looked up uncomfortably.

"It is not our place to fight, it is our place to protect and to advise, not to draw their blood. Let our Qarths do that."

Did not Hulagar feel it? Tamuka wondered. This was not battle for sport, the proving of names. This was beyond war, this was the survival of the Horde, all the Hordes, even of the disgraced Tugar and the accursed Bantag who still pursued their own ride eastward, letting the Merki take the bloody burden of salvation for all of them.

It was strange, this lust. A year ago he had believed he'd achieved detachment from all things except the path to understanding, the rising to the pure crystalline light of the shield-bearer.

He looked at the gathering, Vuka by his father's side, and felt contempt. He remembered Vuka in the charge, riding to the fore when all could see. But in the moment of shock, when they rode through the pit traps, horses falling, screaming, then up the sides of the ramparts, with cattle rising up, and shooting into their faces; at that moment Vuka had hung back, not enough to truly be noticed, but just enough.

It was not the wise decision of a Qar Qarth, a leader who knew there were times to let others go forth ahead, to save himself a danger that was senseless. No, this was different, there was a lingering fear. It was all right when cattle behaved like cattle, sport for a quick wetting of a blade. But when they could deal death, a death that ultimately was ignoble, without honor, then Vuka had shown fear.

It had spurred within him a madness and he had leapt ahead, lowering his shield from Vuka's side, drawing scimitar and crashing up over the battlement. His mount had gone down, rolling into the enemy fort, kicking, screaming, the cattle who had shot the mount standing there, wheezing, his face pale and drawn. The cattle had raised his handgun and squeezed again, but the hammer had fallen on an empty chamber.

Tamuka remembered that with an inner shiver. He thought himself dead in that instant, dead by the hands of a lowly animal, and it had filled him with rage.

The cattle had not died quickly, he had seen to that. The slashing lasted for a long moment—first the arms, before the death-strike to take his head.

Vuka had laughed at the sight, dipping his sword into the cattle's open wounds as if the kill were his, and then he had gone on.

No, Hulagar had not felt that, he still did not feel how deadly this struggle truly was.

"If we press on," Tamuka said coldly, "we could cut both their roads of iron strips by dawn."

"The umens have ridden since afternoon of yesterday, a hundred miles," Hulagar replied sharply. "We have fought a battle, our mounts are dropping with exhaustion. If we press through the night all could be lost at dawn, our warriors too drawn to fight, our horses too tired to move. Already thousands of them have died."

Tamuka snorted with disdain, even as he fought to control the trembling of his limbs. He looked up at the night sky with the rain washing his face and running down inside his armor, and he shivered from the cold, clammy feel of wet leather.

"Why could not the night be day, for just this one moment?" he cried. "For just these hours? They will escape!"

Hulagar, shocked by the dark intensity of Tamuka's emotions, said nothing.

"It could be finished here," Tamuka snapped. "We could cut them off, far beyond their cities, and in half a score of days march into their lands unopposed."

"Our lord Qar Qarth believes that to be the case already."

"Then he is a fool," Tamuka hissed softly.

Stunned, Hulagar turned his mount back around. He pressed up to Tamuka's side, his hand reaching out and grabbing Tamuka by the high collar of his leather tunic.

"You go too far, shield-bearer of the Zan Qarth."

"You forget," Tamuka replied, "it is we who hold power as well. You forget that it is we who can decide even to remove the Qar Qarth himself if he is not worthy to rule, to clear the way for one who is better."

"I am the shield-bearer of the Qar Qarth," Hulagar hissed. "I alone bear that power. I alone am the Qarth of our brotherhood. It is I alone who can voice such thoughts, and then only in the silence of my own mind."

Tamuka pulled back from Hulagar's grasp.

"One night's push. Cut the enemy iron strips ten miles to the northeast, fifty miles to the southeast. Place them in the bag now."

"He has decided," Hulagar replied, "and I agree. We have won much. Though our numbers are great, still we must remember that after this war there will again be the Bantag, despite what promises you thought you created. Our warriors are falling from their saddles with exhaustion. There are no stars to guide us. How can they even known which direction to march in this darkness? You ask too much. Come the light of day, they will not be able to fight—scattered, in danger even of being attacked in turn.

"We must win this fight, but we must win it so that we can win the next one as well. You act like the lives of ten thousand, or fifty thousand, are of no difference in this war of cattle slaughter. Did you hear of the bill of the Vushka Hush?"

"Half dead," Tamuka said dryly, "but they did well."

"Yes, they did well."

Startled, Tamuka turned to see Jubadi drawing up beside them. He felt a moment of inner panic, ashamed that he should feel fear, as if his father had overheard an indiscretion.

Jubadi looked at him closely.

"My son said that you slaughtered one of their leaders," Jubadi said dryly.

Tamuka nodded.

"A strange role for a shield-bearer."

"He was in the way," Tamuka replied.

Jubadi smiled.

"Do not forget your other role, Tamuka."

Tamuka nodded, saying nothing.

"It is time to rest," Jubadi said, looking up at the night sky. Another bolt of lightning streaked overhead, dancing between the clouds. He gazed at it without moving, the rain matting down his flowing mane.

"War at night has never been our way. And when Worg speaks, it is not a time to fight either. Thus have been the words of our fathers."

"Against each other," Tamuka replied. "But against cattle?"

Jubadi looked back at Tamuka.

"We will finish them tomorrow; they are as exhausted as we."

"Let us hope so," Tamuka replied quietly.

Jubadi said nothing, and turned away.

"Burn what's left!" Hans shouted, pointing to an open-sided warehouse, crammed with tons of rations.

A shrill venting of steam slashed across his legs, a shower of sparks rising up behind him. He turned to watch as the train, wheels spinning for several seconds before getting traction on the wet tracks, started out of the depot, heading straight east.

Boxcars slipped past. In the lamplight he could see them crammed full with wounded. Half a dozen flatcars were at the end, each one packing two field pieces, their caissons left behind.

A sudden impulse seized him and he looked over at young Gregory, who stood beside him.

"Boy, I need you to get things organized. Get aboard that damned train. Get the troops straightened out once they get back to the Neiper."

"But, sir, I'm needed here."

"A hell of a lot of good you'll do me now," Hans growled. "Now get a move on ya!"

Gregory hesitated, looking at the train as it slowly clicked past.

"Move it!" Hans snapped.

Gregory saluted and ran to the side of the train.

"When you get back there," Hans shouted, "marry that girl I heard about!"

Gregory looked back, hesitated, then snapped off a sad salute and leaped aboard the last car as it rolled past.

Hans watched him wistfully, barely noticing Ingrao, who had come up to stand beside him.

"Getting sentimental," Charlie said.

"He's got the makings of a good commander," Hans replied softly. "He deserves the chance."

Hans looked over at Ingrao, who silently watched as the train disappeared into the mist.

"That's all of them," Charlie said sadly. "I'm sorry about the others."

"You got out what you could," Hans replied.

"I lost half the corps artillery today—three batteries of Napoleons, twenty of the four-pounders."

"You stopped the Vushka."

"Half our artillery to tear up an umen? At that rate we'll finish off eight umens and they'll have thirty left."

Hans turned away. Again there was the flutter, the lightness, the streak of pain.

He started to bargain with himself yet again: Not now, just let me get us through this.

"We still need eight more trains," Hans said, looking back at Charlie as if by voicing the wish, they would suddenly appear.

He looked up at the sky, a slash of lightning streaking the heavens. A gust of heavy rain swept past, lifting his poncho and drenching his legs.

"What time?"

Charlie shook his head.

"Must be past midnight."

Six hours, then.

He started to turn away, but Charlie grabbed him by the sleeve and pulled him around.

"Someone's getting left behind," Charlie said. "You know it, I know it. Someone's got to cover the retreat. We'll never pull everyone in, load them, and get out. You can smell the beginning of a panic around here already."

Hans nodded.

From the break up to the north he had been pulling the men in all night, what was left of two and a half divisions. Concentrating them at the depot, loading them on the trains, and running them east and out of the pocket being formed by the Vushka on the north and the mass of the Horde to the south. Only two brigades had left. Come dawn, it might be chaos.

"We'll get them out. Pass the word, I want all units formed up within the hour along this track. Abandon the entire line," Hans said quietly.

"Abandon the line! What if they come through?"

Another slash of rain came down, the cold wind driving it into a near horizontal sheet.

"This stuff is heaven sent to cover us," Hans said. "I doubt the filthy buggers will attack at night in this. We're going to march the boys straight east to meet the trains as they come in. At dawn the Merki will close the pocket, and with luck we'll be on the other side. Now move it!"

Ingrao, breaking into a grin, saluted and ran off.

Hans fumbled in his pockets for a chew. He pulled out the small end of a plug, and cursed. It *would* be at a time like this that he'd run out. He put the last bit back in his pocket.

"Two hours to dawn."

Andrew nodded and said nothing.

The rain was coming down in sheets, and he gave a silent prayer of thanks.

Crouching low, he peered into the driving mist, the waters of the Potomac washing over his boots.

He could hear them on the other side, their shouts echoing. They were still at it, even though the waters must already be rising from the all-night storm.

A snap of light erupted on the other side, the spray of canister ripping across the river, the shot slamming into the mud-caked walls behind him.

They had yet to make their move. The night and the weather, at least for this moment, had agreed to help save his army.

"Let's go," Andrew whispered. He turned and struggled back up the slippery slope, mud-caked orderlies half pulling, half pushing their commander back over the wall.

Barney stood before him, barely visible in the storm.

"You know what to do now," Andrew said.

"Keep up the firing till an hour before dawn. Spike the guns, and get the hell back to the rail line."

"I don't think they'll move till dawn. It's simply too dark to try and run the rafts down."

"For my sake, I hope so," Barney said, forcing a grim laugh.

Andrew clapped him on the back.

"See you at the Neiper," Andrew said. Returning Barney's salute, he went off.

Returning to his headquarters he kept his poncho on. It was an old Union Army issue, the one-size-fits-all. Whoever had approved the design must have been a dwarf, Andrew thought coldly. For anyone over six feet the poncho barely came to mid-thigh, and the wet wool of his trousers clung to his spindly legs.

He looked around the cabin. All the maps, and his personal effects, had been loaded. He went to the back room and the telegrapher looked up anxiously.

"Any word?"

"Short on trains at Bastion 60. As per your orders, they're spiking four batteries and pushing them off the cars to get the last regiment out."

"Wait a minute." He held up his hand as the key started to chatter again.

He tapped out a quick reply and looked back up.

"Bastion 60 telegraph station is shutting down. The last train is pulling out now. All men are loaded."

Andrew nodded, and the telegrapher looked back at his tear sheet.

"All positions east of here are abandoned and cleared. The two trains coming down from number 60 should switch through the line back home within the hour. Some Merki managed to cross ten miles west of here, but were stopped short of the rail line. Everybody on our front is out, except for Barney's two regiments. That's all, sir."

"Shut it down and let's get going."

The telegrapher gave an appreciative nod and tapped out a quick message. Seconds later he ripped the key from the line and gingerly picked up the wet batteries. He set them in a carrying case.

"All set, sir."

"Then let's go," Andrew said.

Stepping back out into the storm, he gave a last look around.

"A year of planning," he whispered, and with a quiet curse of self-reproach climbed into the waiting car.

His staff sat huddled around the smoking stove, the room thick with the smell of wet wool. More than one of the young officers was already asleep, curled up between piles of equipment.

"Let's go home," Andrew whispered. Seconds later the train lurched forward, moving up the spur line to the main switch yard and the road back to Suzdal.

"What the hell do you mean, you can't get another train up there?" Pat roared, standing over the stationmaster as if he were ready to kill him.

"We had several washouts from the rain, undermined the tracks. One ten miles down, the other behind the trains coming out. It's tied the line up. It'll take a couple of hours to fix the break. We've got to run the six trains coming out past here, clearing the track, before we can send anything back down the line."

"God damn it!" Pat roared, his fist crashing down on the table. The station master leapt backward in shock.

"While you sit here, Schuder and damn near three brigades are waiting."

"We're working on it," the stationmaster gasped.

"Do something!"

"I've got a son up there!" he cried, his voice breaking. "Don't you think I'm trying to do something?"

"Unload the trains up there, and back them up the line."

"We thought of that," the stationmaster replied. "There's still the break behind them to fix as well. They'd only back up ten miles and wait anyhow. Backing up, they'll have to go slow. The tracks are a mess as is—damn frost's barely out of the ground in these woods. Pushing all those cars will most likely mean a derailment. It's quicker to fix the washouts, clear the line, and then go straight in. Believe me, we've thought of it."

Pat looked at the man who stood before him,

frightened at Pat's rage and yet filled with frustrated anguish as well.

"Do what you can," Pat said, and stalked over to the rain-streaked window to look outside.

The siding was a sea of chaos. Rain was slashing down in sheets. On either side of the rail thousands of dejected men sat in huddled groups, pushed off their train, which was waiting to go back up the line and bring the rest of their comrades out.

"Six lousy trains," Pat said, looking at the engines lined up, the rain hissing against their sides, clouds of vapor rising around the engines. The lead train was packed with fresh troops—two regiments, ready to form a front if need be to protect the pullout.

He looked up the line, picturing in the darkness the men laboring to shore up the last section of track.

He looked back at the clock ticking on the wall. Six hours ago he'd been in Suzdal, and now he was stuck out here in the middle of the line, halfway between the Neiper and the front, just fifty miles from getting in. He felt impotent.

The distant cry of a whistle cut the air. Pat tore the window open and leaned out.

Coming out of the mist, a headlamp appeared.

"They're coming in!" he shouted. Both he and the stationmaster rushed to the door.

The first engine rolled past, illuminated for a moment by the bonfires that smoldered along the side of the track. The cars were packed with troops, the look of defeat on their faces. Behind it came the second train, and then the third.

Pat looked up at the clock ticking on the wall.

"Get ready to switch us through!" he shouted.

Splashing through the mud, he ran to the siding while the fourth train rolled through the station. He leaped up into the cab of the first train, waiting to go back in.

"Get ready to move!" he shouted.

The sixth train passed at a crawl. From the last car on the train Gregory leaped down. Sliding in the mud and seeing Pat, he ran up to the side of the car.

"We barely got it passable," Gregory shouted. "The line's bumpy as hell. By the time you get down there, the other breaks should be cleared."

"Get up here!" Pat shouted. "Guide us back!"

Without hesitating, Gregory climbed aboard the engine and grasped the mug of hot tea offered by the fireman.

"I thought the rain was sent by Kesus," Gregory gasped. "Stop them damned aerosteamers. But it's playing hell with the washouts on the track."

The stationmaster came running out of the shed waving a lantern. Down the line a green lamp was raised up on a post, announcing that the switch was clear.

The engineer pulled down on the throttle, and the train lurched forward.

"What time is it?" Gregory asked.

"An hour and a half till dawn," Pat said softly.

"We'll never get up there in time."

"We have to," Pat said coldly.

Gregory said nothing. Cupping his mug, he turned away with shaking hands.

There would be no dawn this morning.

Tamuka stirred uncomfortably as the first nargas sounded. Pulling back the heavy felt blanket that had sheltered him from the worst of the rain, he stood up. The world was gray, the sky and horizon one. Everyone soaked, rain dripping down the flanks of his mount.

He grabbed hold of the saddle that had served as his pillow and slung it up over the horse's back, cinching the wet slippery belt under the beast's belly.

Slinging his oil-skinned bow case behind the saddle, he then buckled the sword around his waist. Drawing the chain armor out from a greased blanket of felt he quickly donned it and put his helmet on, before finally uncovering the bronze shield and slinging it over his back.

The nargas sounded again. Turning to what he judged to be the east he bowed low, intoning the prayer of the new day toward the direction of the everlasting ride. He then went to his knees on the wet grass and bowed to the west, to the departing of the night, the everlasting haven of the ancestors.

Pulling a leather bag out from under his tunic, he scooped out a handful of dried meat and curds. Munching on them absently, he washed the meal down with a gulp of stale water. Stepping away from where he had slept, he faced north to relieve himself. Ready at last, Tamuka climbed into the saddle, grimacing slightly at the cold discomfort of the wet saddle.

He looked down at the grass. It would be hard to tell direction. Normally the blades leaned slightly to the east, growing with the wind that drew them out of the ground. Maneuvering would be difficult, so thick were the clouds which completely hid the sun. They would have to judge by the wind on their backs. Signal pennants would have to be spaced every fifty yards, at least until the heavy mist had lifted with the passing of the storm.

This had not been planned for.

The nargas sounded yet again, and from the encampment of the Qar Qarth the bearers of the blue flags, marking the line of advance, galloped out. The army would split now. Half swinging straight east, the other half turning northward to cut off any who were left in the trap, to link up with the Vushka and from there ride northeasterly along the Tugar trail into the woods to where the crossing of the river was.

Vuka, stepping out of his father's small field yurt, swung into his saddle without comment, and Tamuka fell in silently behind him.

"Pass the word to halt, and keep it quiet."

Hans reined in his mount. Shadowy forms shuffling to either side of the track stopped; commands, muffled in the rain and fog, drifted down the line. Cursing soldiers collapsed. Soaked clean through, they sat on the ground, in the mud, oblivious to discomfort.

A dull thump echoed through the mist.

Hans looked up, trying to gauge the direction.

Another thump, deadened, washed through. Men stirred, looking back in the direction from which they had been marching since after midnight.

"Gunfire," Ingrao said, looking off to the west, trying to judge where the sound had come from.

Dark gray ghosts moved in the clinging mist. The world was only one color now, all of it shades of gray. Men, horses, moving like shadows.

"I can feel something," a young soldier said, going down to his knees, pressing his ear to the ground.

Hans swung down from his mount and squatted down by the boy. It reminded him of an Indian scout, listening for the sound of hooves out on the vast prairies of western Kansas.

"Something's moving . . . Horses," the boy said.

Hans nodded.

"Horses, lots of them," he said.

"Lines dead."

Hans looked up at the telegrapher, dangling from the pole beside the track, having just hooked in to the line.

"Did you get that last message out?"

The boy nodded.

Hans looked back at Ingrao, the only general officer left, both division commanders and the three brigadiers of the units now left having gone down the day before.

"Most likely their advanced parties have crossed the tracks."

"We're cut off, then?"

Hans looked at the artilleryman and said nothing.

A soft metallic clang rippled past him and he looked down at the rails.

"Something banging on the track," Hans whispered. The men sitting along the embankment looked at the rail as if it had taken on a voice that spoke of impending disaster.

"Definitely in front of us, most likely moving up behind us as well. Hell, it's the only way we could have gone—our trail's easy enough to follow."

A faint breeze stirred through the overhanging trees. In the gradually brightening light the guidon next to him stirred, its colors muted, silken folds hanging heavy.

A slash of rain washed over him, and Hans shivered.

"It's getting colder," he whispered. "Storm should be clearing soon."

Reaching into his jacket he pulled out a pocket watch and unsnapped the cover. Like all the watches that had been brought through the tunnel, every day it registered an extra hour compared to time on this world. He did a quick calculation.

"Dawn nearly an hour ago."

He put the watch back in his jacket and looked eastward.

Should have been here an hour ago. Where the hell are they?

Six lousy trains. All I need is six trains. To hell with the equipment, just get these men out.

"How far do you think we've gone?" Ingrao asked, leaning forward in the saddle, swaying with exhaustion.

"Six miles, maybe seven or eight. Hard to tell."

A horse neighed and Hans turned. Shadows swirled to the south. A horse rider appeared for a second, sitting motionless.

A Merki.

"Bastards must have swung in behind us, figuring to cut us off. Now they're on the hunt."

A gust of wind stirred, rolling the mist back as if drawing a curtain aside. Several dozen riders were visible, racing parallel to the track, several hundred yards to the south.

"They've found us," Hans snapped. Standing, he climbed back into the saddle.

"We fight it out here!" he shouted, and with a vicious pull drove his mount up onto the tracks, motioning for the regimental commanders who had been riding with him to come to his side.

"Those are scouts; the main van should be up shortly. I want a full division square, first brigade north and east, second brigade south and west. Five company front to each regiment, other five companies forming a second line. I want this thing four ranks deep, two ranks kneeling, other two standing. First brigade, second division, is to form a reserve in the center. Charlie, post what guns we've got left on the four corners and keep a battery in the center. We've got men spread out for more than a mile alongside the tracks, and we've only got minutes to get them ready. Now, ride!"

Bugles echoed out commands and officers galloped off, shouting orders. Men stirred, officers urging them on at the run. The square started to form. Regimental groups were forgotten, the men simply falling in where placed. The soldiers looked grim-faced, pulling leather cartridge boxes to their side and fumbling gingerly with the double flaps that had been clamped down tight to keep the rain out.

Hans galloped up and down the inside of the forming square, marking positions, shouting out encouragement, cursing any who were too slow.

The smattering of Merki scouts started to grow into clusters, a gradual line of skirmishers moving around the square, staying out of range. Riders with blue pennants started to gallop along the south side of the square, barely visible in the mist.

Another two miles and we'd have been into the woods, Hans thought coldly. Two goddamn miles, and now we're caught out in the open. He looked northward. The trees of the forest were clearly visible. A mile northward and they'd be into the woods. For several seconds he thought of moving them that way, but knew instantly that it would be suicide. The Merki would cut him off up there. Once the square was formed he'd have to keep pushing eastward straight along the track and cut a way out.

Another sound echoed, and all stopped for the briefest moment. A whistle, high and urgent in its calling, drifted in from the east.

A ragged cheer swept the line, to be stilled when another sound, dark with menace, rolled over them. It was the sound of a rising thunder, the ground trembling. From out of the dying storm the Horde emerged, and at the sight of their hated foe the Merki broke into song.

"Skirmishers, cover the flanks!"

Pat leaped down from the cab of the train, barely noticing the arrows arcing in.

From out of the twenty boxcars behind the engine two regiments piled out, men already running to cover the flanks. The armored car forward of the engine cut loose with a spray of canister that sliced out into the dying mist, the concussion and swirl of shot spinning the wisps of fog into eddies.

Pat raced down the track, screaming for men to follow, cursing wildly at the sight of a section of missing rail.

In the shadowy mists he saw a cluster of Merki riding slowly off, dragging something between them.

"Stop them, goddammit, stop them!" Pat roared.

A young soldier stood beside him. Snatching the rifle out of the youth's hand, he raised it to his shoulder and fired. A rider pitched forward out of the saddle.

"Come on!" Pat screamed.

Leaping from the roadbed he started to run through the knee-high grass, his leather-soled shoes slipping. The ground was torn up in front of him from something being dragged over it.

"Stop them!"

Several soldiers paused and fired, and another rider went down. A Merki turned in the saddle, bow drawn. With the release Pat saw the spray from the string. The arrow came in slow yet still found its mark, dropping the man next to him.

Screaming with a wild rage, Pat rushed on into the open field, men racing by his side. A flurry of shots snapped out and another rider fell, the burden dropping into the grass.

He pulled his revolver out, firing as he ran. The warriors scurried off.

Gasping for breath, his stomach knotted, Pat slid to a stop by the twenty-foot section of rail.

"Now, pick it up! Let's get the hell back!"

A dozen men gathered round, hoisted the section of iron up, and started at a slow run back to the track. Another low thunder was starting to build, and suddenly there was the loud shriek of the train whistle.

Pat looked back over his shoulder. From out of the disappearing fog a dark wall appeared, moving fast, sweeping to the west several hundred yards away, weaving their way past the occasional clumps of conifers that marked the edge of the great forest. The wall started to turn, horns sounding and chants growing. From out of the mist a line of Merki appeared, scimitars raised. They came in at a charge.

"Run!" Pat screamed.

Alongside the engine the first regiment was forming up, deploying lines to either side of the track and forward of the armored car, which was holding its fire, waiting for the struggling party to get in.

The charge continued to surge up the slope. The men around him looked over their shoulders, panic in their eyes, but not one let go of the precious rail.

A snap of light appeared off to the south. Seconds later the shot screamed in, the range high, the round snapping through a treetop to the north of the track.

"Move it, move it!" The chant roared up from the line of Roum infantry, who now formed a wall in front of the train.

Pat looked over his shoulder, and saw that they were less than a hundred yards away and closing in.

A shower of arrows snaked up from the line, slamming into the ground around him. A man holding the rail dropped without a sound.

"First rank, aim!" The command echoed out in Latin. Muskets flashed up and were leveled.

The line parted as they raced into its protection.

"Fire!"

The volley snapped out, horses shrieking, skidding on the wet turf, going down.

The six guns inside the armored car snapped off a volley of canister, cutting gaping holes in the line.

Pat directed the gasping men to lay the rail back in place.

"The spikes are gone!" one of the firemen shouted, barely audible above the crash of the second volley.

"Bayonets, then!" Pat shouted. "Drive the bayonets in! Use the musket butts as hammers!"

A horse, coming forward under its own momentum though already dead, crashed into the volley line not twenty feet behind him, crushing down the double rank, the body slamming alongside the track. Several Merki waded in through the gap, mounts and warriors dying under bayonet jabs but slashing men down in their dying. The wave receded.

A deep, booming roar was now plainly heard. Climbing up the side of the armored car, Pat looked forward. Another line of Merki cavalry was setting up astride the track a hundred yards forward. And beyond them, not a half-mile away, barely visible, he saw the sharp flash of a volley. Several seconds later a patter of bullets snapped past.

A gust of wind swirled through the light scattering of trees, drawing the mist away. An entire division in square had been formed down in the gentle drop of the valley just ahead. Pat unsnapped his field glasses then raised them, ignoring the rain of arrows dropping in from the riders who ranged a hundred yards out, galloping down the length of track, firing bolt after bolt.

From all sides of the square down in the valley Merki were surging in, scimitars flashing. In measured pace, volley after volley rippled down the line, holding them at bay.

In the center of the square he saw a cluster of horsemen, the guidon of the corps planted in the middle, fluttering alongside the dark blue flag marked with the chevrons of a sergeant major.

"Hans!" Pat screamed, slamming his fists against the side of the car with impotent rage.

The men working on the track struggled to pound the bayonets in, to anchor the rail in place so they could advance the last short distance. Musket butts shattered from the blow, barrels bent, but ever so slowly the bayonets inched their way into the rain-swollen wood.

And with every passing second more and yet more Merki filtered out alongside the trains, and dense columns moved to fill the few hundred yards that separated the division from safety. Pat swung his glasses to the south. Coming across the field, he saw battery after battery of guns advancing at the gallop, wheels bouncing and careening, the Merki gunners lashing their mounts on.

Tears of frustration clouded his eyes.

"There's the train!" Ingrao shouted.

Hans spared a quick glance up the long gentle slope to where the lead engine was stalled, the dark tan line of Roum infantry fanning out to form a line before it.

"Something's stopped them!" Hans shouted. "They most likely cut the rail."

A volley crashed out, and then from all sides a continuous roar of musketry swelled.

A steady hail of arrows was winging in, but the arrows came down in a high arc rather than in a deadly flat trajectory. Hans watched their fall.

Wet weather affects their bows, he thought. Not as much punch, thank god.

Charge after charge came in. The fire to stop them was nearly continuous, and hundreds of bodies piled up, formations breaking apart.

Hans looked back up the hill to where a sharp volley had kicked out.

"Charlie, we'll have to fight our way the last half-mile!" Hans shouted.

Charlie looked over at him.

"Holding square's one thing, Hans. Marching and fighting that way is another."

"Ney did it."

"Who?"

"Dammit, didn't they teach you anything?" Hans shouted. "Now pass the order. North and south walls to sidestep, west to back up, east to move forward. Keep them tight. If we start to break in, those bastards will ride right through us."

A hissing whine kicked overhead.

Startled, Hans looked to the southeast. The smoke from a field piece was rolling out on the wind, the Merki gunners leaping forward to reload.

From across the field, screened by a column of horse warriors, a long line of guns was being driven across the field, moving between the division and the trains atop the low ridge.

"We've got to move!" Hans shouted, edging his horse to the east side of the square, raising his carbine and pointing toward the train.

Bugle calls sounded. The men looked about in confusion as officers shouted to hold the formation.

The square started to move. Another flurry of shot crashed into the line as two more guns opened up. Casualties went down, men breaking formation to help the wounded.

"Walk or die!" Hans screamed. "No helping the wounded!"

On the flanks the Merki charged in, regardless of loss, nargas braying their insistent call. A vast wedge formation turned and started in from the south, riding at full gallop, hundreds of Merki on foot racing to keep up.

The musketry rose to a crescendo. Horses dropped,

pitching their riders to the ground, flailing hooves kicked their owners to death. The foot warriors charged on, leaping over the dead and dying, screaming their chants, scimitars raised high, flashing through the air.

The charge crashed into the southwest corner of the square, the line collapsing, Merki pouring into the hole. Part of the reserve brigade, turning about, raced back in a solid line, bayonets at the level, desperate to seal the breach.

Like carrion drawn to death, the Merki charged toward the breach, struggling to crack the line clean apart. Forward, the line of guns moved to deploy, the first piece kicking into the air as the team drove it up over the grading, the iron-shod wheels striking sparks as it slammed over the rails.

A second line of guns was beyond the first. Crews swung the pieces out to face east, back up the hill toward the train.

"Keep moving!" Hans screamed.

He swung in beside the regimental colors of one of the two regiments on the east side.

"Men of the 7th Novrod, we've got to take those guns!" Hans roared, pointing his carbine forward.

He looked back over his shoulder. The breach was closing, but nearly an entire regiment was gone, the square curving in as if a surgeon had sliced off part of a body to save the rest. A knot of survivors outside the protection of the formation fought on and were finally swarmed under.

"Bugler, sound double time!"

Tamuka reined his mount in, grinning with satisfaction at the battery commander, who bowed a salute and then turned back to his guns.

"Load double canister!"

Merki gunners leaped to their work, racing to

load, oblivious to the screaming wall of cattle rushing toward them.

Now they will see what we can give back, he thought with a smile.

The square lurched forward. All around him it was starting to come apart as they swept up the slope, racing to beat the guns before they were unlimbered—and loaded.

A hundred yards! Hans thought. Through the guns and we're home. Thirty seconds, and he saw the rammers stepping away from their pieces.

Fifty yards, and before him the batteries were silent, waiting, and in his heart he knew.

"Home, boys, home! Home's just on the other side of the hill!" Hans screamed.

Thirty guns fired at once. Six thousand iron balls snapped across the field into the line not thirty yards away.

Groaning with anguish, Pat could not look away. The entire east side of the square seemed to go down, the formation stopping as if striking into a stone wall.

The second line of guns facing in his direction fired, shot screaming up the slope. The volley line before him riddled, bodies disintegrating, tumbling into the air.

An explosion of steam shot out around him, the boiler of the train exploding as a solid shot tore through its guts.

Pat stood in numbed silence.

"Rally, goddammit, rally!"

He was on foot. How he had gotten there he couldn't tell. Someone was next to him. The flag-bearer, the staff broken, the boy sobbing as he waved the colors over his head.

"Once more!" Hans screamed.

From out of the confusion individuals rose up, staggering forward as if going into the teeth of a gale.

Flashes rippled in front. Iron hail smashed through, unable to miss. Hans felt as if he were walking in a nightmare. It was a nightmare.

He looked back into the center of the square. What had missed the line had smashed into the reserves, staggering them. Men were streaming back into the center of the formation. The east side of the square was gone. Like a dying animal the three brigades started to curl up into themselves.

"One more time!" Hans screamed. "We can't stop!"

He snatched up his guidon, holding it high, and started to run forward.

A storm swept past him, picking him up as if he were a dried leaf in a gale, tossing him down.

Hands were around him, dragging him back. His leg felt numb.

"Let me go!" He kicked and struggled, but they would not let go. Men closed around him. He struggled free at last, hands releasing him.

"You're hit, sir."

Ignoring the cry he gingerly stood up, grimacing with the pain.

Same damn place the reb sniper got me, he thought coldly.

A regimental commander came up, leading his mount. Without asking, Hans climbed into the saddle, stifling the groan of pain.

The square was going fast. The southwest corner was torn open again, with Merki pouring in. The eastern line was gone, the field a carpet of white-clad bodies, tunics stained red, hundreds of wounded screaming, crawling, staggering back. Up the slope the artillery continued its deadly fire, sweeping in. All that was left was the knot of men around him, the last of the reserve, the survivors running in from the disintegrating line. Officers struggled, pushing the men into lines, plugging the holes with bodies. The air was alive with shot.

And above the wild screams of battle, the nargas sounded.

As if guided by a single hand, the riders swarming through the broken lines turned and galloped out, slashing at all in their way.

The artillery facing the trains continued to pound the line cresting the hill, a high plume of steam venting up from a smashed engine, but over what was left of the three brigades an eerie silence prevailed.

As the smoke momentarily cleared a Merki rider came out of the columns surrounding them, waving a white flag.

"Hold fire!" Hans roared.

The rider came up, reining in his mount.

"My Qar Qarth offers surrender. You will be spared the feasting pits, but subjects of the Merki you will be for the rest of your lives."

Hans looked at the grim-faced men who surrounded the torn standards of what had once been fifteen proud regiments.

The men looked up at him expectantly, their eyes hard and dark, and he smiled.

He leaned forward, shooting a stream of tobacco juice toward the envoy.

"Shit," Hans snarled, and a defiant shout greeted his words.

The Merki snarled angrily, turned his mount around, and galloped back.

"You took that from the Imperial Guard at Waterloo."

Hans looked down to see Ingrao, blood pouring from a slash to his face, standing by his side and smiling.

"Couldn't resist it," Hans said quietly.

"You have a touch of the romantic in you after all," Ingrao replied.

"Don't insult me," Hans said.

He reached into his jacket and pulled out what little was left of the tobacco plug. He bit off half, then offered the rest to Charlie.

Charlie took the plug and nodded sadly.

"I'll see you in Hell," Charlie said defiantly, then went to stand by the one four-pounder still left in the square. He picked up the lanyard and waited.

"Mine eyes have seen the glory . . ."

It started off with a deep bass, the men picking up the words, their voices echoing across the plains. Ramrods clattered in fouled muskets, cartridges were run home, pieces were raised, bayonets poised.

He clicked open his carbine, which he had somehow managed to cling to. Sliding a last round in, he cocked the hammer and rested it across his knee, oblivious to the red stain running down his trousers.

The breeze was blowing fair and clear, the standards fluttering in the wind, the air washed clean by the rain.

There seemed to be a far-off place now. It wasn't here. No, it was Antietam again. The young, terrified officer standing there, looking at him like a lost boy.

He had watched him grow, grow to lead a regiment, an army, an entire world.

The son he'd never had, the son in fact that he now did have. That was enough to leave behind.

"He has loosed the fateful lightning . . ."

"God keep you, son."

The nargas sounded.

"Get the men out of here!" Pat shouted. "back to the next train!"

Gregory looked at Pat, unable to move, his gaze shifting back to what was happening down in the valley.

"Goddammit, Gregory, move them!"

The young officer, unable to speak, turned away and fell in with the retreating infantry.

The Roum infantry, many openly weeping, raced past. Gunners from the armored car leaped out, joining the push to the next train back.

Shot screamed past them, the growing cordon of Merki on their flanks pressing in.

The singing reached up the hill and Pat stood as if struck, his vision blinded by tears.

The massed battery fired as one, the tattered remnants of the square dropping, a cry going up, and yet still the song wavered and held.

"Glory, glory . . ."

The thunder of the charging host stormed in, scimitars flashing. A final defiant volley snapped out, its voice weak. For a moment he saw him, sitting alone, carbine raised. And then the song died away, and there was nothing left but the flashing of the scimitars, rising and falling, rising and falling.

Bell tolling, the engine backed into the station.

Andrew felt alone, completely alone. The empty trains that had come back up the line had been enough to tell the tale, but he had had to hear.

The boxcars of the last train were filled with Roum infantry, gazing out at him hollow-eyed, wounded holding bloody limbs, ashen-faced soldiers with defeat on their faces.

The engine hissed to a stop, and he saw him climb down from the cab.

Andrew walked up to Pat, who came toward him as if carrying a burden impossible to hold.

"Hans is dead," Pat said woodenly, struggling to blink back the tears.

Andrew said nothing, turning away. God, he wanted to cry, to beat his fist upon the ground, to crawl away into a dark corner and hide away forever. But he couldn't. Not now.

Hans had stood by his side at Gettysburg, stood by him as he looked down on the body of his only brother.

"Not now," his old friend had whispered. "Mourn later, but not now."

Hans was dead. He stood by me for over six years, he taught me everything, he was the strength that helped to make me. And now he's gone.

Andrew turned to look back at Pat.

"So close, God forgive me, so close," Pat said, his voice flat, rambling in the dull, numbed tones of one in shock.

"The three brigades?"

"No one got out. Forced into square, then ripped apart by artillery."

"Ingrao, Anderson, Esterlid, Basil Alexandrovich?"

Pat shook his head.

Andrew stood in silence.

"Sweet Jesus, you should have seen them, though," Pat sighed. "Sing they did, the voices of angels bent on killing to the end. That damned Dutchman in the middle of them, surrounded by the flags. I bet chewing a plug, cursing the saints."

"Oh God, forgive me, Andrew. I stood there and couldn't save them," Pat gasped. He sagged forward and wrapped his arms around Andrew's narrow shoulders, his body racked with sobs.

Hans is dead, Andrew thought dully. Somehow, he'd thought the old man would live forever. Hundreds, he had heard hundreds of names spoken with the pause, and then the whispered words, "He's dead." But not Hans . . . No, he had never dreamed that nightmare.

Hans, gone forever.

"Do you have a chew?" Andrew whispered.

Pat nodded. He stood back and pulled out a handkerchief, blowing his nose noisily. He drew out a plug and proffered it. Andrew took a chew, and the biting sting brought with it a flash of memories.

"They're moving fast," Pat said, trying to force himself to regain his composure. "We damn near didn't get out. They'll be here by nightfall, maybe to the Neiper by tomorrow. What happened with the rest of the army?"

"Back across the Neiper by now."

Pat nodded absently.

"We've still got a war to fight," Andrew said, and putting an arm on Pat's shoulder he walked back to the train, while behind him the station was put to the torch.

Chapter 7

"Blow it."

Mina touched the torch to the fuse and watched in silence as the powder train snapped to light, racing down the side of the bank and then on to the trestle. Seconds later the first charge snapped off and timber, rails, a month of work rose upwards, charges further on the bridge flashing off with thunderclap detonations.

The Neiper bridge collapsed. Several hundred yards upstream a second flurry of charges went off, and moments later the first crest of the flood came around the bend of the river, the mill dam torn away, the water washing through the ford.

Mina tossed the torch aside and walked over to the train where Andrew stood.

"Had to do it myself," John said quietly.

Andrew nodded without comment and followed John up into the train car.

He spared a quick glance to the chair in the corner, brass spittoon resting beside it. Clearing his throat, he went to the head of the table and sat down.

"How bad are the losses?" Kal asked.

"Eight hundred casualties in first corps, three hundred in the second," Andrew said, looking down at the roster reports. He paused for a moment. "First division, 3rd corps, and half of the 2nd and 3rd divisions gone."

Kal leaned back in his chair, looking at the ceiling.

"Ten thousand boys."

Andrew nodded.

"Nearly all the corps equipment except what they carried out—sixty field pieces, half a million rounds of ammunition, tentage, two hundred thousand rations."

"And Hans," Pat stated softly. "And twenty-five more of the men from the 35th and 44th."

John shook his head.

"I know that," he whispered. "It's not my job to report the flesh and blood, only the rest."

Kal extended his hand in a consoling gesture.

"Now what?"

The room was silent.

"Now what?" Kal snapped, his voice sharp, jarring Andrew from his thoughts.

He looked over again at the empty chair, as if someone were still sitting there, quietly judging, ready to reproach him if he lost his nerve, especially now.

"We continue to fight," Andrew said coldly.

"Forgive me if I seem unduly pessimistic, Andrew," John said, "but we've lost nearly twenty percent of our best trained troops in the last three days. The plan was that we wouldn't be fighting on the Neiper till midsummer, and that at that point we'd have two, maybe three corps more, ready and equipped. The rail line up the river would be completed, and the entire river from the Inland Sea to a hundred miles upstream fortified."

"Well, the plan is finished," Andrew said quietly.

"And our alternative?"

"Fight to the death," Pat snapped angrily. "Hans

piled them up in mounds around his square. By God, I'll take a dozen with me when they come."

"You're talking defeat," Father Casmar interjected.

"When you're staring forty umens armed with artillery in the face," John replied, "it's hard to think otherwise."

"We beat the Tugars, we beat the Merki fleet last year," Casmar reminded him reproachfully.

"Father, we won both by the skin of our teeth," John replied.

"And the grace of Kesus and Perm," Kal interjected.

"Well, the grace is gone," John said coldly. "In two days they'll be building batteries across from Suzdal and be on the other side of the river, not a half-mile from where we sit. Within the week they'll have patrols a hundred miles farther up the river. Within ten days they'll have tens of thousands of Cartha slaves working like moles at a dozen different places. We saw that on the Potomac."

"May their souls find peace," Casmar whispered.

"Work them till we kill them, and in the killing we fill their pots," John snapped.

"We knew three years ago when we faced the Tugars that we couldn't defend the upper Neiper, that sooner or later they'd get across and any troops above the cut would be annihilated.

"Once they cross the river, I'd say in under two weeks, their numbers will bear us down. They'll invest Suzdal, and they'll remember what we did to the Tugars. They'll blow the dam, the city gets washed out, and then they charge in for the kill."

"Start dropping the water in the reservoir right now," Casmar replied.

"I ordered it this morning," John replied. "It'll still take weeks. Even if we drain it down, there's no way we'll hold the city. Remember, this time they have artillery. They'll smash a way in, even if it takes all summer."

Andrew, who was staring dully at the empty chair, listened without comment. "Always play your advantages, do the unexpected. If you lose your nerve, everyone will lose their nerve," the now silent voice whispered.

Losing my nerve. He felt an inner tremble. That was the core of it. He had gone to the bank once too often. Long years of going to the bank, knowing that a mistake might kill the men of his company, the regiment, the army, the nation.

Well, Hans, I just killed you and ten thousand others—a hell of a mistake. You saw it coming, and I didn't. You could have told me to go to hell, could have refused to obey, and god damn you I would have listened.

But no, you never would have done that. You didn't, even when you saw it coming.

"You'll make an officer some day, if you don't get kilt over first"—his favorite line.

Well, Hans, I've been "kilt over" inside, but did I ever make it to being an officer after all?

The bank's empty, and I finally made a mistake that cost you your life.

"My fault, all my fault"; a reb prisoner had told him that's what Lee said after Pickett went down. Ten thousand rebs lost in a half-hour, the turning point of the war.

Was this the turning point, Hans, the end of all of us, because I left you out on the limb, because I did not send up that one extra division?

"Are you saying the war's already lost?" Casmar asked, staring at John. "That tomorrow I go into my cathedral and tell my flock to prepare, to dig their graves, to cut the throats of their own children to spare them the horrors of the pit?"

John spread his hands and looked to Andrew.

"I'll smother Maddie and then hang myself!" she had shouted.

"Andrew?'

He looked back to the table. Kal was watching him.

"Let it rest," Kal whispered.

"What?"

"Let it rest. You can't go back, you can't change it."

"He put up a hell of a fight, he did," Pat said, looking to the chair and then back at Andrew.

Their gaze held for a moment, and Andrew felt as if the look in Pat's eyes were piercing right into his heart.

Do something! You're the one who thinks! I'm just the loudmouthed brawler!

Andrew got up from his chair and walked out of the car to stand alone on the rear platform.

Along the bank of the river troops stood in silence, watching the bridge burn.

He leaned back against the side of the car, pulling his kepi low over his eyes.

The door creaked open behind him, and Kal came out. He wanted to tell his old friend to leave, but he didn't have the heart to do so.

"Still shaken by it, aren't you?"

Andrew forced a weak smile.

"I lost. I killed ten thousand good men and lost my oldest friend. I most likely lost the war in the process. You heard John in there."

"You've lost something else," Kal said.

"Go on and tell me," Andrew replied coldly.

"Your nerve, of course."

"Thank you for enlightening me."

"I'm President of this country because of you," Kal said sharply, coming to stand in front of Andrew.

"If it hadn't been for you and your people I most likely would have survived the Tugars—they would be long gone by now. Ivor and Ragnar would still be squabbling for power, and I would still be a dirty peasant making up bad verse in order to stay alive."

"I didn't want all of this," Andrew replied.

"I did. I still do. And by Kesus, Andrew Lawrence Keane, I need you."

"Do you?"

"What's the alternative? Fire you? I can, you know, after all, I am the President."

Andrew looked down at Kal, who stood before him, a miniature Lincoln. A foot too short, but a Lincoln nevertheless, in black frock coat, chin whiskers, stovepipe hat, even the broad streak of earthy humor and touch to the common folk.

"Old Abe fired more than one."

"He kept your Grant."

"Grant. 'The Butcher,' we called him—he carpeted the fields with our bodies. I lost half my regiment in twenty minutes at Cold Harbor because of him."

"And yet you still followed him, because you were soldiers."

"We lost the best under him," Andrew said softly.

"That's war. Sometimes generals make mistakes and good men die for it."

"I lost too many good men. We couldn't afford a thousand dead, let alone ten thousand."

"So who the hell would I replace you with?" Kal asked ruefully. "Pat. A hell of an officer, as long as someone tells him where to go first. John? A desk commander, the best organizational mind we've got, even better than you in that area, but he doesn't have the spark. Maybe Vincent someday—needs a lot more seasoning, and there's a terrible fire in that boy's soul that needs to be doused first."

"He needs seasoning, but maybe someday," Andrew

said quietly. "I'd already thought of that, even though he wants out the same way I now do."

"It's you or nothing. Just why the hell do you think Hans picked you to start with?"

Andrew looked at Kal, unable to answer.

"He's expecting you to win even now. You have to Andrew, because I'd sure as hell hate to face him if you didn't."

"Thanks for the guilt," Andrew said quietly.

"If it works, I'll use it."

"You son of a bitch. I was the one who made the mistake," Andrew snarled.

Kal chuckled, shaking his head.

"Most combative thing I've heard from you all day. It'll make great history some day, how my general called me a son of a bitch. A heroic painting perhaps, a wood carving on the side of a train car entitled 'Colonel Keane calls the President a son of a bitch.' "

A smile creased Andrew's features.

"Hans picked you. I need you because, by Kesus, you can think, and you can lead. Look at those men back in there. Pat talking about the pile of Merki dead around his corpse, John weeping doom, Casmar whispering that the end of the world has come. You alone can change that."

"I've never lost before," Andrew whispered, looking past Kal to some distant point. "No matter what, I've always won. I always got the boys out, even at Cold Harbor."

He shook his head sadly.

"I got to the point where it was impossible to think otherwise, yet there was a cold nagging inside me, whispering that this time I was reaching too far. I was asking more than we could possibly do. And it caught up with me. I hesitated at the key moment. I got rattled and didn't act when I should have."

"That's history now, Andrew. I'm not worried about history, I'm worried about next week."

Kal pointed to the ford.

"In a week, ten days, four hundred thousand Merki will be crossing through here, and farther up they'll be like a herd of locust consuming everything in their path: the grass, the crops, ourselves, our children.

"You alone can stop it. You're not the first general to lose a battle, a campaign, even a war. But by heavens, I dare say you'd be the first one to win a war while inside you we're already defeated," Kal whispered. He fell silent, and climbing down from the train he walked toward the riverbank, nodding as the soldiers saw him, waving for them to stand at ease, to come over and chat.

That damned peasant can outthink us all at times, Hans, Andrew whispered to himself.

All right, we certainly won't stop them on the Neiper, he thought, forcing his thoughts to clear, we knew that all along. Our only hope was to hold them back for so long that they'd start to starve, forced to eat their own horses, their families growing thin until they finally gave up and turned away.

Starve.

An amateur studies tactics, a professional logistics.

In the end we'll lose the Neiper line. We'll all die in Suzdal. At least Vincent will live a while longer in Roum.

We need time, precious time. There was the other idea, the one that had been forming since his talk with Yuri. It still bothered him in a way, so much so that he had spoken to no one about it. He needed time.

He felt as if the old eyes were looking up at him, waiting for the flash of understanding, like the first time at Antietam when the rebs had come crashing in from three sides.

"Son, you'd better lead these boys out of here," he had said.

"God damn it."

Kal turned to look back at the car. Andrew was already turning away, pushing the door open and going back inside.

"I better be going along, boys," Kal said, patting a drummer on the head and shaking hands with an old gray-bearded captain whom he remembered for a guard in Ivor's retinue.

"What's going to happen to us?" a young private asked, his face speckled with the first faint wisps of a beard.

"Why, we'll win of course," Kal said with a smile. "That's a promise. If I'm wrong, you can elect somebody else President in the next election."

The men chuckled ruefully as he turned away.

Gaining the car, he stepped back inside. He interrupted what was already turning into an argument between Andrew and John.

Andrew looked up at Kal.

"You damn well better be right," Andrew said.

"About what?"

"About not firing me."

Kal smiled, saying nothing.

"I'm sending you up to Roum right now," Andrew said. "We'll arrange an express train to take you through. I think Marcus needs to hear this one personally and agree before I announce it. If he does I want you back here at once, with him along if possible. You can do it round trip in two days if we clear the line and hook you in to our fastest engine."

"Just what am I being the messenger boy for?" Kal asked, the tone of his voice expressing an agreement before he had even heard what it was.

Andrew told him, even as John snapped about the impossibility of success.

Kal looked at John.

"Defeat is just as impossible an alternative. Let's get this train going. I have a message to deliver."

"You mean to say you funneled your entire Horde up this miserable track?"

Muzta nodded, looking to either side of the wide trail that was now bisected by the rail line that disappeared into the woods beyond.

"The first umen could move up it at fifty miles a day," Muzta said. "But after that things slowed, the track gets turned into mud. It took nearly seven days to move all my umens up to the ford of the Neiper."

The mud.

Jubadi leaned over and looked down. His mount was buried nearly up to mid-hock, the ground churned to a thick soup by the first umen.

"And the horde behind us?" Hulagar asked.

Muzta smiled, shaking his head.

"We were but a third your size, and still it took nearly a moon passage to move through the hundred miles of forest, cross the river, and get back onto the steppe beyond Suzdal. It's as bad as a mountain pass, worse in some ways."

"I did not think it would be this difficult," Jubadi whispered.

"We did not expect the rain," Vuka sniffed, looking up at the canopied branches, which were still dripping with moisture. "It is the mud that slows us. Let it dry, and we shall move faster."

Muzta moved his mount up to the grading of the rail line, his horse slipping on the slope till it gained the limestone ballast beneath the tracks.

"And they got away," Jubadi thought to himself. He had hoped to end it on this side of the river, and then cross unopposed. Their damned iron rail machines had saved them. Eight thousand bodies were taken, enough to feed the army with all its meat for four days at best. The salters were already preparing that which could not be consumed at once.

The trees overhead swayed with the wind, sending down a cold shower of mist. No airships would fly today. Another problem. They were to bomb the rail tracks, to slow the retreat.

Never plan with the weather. A bank of fog, rain at the wrong time, a sudden blizzard, these had ensured more than one victory, or defeat.

He could not even communicate with the southern wing, riding along the edge of the forest thirty miles to the south, sweeping forward to the sea and then pivoting north. Against the retreating cattle, there was not much worry in that. They were on foot or wed to their iron rails. Against the Bantag—and he looked over at Muzta—or against the old Tugars, to split an army like that was to beckon disaster.

That is how they beat us at Orki, forcing us to divide between three passes and then defeating each column in turn.

The trail ahead was obscured with dank smoke roiling across the trail, blinding him for a moment as he rode through it.

The narrow clearing was filled with wreckage. Several log huts still burned, a water tank was on its side, smashed in. An iron rail car, one of its wheels broken, was up on its side. Fresh-turned earth behind the burning cabins was piled high. Half a dozen warriors were digging the graves up, dragging the still fresh bodies out.

He grimaced. Distasteful, but a waste of good food otherwise.

Muzta reined in his mount to watch the disinterring. He edged down off the rail embankment to join him, motioning for his entourage to continue.

The cavalcade continued on, gold standards of the Horde in the fore, the silent ones reining off the trail to wait. Drummers, signalers, nargas-sounders, shamans, servants, message riders, all continued on, slipping through the mud, cursing.

Captured flags of the cattle army passed, white-and-blue standards marked with stars, strange-shaped words emblazoned in gold—7th NOVROD, 15th KEV, 44th SUZDAL, battle honors listed beneath: THE FORD, SIEGE OF SUZDAL, RELIEF OF ROUM, BATTLE OF SAINT STANISLAV. A blue guidon, riddled with shot and marked with sergeant major stripes went past, but all of the words and markings were undistinguish-able to him—the panoply of animals, and as such not worthy of note.

Muzta looked back at Jubadi, then returned to gaze at the corpses being pulled out of the earth.

"It got so that my warriors would creep into the killing ground before the city, to hack off strips of flesh from dead and rotting horses," Muzta said, his voice flat and distant.

"Why such memories now? We'll be in their city before the next moon feast."

"Old terrain, old memories coming back. I rode this trail once with my sons, my horde arrayed behind me. I remember our laughing, the feeling one has when the nargas sound not for battle but rather for a hunt. Little risk to be had, a pleasant day's sport, and then meat on the table."

"You saw the way we slaughtered them this morn-ing," Jubadi said.

"It was almost too easy. They made a mistake."

"They are only cattle!" Vuka shouted, edging his mount down the slippery side of the railroad embank-ment, coming to join his father.

"First time I've seen them caught like that," Muzta acknowledged.

"Because this time they face Merki," Vuka retorted.

Muzta looked back at the Zan Qarth. There was a motion of rebuke from Jubadi, but nothing more.

"Of course," Muzta said with a smile.

A slash of rain burst from above, the heavy drops washing the mud from the frozen features of the cattle lying by the edge of their graves.

Jubadi looked at the cold bodies staring up with sightless eyes, muddy water pooling in their sockets.

"It'll be eight, maybe ten days to get the Cartha cattle up, to start them working at the crossings," Jubadi said, as if speaking to himself.

"Use the prisoners we took this morning for starters," Vuka interjected with a cold laugh.

"They're useless," Hulagar said. "There's less than a hundred, all of them wounded and unable to fight. That's how we took them."

"Then why keep them alive?" Vuka snapped.

"They might prove to be useful yet," Jubadi replied, dismissing the subject.

He looked up the trail, the last regiment of the Navgah umen lost to sight in the gathering mist of evening.

"Pass the word up to the Navgah to press up to the Ford by dawn, start scouting the river for crossings, try and force a way across. Maybe they are demoralized and will rout.

"I doubt it," Muzta stated.

"They face Merki this time," Vuka whispered, just loud enough for Muzta to hear.

The Tugar Qar Qarth turned to look back at the heir.

"But of course," Muzta said softly.

*　　*　　*

"Grandpapa!"

Andrew Hawthorne escaped from the grasp of his mother and raced across the room, nearly knocking Kal over in a wild embrace.

Smiling, Kal kissed the forehead of his grandson, and then was almost swept away by the embrace of Tanya and the tottering hugs of the year-old twins.

"How are you, daughter?" he sighed, breaking free for a brief second to make the sign of blessing before the icon and to accept the sliver of bread, dipped in salt, that she offered in greeting.

Smiling, Tanya patted her stomach.

"Another one started," she whispered.

"That boy certainly has been active," Kal said with a sly grin, and she blushed.

"Daughter, this home is a mess."

Tanya broke free from Kal and raced into her mother's arms, Ludmillia surrounded in turn by the children, all three crying to be picked up.

"Three children," Tanya said apologetically. "Would it be anything less than a mess?"

"A fourth on the way," Kal announced proudly.

Tears clouding her eyes, Ludmillia went up to her daughter and kissed her lovingly on the cheeks.

"Then get a helper."

"I'll have no servants," Tanya replied defensively. "Neither will Vincent."

"A good republican attitude," Kal said, going over to sit by the open window facing out on the forum.

"The devil take politics," Ludmillia announced. "She's the daughter of a president, the wife of a general and ambassador."

"Exactly why I won't have any servants," Tanya stated sharply, her tone indicating that the subject was closed.

"Always was your daughter," Kal said with a soft chuckle.

Kal leaned back in the chair with a sigh, taking off his stovepipe hat and putting it on the table.

"Daughter, something cool to drink perhaps?"

"I'll attend to it," Ludmillia said. "Come along, angels." She swept the children with her into the kitchen.

"What brings you here?" Tanya asked, and as she drew closer he took her around the waist, setting her on his knee.

"I'm a big girl now, Papa," she whispered shyly.

"You'll always be my little one," Kal said, kissing her lightly on the cheek and affectionately tucking a wisp of her hair back up under her fading blue kerchief.

"You look exhausted, Papa."

He nodded, still brushing her hair back.

"Something's wrong, otherwise you wouldn't be here like this."

"Something's wrong," Kal said softly.

"What is it?"

"We lost. We lost badly, nearly an entire corps." He paused. "And Hans."

"Oh, God!" She looked away.

"Basil Alexandrovich, Ilya Progoniv, Boris Ivanovich, Sergei Sergeievich, Yuri Andreievich, Mikhail Ernestovich—all of them dead."

"Yuri?"

He nodded, and she fought a losing battle to hold back the tears for the one she most likely would have married if all had been different.

"Zemyatin Rasknovich lost an arm, Gregory Basiovich has not woken up since he was struck in the head."

"And Andrew Keane, Pat?"

"Andrew is shaken, badly shaken, my dear. You see, we'll most likely lose Suzdal before the next moon. Oh, we'll fight them tooth and nail for it, but the mouse cannot stand in his nest when the wolf starts to dig too deep."

"Is that why you are here, Papa?"

"I'll tell you later. I have little time. I came here in secret. I expect to be with Marcus shortly—he needed to hear this news personally, and not by a message clicked out on a wire."

"Everyone knows something has happened. No messages of the battle have arrived since yesterday morning."

"My orders," Kal said. "It might only start panic."

"It's half there already."

"But at least, my little plum, you and the babies are safe for now."

She wanted to protest, to express some guilt, thinking of Kathleen, of all her friends, but it was different now. There was no room for such heroics when there were three children to protect, and a fourth already quaking inside her.

Smiling, he fumbled in his breast pocket and pulled out a small package wrapped in a stained cloth. She opened it to reveal a tiny chunk of honeycomb.

"Papa, I'm not eight anymore."

"Let's just play the game for now," he sighed. Smiling, she took a bite and leaned her head against his shoulder.

"Our Vincent?"

"The same," she whispered.

Kal nodded slowly.

"He's distant. The innocence . . ." she sighed, and looked away.

"We all lose our innocence. Even my little girl's lost hers."

"Papa, you know what I mean. There was a gentleness, a certain wonder at what Kesus and Perm had created. It was impossible for him to hate."

"And now he hates," Kal asked.

She nodded sadly.

"This war, before it's done, it'll teach a lot more of us to hate," Kal said coldly. "Maybe we need that hate to win. Kesus tells us to love our enemies. Father Casmar says that even the Merki, the Tugars are His creations."

"And do you believe that?"

"Hard to believe it if they take my grandchildren and throw them alive into the feasting pits."

"Don't say that!" Tanya whispered, making the sign of blessing.

"It's just that the hate has eaten his soul. Old Dimitri tells me that no one can talk to him as they once did. He's cold, aloof, obsessed with killing Merki, and merciless to any who cannot match him in that hatred."

"And to yourself?"

She forced a smile.

"He's tired. I think underneath it all there's still the young man I loved, afraid of what he might become. But somehow he's turned away, building a wall, a distance between us. Where before he'd take Little Andrew, play and wrestle, walk hand in hand, now he comes home, when he does come home, and sits alone in the shadows."

"And the dreams, Papa, the terrible dreams. Nearly every night he wakes up covered in sweat, sometimes screaming, often crying. I try to hold him then, but he won't let me."

"So much has happened to him," Kal said soothingly. "Much more will happen before it's finished."

He paused for a moment.

"I need men like him. I could use a hundred more."

"You're talking about your son," Tanya whispered.

He patted her on the knee.

" 'When This Cruel War Is Over,' I think that's the title of the song some are singing now."

"How about 'All Quiet on the Potomac'?"

The two looked up to see Vincent coming into the room, cape dripping with the rain that had rolled in at dawn.

"Very popular song back in the old world."

"It's nothing to joke about," Tanya said softly, leaving her father's knee to take his cape and hat.

"We lost the Potomac front yesterday morning," Kal said quietly.

Vincent hesitated. There was a shimmer of emotion, and then a silent withdrawal.

"How bad?"

Kal told him as he walked over to the window.

"That's why you're here."

"Partially."

"Care to tell me the rest?" Vincent retreated into the kitchen, to return a moment later with an earthen jar. Sitting down at the table he poured out a mug of wine, offering it to Kal, who refused.

"A bit early in the morning for that, isn't it, son?"

"I just heard that we might very well have lost the war yesterday, and you're lecturing me about a drink," Vincent chuckled, draining off part of the mug and setting it back down.

"How soon before your two corps will be ready for action?"

Vincent shook his head.

"At least a month, and even then barely ready. I sure as hell wouldn't trust them in a standup brawl. We'll have weapons—mostly old smoothbores, no artillery. If they get hit hard, I think they'll fall apart, more danger than help to us, and get all their hides slaughtered in the process. I need more time."

There was a knock at the door and Tanya went over to open it.

"Your excellency."

Marcus came in, as soaked as Vincent, and Tanya took his cape.

"Formalities state that I should wait downstairs in my audience chamber for a foreign dignitary to visit," Marcus said coolly.

Kal came to his feet and extended his hand. A slight smile crossed Marcus's features.

"But after all, the ambassador from Rus does live under the same roof as I, so we could say you are paying me the first visit as well."

"I was told you were out drilling with the troops, and would return shortly," Kal said apologetically. "I wanted to see my daughter and grandchildren while I had the time."

Marcus nodded his greetings to Tanya and to Ludmillia, the children rushing back out to greet "Uncle Marcus," who hugged each in turn.

"I take it, if you came this far, the news must indeed be bad," Marcus said, putting the children back down.

Kal nodded to Tanya, who took the three youngsters and left the room, not without a defiant look at Kal, who shook his head.

"Yesterday we lost ten thousand men, the Potomac front, and Hans Schuder."

Marcus said nothing, but took up the other empty mug, poured a cup, and drained it in silence.

"They'll be in front of Suzdal within a fortnight," Kal said coldly.

"And then?"

"They'll be in Roum by the end of the summer," Vincent replied.

Marcus nodded.

"You're coming back with me to Suzdal—the train leaves in an hour. Vincent, I want you as well."

"Well, thank you for the orders," Marcus said,

putting his cup down a little too loudly. "Perhaps I should stay here and start building my own defenses. Remember, Rus was to be the shield for us."

"I hope it still can be, but we're going to have to ask for everything from you if we're to have any chance of survival."

Marcus nodded.

"I promised that to you. We're linked to this."

Kal leaned back in his chair.

"You might not like what you'll hear." He started to explain the plan.

Andrew settled back into his chair and nodded for Yuri to pour himself another drink.

"So he beat you," Yuri said in a detached manner.

"Soundly," Andrew said, a bit shocked by Yuri's bluntness.

"I figured he would," Yuri replied, looking at the vodka for a moment before downing the mug. He coughed slightly and set the cup back on the table. He looked at the grandfather clock ticking in the corner, as if lost in thought.

"Why did you assume that?" Andrew finally ventured.

"He still understood you, better than you him."

"God damn it, that's why I need you."

"I know."

Andrew came to his feet.

"Just who the hell are you?" Andrew shouted. "Why the hell did you come back?"

Andrew slammed his fist on the table.

He heard Maddie stir upstairs, a thin cry echoing at being thus disturbed. He listened as Kathleen walked across the room, and the crying died away.

There was a pained look in Yuri's eyes as he looked up to the ceiling, listening.

"A pleasant sound," he whispered. "The cry of

an infant at night, quieting down in its mother's embrace."

He quickly reached over and poured another drink, closing his eyes as he drained the cup again.

Andrew watched him. Something had surfaced for a moment, he could sense that, a flicker of emotion behind the outer mask that was devoid of all feeling, as if the warmth of life had momentarily pulsed back into the cold body of a corpse.

"I would dare say that part of his plan was to catch not only the army but you as well," Yuri finally said, looking straight back into Andrew's eyes.

"Why?"

"Standard Merki approach to war. Cut the head off even as you dig out the heart. In action against the Bantag, they assign a regiment of a thousand the sole task of searching for the Qar Qarth to bring him down."

"That seems logical enough," Andrew replied. It was anathema to his own military thinking. He realized it was an illogical bit of European tradition regarding warfare, for after all, kings and dukes realized that to use such a policy would mean they would be hunted as well. Gentlemen have better things to do than shoot at each other, Wellington had once said. Yet somehow it had always struck him as a bit illogical.

"Remember, war is tradition to the Merki, every action prescribed by their laws, from which direction to piss, to who will scoop first at the beginning of the moon feast."

"I assume you fought the Vushka on your right."

"How did you know?"

Yuri smiled.

"The Vushka are accorded the right of first entry into a war. They are the oldest of the clans of the Merki, and guard that distinction with jealousy."

"They were chewed up—we estimate we got two-thirds of them. Foolish to waste your elite for an opening move."

"Not foolish to them. The only drawback is that when their spirits were swept up by Bugghaal, there was nothing to boast of."

"Who?" Andrew interrupted.

"Bugghaal, goddess of the dead, the spirit who rides the night, sweeping up the souls of the slain into her quiver, bearing them to the everlasting sky. The problem was that when she rode past, none would be able to boast of their kills to gain her attention first."

"Because we are cattle."

Yuri nodded.

"The shamans puzzled hard over that one," Yuri said with a chuckle. "They declared that since it is obvious that all of you have been driven into some madness, the death was honorable, since they were fighting against evil spirits who had possessed the cattle."

"So they think we are evil spirits," Andrew said softly.

Yuri chuckled, his head bobbing up and down.

"Weak cattle-spirits though. The world is full of spirits, good and evil. The Merki find protection in that realm through the intercession of their ancestors, who ride the everlasting sky above them."

"If our spirits are so weak, how then did we defeat the Tugars?"

"Tugars. They were viewed as being foolish, too prideful. Though all were appalled, inside they rejoiced, for they saw it as a vengeance for the battle of Orki when the Tugars shattered the Merki Horde."

"The Tugars are reported to have two umens with the Merki," Andrew said.

"Your intelligence is good."

"We have several hundred refugees a day coming out of Cartha. We get daily reports from Hamilcar."

"I'd be careful."

"Why?"

"Another standard Merki trick. To somehow infiltrate the enemy. There is a story how, several circlings back, a pet was traded to a Bantag Qarth. The pet poisoned his master."

"Why?"

"He was promised that if he succeeded his family would be spared the moon feast."

Andrew nodded, looking at Yuri sharply.

Yuri laughed, looking down and rubbing the ring on his finger.

"Now, I might have told you that information as a demonstration of my loyalty, though in fact I truly have been sent to spare someone still in their camp after all. A game within a game."

"I've already heard the story. Hamilcar repeated it to me the night you were brought in."

"With advice to cut out my tongue, jam it back into my mouth, then crucify me on the walls of the city—the traditional punishment for an eater of flesh here in Rus."

Andrew said nothing.

"As we were saying, the Tugars ride with the Merki. I made a bracelet for Muzta Qar Qarth. I stood in his yurt when it was presented."

"Muzta."

"You know him?"

"We met once."

"Perhaps we will meet again, one called Keane," Muzta had said. He had spared Kathleen and Vincent, a strange chivalrous act. Out of character for all Andrew thought the Horde to be.

"I'm surprised they let him live after his defeat," Andrew said.

"There's almost a tone of affection in your voice," Yuri replied.

"Let us say that, in spite of everything, he did me a favor once."

Andrew listened for a moment. She was asleep, most likely with Maddie back in her cradle. She was safe, at least for the moment.

"I heard about that. A sign of weakness, some said. Curious that his own people have not slain him. He must still somehow hold power over them."

"It is hard to kill a Qar Qarth, even among the more barbaric Tugars."

Andrew detected the slightest note of superiority in Yuri's voice—again, the identification with his old masters.

"Does a Qar Qarth ride at the lead in battle?" Andrew asked.

"Rarely. He is the planner, the center of thought, the master hand pulling the strings of battle.

"You noticed the flags."

Andrew nodded.

"We assumed they were for signaling."

"Incredible. Blue flags for marking the line of march. Red for battle information. A message can fly miles in a matter of minutes, and is not tied to your wires that clatter. All goes back to him.

"The Vushka are at the point of the first attack. The Qar Qarth usually remains at the center, so that neither horn is beyond his quick reach. The Zan Qarth is expected to range forward to gain blood and training."

"Vuka?"

Yuri nodded.

"I heard he was the reason for the riot in Roum."

"Hotheaded. Prone to be rash, yet down deep perhaps a coward. The opposite of his father, who is cautious, thinks out his plans, calculates his moves, and has the courage worthy of his office. It is something Jubadi learned when his father was killed at Orki, a lesson he has never forgotten. That is why, whatever tricks you have, he has already thought out the response. He expects to be surprised, and thus the surprise is lessened. His campaign against you last summer was designed for a victory, but it was also to probe you, so that even if he lost he would better know your thinking."

Andrew leaned back in his chair, his right hand resting absently on the stump of his left arm.

"He knows that you will fight to the last, that is assumed. It is hoped, though, that if you are soundly defeated here in Rus, the Roum will accept the offer of surrender and a return to the old order. That, when your situation is hopeless, you will surrender as well, under blood oath that you will not be slain."

"He doesn't know us very well, then."

"You see defeat as almost inevitable. You might change your mind before this is finished."

If we are wiped out, Andrew thought, Marcus would be a fool not to accept the offer. At least there would be a small hope, rather than the inevitability of annihilation.

"And Vuka would rush in headlong."

"Not himself, but he would send others in, and without the guile of Jubadi. Down deep I think he fears you. You are outside his understanding, again beyond the confines of tradition. He is far too unpredictable—sly, but lacking some of the calculation of Jubadi and his shield-bearer Tamuka, whom I served."

Andrew stood up and walked over to the window. Not more than a week and a half ago they had danced out on the green. Tonight it was empty.

Completely empty, as if already all of them were ghosts.

Jubadi. He was the enemy. He had thought too much of them as the faceless Horde. He had to focus more. He was the enemy to be defeated.

He thought for a moment of the package that still rested in the cabinet in the corner of the room. This was the time, but he had to be sure before he asked.

He looked back at Yuri.

"You saw Jubadi often."

"Every day, my lord, since I was of the yurt of Tamuka. Where the bronze shield of Tamuka was, usually there was Vuka and Jubadi."

Andrew nodded again, feeling a cold sense of calculation.

"Why did you come back to us?"

"My own reason," Yuri whispered.

He paused again, his eyes distant, and then he looked back up to the ceiling.

"How old is the baby?"

"Why?" Andrew asked, his voice soft and very cold.

"Just curious. Interesting, that you've had me over here several times and never have I met your child."

Andrew felt an inward chill. He found repulsive the thought of the hands of a cannibal, one who had eaten at the table of the Merki, holding his child.

Yuri smiled and shook his head.

"I understand."

Andrew, feeling embarrassed, looked away. Irrational. The man had been forced into it. He'd had to survive, everyone had wanted to survive, even when in the pit of Hell.

Prejudice. I thought I was above it, he thought. Yet he felt his skin crawl at the thought of Yuri holding Maddie, his hands stained with the flesh of how many children?

He looked back at Yuri.

"I'm sorry."

"Down deep, I know you're not."

Yuri held up his hand.

"It's all right, don't apologize. The winter before I was taken I saw the Tugars winter in Suzdal."

He looked far off, again with that serene, detached look.

"I was almost taken by them for the pits, the feast. I took my gold, the things I had fashioned, out of hiding. I groveled, presenting them. One of their women laughed, and with the flick of a finger pointed me away from the pit. I was set to work fashioning a necklace for her, for her old pet had died. She was going to take me as her new pet, but she died during the winter and I hid then till spring.

"I saw those who traveled with the Tugars, tens of thousands of pets, I saw them grovel as I did. I saw them eat the leavings of the pots as well, struggling for a morsel while their masters laughed. I loathed them.

"They loathed themselves," he whispered. "None would gaze into my eye, they were the damned. When alone with them, I spat in their faces if one dared to look at me. I reviled them, called them traitors, asked them why they did not draw a dagger in the night and at least slay one, for there were no families or villages which could then be taken in vengeance. They crawled away, whispering that I did not understand.

"Now I understand, even as you do not."

Andrew sat in silence, not looking at him but watching the pendulum of the clock ticking off the seconds of time.

"I hate them for it," he sighed. "I hate myself. I even hate you, for never knowing what you could finally be reduced to the way I now know."

His features did not change as he spoke. Still, there was the slightest of smiles, as if he understood some vast secret that Andrew could never fathom.

"I want my vengeance," Yuri whispered. "In that, our paths have crossed."

Andrew reached the point of decision, feeling a slight qualm of guilt, for after all this was different from what he had believed war should be. But this was survival. Yuri had finally reached the point he had been quietly maneuvering him to since they had first met.

"I shall help you have it," Andrew replied. Standing, he went over to a cabinet in the corner of the room, opened it, and pointed within.

"You'll do it with this."

"It's dangerous to go further," Hulagar said, pushing his mount in front of Jubadi's, and the Qar Qarth nodded in agreement. A grin of satisfaction lit his features as he looked through the scattering of trees to the flowing river beyond. In the middle an ironclad rode at anchor, its guns pointing toward the woods. A spattering of skirmish fire puffed along either bank, punctuated by the deeper blast of artillery.

"Well, we've finally come back, my friend," Jubadi announced.

Hulagar, his features breaking into a smile, motioned for a guard who had been waiting for them to come forward. The warrior bowed low, offering up a leather-wrapped case. Jubadi tore the covering off, and grinned as his hand gripped the hilt of the sword.

"I marked where you threw it in the river," Hulagar said. "This warrior was with the advance guard of the Darg Umen that deployed before Suzdal. He dove in the river under fire, until he retrieved the blade."

Jubadi looked down at the warrior, nodded his thanks, and then climbed down from his mount.

"A gift should be matched in kind," Jubadi said, pointing to his horse.

The warrior backed up, hands extended.

"My Qar Qarth, I cannot."

"Take it, and ride well," Jubadi said with a smile.

Grinning, the warrior leaped into the saddle.

"Now go back and kill cattle."

With a shout of joy the warrior reared the horse up then galloped off through the woods.

"A generous mood, my Qar Qarth."

"Reward loyalty and bravery," Jubadi said. He motioned for Hulagar to follow, as he walked down closer to the river's edge.

A minié ball flickered through the branches above his head, the shot hissing with a cold cry.

Hulagar stepped in front of Jubadi and motioned for him to stand behind one of the trees.

"And yet I never reward you," Jubadi said, doing as Hulagar had requested.

"I am your shield-bearer. It is not for me to be rewarded with trinkets or horses."

"Well said," Jubadi said softly. "Loyalty of the shield-bearer is his lifeblood, as guided by his *tu*."

"Something is troubling you," Hulagar said.

"Tamuka."

Hulagar said nothing, knowing that this had been coming.

"In battle he left the side of my son to seek blood, and I see the hatred that simmers between the two. This is not as it should be between shield-bearer and Qarth."

"No, my Qarth," Hulagar replied, unable to say anything else.

"Why is this?"

"What do you think, my lord?"

Jubadi laughed softly.

"Turn the question back to me, since you believe I might know the answer already."

Hulagar nodded.

"Because he despises Vuka, believing that Vuka murdered his brother."

"Your words, not mine," Hulagar said cautiously.

"Somewhere along this accursed river," Jubadi said quietly, and despite Hulagar's protest he stepped out from behind the tree to look at the Neiper flowing past, the ironclad not a hundred yards away.

"Do you believe that Vuka did this thing?"

"It is not my place to say," Hulagar replied cautiously.

"Hulagar, yes or no."

"Yes, my Qar Qarth."

Jubadi held Hulagar's gaze, the shield-bearer not turning away.

"I see," Jubadi sighed.

"If I should fall in this campaign, would he be fit to lead my people to victory?"

"His *ka* is strong," Hulagar replied.

"Too strong."

Hulagar nodded.

"He went into the charge against my orders and then he held back at the last moment, at least that is what I heard."

"That is what I heard as well, my lord."

Another shot whistled past, but he ignored it.

Turning, he slammed his fist against the tree.

"Why was it not Mantu who lived?" he gasped.

"Bugglaah called his name," Hulagar said. "Fate is fate."

"Now Vuka is the only son of the bloodline left to

me," Jubadi said, looking straight into Hulagar's eyes. "When I die, he will be the Qar Qarth."

"Speak not of your death, Jubadi," Hulagar cautioned, "for the ancestors might heed it as a wish."

"Tamuka must swear to protect him, to guide him."

"He shall."

"There is no one who can replace Vuka."

Hulagar was silent.

"No one!" Jubadi roared, grabbing hold of Hulagar.

"I have served you, my Qarth, for more than a circling, but I am not the shield-bearer of the Zan."

"And if Tamuka should decide differently?"

"My lord, only the father may order the death of the son, only the council of my clan may order the death of a Qar Qarth. It is not Tamuka's to decide."

"I know that," Jubadi whispered.

Hulagar looked down at Jubadi's hands, and almost apologetically the Qar Qarth let go and stepped back. Another shot hummed in, slapping into the tree above Hulagar's head.

"To lose a shield-bearer to this type of shooting is one thing," Hulagar said, forcing a laugh, "but quite ignoble for the Qar Qarth."

Jubadi stepped back behind the tree, and Hulagar breathed easier.

"I know that Tamuka does not agree with how I fight this war," Jubadi said, leaning back against the trunk and taking the flask of fermented horse milk offered by his shield-bearer.

"He speaks from his *tu*, and that is how it guides him."

"I still do not understand it. We fight the cattle to preserve our way of life, the way of our ancestors, and yet he wishes to destroy that in the end. Granted, the Rus will most likely be destroyed, perhaps the Roum will live on as pets—they have been too infected with this thing—but to slaughter all cattle around the world? And the hatred that burns in his heart, it is not something I understand, especially from a shield-bearer. There is a cold calculation there, not born of hot blood but rather out of the icy, rational mind of your order. Yet if we kill all cattle, then in the end we starve."

"It is a problem I see no answer to," Hulagar replied.

"Yet it must be answered," Jubadi replied. He looked down at the sword in his hand, the blade burnished, the leather of the grip rewrapped and fresh, and then he looked back across the river.

The forest started to lighten, and looking overhead Jubadi saw the gray clouds thinning, a patch of blue appearing for a moment.

He smiled.

"Storm's lifting."

Hulagar nodded, turning his face upward as a thin shaft of sunlight filtered through the trees. The smells here were so different. Unlike the endless sea of grass, here it was dank, rich with damp earth, trees that never shed their thin needles. He could not decide if he liked the smell or not.

"Ground should start drying out tomorrow; we'll be able to move up."

"I want us across the river within seven days," Jubadi announced, looking out on the flood-swollen river. "I don't trust these Yankees to stay beaten for long."

"Is everyone here?" Andrew asked, looking around the nave of the cathedral.

Kal nodded wearily, motioning for the guards to close the doors. Outside, the square was in turmoil. Casualty lists had at last been posted, and the screams of lamentation echoed through the building even as the oaken doors slammed shut. Three Suzdalian regiments had been entirely wiped out—fifteen hundred men gone in an instant. Similar lists were going up throughout Rus, and panic was in the air.

"A hard day out there," Casmar said. Rising, he offered his blessing to the assembly of officers and senators, all going to their knees except the non-Catholic New Englanders and Marcus.

Andrew nodded his thanks and stepped before the group, looking around the church.

A strange place to be holding a council of war, but the Senate Hall had been hit by an airship only the hour before. If the timing had been slightly different they might have succeeded in annihilating the high command in one stroke. The high stain-glassed windows, depicting the lives of the Saints, of Kesus, shone with a soft translucent light, the church smelling of thousands of candles and incense burned down through the centuries. It had stood as the focal point of the Rus since they had come through the tunnel of light nearly eight hundred years before. Its time was finished.

"You all know that we are in serious trouble," Andrew began.

The men were silent.

"I fully expect that even if we fight it out on the Neiper we will lose that position as well—it is far less defendable than the Potomac. After that, I expect they will invest this city. They will have artillery unlike the Tugars. Even if we hold against that, it is only the middle of spring. The first harvest will not be in for months, and when it does come in it will be in their hands and not ours. We might hold out here for weeks, maybe even for months. But in the end . . ." and his voice trailed off.

"And what about Novrod, Kev, Vyzama, all the other cities of the Rus?" a senator shouted from the back of the room. "Are you saying that Suzdal will be defended, and we will be left outside to fend for ourselves?"

Andrew held up his hand, nodding in agreement.

"I will not do that. To start with, all the Rus could not possibly hide in the city. Second, I will not ask regiments of Kev to abandon their city and defend this capital. We built fortifications around those cities in case a raiding group should break through. But if we try to defend all the cities, they will simply reduce them one by one."

The men looked at Andrew with open curiosity.

"Then what are you saying?" the senator replied.

"I propose to evacuate all of Rus, and move it east before the Merki arrive. All noncombatants will be shipped to Roum—half a million people. Marcus Licinius Graca has come back here to voice his agreement to this, to offer shelter, food for our people. All involved with the army, or who can work in any way, will be moved to our eastern borders of the White Hills, where we will make our next stand outside Kev. Anything we can use will go with us, that which they can use we will destroy. All factories will be torn apart. The tools, the engines, even the raw material will go with us, and will be rebuilt, if need be, in the open fields and kept working. Anything we can eat—cows, pigs, grain—all will go, and that which we cannot take will be destroyed. The wells we'll poison, we'll sow the ground with traps. We'll leave them nothing. With our navy the river, the sea, will still be ours, and we'll harry their every movement. The army will fight it out on the Neiper and buy the time for the rest to escape, to rebuild and to fight again. I am asking for two weeks from all of you, to give our people that time to escape.

And when we are gone what we leave behind will be a wasteland, in which those bastards will starve!"

Pandemonium broke out in the cathedral, and Andrew stood silently. He looked over at John Mina, with Ferguson and Bob Fletcher by his side. John stared straight ahead, not saying anything.

Andrew held up his hand and the room fell silent.

"It is the only alternative. We cannot hold the Neiper. I realize now that my dream of holding the Potomac was a vain hope as well."

He paused, waiting for the condemnation, the bitter recriminations to echo forth. He had already resolved within himself that if they came he would tender his resignation.

The room was silent. He looked into the eyes of all his generals, the ones whom he and Hans had elevated, to the senators he had created in writing a constitution, and at last to Kal, who had quietly risen from his chair to stand beside him.

"Lead us, Andrew Lawrence Keane," Kal said, his voice cold and clear, "Lead us and we shall follow."

The church was silent, and Andrew looked over at Father Casmar.

"Lead us, and I will follow."

He turned his gaze back to the others. Marcus stepped forward and grasped his hand. The men looked at him, grim-faced, filled with coldness, as if they had heard a call to battle. They came to their feet—first one, and then in seconds the entire assembly—and a cheer of defiance rang out.

Andrew turned away, blinded by tears.

Chapter 8

"All of your ideas were easily stated," John Mina said, "but I do hate to be the one who starts to throw the cold water."

Andrew struggled to keep from falling asleep. The grandfather clock in the parlor ticked in slow rhythmic time. He picked up the hot tea that Kathleen had placed on the side table by his chair and took a sip. The parlor was almost too warm, for the fire in the stove which had been lit to drive out the cool chill of evening had made the room feel stuffy.

He unbuttoned the collar of his shirt, glad to be out of the heavy woolen uniform and vest. Outside, in the town square of their little New England village in the heart of Suzdal, all was quiet. The mass meeting had gone smoothly enough, the men and their families going back home in silence. Ten of the men lost with Hans had families, and their homes were now dark. He tried not to think about the simple log cabin on the other side of the square, where he had spent many an evening in quiet talk. A guard was at the door, the inside dark and cold. He'd have to go over there to decide what should be done with the personal effects. He pushed the thought out of his mind. There was too much to worry about to allow grief to creep back in.

He had told them that all of it was lost, that they were to abandon their homes, which they had built with such a loving recreation of an older life, and go east into an unknown fate.

He looked around the room at his old friends, the companions who had been with him in this adventure from the beginning: Pat, John, Emil, Vincent, Chuck Ferguson, Kal, the staff officers, and the two new leaders, Marcus and Hamilcar; and of course Kathleen, who sat down beside him.

"Throw all the cold water you want," Andrew replied. "That's part of your job, John, to tell me what we can and cannot do. But this time I'm telling you it *has* to be done."

"I know that, Andrew."

"Then tell me how we'll do it."

"We have sixty-six locomotives, and of all rolling stock just about eight hundred cars. That's what we'll have to base all of this on.

"In all of Rus the census counted just over three-quarters of a million people. That's increased somewhat since last year." He looked over at Hamilcar. "By about thirty thousand."

"About two hundred thousand of those people live within a hundred miles of Kev, with fifty thousand of those within twenty miles of the city. Except for the infirm and the old, I'm proposing that nearly all of them walk out."

"What about their provisions?" Emil asked.

"I'll get to that, doctor," John said wearily.

"It means we'll have to move at least five hundred and fifty thousand people by rail. I'm proposing that we do it in two steps. We go first to Kev—that'll put us two hundred and fifty miles east of here. From there, we'll stage all noncombatants the rest of the distance to Roum."

"Two hundred and fifty miles can be covered by the Horde in five days," Hamilcar said coldly.

"On what?" Andrew asked. "They expect to live off the land when they get here; if we turn it into a desert as we leave, it'll make that somewhat more difficult."

"You can't burn green grass," Hamilcar replied.

Andrew nodded in agreement.

"They'll have a million horses with their army. John, what does it take to keep one horse going?"

"I remember hearing that for one of our regular-size horses, not the monsters we have here, that it comes out to about twenty-five acres a year. I'd say at least thirty, maybe thirty-five acres of prime pasture land."

"They'll not be quartering for a year," Emil said quietly. "They just need to cut through us. Seventy pounds of hay a day for horses that size will do it."

"A million horses, four hundred thousand warriors, four hundred guns, all funneling in through Suzdal," Andrew said forcefully. "And remember, this is not just an army marching, it's an entire people, a *Volkswanderung*."

"A what?" Pat asked.

"A people movement," Emil said. "You know, like the Huns. Women, children, old people, wagons, everything."

"Another million horses with them as well, at the very least," Andrew added.

"They'll eat horse flesh. The Tugars refused that, but I think these people know better now."

"Two thousand horses a day, if there isn't any other foodstuff available. It'll start to hurt fairly quick, if we can slow them down. They can't abandon their yurts, so they'll have to keep those beasts of burden alive. It'll come out of their remounts."

"Even with the sweet grass of spring," Pat said, a

glimmer of optimism in his eyes, "ten horses will eat through an acre of this farmland in a day. It'll drop off like mad, maybe down to an acre a horse in a couple of months."

"A hundred thousand acres a day, just for the army mounts, a million acres a day by midsummer," Andrew said, a thin smile lighting his drawn features.

"You still haven't answered my earlier objection," Hamilcar said, barely giving his translator time to work. "They can still rush a dozen umens across the entire length of Rus in five or six days, then smash into the disorganized mass around Kev."

He lowered his voice.

"It'll be a slaughter."

Everyone looked at Andrew.

"They'll be slowed down. You can be sure of that." Andrew's tone was emphatic.

"How?"

"It'll be done," he replied, his manner indicating that the topic was closed.

"They'll continue to feed off my people," Hamilcar said angrily.

Andrew looked over at the Cartha leader, unable to say anything, still ashamed of the slaughter on the Potomac.

"I'm still in the fight, though," Hamilcar said quietly.

"If we hold the river with our ironclads, even after we retreat it'll force them to go further upstream to cross, and the river road will be untenable. They'll have to cut another road entirely through the woods for fifty or more miles to move their wagons up."

"And our food?" Emil asked.

Andrew looked back to John hopefully.

"With the trains I have, we can move eighty thousand people a day to Kev, each with ten pounds of belongings.

"I estimate that we have approximately a ninety-day supply of food in all of Rus at this moment. Roughly one hundred thousand tons of food—that's counting everything on hoof or in the barns. Considering the bulk, it comes out to at least six hundred trainloads."

John shuffled his notes for a moment.

"We'll need at least thirty days to move everything by rail, just for the people and food up to Kev. But there is one hell of a lot more. We have all the tools and machinery from the iron mills, foundries, shot works, the locomotive yard, and sawmills. And I recommend all farm tools as well, if we wish to survive—and if, on the off chance, we win.

"I figure forty days of trains running nonstop can do it, and that's assuming that every locomotive keeps on running. We cut a lot of wood this winter, but I'm not sure it'll be enough. And we've only converted six of the engines to coal-burning."

The room was silent.

"And after that, Andrew, don't forget the army. We'll need to keep the river posted throughout, and when the line finally breaks all rolling stock will be needed to get the army out. That is, if we want an army and its equipment, which we've worked three years to build. Just to get the field artillery out will take every flatcar for two days. Another day for guns emplaced in the cities."

"What about the navy?" Bullfinch asked.

"Every ironclad will be on the river or patrolling the sea," Andrew said.

"The galleys?"

"If we land them further up the coast, we could evacuate all my people and some of the Rus living nearby," Hamilcar said.

Andrew nodded his thanks.

"Then we start tomorrow," Andrew said. "Those that can start to walk out will do so. Children, mothers with infants, anyone over sixty, the infirm, all the wounded—they go out by rail starting tomorrow morning."

"Jesus, Andrew, we have no contingency plans for this type of thing. It'll take days to figure it out."

"We don't *have* days!" Andrew snapped. "You just said it."

"It'll get tangled as hell. These people won't have a place to live in Kev."

"Then stage off several trains, take the dormitory cars the rail workers used, and start running them all the way up to Roum right off. If we did that, we could get at least a hundred thousand up to Roum in thirty days."

John nodded in agreement.

"First step is to load on all food after the first wave of evacuees. Though I hate to do this, Mr. President, I'm going to declare military law as of this moment."

Kal smiled.

"I assumed it."

"We have to. All food will have to be pooled. Webster, you and Gates start printing up voucher forms tonight. I'm nationalizing all food. Everyone will receive a receipt, and after this is over we'll try and sort out compensation. When a farm is cleared out, the farmer and his family start walking east. If there's room on a train, we take them out."

"There goes capitalism," Webster sighed, bringing rueful smiles to the group.

"We tear down the factories. If we lose the tools and the machines, we lose the war. Once the factories are torn down they receive top priority—all the workers and families still here go out on the trains with them. We don't want those people getting separated from their equipment, since they'll be the only ones who know how to put it back together.

"Finally, we pick up everything else that we can move. Wagons and their teams, even the rails from the tracks, and then the army, when it can no longer hold."

"It'll have to be done in three weeks," Andrew said softly, looking back at John. "I can't even promise you ten days, but we'll try to hold longer."

John said nothing.

"And if they break through before we are done?" Casmar asked.

"The priorities stand," Andrew whispered. "As we organize, noncombatants go first, then food as it's moved in, and the factories once they're torn down, and finally the army and what's left. If they break through before that, the army goes out first along with the factories, and the rest will have to move to Kev by foot."

Casmar nodded and said nothing.

"Fire the cities," Emil said quietly.

"Moscow?" Andrew said hesitantly.

He looked around the room.

"No," he whispered. "Cities are useless to these people. Maybe something of what we have will still be standing when it's over at last."

He looked around his home, realizing for the first time what he had ordered and how it applied to himself. The clock ticking in the corner, the desk carved by a Rus peasant and left on his doorstep one morning, the simple plates in the kitchen, even the jewelry box, the one he had given to Kathleen so long ago, when they had first walked the streets of Suzdal together. All of this, left behind. He struggled with the thought for a moment and looked over at Kathleen, their hands touching.

"Emil, I want you to go out tomorrow to Kev with

all the wounded. Start setting up a hospital there, and organize sanitation. Fletcher, you go with him— you're responsible for organizing food storage and distribution. We'll need to get warehouses up to store everything."

For once, there was no argument from the doctor. Andrew looked over at Kathleen.

"Maddie and I leave when you do," she whispered. He said nothing, and squeezed her hand.

"There is a final point," Andrew said. "This is to be done in secret. The Merki are not to know until they cross the river and get in here."

"A hell of an order, Andrew," Kal said. "What with them damned aerosteamers buzzing about."

"That is a point," John said. "We had some defenses along the military railroad down to the Potomac, but past the Novrod turnoff the road is empty for miles. Once they get wind they can swoop in, bomb a section, maybe even land and tear up a rail or two. One derailment could cripple the line for a day or more."

Andrew looked over at Chuck.

"You flew a machine last week?"

"Well, sir, Jack was the pilot."

"I knew all along you'd go up, in spite of my orders," Andrew said, a note of reproach in his voice. "Is it ready to fight?"

"We're still getting some minor problems ironed out."

"I want it in the air over Suzdal in three days. And move the other ships up as fast as you can."

"The hangers above Vyzima are barely up, sir. Also, sir, it'll depend on the wind. We need a north-easterly, better yet an easterly to get up here."

"Get them up, and get those ships in the air, son. We won't have time to build up a fleet to surprise them, as we'd originally planned, but if they figure out what we're up to they'll swarm across the Neiper regardless of casualties.

"This Jubadi learned from Muzta's mistakes. He's being methodical, sparing his men. But he won't spare them if he thinks we're escaping. I need air protection."

Chuck smiled cautiously.

"I have a full card to do whatever I think necessary?"

"Of course. Your orders will be cut and ready for you when you leave."

Chuck smiled and sat back.

"Whatever you say, sir."

John looked over suspiciously at Chuck, sensing that Andrew might have given a far more sweeping order than he'd suspected. but he was too tired to care and said nothing.

John turned his gaze back toward Andrew. He realized that the entire operation was a fool's dream. Though Andrew had brushed it off, once the Merki broke through there would be nothing to slow them from a sharp run east with part of their forces. Positions along the White Hills would barely be ready to receive their attack.

He was feeding all of them a fantasy. This was the end of it all. He wanted to say something, but a sharp look from Andrew told him that now was not the time to say anything. He lowered his gaze, numbed by what was being asked of them yet again.

Tamuka grabbed hold of the branch, feeling it bow slightly with his weight. He pulled himself up and leaned back to sit against the trunk of the tree. It swayed slightly, the breeze coming out of the north, cool and fragrant. He looked back to the west. The wide trail through the forest, as far as the eye could carry, was packed with horses, warriors, and batteries of artillery, all of it moving forward like one slow, undulating serpent.

A terrible place this, he thought. His memory flashed back to the charge: the lone line of the Navhag sweeping forward, behind them column after column of umens, sweeping across the open steppe. And now this. Four days, and still less than a third of the northern wing up to the river. Below him the forest was packed with horses pawing through the leaves, the riverbank lined for fifty miles or more with the gathering host.

A shot fluttered through the night air trailing sparks, then burst above the trail. A scream of pain, then a warrior and his mount going down in a bloody heap, their torn bodies ghostly in the red moonlight.

Another gun fired, and he looked eastward. A ripple of fire raced down the line. Shells winging overhead, bursting along the trail, in the treetops. He felt foolishly naked. A hiss of shrapnel screamed past, cracking through the branches. More warriors went down, the column in confusion. The cattle guns fell silent.

Masterful, Tamuka thought grudgingly.

The fortifications across the river were imposing: two lines on the rising slope, the front of each a near impenetrable maze of sharpened stakes and brush. The shore line was covered with the bodies of three regiments that had attempted to storm across, only to be annihilated by the crossfire of the iron ships and the batteries lining the shore.

He closed his eyes, blocking out the cries of pain from below. His breath came strongly, pulsing in and out, rapidly and yet more rapidly. The tree swayed and the wind whispered a gentle voice through the branches, sighing, drawing each breath out, pushing each breath in. It seemed to say that he, the wind, and the sky were as one.

Tamuka's spirit soared.

He felt himself falling away, and though his *tu* knew it not, his hands clung yet more tightly to the branch, the husk preserving itself for the return.

There was a pulse of light flowing up out of the west, stretching back hundreds of miles. The life-blood of his people, the Horde, relentlessly moving ever forward, the scent of the horses, of the peoples, the smell of the yurt, of the fires, of the open grasslands, the endless steppe floating about his *tu*, focusing his energy.

The spirits of the ancestors hovered, a vast river as well, forever flowing through the heavens above them, guiding them onward in their endless ride. His sightless eyes turned to the heavens, and could see. Again that longing, a memory locked into his very soul, the memory arching out across the very heavens. The ancestors of the ancestors calling. We were once this, we who traveled the stars, who fashioned the tunnels of light to leap between worlds. Even unto the world of the cattle that we once trod in our youth, building the gateways upon its green surfaces, building the gates upon lands now buried by the seas, gateways upon their open steppes, in their vast mountains, in realms beneath turquoise oceans.

And it is gone, all of it gone—destroyed by our pride, our self-hatreds torn down ten thousand generations ago, until now all that is left of us rests here upon Valennia, the remnants of what we were in our greatness.

He felt his heart bursting with anguish—the understanding of all that had been lost, the memories seeping through his very bones, passed by the blood of his fathers into his own heart. A universe once in our hands, and now we are but this, struggling with those whom we did not even deem to notice, when once we were masters of the stars. And now the ancestors whispered to him, they who were but in their dawning while we were at midday have risen. They have risen to come out, to come out to hunt us down thus, and to kill us.

The ancestors thus spoke to Tamuka, shield-bearer, spirit-walker of the *tu*, to the path of knowledge, and his soul wept bitter tears, the *tu* crying out in rage, so that even the husk, the *ka*, trembled as it clung to the tree, tears clouding its closed sightless eyes. For we are now in the evening of our days, and they shall leap into their bright morning.

O fathers! he cried with a soundless voice, cast back the suns in their turning, guide me back to the brightness of our noonday!

That, o Tamuka, was what we once were, the ancestors whispered in reply. Gaze upon our greatness and weep, for the circling is but a pale reflection of our greatest rides, when the universe was like the steppe and we gloried in our power. And now those whom we disdained have risen. Almost as if in taunting, sad, pained faces floated before his spirit, pointing to the heavens.

His spirit turned eastward, away from the realm of the ancestor who floated yet beside him, unable to bear the ineffable pain of his knowledge, focusing on the here, the now, and not all that had been lost in the distant past. For it was the past, one he had already gazed upon in tears, a glory he kept unto himself. To speak of it was to no purpose. He looked away from the dream-memories of ancestors not even born upon Valennia, guiding his spirit back up, up through the memories of the coming. Again he rode across the world, the endless generations trapped, living upon the memories of their past, and

then came the cattle, and with them the gift of the
ancestors, the horse, the liberator that had given
them all the world to ride upon. Two hundred circlings, and what glory there was, the spirit of the *ka*,
the warrior, the horse-rider, feeling the wind in
one's face, the lamentations of their enemies, enemies though brothers, the glory of the charges, the
celebrations of triumph, the lamentations of defeat,
yet knowing there would be triumph yet again. For
after all, was it not all an illusion, the glory of this
living? The circlings spun past through his wander-
ing soul, images of a hundred ancestors whispering
to him, laughing in their joy, crying in their anguish,
rising to the endless ride of the everlasting sky when
their brief moment had passed.

And then, at last, the image of his own sire drifted
past, coming into his own. All of the generations of
the Merki, the chosen ones. And in his heart was
the warning, that the twilight of the ancestors, of all
that they were, might very well be upon them, the
realization shaking into his soul. The responsibility
of halting it thrust into his heart, calling to his *ka* to
seize what must be taken.

He looked eastward and the world ahead was
dark, as if a curtain had been drawn across his sight.
The powerful spirits of the cattle, blocking what he
could see.

What is happening beyond the river, the boundary
between us? He strove to go forward to see.

There was nothing but darkness, and yet even in
the darkness there was a swirling, a strength, pulsing
away, moving away, following the trails of iron. He
felt a vague foreboding. If the strength was moving
to the east, what could this mean?

He looked back to the heavens, the Great Wheel
which blazed through his soul, filling him with long-

ing. But there was nothing to be heard there, no ancestor to help him pull back the veil.

They are far from finished, his *tu* whispered. Far from finished. They come to this world each time more powerful, coming out of our own past to haunt us, for if it was not for the Tunnels they would never be here.

He felt the clouding of spirits, the memory of all the Hordes, Merki, Bantag, Tugar, Kuvak, Org, all the peoples. We are old, he realized, old unto a million generations, of which our time here is but the briefest of flickers, a dying race upon a last lonely world.

And they are young, these cattle, rising up new, streaming with life, sweeping through the devices we have left behind, coming even unto this world as our slaves to turn and kill us in their defiance.

The ancestors were silent.

He felt a cold rage at their resignation, their blood which was one and now trembled.

Fate is not fate, he hissed, startled as his silent words echoed through the firmament. He bent his thoughts back to the east, to where they waited, the defiant few, the first trembling of the storm, a race coming out of the cradle to challenge.

They were drawing their strength eastward, but to what goal?

It would not form—only the foreboding of understanding whispered to him.

Then let the dying race suck the strength out of the new, and cast aside their dried husk.

We have grown fat and old in our ignorance of what we have lost, he realized. Then let us take that strength, that knowledge back unto our selves and seize all that we once were.

He looked back to the heavens, and suddenly the steppe, the endless ride, were as nothing, the tottering of an old one whose mind had fled while the *ha* staggered blindly.

There was a snap of light, a whistling shriek. He felt a warmth, a sting.

The *tu* returned inward, the vision fading.

He felt a throbbing pain in his arm. Opening his eyes, he saw the trickle of blood coursing down his sleeve, his leather armor torn open at the shoulder, the flesh of upper arm laid open in a shallow cut. The jagged fragment of shell that had struck him was sticking out of the tree trunk.

There was another flash overhead, and yet more screams from the trail below.

With a grim understanding at last, Tamuka climbed down from the tree and stalked away into the shadows of night.

He had laid out his plan, the *tu* whispering to him. He had groomed his chosen one for years, tormenting and then rewarding. If the cattle acted either way, the plan in the end would be the same, and Tamuka smiled.

"Line is cleared up to Kennebec station!" the telegrapher shouted, standing outside his office and looking up with awe.

Jack Petracci nodded, tapping the exhaust vent. The *Flying Cloud* lowered ever so imperceptibly.

Ground crews, standing on the empty flatcars, waved the all-clear, securing the last line in place.

Anxiously, Jack looked at the locomotive engine a hundred feet below.

"Feyodor, cable release secured?"

Feyodor leaned out of his chair, hanging nearly upside-down.

"Looks in place, Captain."

Jack reached down with his right hand and grabbed hold of the ring bolt. According to Chuck, one yank would release all the cables holding the aerosteamer to the train below.

"All ready!" Jack shouted, trying to conceal his outright terror at this mad plan. Chuck had outlined it months before, and it had seemed all so simple on paper. But like everything else about this insane project it was a first, the testing would be in the doing, and if something went wrong it'd be his life that was forfeit.

Towing the ship by rail all the way back to Vyzima had seemed easy enough when sitting around a table. Get a train, hook some cables, and away we go.

Now it was real. A hundred feet below, the engine was hissing, occasional sparks wafting up from the smokestack, a light breeze coming out of the north and pushing the ship south of the track. Feyodor revved the engine up slightly and Jack pushed the rudder over to keep the ship stationary.

The hundred men of the ground crew were standing on the flatcars, looking up anxiously. All of the equipment for the *Flying Cloud*—barrels of fuel, hopper cars loaded with zinc, a lead, line-sealed tank full of sulfuric acid for making hydrogen—all of it had been loaded up and moved down to the main line of the MFL & S railroad.

Jack looked off to the north. The entire city of Hispania seemed to have turned out for this one. The secret of what was going on in the woods above the city had been revealed at last.

"Waiting for you, sir!" the locomotive engineer shouted through a speaking trumpet.

Jack looked over his shoulder at Feyodor.

"All set, Captain."

Jack gulped hard and, pulling a green signal flag out from under the seat, waved it.

The engineer disappeared back into his cab. A puff of smoke shot up, and Jack winced.

The train started to inch forward.

The cables went taut, the aerosteamer straining against the pull and dropping down slightly.

He looked back over his shoulder again at the long shadow cast behind him by the setting sun. The shadow moved over the water tower behind the station.

The puffing from below came at shorter intervals.

The brass gauge, fashioned by his recommendation to measure the flow of wind, started to move, the pointer on the dial shifting past five miles an hour.

As the engine picked up speed, the balloon continued to shift down closer to the ground.

"Give us some throttle!" Jack shouted.

Feyodor responded and the propeller, which was clicking over slowly, shifted into a stuttering blur.

The balloon rose back up.

Jack continued to wave the green flag. The engine below accelerated.

"Fifteen miles to the hour."

Telegraph poles, by pure luck laid out on the north side of the track, started to drift past. The engine continued to move forward, the sound of the clicking rails echoing up.

The ship shuddered, a gust of breeze shifting it out to the south. Jack pushed the rudder over, lining back up, the aerosteamer now pulling back astern. He pulled out a yellow flag and waved it.

The engine speed leveled out at just over twenty miles to the hour.

It was going to be one hell of a long trip, and Jack tried to settle back in his chair and let the tangled knot of queasiness in his stomach loosen up.

*   *   *

Chuck stood to the side, watching as the first of his aerosteamer fleet gradually disappeared westward, back to the front from which he had returned.

"Think it will work?" Vincent asked, standing beside him with arms crossed over his narrow chest.

"Got to. We built them out here where they'd be safe. If the Merki ships found out what we were doing before we got into the air, we'd be sunk before we even got up. Tricky maneuver, this—too much strain and it could tear the ship apart, or maybe even derail the train. Try it alone and we'll burn through engine time like mad, might not even make it.

"Those damn Merki aerosteamers can stay up forever with those engines they got, wherever the hell they got them from. Love to get a hold of one and tear it apart."

"You know the orders," Vincent said quietly. "Some sort of poison in them. They're to be buried."

"Damn it, I know."

"The first battle between aerosteamers . . . I'd love to see it," Vincent whispered.

"Did you like flying?"

Vincent smiled.

"The last ride I took was interesting."

Again that smile, and Chuck said nothing.

The whistle of the train on the siding sounded.

"Time to get going," Vincent said, looking back at the train. It was packed with the first load of refugees moved out of Suzdal the morning since the conference. Every car was crammed to overflowing. Kal had loaned his personal car to Chuck, Marcus, and Vincent for the return, and they had shared it with fifty mothers and over a hundred screaming infants.

Chuck wrinkled his nose in disdain—if that's what being a father was all about, they could keep it. The smell of swaddling clothes, spit-up milk, and a hundred unwashed babies had driven him out to the platform on more than one occasion. Marcus had surprised him by acting almost like a politician. He'd held more than one wailing child. A strange sight: A true patrician—gray haired, chiseled features, still holding to the traditional breastplate and red cape—rocking a screaming child in his arms.

"Hell of a fight coming up," Vincent said quietly, looking back to the west.

"You sound like you're looking forward to it, Vincent."

The general looked over at Chuck and smiled.

"I am."

He turned and walked away.

"A strange fish."

Chuck looked over at Theodor, who had watched with open envy as his twin brother flew off to war.

"Too much war either kills you or makes you crazy."

"Or both."

"Perhaps," Chuck said quietly.

A high-pitched tooting cut through the yard.

"Our train," Chuck said. He started toward the toylike engine waiting to take him up to the aerosteamer hangers and his factory.

"Do whatever you want," Andrew had said, and he smiled. John would be far too busy now to miss some powder, some high-grade steel, a couple of boring machines. Mark it off to the aerosteamer program.

"Why are you laughing?" Theodor asked.

"You'll find out. Now let's get back home and get *Yankee Clipper* launched."

"Jesus Christ, what a mess," Pat groaned.

Andrew could only nod his head in agreement. The rail yard was bad enough. The city was empty-

340 William R. Forstchen

ing out already, so that after only four days the
streets seemed empty. No longer did the sound of
laughing children, the bustle of the market, the singing in the churches, the hum of life echo through
the streets. Six thousand more had left before dawn,
all semblance of order nearly disintegrating as hysterical families were pulled apart—men staying behind
till the last, women and children leaning out of car
windows or sitting forlornly on flatcars that were
heaped with their meager possessions. Their only
connection to the future was a numbered card held
by the males telling them which train their family
had departed on. The trains had pulled out in
silence, so that the watchers on the other side of the
river would not hear.

A battery had opened up the evening before,
dropping shells across the river. The guns were light
compared to the fifty- and seventy-five-pound shot
that the ironclads and the south bastion had hurled
back at the position. But it was evidence enough that
the Merki were there, watching, undoubtedly able to
see the sparks as the trains crossed the trestle over
the flooding Vina, which was swollen with the runoff
from the reservoir.

The vast foundry was a nightmare of confusion.
Hundreds of workers, who but days before had been
laboring on twelve-hour shifts to turn out artillery
pieces, muskets, and rifles, were tearing their
machines down, packing the precious equipment
into rough-made crates, pushing and shoving the
crates out the doors and onto the rail sidings. A
train waited by the brick building, with gangs of men
struggling to heave the larger pieces of equipment
up on to flatcars, where they were covered with tarps
and roped down.

"Every day we lose like this is another three hundred rifles and muskets, another two field pieces not

turned out," Pat said ruefully, turning sideways to let a team of men manhandle a press forge through the door.

Andrew looked around and forced a smile of encouragement as he stepped into the cavernous building.

This place had been the core, the heart pulse of all their efforts. Only days before it had been a place of smoke and showering sparks. Sweating gangs of men had pulled the raw iron out from the blast furnace next door, moved it in here, cooked it down into steel and cast. They'd poured it into molds, turned the barrels on lathes, and bored the tubes out, all to build the coiled spring sinews of a modern war machine bent on the salvation of a people.

It was here that any dream of survival had rested. How it had grown! He remembered the first foundry in comparison, but half the size of this, the building swept away with the flood from the blown dam. The fires were still going, a ruse for the watchers beyond the river, smokestacks still coiling out black plumes.

Next door at the rail foundry the chaos was the same. After the naval war it had reached a peak of nearly a hundred and fifty tons of rail a day, forty lengths of track an hour, twenty-four hours a day. The shiny iron had been loaded straight from the molds and forges onto waiting flatcars, which were rolled straight into the building. For months the trains had rolled eastward, one every eight hours, moving eastward to repair the Roum track torn up to make the ironclads. With the coming of late fall the trains had started to move north, up the river road line, across the Neiper and then west onto the military railroad for the Potomac. Ten thousand men had labored to build that line, which was completed only days before the Merki attack. And all of that effort had been for naught.

Beyond the rail foundry, where crews were tearing down the presses and molds, was the latest addition to their factories, the turning out of sheets of one-inch-thick armor for the ironclad fleet. The plates were moved down to the naval yard on the Neiper, now under bombardment, or by rail all the way up to Roum, where the second yard on the Tiber was turning out two more ships of the latest six-gun design.

On the west side of the naval armor forges was the shot factory, where one-inch ball was molded and packed into tin cans as canister, and next to that the molding rooms for four-, twelve-, fifty-, and seventy-five-pound solid shot. Another brick building alongside was built more like a bunker. There the exploding case shot for the Napoleons, and the percussion shells for the three-inch rounds were packed with powder, fused, and crated up in ammunition chests.

Down the slope were the rail yards, where the locomotive factory was located. Within it some of the most valuable and best-trained men in all of the Republic raced to finish the two engines on the assembly line, while others packed up the tools and forges and stripped down the other three engines, only partially built, to be shipped east for completion later.

The rolling stockyard had already been stripped. The molds for wheels and frames for the rolling stock had been shipped out that morning, to be moved back to Hispania. Hispania had become the second major rail yard before the war had even started, and now would be the center of the rail industry.

Andrew passed through the last of the factories, this one dedicated to producing a wide variety of miscellaneous items: reapers and plows, tire irons for the guns, bolts, nails, bayonets, wood stoves, and even the bells for the churches.

Everywhere it was the same, the chaotic, insane look of a vast moving operation, arrived at that terrible point where one looks around one's home, cursing the fact that one has acquired too many possessions, believing that it will be impossible to have everything ready when the moving day actually arrives.

"God, do you think we'll ever get it done?" Pat whispered.

Andrew looked over at his friend. Something had weathered in the burly Irishman. It had started when he had gone through the long, slow recovery from the gut-shot wound. It must have tempered out when he had stood on the hill, watching Hans and the brigades go down to defeat. The boisterous swagger was gone and the feigned act of being a slightly dumb, belligerent drunkard had fallen aside. It was as if Pat sensed that Andrew now needed a rock-stable companion rather than a humorous foil and gadfly.

"We have to get it done, Pat. We can evacuate out all our people, all the food, but if we lose this"—he gestured back toward the factories—"we might as well crawl into the woods or become like the wanderers, forever fleeing in front of the Hordes. It's taken us damn near four long years to build all of this, and I refuse to see it be lost. The buildings we can replace, but these men and their tools can't be replaced."

His voice rose with passion as he spoke, and in anger he turned away to look to the west.

"I'll be goddamned if they'll get it from us."

Pat smiled as Andrew walked away. There was something of the old fire coming back in the man. He looked like hell to be sure—burned-out, face pale, eyes hollow—but at least the eternal spark, the spark of a professional killer, was flaring.

An engine puffed into life from alongside the gun foundry, the flagman racing down the track and waving for the switchman to clear the way.

The engine's wheels spun for several seconds, and then with a lurch the train started forward. Its long line of fourteen flatcars was piled high with crates, half a drop-forge resting so heavy that the car beneath it had been reinforced with six-by-six beams. The cars were packed with men who rode with their equipment, their families packed into three boxcars tagged to the end of the train.

At the sight of Andrew standing alone, the men came to their feet, defiant fists raised in the air, hoarse shouts echoing. Andrew raised his hand and saluted as the train rolled through the switch, picking up steam for the run up along the bank of the Vina, where it would be switched through to the trestle and then eastward to Hispania.

Pat raised a meaty hand, held a clenched fist aloft as the cars rumbled past.

"Get that damn thing working!" he shouted. "I need the bloody guns!"

The men, who were part of his corps, recognizing their commander, gave him a cheer. Then the boxcars rumbled past, silent and frightened families looking out, and the train was gone.

"Five thousand of our best men tied up here—an entire division," Pat said.

"We need them more in the factories," Andrew replied. "Let's just hope we don't have to put guns in their hands as well, before this is done."

From the town the cathedral bell started to ring, the soft, melodious peals sending a shiver through Andrew.

"Aerosteamers . . ." He looked around at the

laboring crews, which had stopped to look to the southwest.

A messenger came running up and breathlessly handed Andrew a telegram.

"From our watch station above the mine. Four aerosteamers coming up along the coast of the Inland Sea," Andrew said quietly.

"Well, we might be seeing our first air battle," Pat replied, and there was a glimmer in his eye.

"At four-to-one, it should be interesting," Andrew said coldly.

"Get her up!" Jack shouted, racing out of the telegraph shed. The crews were already scrambling, alerted by the clanging bell.

Feyodor came running out of the hanger shed, waving the ground crew to their tasks.

Cables were grabbed hold of and the vast doors to the shed were rolled back. The ground chief looked to the watch tower and the banner fluttering atop it.

"Wind northerly. Haul it out slowly, now."

"Where are they?" Feyodor shouted, coming up to Jack's side.

"Coming up the coast of the sea." He paused. "Four of them."

"Kesus damn it!" Feyodor snapped.

"Boiler on?"

Feyodor nodded. "Full load of fuel on board."

"At least we'll have the wind at our backs going down."

Assistants came running up to help Jack and his assistant engineer into heavy coveralls and wool caps. The nose of the aerosteamer cleared the hanger door, bearing against the wind. More than two hundred men, most of them the original Roum crew, struggled to keep her centered.

Jack paced back and forth anxiously, trying not to think too much about what was coming. Flying it was bad enough, but the rest . . . He pushed the thought away.

The wicker cabin, engine section, and propeller appeared, and Jack and Feyodor raced over to the craft, which was now riding with wheels floating above the ground.

They climbed up into the cab, the aerosteamer coming back down to the ground, wheels beneath the cab hitting the ground.

The tail cleared the hanger and the balloon weathervaned around into the wind, crews struggling to keep her steady.

"Boiler on full power?" Jack spoke into the speaking tube, an addition put in only yesterday at his suggestion, the tube hooked up to Feyodor's ears. Only three feet separated them, but in the long and exhausting ride being towed by the train he had found it difficult at times for them to hear each other.

"Boiler on full power."

We must look like two elephants in a passionate embrace, he thought, with these tubes running back and forth between us.

He sat shaking with excitement and fear, waiting for the hot-air bag to provide the necessary lift. The crew chief stood beside him, looking down at the wheels on the ground.

The chief raised his hand. Jack nodded, and the man reached under the cab to pull the release lever that dropped the dolly wheels off. The aerosteamer started up.

"Slow forward!"

"Slow forward it is."

The propeller started to flick over, the warship rising straight up. Ground crews cast off lines, and a priest stood in the middle of the clearing waving a branch laden with holy water as a blessing.

Jack made the sign of the Catholic cross in response and the priest nodded, even though it was backwards to the Rus rite.

The aerosteamer field started to drop down from beneath him. The four hangers formed a rough square, and fake chimneys on the side spewed smoke to make the buildings look like factories. It had fooled several inquisitive runs by the Merki ships, which had merely passed over and continued on. But after today he knew they'd be coming back, surmising that this balloon had to come from somewhere beyond Suzdal.

The valley floor was now a hundred feet down, the trees lining the hills wavering slightly in the breeze.

"Bring her up to quarter speed."

The engine surged louder and he gave a bit of up-rudder to the machine. The nose tilted up, the cheers of the crew echoing from below.

With a light touch he turned the aerosteamer to the left, the nose swinging around, the valley dropping away.

"Three-quarters speed!"

The propeller humming, the *Flying Cloud* now climbed upward at nearly two hundred feet a minute. The valley cleared, the steamer's shadow raced across the open fields, growing ever smaller. The town of Vyzima passed by to the east, the streets packed with refugees pointing and shouting.

Jack could only hope that the huge flag of Rus painted on the underbelly, with the name *Flying Cloud* in Cyrllic and English painted on the bow, would prevent the soldiers from opening fire.

Feyodor leaned far out of the cab, waving, and the realization sunk in on those looking up gape-mouthed that the aerosteamer was on their side, the crowds screaming with delight, leaping up and down excitedly, children racing through the streets of the town, waving. The church bells started to peal, the air trembling with their harmonic rolls.

"Almost makes you feel like a hero," Jack said.

"Well damn it, we are!" Feyodor cried excitedly.

All of Rus is going to know the secret now, Jack realized, their efforts of the last nine months revealed at last. Damn it, if he survived this day he might very well be a bloody hero, and the fear dropped away for a moment as he imagined his triumphant return. He imagined Svetlana, the young Rus girl he had noticed at the Vyzima station, whose father was the telegrapher, coming out to greet him with shining eyes. Leaping into his arms, her heavy rounded breasts pressing into him.

It just might be worth this, he thought.

The ship continued to climb, the fair rolling fields of Rus undulating below him. Small farmsteads, villages, tiny chapels to Perm, streams lined with trees, all rolled by beneath him. He felt like an eagle.

The main rail line back to Suzdal rolled into view—the track cutting through the side of a hill, a train laboring eastward, puffing down the grade, the boxcars crammed with people, hundreds more riding on the roofs, pointing up fearfully at first and then waving with delight.

Hills rose to the west, clad with the heavy forest that marched on in scattered clumps across the rich black land. Far away to the northwest he saw a tracing of smoke on the horizon which climbed lazily into the sky. Barely visible beyond, a high ridgeline, green-blue.

Battle, somewhere along the Neiper.

There was a flicker of light on the horizon, reflecting off water. The reservoir above Suzdal. He kept a close eye on the ground, picking out distinguishing landmarks, quickly marking them down on a sheet of paper pegged to a board resting on his knees. It was a crystal-clear day, the horizon limitless, but as he might have to negotiate this in far different weather it was best to build the charts up now. He continued to sketch in details. A high-spired church, a small village with an old boyar manor house, its roof a gaudy red, the peak surmounted with carved bears marching in procession. Another village, burned huts replaced with Tugar yurts salvaged from the war. Wagons burdened down with supplies were moving across the countryside, heading to the nearest section of track where trains would come through, picking up the precious supplies. In an outlying village, near the great forest, several barns were on fire, bulk fodder being put to the torch. A procession of antlike creatures was moving out of the town, heading south to the rail line, a drove of pigs, cattle, barking dogs, and several horse-drawn wagons following behind the group.

If any of the Merki airships should come over the countryside now, they would have to be blind not to surmise what was being done. He sketched in the position of the village, noting the burning barns. Feyodor was behind him doing the same, and they would compare charts later.

"Novrod!" Jack shouted, his voice too loud in the voice tube. He pointed to the city, nestled in on a gentle southward slope, going down to the banks of the Vina. A long train of passenger cars was rolling out of the station. Behind it another train—a long line of flatcars piled high with machinery, several boxcars on the end—was slowly climbing the slope into town.

"Not far now!" Feyodor replied. Leaning out of his chair, he bathed the engine drive shafts with a long-necked oil can. He eyed the float gauge of the first tin drum of fuel and quickly calculated out their remaining supply.

Jack uncased his field glasses and trained them southwestward. Within seconds, he saw the four dark ships on the horizon.

"I see them!"

Feyodor leaned around, taking his own glasses and training them on the spot where Jack had pointed.

The Rus engineer nodded, saying nothing.

"Taking her up higher." He pulled the up-rudder back slightly, letting the nose rise, and then centered it while the ship continued to climb.

He had spent countless hours debating tactics with Feyodor, both of them often screaming at each other, reminding their companion that if the other was wrong, they would both go down in flames cursing each other.

They had at least agreed on one thing, that whoever came in higher and faster, and with the wind at their backs, would have the advantage.

The rest was all a mystery. He suspected they could climb faster than the Merki, but wasn't sure. The Merki ships were certainly bigger, and he feared their engines were far more powerful. Colonel Keane had given strict orders not to destroy one over a city, fearing whatever mysterious poison was inside the engine if it should break open, but Jack knew if battle was joined that would be the least of his worries. But the Merki ships were simple balloons kept rigid by the gas inside, while the *Flying Cloud* had a wicker-worked structure woven out of a bamboo-like plant that was hollow, light, and extremely tough.

Coming almost to the northwest corner of the reservoir, he turned more westerly. Suzdal was now clearly in view, the gold roof of the cathedral catching the noonday sun and reflecting the light with a golden red. The high log buildings of the old town looked fairy tale-ish, their multicolored roofs a riot of color, while the section rebuilt after the war was dominated by the Yankee Quarter, the twin spires of the Methodist and Congregationalist Churches shining white.

It all had a toylike appearance, which fascinated him as the ship climbed ever higher. The reservoir was now below, stretching for several miles through the low, tree-lined hills. Farther to the south he could see the low ridges above abandoned Fort Lincoln, where the ore and coal mines were. Atop the highest of the hills the slender line of a watchtower jutted up, the position from which the enemy aerosteamers had first been sighted.

Near the earthen wall of the dam, the valley below revealed the vast factory complex, the tracks bordering each building aswarm with workers, disassembled machines piled high, engines backing in to the siding, pushing a long line of empty boxcars. A sea of tiny oval faces was turned upward, and Jack felt a surge of pleasure. He and Feyodor were alone on the stage, like the knights of old going forth to single combat, a David facing four Goliaths. Even at this great height he could hear the faint echo of their cheering.

"Well, now everyone knows!" Feyodor shouted.

"Let's hope we get back to bask in the glory."

The enemy ships were already above the mouth of the Neiper, slowly moving up the river in single file, each ship a mile behind the one in front.

Jack had yet to learn how to gauge relative height and distance, for all the sensations in their realm, both physical and visual, were far too new. But it was obvious they must be having some sort of effect on the Merki ships. The lead vessel was at a near stop, the three behind coming up and spreading out to the east.

Continuing to climb, they rose above the factory and headed straight over Suzdal, the church bell ringing below, those still in the city looking up, shouting and pointing. It was a lovely sight; the old city a warren of narrow lanes leading to the great square, the cathedral, and the partially bombed ruins of the Presidential and Senate building.

"Prelate Casmar!" Feyodor cried, leaning over to point straight down at the cathedral tower, where a lone, black-robed figure stood, waving excitedly. Feyodor again made the sign of blessing, and Jack wondered if prayers could float up to be captured and held.

On the far bank of the river the low hills rose up, their crest marked by felled trees and the raw slashes of gun emplacements. The forest rolled on for miles, the open steppe beyond visible on the horizon, the southward run of the Potomac military railroad an arrow-straight line through the woods, crammed now with a long column of Merki horse warriors. He was tempted to push on, to do a little reconnaissance of his own, but the orders were clear there as well: Do not risk the ship over enemy territory. If the engine should cut out now, the wind would bring them far across the river before Jack could bring her down. He didn't relish the thought of landing inside Merki lines.

The enemy aerosteamers were gathering just above Fort Lincoln, as if waiting to see what he would do. He pushed the rudder over to the left, the *Flying Cloud* turning to run southward with the wind at its back.

"We're definitely above them!" Jack shouted.

The south side of Suzdal passed below, the river

just to his right with two ironclads anchored in mid-
stream. The bed of the MFL & S traced southward
the few scant miles to Fort Lincoln, which now stood
covered in high grass, the old cabins of their first
home on this world sitting abandoned and derelict.

The four enemy aerosteamers were drawing up
abreast, their noses pointed high, struggling to
climb.

"Get ready, Feyodor!"

The Rus engineer tore open a wicker basket lined
with straw and gingerly lifted out a thin-walled jar,
a linen wick sticking out of the wax-sealed top.

Nervously, Feyodor looked over Jack's shoulder as
the range closed.

"A good thousand feet above the bastards!" Feyodor shouted.

Jack nodded and pushed the rudder forward. The
nose of the *Flying Cloud* dropped and its speed
increased, as the ship went into a slow dive, engine
howling.

"I'm lighting it!" Feyodor shouted. With a gloved
hand he pulled open the door to the engine boiler
and stuck the linen wick inside. Pulling it out, he
held the pot nervously, watching the wick flicker,
terrified that a burning ember might snap lose and
get whisked astern to lodge against the underbelly
of the aerosteamer.

He looked back over his shoulder.

"Dropping now!"

He released the jar, flame snapping around it.
With a groan, he watched as the jar fell far forward
of the center airship and continued to plummet to
the ground, the wick going out. The enemy ship
soared by beneath them, nose still high, the eyes of
the eagle that were painted forward barely visible.
Jack steered straight on.

"Give us full power, Feyodor!"

He pushed the rudder hard over, the *Flying Cloud* turning eastward, drifting astern of the enemy ships, which were still climbing.

The enemy airships continued to climb slowly, like black whales of the sky. Reaching a full easterly heading, the wind continued to push the *Flying Cloud* aft of the enemy ships. Jack continued the turn and leveled the ship, coming out a good half mile astern of the enemy vessels, which were still pushing northward and slowly rising.

He singled out the ship farthest to the east and headed straight for it.

Directly below the old forge, the first iron foundry of Valennia passed beneath, the crew of workers out on the track jumping up and down, shouting, urging them on.

The climbing race continued, with the enemy ships slowly pulling ahead, though Jack found he climbed at a slightly higher rate with the exhaust vent fully closed off.

Running parallel to the MFL & S rail line, the five ships moved up toward Suzdal.

"Can't you get any more speed?"

"At full throttle already!" Feyodor cried.

Jack pushed the ship into a shallow dive, wind buffeting his face, the ship rippling up and down in the northerly breeze, a thermal rising from an open field causing an upward surge. They started to gain, and he nosed over even further.

Hands white-knuckled on the controls, he guided the *Flying Cloud* in, coming up astern of the most easterly ship, which was still rising as he dived down. He pushed hard rudder over to the right to avoid smashing into the tail, and then hard left.

"Now, Feyodor!"

The aerosteamer mechanic lifted up a revolver as the cabins of the two ships came alongside with not ten yards separating them, the air bags above brushing alongside each other.

The two Merki looked over at him wide-eyed. Feyodor leveled the revolver and squeezed, cocked, and squeezed again and yet again.

One of the Merki flinched and the other shook its fist, its cries of rage heard above the roaring of the caloric engine. The enemy ship continued to rise as they shot past. The revolver empty, Feyodor lifted a musket, the barrel sawed off. Leaning far out of the cab, Feyodor fired it off with an explosive roar, the recoil of the double load of buckshot slamming him back with such force that he dropped the weapon, which tumbled end-over-end to the ground below. One of the Merki slumped back, clutching its shoulder.

"Got him!" Feyodor screamed.

Shouting with joy, Jack pointed the nose of the *Flying Cloud* up, as the enemy ship started to turn to the west and continued on through, putting its stern to the wind.

Jack swung the *Flying Cloud* into a shallow turn to the left, then pulled the nose up again, angling in toward the other three vessels. The nearest one suddenly turned head-on, nose pointing up at a forty-five-degree angle, the two Merki engineers hanging in their side-by-side chairs.

Jack was tempted to run head-on, plowing the nose of the *Flying Cloud* straight into the cabin dangling below the balloon, but the thought of what might happen caused him to push the rudder forward, dropping *Flying Cloud* back down, pushing it hard over to the north again. The two vessels crossed, the Merki above. He felt a thump.

"Bloody Kesus!" Feyodor screamed.

Jack looked aft to see a Merki bomb tumbling end-over-end toward the ground, sparks trailing from its fuse. The bomb turned into a black point, an explosion detonating in a field just south of the city.

"Dropped it on us, and it didn't explode," Feyodor gasped.

Jack's legs started to tremble, feeling as if they had turned to jelly. The other two ships were turning as well, coming straight at him.

"Hang on, Feyodor!" He pulled the up-rudder full back.

The ship started to surge upward, and he prayed that the Merki ship that had bombed them had cleared, since the vast bag overhead blocked all view in that direction.

The nose climbed past forty-five degrees up to sixty, and he leveled the rudder and pressed back in his chair, Feyodor behind him cursing wildly as he dangled from his safety belt.

Like two lines of a triangle climbing toward the apex, the Merki and Rus ships rose heavenward. Jack pushed the rudder over to the right, pivoting the vessel toward the northwest. The next Merki ship passed to the right, climbing in the opposite direction, the engineers on board shaking their fists in rage. Jack pulled out a revolver and, Feyodor following suit, they blazed away. The two Merki ducked down as the ships passed, and when the shooting had stopped they rose back up, shouting insults.

The last ship was before him, and he could see they were climbing at a slightly faster rate than the enemy.

"Get another one ready!"

Feyodor reached over to his side, this time cutting free from alongside his chair the wicker basket filled with the fragile jars. Balancing the basket on his lap, he pulled a jar out. He stuck the wick into the boiler for a moment, then pulled it out and placed it back in with the other containers.

He held the basket over the side as it started to flame.

"Hurry up!" Feyodor roared.

Jack turned the ship back toward the southwest, and the nose of the enemy ship passed by not a hundred feet below.

Feyodor dropped the flaming basket. It slammed into the top of the enemy balloon, even as the Merki pilot started to turn to the west in a vain attempt to run parallel with the *Flying Cloud*. The basket slid off the side of the balloon, a burst of liquid flame trailing behind it.

The enemy ship continued to turn, the flame licking the silk covering. It seemed to wink out with a wisp of smoke.

Feyodor leaned out of his chair, watching. The silk top of the ship suddenly appeared to melt open, a barely visible tongue of blue flame rippling along the top of the ship where a river of benzine from the broken jug had soaked the silk.

"It's catching!" Feyodor roared.

Jack looked over his shoulder.

The melted circle of silk rolled back, and a jet of blue flame roared up.

"She's going up!" Jack screamed.

A shudder passed through the Merki ship, the bag buckling in. It started to nose over, wisps of flaming silk shooting skyward on a river of heat, soaring straight up into the underside of the *Flying Cloud* which surged upward, bucking wildly.

Terrified, Jack pushed the rudder hard to the right and turned to the northwest, going straight over the Neiper. The enemy ship started to fold in, pointing a trailing arc of fire down across the river, which caught and reflected the fiery glow of the death plunge. In a river of flame, the ship tumbled from the sky in a fireball. A smoke-wreathed body leaped free, and even though it was a Merki Jack felt sick at the sight of it tumbling, trailing smoke, its arms flung wide. The body slammed into the west bank of the river, followed seconds later by the rest of the ship, which crashed into the woods and ignited the forest in a smoking inferno.

"Kesus and Perm protect us from that," Feyodor whispered.

Awed by what he had done, Jack let the ship continue straight on for some seconds, silently contemplating the flaming wreck half a mile below.

"The others are getting the hell out," Feyodor said. Looking back over his shoulder, Jack saw that the ship with the wounded engineer was already a couple of miles astern, the other two swinging in behind it. They themselves were now more than a mile over the west bank, looking down on the line of Merki guns dug in on the crest of the hill. Far out to the south, more than thirty miles away, he could see dark, serpentine lines, columns of the Horde.

"We'll hold station over the city," Jack announced, suddenly anxious at being over enemy territory, where a sudden engine failure might bring on a decidedly unpleasant conclusion.

He turned the ship eastward, passing north of the still flaming wreck.

"Scratch one," he said coldly.

"They've only got about twenty more," Feyodor replied.

Jack nodded, saying nothing. This first one had been a surprise—next time, they'd come up ready for battle. It wouldn't be so easy the second time around.

Crossing back over the river he turned *Flying Cloud* into the wind, Feyodor throttling the engine down till they had matched the breeze from the north and hovered above the great square. The cathedral bell was pealing, and the square below was filled with upturned faces, their cheers rising up. Looking back over his shoulder, Feyodor watched as the enemy ships continued southward, growing smaller and smaller.

"They've had it for today," Feyodor announced.

"Well, let's bask in some glory!" Jack cried. Reaching up he pulled the black vent cord, letting the ship settle, then closed it off till they were only a couple of hundred feet above the square.

Leaning out of the cab, the two waved and bowed like triumphant knights returning from the joust. With a kick of the rudder Jack turned the ship northeasterly, and moments later they were slowing, to hover above the factories as thousands cheered.

"Time for supper!" Jack finally shouted. "Let's head for home!"

Feyodor gave him full throttle, and pointing her nose heavenward the *Flying Cloud* climbed upward to race back to its hanger.

"Well, now we've got to figure out how to fight them next time," Feyodor announced gravely.

"Jesus, one thing at a time," Jack replied, his mind still filled with the sight of that burning body, tumbling end-over-end to its brutal death.

Raging, Jubadi watched as the cattle airship swung to the northeast and climbed into the afternoon sky.

"How, by the hide of Bugglaah, how?"

"It is always the same," Hulagar said. "They build something, we take it and build. And then they create something new to best us. We gained the advantage with the cloud-flyers. Now they have figured out the same."

"We should have anticipated it!" Jubadi snapped.

"We did. It's just that we did not find where they were building them."

"But the engine! We found ours in the barrows of the ancients. Where did they find such a thing?"

"They made their own," Muzta said.

Jubadi looked over at the Tugar angrily.

"I need to know where they are, what they are doing beyond this damned river."

"Don't blame me," Muzta said with a smile.

"Perhaps we should," Vuka interjected. "If you had taken care of your own cattle at the start we would not be troubled by this now."

"I'm eager to see you try them, o Zan Qarth. Perhaps you would care to lead the charge across the river, as my own youngest son once did."

He paused for a moment.

"He died, of course."

"Doubt my courage, Tugar?" Vuka snarled. He stepped up closer to Muzta, the Tugar guards around him stepping forward, hands leaping to hilts.

"The Yankees are laughing twice as loud," Tamuka said coldly. "Laughing at their triumph. And if they can see us argue thus, they are laughing about this as well."

Muzta grinned sardonically at Vuka.

"Of course I would never doubt your courage," he whispered. "All know how well you fought on the river before us."

Vuka bristled, yet there was a sudden nervous look in his eyes.

"Zan Qarth," Jubadi snapped. "The enemy is across the river."

With a bitter curse, Vuka let his hand drop from his blade and stalked away.

"We must find where their cloud-flyers hide, where they are made, and smash them," Hulagar said. "Let weapons to kill other cloud-flyers be made."

"By whom?" Tamuka said quietly.

"By the cattle who made the machines in the first place," Jubadi replied.

"Oh yes, but of course," Tamuka replied.

The cracking of a whip disturbed the group, and Jubadi turned to look back down the slope. Along the rail bed a long column of Cartha cattle were coming into view, staggering forward.

"Tomorrow they will be at the first ford. We can start building another mole. Within five days I want the river covered for a hundred miles. We must keep the pressure on. If we stay pent up in these woods beyond then, disaster will start to loom."

Tamuka said nothing but looked closely at Muzta, who was gazing at the flaming wreck, a thin smile lighting his features.

Chapter 9

"What a mess, what a godawful mess!"

John Mina slapped his gauntlets against the side of his leg, as he waded through the sea of refugees climbing down from the train.

As far as the eye could see, the hills rising to the south and east of Kev were carpeted with a ragtag tent city. The air was filled with incessant hammering, shouting, the sounds of squalling babies and shouting women, a mad cacophony of noise. A team of horses pulling a wagon laden down with fresh-cut lumber went past, splattering him with mud. He looked down at his stained, bedraggled uniform and cursed. It was one thing he had always hated about the army, one could never get clean. Back in the old Army of the Potomac days he had been filled with self-loathing and embarrassment the day he discovered that he was lousy. It did not matter that everyone else, from Andrew on down, was vermin-ridden. The abominal creatures were on *him*, and that's all that mattered.

Nervously, he scratched at himself. Was the itching from being in the same clothes for five days and nights without a change, or had he caught *them* again?

He pushed his way through the crowd, ignoring

the delegation from the town council, which always attempted to grab any official it could find to scream out its complaints.

He paused for a moment to look at a pile of ground wheat in canvas bags that lay by the side of the road, half-buried in mud and soaked through from the rain.

"What dim-witted, son of a goddamned devil's spawn is responsible for that?" John raged, pointing at the ruined food.

The unloading master stood mute.

"Enough wheat there to feed a thousand people for a day, and it's ruined!" John shouted.

"We've got seventy-five trains a day stopping here!" the stationmaster protested. "It's chaos!"

"Of course it's chaos!" John shouted. "It's madness, bloody madness!"

He looked around at the men lining the platform. "Who's second-in-command here?"

A bent-shouldered old man came forward.

"Petrov Gregorovich, your excellency." The man took off his cap, his bald head bobbing up and down.

"Well god damn it, Petrov, you're now Colonel Petrov. If you don't improve this by tomorrow you'll be fired too, until I find someone to get some order here."

He turned to look back at the fired manager.

"Your regiment? And where is it located?"

"Fifteenth Kev. Last I heard, north of the Ford."

"Find your rifle, and take the next train up and join it," John snapped and he stalked off, leaving the gape-mouthed man trembling.

"He was doing the best he could," an aide argued.

"Not good enough," John snarled in reply.

He shouldered his way out of the station, climbing over the temporary tracks laid down to act as sidings.

The high pierce of a whistle cut the air, and he looked back to watch as a long train came into the station, moving hard. People, squealing pigs, squawking chickens, and lumbering cows scattered before it. The train thundered through, the red-and-gold pennant of an express bound straight for Roum flying from its smokestack. Behind it were ten dormitory cars, swaying violently from their topheavy loads. The cars were crammed to overflowing with the lucky ones, destined straight through to the relative safety three hundred miles farther on.

"Mina!"

John turned with a groan as Emil Weiss stepped out of a shack and came up to his side.

"Where the hell are my tents?"

"Somewhere back in Suzdal."

"I've got three thousand wounded from the last battle, a lot of them lying out under blankets in the open field. I'm losing thirty boys a day I could be saving."

John held up his hand as if to beg off.

"And beside that. We need tents for the people, lumber for barracks, and water, John. They're taking it straight out of the Volga—no filtration, nothing. I already got a couple of typhoid cases—soon it'll be a damned epidemic."

"Later, doctor."

Emil fell in by John's side as he walked down the track. On the far side of town the line turned northward, starting up the long grade along the flank of the White Hills. John went straight on, stepping over the track and wading down a sloppy, mud-caked embankment. He ignored Emil and shouted orders at his staff, pointing out another pile of abandoned food and roaring with anger at the sight of a dead horse, half-butchered, the remains of its carcass sinking into the mud. Emil wrinkled his nose at the smell, and simply followed John as he started up the long slope beyond the town.

"I know you're doing the best you can," Emil said, his voice suddenly gentle, and John looked over at him in surprise.

"How are you holding up?'

"As usual," John replied, not wishing to even think about how he was feeling. His stomach felt as if it were in a knot. It had started the moment Andrew had mentioned evacuation and had stayed that way for the last ten days.

"When was the last time you slept?"

John laughed, shaking his head, and made no reply.

Emil was silent, looking at him closely.

John slowed going up the hill, and Emil turned with a solicitous look.

"How old are you, son?"

"Thirty-three."

"I'm twice your age, and you're getting winded. Boy, you're run down and out."

John held up his hand as if to ward Emil off.

The rail line swept up the side of the hill before him, turning northward on its long four-mile climb to reach the pass through the White Hills. It ran nearly eight hundred feet above the valley floor, where it would turn through the cut and run back down, straight as an arrow, to the Kennebec crossing a hundred miles farther on.

The hills were still heavily clad in towering pines, although in the last week they had been falling by the thousands, both slopes of the hills being cleared for the needs at hand—the west slope for the construction of fortifications, the east slope for where the temporary factories and shelters were going up. In another day the rail turnaround on the far side of the hills would be complete, eliminating the need of running the trains up through the hills, to off-load and then slowly back down.

Slowing, John stopped to watch the refugee train that had passed through Kev continue its laborious climb, engine puffing dark plumes of smoke, one of the first of the coal-burners to join the line. The burden it was carrying was almost too much—the engine was straining hard, showers of sparks were spraying up and flame shooting out from its belly. The acrid smoke rolled off to the south in a heavy layer.

Around the bend out of Kev another train started to move up the slope, flatcars piled high with turning lathes and molds from the gun works. The engine pulling the equipment would be stripped down to provide the power to get the lathes running again. Nearly half the locomotives were destined to be cannibalized for the factories, once the first stage of evacuation had been completed. He cursed himself silently for not having converted the factories to steam power earlier, and for having allowed himself to stay married to the convenience of the nearly limitless power harnessed from the Vina Dam.

He slowed, pulling out a handkerchief to wipe the sweat from his face. Without any worry about projecting the proper image, he sat down on a tree stump that was still oozing pitch. He looked a mess already, he realized, so getting the seat of his pants covered with pitch didn't matter anymore.

Pulling out his field glasses, he looked back to the west. It was a beautiful, clear view, straight back through the heart of Rus. The showers of the night before had given way to the promise of a warm spring day, the sky a crystalline, fresh-washed blue. The orchards were shedding the last of their blossoms and the hills to the south of Kev were carpeted in pink. If he could only have blocked out the madness it would have been a scene of pastoral splendor, worthy of a painting by Church or Cole. The scent of green fields, of fresh grass, wildflowers, and pine, almost masked the undertone of sweat, unwashed bodies, and excrement.

To the north, half a dozen miles away, the last solid stands of the great forest resting along the high hills dropped away into a scattering of trees, which followed the moisture of the creeks and gullies that cut through the gently rolling landscape. Behind him the high backs of the White Hills, which marched in a straight line from the forest to the inland sea, were crowned with towering stands of virgin growth, many of the trees a hundred or more feet in height.

He tried to visualize the rough survey maps that had been made at the same time the census teams went out. The realm of the Rus ran from the Neiper to here, nearly two hundred and fifty miles, with a few scattered settlements going out into the vast plains that stretched three hundred miles farther on to Hispania and Roum.

If there was a final defendable point, it was here—Andrew had at least chosen well in that. Farther west, back toward Suzdal, the width of open land between the ocean and the great forest averaged more than sixty miles across, a few sections bulging out to nearly a hundred. This was the only other choke point, the thousand-foot crest of the White Hills forming a natural barrier, heavy with forest— twenty miles of front to defend.

The valley floor below was a sea of chaos. Nearly a third of a million refugees had funneled through. Far out on the open plains beyond he could see wagon after wagon moving eastward, piled high with food and the few meager possessions the people of Rus could not bear to part with.

Anyone capable of work was laboring on the long western slope of the hills, felling trees and digging, some with nothing more than sharpened sticks. He looked around at the women, the old men, the children of ten years of age; the long line already running for miles; the staff of engineers who had gained their knowledge on the Potomac front now laying out fields of fire, driving in marking stakes, directing the laboring thousands.

"Just where in the name of God do they get their strength to go on like this?" John whispered in English.

"They're Rus," Emil said, sitting down by John's side, pulling up a wilting blue flower and twirling it absently between his fingers.

"We think we've pushed them to the edge, and still they keep on going. It's part of the peasant soul. Believe me, John, I know—remember, I'm from the old country. A Jew, to be certain. Back in the old world their cousins would have burned my beard off with joy. But the Slavic peasant, you pile suffering on top of suffering on his back and he'll carry it. Oh, God knows, they'll cut your throat if you cross them the wrong way. But they know that they either suffer doing this, or they all die in the end."

"Think how much easier it all would have been," John said, "if we had listened to Tobias. Remember, back in that council meeting we held after the Tugar Namer of Time showed up."

"Can't recall," Emil replied. "Never did care to listen to that pompous fool."

"He said that we should leave, find a place down south and wait for the Hordes to disappear, then come back and take twenty years to build. You know, if we'd done that the Hordes would be gone by now."

"And twenty percent of the Rus, the Roum, and the Cartha would be in the feasting pits."

"My dear doctor, over half of the Rus have died in the last five years, and I bet not one Cartha in ten will be around to see next winter."

"Don't forget that by staying we managed to put an end to the smallpox which would still be preceding the Tugars, so the number of lives saved in Roum and elsewheres more than makes up for it. Cold as it seems, John, it does balance out."

"If we lose here, the Roum will get it by winter. That city is a trap—hills looking down on it from three sides. The Merki would shell it apart."

"Go over and ask some of those folks digging down there if they'd want it different.

"Go on—what the hell do you think they'd say to me?" John sniffed, leaning forward and plucking up a blade of grass, turning it over in his hand.

"You're playing with what if's, John," Emil said forcefully. "That's far too much for a peasant to worry about. All he knows is that he is free, and if need be he'll die fighting. Sure, we could have run. Would we have found a safe place? I doubt it. If we had, would we have found iron and coal sitting on top of each other? And what about being in the hands of Tobias—you saw how he turned out. I'm happy to stick it through as it was played out."

"Even if we lose."

Emil smiled softly.

"Ever see a pogrom?"

"A what?"

"You Americans," Emil said, shaking his head. "I was born in what used to be Poland. My father was murdered by a gang of drunken Hungarian soldiers in 1813, when the French were retreating out of Russia. They spit on my father's body, called him a dirty Jew, and then raped my mother. Of course, she wasn't too dirty to receive that favor."

He was silent for a moment, looking off, eyes unfocused.

"She died from what happened," he whispered, "leaving me and an older brother, who died of the typhus that followed the army. I never forgot what it was like to live in that fear. Even after I grew up with my uncle, became a doctor in Budapest, and went from there to Vienna, I was still in the grip of that fear. Oh, I was a doctor, to be sure, but I still never knew when the Hungarian, or any *goyim*, might be at the door, laughing, knowing he could kill me without fear of reprisal. That's why I finally came to America. You Americans, born in your blessed New England, never knew that kind of fear."

Emil sighed, looking off to the west.

"That's why I loved your Maine, my Maine. That's why I hated what the Confederacy stood for, even though I saved the life of more than one rebel boy, caught in war beyond his making.

"I was terrified when we first landed here and discovered they were Russians—Rus—and breathed a sigh of relief when I found they didn't know what a Jew was. I was just another Yankee to them." He laughed in a self-deprecating manner. "Surrounded by *shiksas*, and they think I'm one of them. Can't even tell the difference in accents."

Mina looked over at him and smiled.

"Better English than a lot of folks I've heard. O'Donald's brogue gets mighty thick at times."

"Exactly what I'm talking about. O'Donald, ask him about watching his older sister starve to death during the potato famine. He knows what I'm talking about, the terrible fear. Well, these people were born and bred to it. Fear of boyars, fear of Tugars, fear of their own church. Give them a taste of living without that fear. That's why they're digging out here till they drop dead from exhaustion. That's why they'll fight them on the river, across those plains in front of us, into these hills, and if need be backwards across this entire goddamn world."

He paused for a moment.

"That's why their sons, their fathers, died with Hans, singing the 'Battle Hymn' as they went down." He paused for a moment, his voice choked.

"So don't ever say we should have left these poor miserable bastards to the Tugars."

John nodded, looking across the plains. He watched the shadows of the cumulus clouds as they floated lazily down to the sea, puffing high with the warmth of a spring day after a night of rain.

"Hard to believe there'll be a war here in a month, it's so damned peaceful."

"Maybe it'll be peaceful for your children," Emil said wearily, climbing back to his feet.

"By the way, John, I've got hospital supplies stockpiled in Suzdal, Novrod, and Vyzima, and I want a priority train to get them out *now*."

John chuckled softly.

"Knew you'd put the pressure on me at some point."

"It's my job," Emil said, extending his hand to pull John back to his feet.

"All right, I'll write the order and send it down the line," John replied. "You'll get them day after tomorrow."

He paused for a moment, looking off to the south to the point where the dark line of earth was turning up through what had once been a forest of pines. If they could get this position finished in time, it would be one hell of a killing ground.

Twenty miles from the sea to the forest, the hills nearly twelve hundred feet high at points. The forest was right at their back—all they had to do was cut the logs and stack them up. The only drawback was the hard, rocky soil, unlike the loam of the Potomac front which was a paradise for digging entrenchments. In a month he could have a single line up; in three months, bastions, a fallback position, fortresses blocking each of the passes, and the slope forward a madness of entanglements. Time, it was always time.

He looked over his shoulder. A hundred yards farther up the slope a crew was working hard. A low, double-walled blockhouse was going up, dirt piled up against its side. The men were doing good work, and when finished it'd be proof against damn near anything.

"How long have we got?" Emil asked. "I've been out of touch up here."

"They hit hard on the ford last evening, got a foothold across and we didn't push it back till morning. We took a thousand casualties—the 1st Orel and the 2nd Roum got badly chewed up. I forgot to tell you, there'll be a trainload of them coming in by evening."

Emil nodded absently.

"I think I better get some rest—it's going to be a long night."

John didn't say anything. His deepest terror was to one day be brought in to Emil, this time to receive his professional consideration. He had gone through the war without a scratch, but he'd been in too many field hospitals—filled with the thunder of screams, rasping saws, and slashing scalpels—to feel anything but a primal dread. He looked over at Emil, wondering how such a gentle man—for after all, beneath the irascible exterior was an infinite well of gentleness—could wield a scalpel against the torn flesh of so many young soldiers. He felt a sick compulsion to ask how many arms, how many legs he had taken off, as he looked at the weathered hands, which seemed to be permanently red from the caustic washes he used to prevent infection.

"Scared?" Emil asked softly.

"Terrified," John whispered.

"We all are, this time around. I thought for a while I might lose Andrew to it. I see it in you, Fletcher, Kal, and down deep, even that young Hawthorne."

"But not in Pat. I think he really loves it."

"Thick-headed, but we need that type. All the rest of us, though. We were scared the first time around, but I think we were too caught up in it all to worry. Last summer, that one hit us off-guard. I think it shook our confidence a bit, even though we won. It made us nervous, and then the disaster two weeks back, the way they sliced right through us, that one shook all of us to the core, it made us realize we really could lose this one."

"I remember this bully in my town, Waterville," John said, his face flickering into a smile. "He taunted me for weeks and I was terrified of him. Finally I just exploded, and by god I beat the living daylights out of him. I felt grand, I did. The next morning, as I walked to school, I saw him, black-eyed. Behind him was his big brother, twice my size, who beat me to within an inch of my life.

"Sort of the same this time with the Tugars and then the Merki. I guess that's why I'm so damn scared. What we're doing here is a last desperate bid, doctor. We're losing all of Rus, everything, to try and beat them. You know damn well if they break this line some of us might get to Roum, but we'll never come back. It'll all be gone forever."

"And you think that'll happen, even after all of this?"

John nodded sadly.

"You know, I know that Andrew is playing out a game," John said, his voice lowering to a whisper. "Once they break through and find the country empty they'll storm forward, supplies or not. They'll have to. Six days after the breakthrough they'll be here, my good doctor, and there isn't a damn thing we can do to stop them."

"Andrew keeps saying a month."

John shook his head.

"Propaganda, a last hope. I just pray to God that *he* knows that it's a dream. Believe me, doctor, those bastards will come on with death in their eyes. Give me a month and I might be able to make a go of it here. But I think, my friend, that in a month's time all of us will be bones in the feasting pits. Nothing will stop them once they're across."

"Let's hope you're wrong," Emil whispered, but John could sense the fear in the doctor's voice.

They started back down the hill. A few soldiers, part of the engineering regiment, saluted as the two passed, but the peasants barely noticed their passage.

Emil motioned John over to his shack, past a long row of tents with their flaps open. John looked out of the corner of his eye at the cots within—casualties of the fight on the Potomac, the incessant skirmishing along the river, lying by the hundreds. He felt it was his duty to go in, to spend a couple of minutes and offer a cheerful word, but the fear, the exhaustion, caused him to look away, stabbing him with guilt.

He could hear their low moans, snatches of prayers, the wheezing gasps of a man shot in the chest, the insane cackle of someone driven over the edge by having seen too much. He felt as if his own knees were turning to jelly.

God, never let it happen. Make it quick, but not

that—not looking up into Emil's eyes, shrieking on the table like a terrified animal.

His memory flashed for a moment to the hospital after Cold Harbor. The boy lying outside a tent, both legs gone at the thighs, screaming, just screaming.

"Are you all right, John?"

He looked over to see Emil staring at him.

"How do you stand it?" John whispered.

Emil tried to force a smile.

"I don't. I just try to remember the ones I put back together. The others . . ."

He waved his hand, as if warding off an evil demon, and continued on.

"I'd best be getting back to the depot," John said.

Emil motioned him over to his tent.

"Have a drink first."

"I've got to catch a ride to the other side of the hills. They'll be laying in the furnace for a temporary shot mill, and I need to be there."

"Take a couple of minutes."

John nodded wearily. Ducking low, he entered the tent and sat down on Emil's cot. Emil went over to a wooden chest and pulled out a bottle, then poured the contents into a beaker and passed it over.

John took the drink, downed it in a quick gulp, and sighed.

"Tastes good. What is it?"

"A good vodka, with a strong dash of laudanum. Was able to mix some up with the opium we found south of Roum."

"What the hell have you given me?" John said slowly.

"A good knockout drop. You'll be asleep in a couple of minutes, my good sir. Doctor's orders. It's either that or I'll be checking you into the hospital with a heart attack or nervous debilitation."

"Damn you, I don't have the time," John whispered.

"None of us do."

John cursed feebly as Emil lifted his feet up onto the cot. Within a couple of minutes he was snoring.

"My cot, too," Emil sighed.

It had been over a day since he'd slept, and he had a long night ahead of him. Amputations—cutting and yet more cutting—and he felt an inner shaking at the red price which war took out of his heart. It seemed like this was all he had ever done.

He looked over at his notebooks and the microscope next to them—the precious research he'd been doing on consumption, typhoid, infectious wounds, and that strange mold he was finding on the side of certain trees which seemed to kill infection on contact. It would all have to wait yet again.

He walked out of his tent and saw John's staff waiting patiently.

"Go on, get the hell out of here and find a quiet corner to sleep!" he shouted, waving his hands as if shooing away a flock of confused geese. "Come back tomorrow morning."

The men looked at each other, first in confusion and then almost gratefully, before going over to a stack of boxes covered with a tarpaulin and settling down.

"I'll get some hot food to the lot of you," Emil said, turned away and heading back to do another round in the hospital. There was a Roum boy with a terrible stomach wound. Ever since he had saved Pat he no longer turned stomach wounds away, sending them to an isolated tent to die. The problem was that an amputation took only five minutes, a stomach wound a half-hour or more. But he could not leave them to die. This time he had packed the wound with the mold, and he was curious to see if infection had set in yet. Perhaps, the lord willing, it just might work. If so, he'd have to get teams of people into the woods to gather more of the mold, and train all surgeons in stomach-wound treatment, something he had skipped over in the past.

Looking up, he saw a train slowly working its way down the hill, another of the huge aerosteamers riding above it.

He gave a sniff of disdain. Yet another way for men to figure out how to kill each other, he thought angrily, then disappeared into the tent.

"A beautiful day," Andrew said, sighing and leaning back against a tree.

There was a distant booming, like thunder on a summer evening, but he barely noticed it. A flash of light snapped over Suzdal, near the Yankee quarter. Long seconds later a dull, muffled thump rolled up against the hills. He tried not to think of Kathleen and Maddie. She'd most likely be in the Cathedral, working in the special surgery ward with several dozen trainees around her. It was a cold thought. His wife, nursing their child, and an hour later her hands wrapped around a saw, cutting a wounded boy's arm off as part of a training lesson. The giving of life in two such different ways—one through love, and yet the other an act of love as well, even as it mutilated. When done, she'd wash and then pick up Maddie yet again.

"A thousand and thirty-two yards to the outer gate," Andrew said, looking over at Yuri. "That's the closest the woods come."

Yuri nodded in reply.

"A bit far," he said, looking down the long tube of the telescope.

"Have you been practicing?" Andrew asked.

"Actually, I'm getting rather good at it," Yuri replied, the slightest hint of pride in his voice.

All Andrew's hopes were tied in to this one effort. It had to work.

"The hidden field you've been practicing at—any problems?"

Yuri shook his head and continued to look down the tube.

"Everything is according to ritual," Yuri finally said. "Suzdal is the same as the golden yurt of a rival Qar Qarth, the taking of it the symbolic overthrow of an enemy. The Tugars captured the great yurt of the Merki at Orki and it was a humiliation that still burns their hearts. It implies that a Qarth cannot protect the circle of fire of his own hearth.

"Though you are only cattle, the failure to defend your great yurt will mystify them."

"And Jubadi?"

Yuri chuckled, rolling up from where he had been lying on the forest floor and leaning back to sit against a tree.

"He somehow felt that taking Suzdal would be the focus—the same as when the Tugars fought you."

"Why not do this from inside of Suzdal?" Andrew asked.

Yuri shook his head.

"They are not that stupid. A full umen will sweep through your town before Jubadi even steps foot into it."

Andrew nodded.

"And when he discovers the city is empty?"

"Ah, there will be rage. It will be perceived as the ultimate action of cowards, abandoning one's own yurts, conceding the hearth circles without a fight. Incomprehensible to a Merki. I daresay that they will leap forward, like dogs on the scent of blood. No matter how good the destruction that you have wrought, he will still send ten or more umens straight eastward. In five days they will be before Kev."

"And we're not ready," Andrew said. "It'll be a month more, at the earliest, before everyone is safely out, and the lines are fortified. All our able-bodied men are in the army, at the front, or in the factories. It's what's left that's digging the line."

"That is where I come in," Yuri replied.

Andrew would have preferred that someone else would "present," as he now called it, the argument to Jubadi. Yet no one knew the rituals, the panoply, the markings of the Qar Qarth as Yuri did. It had to be he. At the suggestion that someone else be with him, Yuri flatly refused. There was no sense in ordering it; besides, Andrew could not bring himself to ask for a volunteer. Yuri's argument that he was as good as anyone else was sound. All hopes were on him.

"I'm telling my people that it'll be weeks before the Merki come on again."

Yuri chuckled, shaking his head.

"Wishful thinking. Jubadi is no fool. He knows that to wait is to court disaster, and besides, you will have outmaneuvered him. That will not sit well. I dare say he dreamed that with the fall of Suzdal the war, for all practical purposes, would be over.

"No, he will come on. Again it will be the horns— two wings striking, one along the shore, the other along the forest, the head in the middle. He has learned to flank you through the forest, and he will do so again."

That is where we will be weakest yet again, Andrew thought, saying nothing.

A shadow passed over them, rolling down from the edge of the thick woods, across the open slopes to the Vina, and then on up over the fortifications along the north wall of Suzdal. Andrew realized that it was a beautiful day, what with the landscape being dotted with shadows and light. Perfect weather for the aerosteamers, which had been strangely absent since their defeat.

"Andrew Keane, you must learn to be a Merki if you are to win."

"I'm trying," Andrew replied, looking over at the man who was part of both worlds, torn between them.

"All the other arrangements?" Yuri asked.

"The seamstress reports that her work is finished."

Yuri smiled.

"Good, very good, that will help."

"Suppose you are still lying?" Andrew asked suddenly, looking over at Yuri. "Suppose that all you have said is merely a ploy within a ploy, a means for your safe return to the Merki, bearing with you all that you know about me?"

Andrew looked past Yuri to where several guards lounged not twenty feet away. They appeared to be uninterested, yet they observed Yuri's every move with intense scrutiny.

"If you suspect that, then why are you allowing me to do this plan?"

"Because you are the only one who possibly could."

Yuri smiled.

"You won't know until it happens," the Rus replied.

A startled cry aroused him from his slumber. Hulagar, torn from his own dark dreams, was up in an instant. Grabbing his scimitar he pulled the curtain back, even as the silent ones rushed into the small yurt. On the other side Jubadi was sitting up.

"A dream?" Hulagar asked.

Jubadi nodded, a bit sheepishly.

Hulagar looked to the guards, beckoning for them to withdraw.

Taking a candle he touched the wick against the glowing embers of the fire in the middle of the yurt. A dim glow of light filled the inside of the small yurt. Going up beside Jubadi he sat down, setting the candle in the top of a skull, and in an almost fatherly manner took up a cloak and placed it around Jubadi's shoulders.

"A drink," Jubadi whispered.

Reaching over to a small lacquered stand, Hulagar took a leather pouch full of fermented milk and passed it over. Jubadi leaned back and took a long swallow, then passed it back to Hulagar, who took a sip before tying the spout off.

"A strange place, this," Jubadi sighed. "This forest, the dank cold, the rain. I hate it."

"In our old realms, the heat of high spring would already be washing the steppe, and the grass would be up to mid-waist, turning golden. Here it is dripping trees and darkness—one can't even see the sky. It is the stink of the cattle weapons, death drifting through the woods unexpected, our warriors dying in the dark, without the sun to shine on their faces as they look to the everlasting sky."

"We will soon be out of it," Hulagar said soothingly.

Jubadi nodded wearily and with a sigh lay back, pulling the cloak around his naked shoulders and curling up under the heavy felt blanket.

"Remember when we were young? My father sent us out."

"To fetch the Qarth of the Fraqu for punishment," Hulagar chimed in, the two friends sharing the memory.

"And the great storm came up. You dug a hole

into the snow, killing your own horse to close the hole over, cutting its body open to give us heat.

"That was your first horse," Jubadi said.

Hulagar looked off, a touch of sadness in his eyes.

"You gave me a thousand as a reward."

"But it did not replace him," Jubadi replied.

"Remember, my Qarth, it was my life I saved too. Do not make too much of it."

"I've been making much of it for nearly two circlings."

Hulagar untied the spout and took another sip of fermented milk, offering it to Jubadi, who refused.

"What troubled you in your sleep, my Qarth?"

"I saw the banner of black," Jubadi said, looking into Hulagar's eyes.

"Dreams are but dreams," Hulagar replied, a bit too quickly.

Jubadi growled out a soft laugh.

"Imagine a shield-bearer telling me that!"

"If you want dreams interpreted, send for Shaga," Hulagar announced with a soft smile.

Jubadi shook his head.

"It would terrify the old faker to hear that his Qarth dreamed of the black banner. He never did have the sense to keep his mouth shut—it'd spread throughout the camp."

"You know what the dream means as well as I," Hulagar finally said.

"Now that I stir again in the world of things real, it holds not the same terror that it had but moments ago."

He was silent for a moment.

"Was it a portent?"

"Possible, my Qarth, but portents appear as a warning, not as a finality."

"Yet are not the chant-singers filled with tales of those who turned from the path, because of a portent, only to have it thus completed precisely because they did turn away from a danger not really there?"

"A puzzling question, my Qarth."

Jubadi reached out for the sack and Hulagar passed it over. He took a long drink and sighed.

"We should be a moon's ride east of Cartha by now, rising up into the low hills of the heavy red flowers. Instead . . ." He motioned toward the entry to the yurt, the dark forest invisible beyond.

"We did what you knew we must. I have never disputed that, Jubadi."

The Qar Qarth nodded, putting the sack down and lying back, hands open behind his head, shaggy arms spread out to either side, the taut muscles rippling.

"The cattle were almost too easy to break, after the fight of the summer, what they did to the Tugars."

"Tugars, they were fools."

"They were still good warriors. Something I would admit only to you."

"I am still uneasy about Muzta. He resists nothing. There seems to be no pride, no spark. He is far too silent for my blood."

"Bears watching," Jubadi replied. "He would be a fool to think that when this war is over, the cattle subdued, that we will turn south to face the Bantag and leave him at our back."

"I assumed that is what you were planning."

"The young ones, the women of choice, they will come with us. As for all the rest"—he paused for a moment—"I have not forgiven Orki."

He sighed again, closing his eyes.

"Are portents true?"

"It is truly troubling you," Hulagar said softly.

"If you had such a dream, would it not trouble you?"

Hulagar chuckled softly.

"Remember, my Qarth, when you die I die too at your grave. I wish to see you live a long time, a very long time."

"Motivated by personal concern, are we?"

Hulagar laughed, patting his old friend on the elbow.

"You have planned this war well, my Qarth. Tomorrow you will be across the river. In a week their great city, Suzdal, will be surrounded. In a month all of the cattle of Rus will either be dead or have submitted, their secrets revealed. Roum by midsummer, then the following spring turn southward, back into our old pastures, with ten times the cattle weapons of the Bantag, and they will learn their place. There is nothing to fear."

"But the unexpected. That, you said, was always my strength, to expect the unexpected. That is how we have won so far, survived you and I through two circlings, a score of great battles, a hundred skirmishes, a dozen plots to kill me. I understand the minds of those like us; I do not understand cattle minds."

"Tamuka's pet will be sure to end that concern when the time comes. If not, he knows what will happen."

"He should have acted by now."

"He will act when he acts. Our cattle spy that got out during the winter says that he is still alive. Keane had turned to him for advice, in the same way you would speak to one of us who had ridden by Keane's side for a circling."

Hulagar snorted with disdain.

"I half wish I could see Keane alive rather than as we planned. He arouses my curiosity. I would make him a pet."

"Like the other prisoners, and the one like Hinsen."

"Hinsen is a traitor. We use him, we reward him, but we never trust him. When he makes a mistake he will go to the moon feast the same as Cromwell."

Jubadi yawned lazily.

"The night must be half-past," he sighed, stretching and then curling back up.

"Tomorrow will be a long day, my Qarth. Rest now."

Jubadi nodded.

"Do you believe in dreams?" Jubadi whispered, his voice drifting away.

Hulagar pulled the blanket up around his Qar Qarth's shoulders and withdrew silently, saying nothing.

Wearily climbing down from his mount, Pat muttered a sharp curse while rubbing his backside.

"Too goddamn long out of the saddle," he snapped, looking around at his old comrades from the 44th who had moved up to serve as his staff.

"A bit of the cruel, Major darlin'." Harrigan, a former gun commander of the 44th who could pass for a double of Pat with his bright red muttonchops, dismounted alongside of him. Laughing, he pulled a bottle out of his pocket.

"Throw that thing away!" Pat growled. "I'm a goddamn lieutenant general, and you, you bloody ass, are a brigadier now."

Harrigan made a mock gesture of tossing the bottle into the woods, then slipped it back into his pocket.

A Rus brigade commander came out of the gloom and saluted as Pat started up the trail.

"What do you have?" Pat asked.

"They're getting set to hit."

"Well, let's go see."

The Rus brigadier pointed up the trail and Pat

followed. Both of the moons were just past full, their light illuminating the forest with twin ribbons of shadows and light. Pat had been up on the ford when both had been at full, and the shrieks of the Cartha prisoners on the other side had curdled his blood, like the wailing of banshees. Just at dawn the Merki had stood one of them up, and he had seen the flames.

He suppressed a retch at the memory, which had sent the Rus troops into a frenzy. Whoever had done it was certainly a fool, Pat realized, for if ever there was a way to harden men to fight to the death, it was the sight of that.

"Get down low," the Rus general hissed. "They're getting damn good at it. Some of them have got our captured rifles."

Enough to arm nearly two divisions' worth, Pat thought coldly. As if to add weight to the argument, Harrigan stood up for a quick look around only to dive into the pine needles when the tree alongside his head was torn open by a minié ball.

They slid into a trench lining the river bank, then moved down its length for a score of paces to the spot where a narrow sniper's slit had been carved between two logs.

Pat cautiously peered through the hole.

The river was less than a hundred yards across, and the moonlight gave a ghostly glow to the corpses, human and Merki, lining the other shore.

The sound of axes ringing on the far shore rang across the river. The mole was only thirty yards into the stream, fronted with a heavy log breastwork, and it had been torn and riddled by twelve-pound solid shot fired at near point-blank range.

Farther upstream he saw incessant flashes of light rippling up and down the shore, both sides keeping up a murderous fire.

"It's been building all night," the general said. "There must be thousands of those poor Cartha devils in the woods, getting ready to push the log rafts in to block off the stream."

Pat nodded.

"All you men up?"

"Haven't slept since early morning of yesterday."

"Get them ready."

"What kind of support do I have?"

Pat smiled.

"They're planning this for all along the line, fifty miles. I'm getting the same reports. They've got six moles like this one, and there's half a dozen other fords. The bastards are even floating across the deep sections on logs. It's all getting set to hit."

"I'm just worried about me," the brigadier said.

"It's gonna be a long day, Ilya, I'm sorry."

"A regiment by mid-morning, that's all I'm asking. Hell, general, they'll be over the river by then."

"You better not let it happen here," Pat said quietly. "You've got a good path running behind you for horses. They'll slice right through us if you fail."

"Well, thanks for the support," the brigadier hissed.

"A pleasure, general, a pleasure," Pat replied, slapping the man on the shoulder.

He paused for a moment.

"Ilya."

The Rus general looked back angrily.

"We need you to hold out as long as possible, do you understand? I'm trusting you to give it everything you've got before you allow your men to fall back."

"Thanks, I understand now." His voice was cold, as if already coming from the grave.

Pat crawled back out of the trench and started for the rear, ignoring the flurry of shots that snapped through the trees above him. Standing up at last, he walked back to his mount.

"Poor son of a bitch doesn't stand a chance," Harrigan said in English.

"Somebody had to take the worst spot, and it's him," Pat replied, looking back sadly as he mounted. "It's the same place where the Tugars first flanked us. They were bound to remember it."

"Will you commit the reserves to him?"

"They're dug in five miles back across a gully. It's all we've got."

"Then you won't."

"Never reinforce what you know will be a defeat," Pat whispered. "We're weak all along the line, and we've got to save most of this army for Kev. We're buying time here, Harrigan. Buying time. Five miles a day through the woods at most—that's what Andrew's asking for, that's what he'll get. We need at least three corps to make any type of stand at Kev, and we need another two weeks to get everyone out. It means a lot of men are going to die in the process."

Trying to still the guilt in his heart, Pat turned his mount and galloped off.

Andrew stepped out of his headquarters into the incessant roar of battle. Overhead a shot fluttered past, detonating at the opposite side of the clearing.

A half-mile away, at the ford, the thunder was reaching a sharp crescendo. The incessant shouts of the Merki boomed above the roar of the artillery and the sharp tearing report of volleys.

Yet this was merely a demonstration.

Andrew looked down at the telegraph message from Pat.

" 'Yerganin Ford breached on half-mile front.

Recommend evacuation of entire 2nd Corps southward.' "

The Merki were across the river, on the fifteenth day of what he had hoped would be thirty.

He slumped against the side of the rail car. In less than five days, Suzdal and the heart of Rus would be overrun.

"The Navgah and Vushka have forced the river!"

Jubadi looked over at the joyful messenger and merely nodded in reply.

He stretched wearily, wishing he could take off his battle armor, but he still had to put on the show. His Qarths and umen commanders grunted their approval of the news.

"It's more than fifty miles through the woods, from the ford down to the open lands near their city of Vazima," Muzta said quietly. "It's gullies, sharp ravines, marshes. The last time they didn't have the men to cover that approach and ceded it to us. It'll be a hard fight, Jubadi."

"We are still driving them back," Vuka replied.

"And we are running low on food," Muzta said. "Horses cannot dig for roots in the forest for long. They cannot eat cattle flesh. Our mounts are thinning."

Jubadi held his hand up for silence.

"We will be in their land. Then we shall eat off of it."

"If they are still there," Tamuka replied.

Jubadi looked over at the shield-bearer.

"Not your vision again?"

"It was the *tu*, the sight; that is what I speak of, my Qar Qarth."

Vuka gave a sniff of disdain and turned his horse around, trotting off.

"We will know of this when the cloud-flyers go up

again," Hulagar interjected. "They are ready, and but wait for a favorable wind."

"Get them up, once the wind changes," Jubadi snapped. "I need to know."

He looked up at the dark skies heavy with rain, and cursed.

His mount slipping through the mud, Pat reined in hard, the horse nearly collapsing.

"You've got to hold here till night!" Pat shouted, pointing with his saber to the crest of the ravine.

The men in the road nodded, moving up to the low ridge and deploying across the trail. From up over the next ridge a mud-spattered mob appeared, men staggering, running hard, many without weapons.

From beyond came a rising, taunting shout.

Pat edged his horse up to the top of the ridge.

In the gully below, men were wading through the marshy ground to either side of the trail. Spilling over the opposite ridge, barely visible in the rain and mist, came a scattering of Merki, some on horse, most on foot, waving scimitars, some carrying Springfield rifles, others with bows.

Pat had thought to keep the next line five miles back from the river, but guilt had finally won, and he had rushed a regiment forward to provide cover for Ilya's broken units.

The forest to either side echoed with shouts, the woods for miles along the river now a breach.

"Bad as the Wilderness."

He looked down to see an officer standing by his horse, gasping for breath. He wore the colonel's eagle of the Rus army, and was dressed in the faded blue of a Union uniform, his corporal stripes still visible.

"Damn near," Pat said dryly. "What happened up there?"

"My regiment was to the right of the ford. We burned off most of our ammunition just shooting the poor Cartha bastards pushing the log rafts and booms in. They jammed the river by the mole, and in minutes they started across. Thousands of them. The whole line broke, sir."

"It had to happen sooner or later," Pat replied, his voice edged with bitterness.

"We got flanked, I ordered the boys back. Got cut off a couple of times, but we pushed out. I told the men to keep going straight south, angle in towards the road, and get the hell out of here."

Pat nodded.

A volley roared down the line, slamming into the Merki on the opposite ridge and slowing their charge. The men down in the gully were running hard, coming up the slope and dragging their wounded along. The survivors came through the line and kept on going.

Pat saw the Rus general and rode up to his side.

"Tried, but they just keep coming," the man gasped.

"You did your best."

"Lost half a brigade back there. It better be worth it," the man said bitterly.

"Let's hope so," Pat replied, reaching over to offer the man a drink.

The officer took the flask, drained it down in a long gulp, and passed it back up.

"Keep your men moving south," Pat said. "Rally them at sundown, then march 'em south and out of here. Once clear of the woods head to Vyzima—a train will pick you up."

"To go where, yet another debacle?" the general

snapped, and without waiting for a reply he started down the trail.

The Merki, stalled for a moment by the fresh regiment, started down the slope at a run, chanting their clan names. They hit the marshy ground and sank knee-deep, but kept sloughing forward. The woods filled with acrid smoke, bullets that missed their mark sending up geysers of mud. The enemy pushed on, climbing over their dead and relentlessly pushing in.

Straight down the trail a heavy column started in at a run, hitting the corduroy road through the low ground. The head of the column collapsed from the volleys and the rear spilled over the sides of the road and leaped past the bodies of their comrades, swarming up the slope. Bows wet from the rain snapped lazy bolts up the hill, still carrying enough power to drive into flesh. Men staggered out of the line, holding still quivering shafts.

"Wounded that can walk, take your guns with you!" Pat shouted. Far too many weapons were being lost in the leapfrog retreat through the woods.

Pat watched the action closely. The fresh regiment was giving a good account of itself, and the torn remnants of the broken units were now safely to the rear.

He rode up to the regimental commander.

"They'll be flanking you before long. Send a couple of your reserve companies back to the next ridge, then get your boys the hell out before you get overrun!"

The commander nodded without comment.

Pat turned to ride away. He had to keep reminding himself that he was not a field commander anymore. He was responsible for the entire right wing of the army, a full two corps, holding over fifty miles of woods bordering the river. If he let this corps go down, there'd be precious little to hold Kev.

He started back. A wounded Rus soldier was hobbling down the road, trailing blood from a gunshot wound to the leg. Pat reached down from his mount.

"Get up here, damn it!" he snapped, grabbing hold of the man and pulling him up across the horse's rump. The soldier grimaced even as he tried to force a smile of thanks.

Pat urged the horse into a gallop. With mud splattering, he cantered off into the mist.

The train rolled silently into the station, the hiss of steam mingling with the light drizzle that marked the ending of the storm that had lingered for two long days and nights.

Wearily, Andrew climbed down from the car. The reception committee looked ghostlike in the fog, silhouetted by a couple of lanterns, the umbrellas above them shiny from the rain.

There was an eerie silence to it all. He had so many memories of other days at this station: the day the first train bearing citizens of Roum came in; the morning he had left here to lead the relief to their allies, or the coming back less than three weeks ago after the defeat on the Potomac. Now there was another defeat in the air. Three days ago the enemy had broken the Neiper. With the coming of morning advanced scouts most likely would be filtering out of the forest, sweeping down toward Vyzima by nightfall. The moment Merki units hit the rail line, the retreat out for everything west of Vyzima would be cut.

"I've been reading the reports," Kal said quietly, coming out of the group to shake Andrew's hand.

"They put up a hell of a fight, but I still don't

think it gave us enough time," Andrew replied softly.

"Is it time to leave?" Kal asked.

Andrew nodded sadly.

"Anyone still in the city has to be out by tomorrow," Andrew said. "We're keeping a brigade at the ford till tomorrow night. Once evening comes in, all trains will be run back up the line to pick up the troops pulling back to Vyzima and those at the ford.

"A couple of regiments will stay in the city till the end. They'll retreat south to the beach on the inland sea, and be pulled out by Hamilcar and a couple of the ironclads. After that, the only ones to see Suzdal will be Bullfinch's flotilla, which will stay on the river for the duration.

"How did we do, John?" Andrew asked quietly, falling in with the group as they started back up the hill toward the Great Square. A shell from the far shore arched overhead, bursting in midair, followed seconds later by a volley of shots that thunderclapped across the square and on northward into the Yankee Quarter.

Andrew tried not to worry about it.

"Only half the food out we had hoped for," John said wearily. "We must of burned tens of thousands of tons out in the barns and fields that we could have gotten out. We've got a pretty good sweep of everything west of Vyzima, but east of that, especially from Nizhil to Kev, maybe fifty thousand tons of it are still sitting there. If the Merki drive straight on east, it's all going to have to be torched."

"The people?"

"Like something out of the Bible. An exodus of them marching east, the roads choked with them. Trains overflowing. Nearly everyone west of Vyzima is out, but if they come on hard, Andrew, I'm afraid a couple of hundred thousand still might get caught.

There's a hell of a lot of people still a hundred or more miles west of Kev, and a huge cluster around Vyzima. Word didn't get to some of the out regions for days. Some of those poor bastards out in the far reaches don't believe what's happening and are refusing to leave, or got started too late. We've got a good fifty thousand along the coast. Hamilcar is running galleys to pick them up, moving them to the Kennebec, where they can walk up to the rail line and catch a train east. Some of the folks are even heading into the woods."

"Maybe they'll get lucky and survive," Kal replied.

"I tell you, it's like them stories you read about the Russians and Napoleon. Some of the peasants even plowed their crops back under before leaving. Trees are getting dropped across roads. I broke up a couple of companies of engineers and sent them to damn near every town. Showed people how to make traps, deadfalls. I saw one smart bastard catch a couple of poisonous snakes and put them in a barrel that looks like it might have food. If it doesn't kill some Merki bastard, it'll sure scare the shit out of him."

John chuckled softly, the rest of the group shaking their heads.

"We took about five hundred defective shells that hadn't been cast right and packed them with powder anyhow, set percussion fuses in them. We'll bury them in the roads as we pull back. That ought to shake them up as well."

"Good work. When they come on to Kev, anything to slow them will buy us time and hurt them further."

"Once they break through, they could sweep up to the White Hills in five, six days," John said. "If only we had a division or two of cavalry, it'd slow them down. We're tied to that single rail line. They'll outflank us anywhere we try to slow them."

Andrew said nothing, and after a long moment of silence John realized that his commander would not offer any information.

"Now the bad news. We're going down on engines. Ten were stripped down to give power to the factories. The first rifles were turned out today in Hispania, and we've got shot getting molded again as well. But twelve of the locomotives are just plain finished—they're back up at Hispania for overhauling. We had to tow three of them in, the others barely could make it under their own steam. We've done a year's worth of hauling in a month, Andrew—the tracks are ready to come apart."

"Well, I don't think it'll be much of a worry after tomorrow."

"I've got crews waiting for a good sixty miles west of Kev. Once the last troop trains go through we're going to start tearing up the rail behind us. At a hundred tons to the mile that'll be six thousand tons of iron. It'll keep the forges going for weapons—we'll even use them in fortifications."

"Good thinking," Andrew said, forcing a smile. "But don't pass the order on that till I give the word."

"But the food, Andrew, that's the problem. At best we've got forty days' worth for the people. Army rations are fairly secure for the next sixty days, though I had to order a lot of them sent back up to Hispania, where we have more warehouses going up. Emil's worried about disease. We're getting a lot of typhoid—it's spreading from that outbreak we had last winter up in Yaroslav. There's even been a couple of cases of smallpox. A lot of consumption, too, what with all this rain."

"A mixed blessing," Casmar said.

"Father, if you could come up with a clear-weather prayer I'd sure appreciate it."

"For tomorrow morning's mass, my son."

Andrew nodded his thanks.

They had reached the great square. It was ghostly, the city dark and eerie as only an empty city can be. Andrew felt as if spirits were taking over.

"What about the factories?"

"Cleaned out, as of yesterday."

"And all the government material?"

"Everything's gone," Bill Webster said. "Presses for money, a full boxcar load of paper for notices, forms, the usual garbage of running a bureaucracy, including all records. The same for the treasury and public corporations."

Andrew shook his head at that. It was hard to conceive that several cars had to be given over to such things, but if they were ever to rebuild they would be needed later.

"What have we forgotten?" Andrew asked quietly.

The circle of men was silent for a moment.

"A way to save our city as well," Yaro, one of the senators, said sadly.

"I wish we could," Andrew whispered, looking around at the square and the cathedral. The wondrous clock designed by Hawthorne ticked away the minutes above them, its chimes silent else they might be taken as a warning of an aerosteamer attack.

Would they come back to nothing but a flame-scorched wreck? Would they ever come back, or were they now condemned refugees, like the tens of thousands of wanderers who forever fled before the Hordes?

"Final pullout starts tomorrow, gentlemen. We all better get some sleep."

Andrew looked overhead. The clouds were breaking, the wind coming up from the southwest, the Wheel standing out clear in the midnight sky.

"Good flying day for them tomorrow," John said. "They'll be up, and most likely figure it out at last."

Andrew nodded and turned away, to walk alone back to his home.

Chapter 10

"I thought I'd come up and talk to you about my muskets," Vincent said dryly.

"That's John's department, not mine," Chuck replied, feeling a bit nervous about Vincent's unannounced visit.

"John's tied up three hundred miles from here. I haven't gotten a response in days. I saw a car loaded down with a thousand of them heading out yesterday, straight out of the factory in Roum, bound west. And god damn it, I want to know *why*!"

The workers in the shed fell silent, looking over at Vincent as if he had started screaming in the middle of a church service.

Chuck motioned for Vincent to follow him out the door and into the early morning light.

"You don't disturb my people," Chuck said coldly. "I've got some precision tools being cut in there. Get somebody to slip, and it ruins a day's, maybe a week's work."

Vincent didn't offer an apology, but looked at Chuck angrily.

"Nearly half of my people are still without weapons! How else am I supposed to feel?"

"I know, Vincent," Chuck said soothingly.

"And just what the hell do you have going up

here? I've heard that you've pulled a hundred people out of the gun works in Roum. That's a lot of weapons not being made, the way I see it. Powder's coming up short by the ton, one of the narrow-gauge engines has disappeared, and tin can't be found anywhere. There's talk that you're building a secret factory up here, out beyond the old balloon works."

Chuck grimaced and shrugged his shoulders, in a poor display of innocence.

"Does John know anything about all of this?"

"I do have authorization from Andrew to take whatever measures I feel are necessary to get certain things going."

"Doesn't sound like Andrew. He's usually precise in his orders."

"Well, he *did* say it," Chuck replied, sounding like a school-boy lying himself into a corner. "And I've got it in writing."

"I want five thousand muskets, Ferguson, ten batteries, and ammunition for the lot."

"Are you asking me, or telling me?" Chuck said quietly.

"I'm telling you. You control resources at this end, all of John's people are down reorganizing the front at Kev. Now pull some strings, fake a form, but I want it."

"Or?"

"One of my staff people will talk to one of John's, mentioning that you've been funneling powder off at over a ton a day. That fifty case-shot rounds a day are disappearing for whatever it is you're producing."

"You son of a bitch," Chuck whispered.

"Exactly," Vincent replied coldly. "Half of Marcus's command is skirmishing on the southern border with a couple of umens of the Merki. I'm expected to form two corps out here, and I'll be damned if I'm going to be nothing more than a training ground stuck behind the lines when the showdown comes. I want in on this war, and by god I'll blackmail Christ himself if it'll get me into it."

"God, Vincent, just what the hell has happened to you?" Chuck said quietly.

He looked past Vincent to where Dimitri stood a short distance away. The old soldier was watching this exchange with interest, though not understanding a word of the English being snapped back and forth.

"Just doing my job," Vincent replied.

"It's gotten way too personal for you," Chuck said quietly. "Sure, I hate the bastards, who wouldn't? But by the eternal, Vincent, I don't let it eat my soul out. I'm breaking the rules right now, going off where I don't have the authority, I'll admit it. But I'm doing it 'cause I've got a gut feeling I'm right and it might help win this fight. But you're doing this because you can't bear to miss out on the kill."

"Don't preach to me," Vincent whispered.

"There was a time when you didn't hesitate to preach to our entire regiment about what was morally right. You convinced more than one of the fellas to vote to stay here back at the beginning, when Tobias was arguing for us to pack up and skedaddle. Now all I see is hate, Vincent. The Merki didn't get your body, but they sure got your soul."

"I don't need to hear this," Vincent retorted, turning away.

"If you want your goddamned muskets, then you better listen."

Vincent looked back at him.

"Look, Vincent, I like you, I always did like you. Hell, we grew up in Vassalboro together. I remember the time you snuck out to go swimming with us older fellows in Webber Pond. Your father caught you, and raised holy hell 'cause you were out there naked with the rest of us."

A thin flicker of a smile crossed Vincent's features.

"And I remember you moon-eyed over my kid sister Alice," Chuck went on.

Vincent said nothing, but dropped his head and nodded.

"We were a bunch of innocent children then," Chuck sighed. "None of us thought we'd grow up to be killers. I just wanted to be an engineer and make machines, you just wanted to study and be a teacher or writer, like the Colonel once was. Well, we got caught in a war. Vincent, I do what I'm doing now because it's my job, but you, Vincent, you're doing it because you love it."

"And that way we win," Vincent replied.

"Look at Keane. Hell, I remember at Gettysburg. . . . I knew he loved it—I could see it, even after his brother got kilt. But look what it's doing to him now. He's the big general now; somebody had to do it, and thank god it was him. But I wouldn't want to be in his shoes for nothing. He's aged twenty years from the strain of it. It's like a cancer, Vincent— don't catch it. Sure, you'll be like Keane, you already are a damned hero, but in the end it'll leave you hollow and dead inside."

"Are you finished with the sermon, brother Ferguson?"

Chuck nodded.

"I'm getting my guns."

"I'll figure out something. I promise you'll have them as soon as possible. But it's going to be hell faking the disappearance of ten thousand muskets," Chuck said quietly.

"Then *your* secret is safe as well. Thank you."

"How are things in Roum?"

"Chaos. Julius is in charge of housing the refugees and moving them out to the countryside. He's doing a good job of it. There's been some problems—a couple of fights, some disease. But the Roum are doing fine by us. I guess peasants understand peasants. Problem is, we have refugees coming up from the south as well. There's not enough Merki to really hurt down there, but it is tying us down on that front. We might lose part of the late spring harvest. The city's like one damned giant nursery. I've got two mothers and five children in our home, cousins of Tanya's."

"Julius's daughter, Olivia?"

Vincent blushed nervously.

"She's all right. Been asking for you."

"Why the blushing, Vincent?"

"Nothing."

"Say, was there something between the two of you? I heard a couple of rumors," Chuck asked, his voice brittle.

"I swear it was nothing," Vincent said, a little too hastily.

Chuck decided to let it drop, really preferring not to know.

"You saw the message that came through this morning?" Chuck asked conversationally, as Vincent seemed to relax.

"About Suzdal being evacuated today?" He nodded.

"Bad business. Somehow I can't imagine that we've really lost the city. It's like hearing the rebs had taken Maine. That place was home. Damn, I had a really nice cabin there, was planning to build a regular home: scrollwork on the porch, a turret, a wrought-iron fence. A place to settle down and start a family. Hell, I guess it'll all be cinders when this is done."

"Fortunes of war," Vincent replied, and his features tensed up again. He paused and looked back.

"What about those sniper guns, the Whitworths?" Chuck hesitated.

"I turned out a couple more. I just couldn't give it up after so much work."

"I saw the one you gave Andrew. I want one."

"Plan to do a little personal killing?"

Vincent merely smiled and walked away.

"Just what the hell was that all about?" Theodor asked, coming up to join Chuck.

"Just doing a little trading with someone possessed."

"He's a good general, that one," Theodor said. "I've got a couple of cousins in the 8th Regiment. They say he's a rare one, filled with fire."

"Fire burns," Chuck replied.

He nodded to Dimitri and went back into the shed.

Dimitri smiled and nodded in return, then fell in alongside of Vincent as they remounted and started the long ride back to Hispania.

"Did you get the guns?"

Vincent smiled.

"What else did he say?"

"Nothing much."

"I really should learn your English—it seems one can get quite passionate while saying nothing much."

"Just that he's sounding too much like you, Dimitri."

Dimitri knew better than to reply.

It'd be a couple of months yet before he was ready for action, but Vincent Hawthorne knew that when the time finally came he would be ready. Whistling a tune off-key, he urged his mount into a canter and trotted off, leaving Dimitri behind in the mud.

* * *

For the first time in months Andrew saw tears in her eyes. Awkwardly he walked up and embraced her, Maddie still asleep in her arms.

"It's just we worked so hard for all of this," she said, her voice choking, her eyes bright as she looked around the simple parlor.

"Ludmillia gave me those curtains when I had my small cabin at Fort Lincoln—her first gift."

She stepped away from Andrew.

"Maddie's cradle. Remember how proud the boys from Company C were when they presented it?" She turned, running her hand along the back of a chair as if saying good-bye to an old friend, her gaze lingering for a second on a framed print of the two of them that had been published in Gates's paper. The only bare spot on the paneled wall was where the presentation papers for his Congressional Medal of Honor, signed by Lincoln, had been. That heirloom was part of her ten pounds of baggage.

"God, we lost all of it."

Clutching the baby tight she fled the room, Andrew following in silence.

A couple of the men from the 35th stood on the porch, holding Andrew's baggage. The regiment was formed up on the village green, the few family members still in the city standing alongside the column, their possessions resting in wheelbarrows or on their shoulders.

Andrew stepped out on the porch and surveyed their ranks. Barely one in five of them was from the old regiment. All the rest, at least those still alive, were out in the field, commanding units. This was the core, the men assigned to jobs with the government, or in the city. The rest of the ranks were filled out with Rus, and now a full company from Roum and even a couple of Cartha. Youngsters of promise, sent up to serve in the elite regiment of the Republic and to return after a time to positions of rank. All were wearing the old uniform: navy blue jacket, sky-blue trousers, blanket roll over shoulder, Springfield at the carry, the headgear a sprinkling of the old kepis with the rest wearing the black Hardee, the number 35 affixed to the crown. The old American flag, carried since Antietam, was at the fore, patched and repatched, the names of over twenty engagements emblazed on its silken folds. Next to it the dark blue flag of Maine, and between them the white-and-blue flag of Rus. Behind it were the colors of the 44th, the same American flag, and the emblem of a New York battery.

Even in this most heartbreaking of moments Andrew felt a swelling of pride. The regiment had endured, it would always endure. If it was fated that they were doomed never to return here, somehow the regiment would survive. If only one of them was able to bear the colors away, to remember the legends, the honor, the serried columns standing proud in the morning, the flame-scorched ranks holding in proud lines; if that was remembered, even if they were driven clear around the world, then the regiment would survive.

He felt as if an army of ghosts hovered around the colors. All those who had fallen beneath its folds were somehow present. The hundreds of names, barely remembered, who still somehow lived with the regiment, his brother John, Kindred, Houston, Sadler, and Dunlevy of the 44th. And of course Hans.

"We'll come back," Andrew said, his voice ringing across the square.

He looked out over their faces as if the ghosts were again in the ranks, swelling it out, joined in a brotherhood of blood and passion.

"This regiment will endure till the ending of the

world. This city, this entire country, may be burned to nothingness, and yet we will be remembered. Our names will be recalled, and when a day comes beyond our own, when grandchildren speak of these days, they will remember you, all of you, for what you sacrificed here.

"It is no consolation, perhaps, for what we have lost, this future memory by those we do not even yet dream of. But it should be enough. Our homes, our city can be destroyed, but we will rebuild them, and this time rebuild them free of fear. That is our sacrifice for those to come. That is what I am fighting for." He paused and nodded toward Maddie, who was still asleep in her mother's arms.

"She is worth far more than all I own and lose this day. And some day she will stand on this place and tell her grandchildren, who do not know fear, the story of what we did.

"Remember that promise, as we march out of here. And remember as well that we will come back, if we have to march clear around the world to do it."

He looked down the street and remembered walking up it the last night before the war started, laughing softly about the performance of Pat as Romeo, of young Gregory as Henry V.

" 'We few, we happy few, we band of brothers,' " he whispered to himself.

He walked down the steps of the porch, Kathleen behind him. He looked back for a moment at what had been home, its door open. Kathleen smiled sadly.

"No sense in locking it," she whispered.

He forced a smile, then kissed her lightly on the forehead and kissed Maddie in her arms, at which Maddie squirmed and nestled back in against her mother's breast.

Holding his hand up he pointed forward, and the column started out, the men grim-faced and silent.

Turning toward the south they passed the Congregationalist Church. The young corporal turned minister was coming out the door, rifle over his shoulder and a Bible under his arm. From out of the Town Hall several men emerged, to fall in with the column. With them they brought the regimental records, the log books going back to the day the regiment and battery had been formed.

A loud buzzing came from out of the south, and Andrew nervously looked up to see a dozen Merki aerosteamers coming up from that direction, moving fast on the southwesterly breeze. He watched them warily, ready to give the order to scatter if one should turn in for an attack on such a tempting target as a close-packed column. One of the ships, riding high, turned and moved off to the west, crossing the river and dropping down low.

"Must be telling them that the city is empty," Andrew said with a soft chuckle. "Won't *that* be a hell of a surprise?"

The rest of the ships continued on several thousand feet above the city, moving toward the northeast.

Reaching the great square, a thin trickle of refugees was moving down the boulevard to the east gate and the rail yard. From in front of the church Father Casmar appeared, with several dozen priests. He paused in front of the doors of the cathedral and made the sign of blessing, while two acolytes closed the doors, a hollow boom echoing through the square. Kal, Ludmillia, and several score of government officials were beside him, kneeling down and making the sign of the Rus cross. Coming to their feet, they moved down to fall in by Andrew's side.

"Holy relics," Casmar said, nodding toward four

acolytes carrying an iron-strapped box. "Hope you can see clear to bend the weight limits a bit."

Andrew smiled.

"Put them in the staff car, Your Holiness."

"Please, Andrew, just Casmar."

Andrew nodded appreciatively at this most unusual and unassuming of priests. He was wearing a simple homespun wool cassock, dyed the traditional black and with no adornment except for a plain iron cross of Kesus and the inverted hand of Perm.

"Will the last one out of the city please close the doors and blow out the lights?" Kal requested, and a ripple of laughter echoed down the column, the men farther back passing Kal's comment along.

There was a renewed flurry of shots from the far bank—shells arcing in, explosions detonating across the square. Anxiously Andrew looked back. No one had been hit.

Bullfinch came up out of a side street, saluted, and fell in at Andrew's side.

"Remember, Mr. Bullfinch, you're on your own. Once we're clear away, I want the battery troops and the last Suzdalian regiment evacuated down to the coast of the sea. You're to hold this river. Give them hell as they move up the Ford road. Force them off it, slow them down, but be sure to let them arrive at the city before sundown. You are under strictest orders not to engage them within two miles of the city."

"I still don't understand that part, sir."

"When you open your sealed orders you will," Andrew replied. "After that, deny them any chance of moving supplies up by sea. If you see a chance to raid ashore, do it."

Bullfinch nodded, looking like a savage pirate with his eye-patch and scarred face.

"Aye-aye, sir."

Andrew grimaced at the affectation of nautical jargon.

"I think you're going to enjoy this."

"That I am, sir. Independent command of a flotilla—who wouldn't?"

"Just get back safe, young man, and don't lose any of these ironclads. Mina's arranging to have food, wood, and coal moved down the Kennebec to keep you supplied. If you can free a ship to support Hamilcar on his raids, do so."

"What he wanted to hear. It'll keep him happy."

"Good luck, son."

"Couldn't you at least tell me why all the secrecy, sir. We've been hearing rumors: an area beyond the city that's been sealed off to everyone for weeks; the no shooting near the city. Just what are you up to, sir?" Bullfinch said quietly.

"You have your sealed orders. Don't open them until you see what I told you to look for."

"Exactly as you order it, sir," Bullfinch said, his disappointment in not knowing obvious.

"Good. Now get a move on."

Bullfinch snapped off a salute and turned to race back toward the naval yard.

Going out through the inner gate the column reached the station at last. The two trains waiting on the siding were already partially filled with the last refugees. The column broke to file aboard the cars.

John came out of the staff car and saluted.

"Pat reports they'll be in Vyzima by nightfall. Advance teams are already filtering out of the woods."

"The army?"

"Falling back in good order. I've got thirty trains in Vyzima to pick them up. The rear guard's going to be tough, though—the Merki are pressing pretty damn hard."

"Pat. Have you heard from him?"

"Not since midnight."

"I need that damned fool," Andrew said. "I pray to god he doesn't get caught like Hans."

John nodded.

"And along the river front, south of the Ford?"

"The last unit pulled out of the Ford just before daybreak—the train should be shuttling through the switch shortly. The Merki are most likely crossing by now."

"Let's get going, then."

John helped Kathleen up into the car, which was soon packed with staff from Andrew's command and Kal's office, plus Casmar's priests.

The assistant telegrapher was hanging from the pole by the station, looking down at Andrew.

"Shut us down," Andrew said.

The boy clipped the wire free, the telegrapher inside reeling the cable in. The boy scrambled up into the car and paused.

"Sir, what about that wire you ordered run out? Is that to stay?"

"Never mind now," Andrew said, shooing the boy aboard the car.

Andrew stood alone on the siding, looking at the anxious faces looking back at him from the window and from open boxcar doors. He walked back into the station and into a small room behind the telegraphers' office.

Yuri was waiting for him, and came to his feet.

"I'm counting on you," Andrew said. "God knows I shouldn't be, but I am counting on you."

"Against the angels of your better judgment," the man replied.

Andrew nodded.

The man reached into his tunic and pulled out a letter.

"I've only told you part of the truth. For my own reasons. Open it later."

Andrew nodded.

There was a nervous nod of reply. Andrew could see there was no sense in dragging it out—it served no purpose for either of them.

Hesitantly, he extended his hand.

"Good luck to you, Yuri."

Almost shyly Yuri took his hand, and then turned away, his eyes bright.

"You'll never know how your simple charity changed everything," Yuri said. His back was turned, and Andrew was already gone.

Andrew stepped back out into the early morning light.

He looked back at his city. It was silent, except for the occasional rattle of gunfire. It reminded him of a village early on a summer morning, when no one had yet stirred. Somehow it should be coming alive shortly, vibrant with life.

Suzdal was filled now only with memories.

He waved to the engineer leaning out of the cab.

A shudder ran through the train.

"Good-bye," was all that he could whisper as he climbed up into the car.

The engine started down the siding, the train before it already through the outer fortress lines.

Andrew stood alone, watching the earthworks fall behind. The train turned and started to pick up speed, the barrows of the Tugar slain on the hills to the right.

The engine rattled over the trestle crossing the Vina. Looking down, Andrew saw the river running turbulent, the floodgates of the dam wide open. The factories were visible for a moment up the valley— smokestacks clean, the last of the false fires set to deceive the enemy now out and cold.

The whole world seemed cold at this moment, though the sun was shining brightly and a warm drying breeze was rolling in from the southwest.

The train cleared the trestle. An enemy shot fell short behind them.

The rails clicked louder, faster. The train turned to the east, running up the grade on the far side of the reservoir. The engine slowed. Clearing the rise they continued on, the train's steam whistle tooting out a quick call. Andrew leaned out from the car and saw a switchman running alongside and leaping into a boxcar. The engineer leaned out of the cab to watch, then pushed the throttle back up again.

The train clicked through the switch. To his left he saw the main line run off toward Vyzima while they continued on straight toward Novrod, to rejoin the main line a hundred miles farther on, beyond the range of the Merki advance.

He looked back to the west. All that was visible was the spires. The train turned up over a low hill. For a moment all of Suzdal was again in sight like the first day he had seen it, fairy tale-like with its wooden spires, ancient walls, and soaring log structures carved into a riot of pleasing shapes and forms. And then it was gone.

A ripple of gunfire snapped along the ridge line. Pat sat meditatively, munching on a sandwich, watching the artillery batteries in action.

The limber teams were moved up, crews hooking their pieces to the back of caissons. The first gun started off down the hill, galloping hard through the fields. Several shells burst on the ridge line. A caisson detonated and was lifted high into the air, the gun behind it careening over, tumbling like a broken toy.

"God damn," Pat whispered.

The rest of the batteries continued down the slope. Not a minute later a thin wave of Merki cavalry crested the ridge, leaning out of their saddles and spearing the few wounded still left behind.

The wavery line of infantry that had supported the guns was now coming up the slope before him, colors snapping in the wind, officers shouting orders. From behind him came the roar of a dozen pieces. Seconds later, plumes of dirt rose along the ridge. The advancing skirmish line of Merki cavalry slowed in its advance, then turned to move back behind the slope.

"That ought to slow the bastards," Schneid said with a cold laugh.

"Your people are fighting well," Pat replied, waving a beefy hand in salute as the rear-guard brigade came up the slope, the men cheering at his recognition.

He raised his field glasses with his free hand, scanning the fields around him. In a vast semicircle the 2nd Corps was pulling back. Ripples of smoke marked the front. The lines were holding in good order, something he would not have believed possible only the day before, when the Merki had pressed out of the woods and broken the continuous front at half a dozen points.

But the fifty miles of forest had played far worse for them than for the Rus and Roum infantry, who knew the territory and were pulling back to their base of supply. The small elements of the Merki were cut off and ruthlessly eliminated. Only this morning had the first organized body come through the trail down from Yaroslav, bursting out, a full umen of them by midday. Pat had wrestled with the temptation to launch a counterattack, but to do so would have gained at best a minor victory, compared to the potential of yet losing his two corps. It wasn't worth it.

Never thought I'd be this cautious, he thought. Must be getting old. A year ago I'd have said charge the buggers and be damned.

Not now, not anymore. Finishing the sandwich, he uncorked his canteen and washed the greasy pork down with a swill of warm water, grimacing at the taste. He raised his glasses again.

Far to the west he could barely discern the low hills to the north of Suzdal, more than forty miles away, thin traces of smoke marking what had to be the banks of the Neiper.

"Aerosteamers coming up!" someone shouted, and he turned to look to the south. A dozen small dots were moving in, high in the air.

Church bells started to ring in the town. The city was already a mass of confusion. Trains were backed up for a mile or more, waiting to take on the troops pulling out. Beyond the city, in a low valley surrounded by woods, Pat could see the high shed roofs of Jack's fleet. A red flag snapped out from the watchtower.

"Damned poor show," Schneid snapped.

"Telegraph line's most likely been cut from Suzdal, word never got through."

"Well, if they hit an engine and block the line we're all for the fire."

Pat looked back to the west and north. Dark columns were moving across the fields—the Merki spreading out, probing for the flanks, ready to move in for the kill.

Jack ran to the cabin of the *Flying Cloud*, the engine already radiating heat. They'd been up twice today already, flying along the front, marking the Merki advance and swooping back low to drop reports to the ground. It had been a chilling sight. Merki columns were snaked through the woods all they way back to the Neiper. It seemed as if the forest were alive, a dark, crawling growth undulating through it. Flashes of metal, tan leather, horses, multicolored standards, the wood trail lined with battery after battery of their guns.

On the other side of the clearing, the *Yankee Clipper* was being edged out of its hanger. The *China Sea* had already turned off to the east an hour ago, running back toward Kev where the new hangers were going up. Jack was planning to follow suit within the hour, his ground crews then moving down to the rail line to catch the last train out. The men were already nervous, but he had reassured them that it would be some hours yet before the Merki closed in.

For two weeks the flying weather had been iffy at best. On the few days they had gone up, the wind had been strong out of the north. Either the Merki ships had been unable to breast it, or they were leery of another fight. Ships had been sighted twice, but had pulled back at his approach. Jack's time thus had been spent flying reconnaissance, keeping tabs on the Merki. Now, at last, they were challenging him again.

"They're coming in fast!" the watchman shouted, pointing off to the south.

Feyodor came running out of the telegraph office and leaped in behind Jack.

The ground chief watched the carriage, motioning the crews to continue forward.

Behind Jack the boiler was hissing, the metal crackling as it expanded from the heat.

"You got lift!" the chief shouted, reaching under to pull the ground wheels free.

Jack looked over to the tower, watching the flag.

"Give us quarter-speed, Feyodor!"

The propeller started to crank over.

"Cast off all lines!"

The *Flying Cloud* started straight up, holding steady against the wind. Jack looked over to the *Yankee Clipper*, its crew still waiting for their ship to gain lift. Something wasn't quite right in her design, though he had spent hours puzzling over it. Most likely some of the seams were a bit loose, leaking out gas and hot air. It took way too long for her to get up, but there was no time to worry about that now. He edged the nose up slightly.

The Merki were coming in not five miles away, several thousand feet off the ground. Jack was tempted to turn with the wind and run out for several miles. It'd take a good fifteen minutes or more to get up to their height. But if he did so, they'd be over Vyzima unopposed. One of their bombs into the rail line could wreak havoc, perhaps even jeopardize the final pullout.

"Full power, Feyodor. We're going straight up!"

He pushed the nose up high, engine roaring. The enemy ships started to drop down, forming a line more than a mile across. He nervously fingered the rack by his side. Half a dozen revolvers were hanging from it. Behind him Feyodor had his supply of benzene bombs, along with two short-barrelled blunderbusses that one of the ground crew had fashioned. They were deadly-looking affairs. He feared they'd be as dangerous for Feyodor as for anyone downrange.

The ships continued in and the formation changed, with six of them falling astern and the other six pressing on in.

Curious. Why would they do that?

He looked back over his shoulder to see that the *Yankee Clipper* was finally clearing the ground.

"They're going to come in high of us!" Jack shouted. The bastards had the wind at their back, and, dropping down, their speed was at least twice his own.

He grimly hung on in what he felt was a high-speed dance of death. The eyes painted forward of the enemy ships looked dark and menacing.

The range was less than a mile. Vyzima was almost directly below, the activity in the rail yard a mass of confusion, as if a nest of ants had been spilled over. The closing arc of battle was clearly visible several miles away, smoke ringing the lines as the Merki closed in on the main base, the last point out from Rus. Above the howl of the engine, the constant thump of guns was clearly audible. Jack forced his attention back to the enemy ships.

He felt a moment of panic, as he raised his field glasses to study the closest ship. There was a flash of metal in front of the Merki engineer.

"God damn, they've got a cannon on her!" Jack shouted.

In a near panic he pushed the nose down, slamming the rudder hard over to the right. Three of the ships were continuing straight on to his left, obviously closing in on the *Yankee Clipper*, while the other three were lining up to pass straight over him.

There was no place to go except down. He pushed the nose forward and went into a dive, pulling open the vent.

The first ship passed overhead. He heard a faint crack but saw nothing, and started to breath easier. Unable to see the ships above, he randomly kicked the rudder back and forth as he dived, the ground rushing up. He closed the vent.

A flash of flame appeared off to his left. For a brief instant he saw what appeared to be a metal barb, like a harpoon, falling to earth, trailing a short length of rope with a flaming torch on the end.

Like hunting a sky-whale, he thought, feeling his knees go weak. Harpoon us from above—the shaft goes in, the torch gets dragged to the hole where hydrogen is leaking out.

Feyodor looked over at Jack and nodded, as the two watched the harpoon slam into the ground just north of the rail yard.

Not twenty feet forward, the bottom of the bag tore open as if ripped by an invisible hand. On the ground several hundred feet below, a plume of dust snapped up from the spray of canister striking down from above.

"Jesus Christ, the bastards are shooting at us too!"

"Well, what the hell did you expect?" Feyodor shouted. "They had to do something back."

Jack pulled the rudder back, the nose lifting, the aerosteamer skimming over the rail yard and starting to climb back into the heavens. He leaned forward and looked up. A couple of dozen holes were in the bottom of the bag, and a section of splintered spar was sticking out. It would be the same on top, and he tried to calculate just how long it would take for the gas to escape.

"It's not that bad!" Feyodor shouted. "We can stay up for some time yet!"

"It still means we'll never get her back to Hispania now."

"Just keep flying!" Feyodor cried.

Nose high, Jack saw that the three aerosteamers that had hit him were now going into a turn upwind. He looked back to his right where the other six ships waited, still a couple of miles up-wind.

He had a flash of insight.

"The other six must be loaded with bombs! They

most likely can't carry both! That's what we're going for!"

There was a rattle of cannon fire, and Jack looked down to see the four-pound anti-aerosteamer guns mounted along the train track go into action. They fired away at the enemy ships which were now running low, three of them turning, the other three pressing in toward the hangers, where the *Yankee Clipper* was struggling to get up.

He continued to climb, cursing as the ships behind him came about to start in on a stern chase, their advantage in speed now showing. But at least he had the advantage in climb, and he pressed it to the fullest. The bomb aerosteamers waiting out of range started to turn into the wind, trying to keep their distance.

The three aerosteamers behind continued to gain. They were now nearly at the same level, several hundred yards astern.

There was a snap of light from the lead one and Jack hunkered down, feeling naked as a solid shot whistled by. The race slowly continued, with the *Flying Cloud* now above her pursuers but still far out of reach of the pursued. The enemy ships were tantalizingly above him.

"I wish the hell we had a gun to reach them!" Jack shouted. He pushed on for long minutes with little hope of finally closing the gap—they were too far up-wind. Well over a thousand feet up, he looked down as they started to cross over the edge of the battle line. On the next ridge a long line of Merki skirmishers were advancing on foot, carrying muskets. It was the last thing they needed.

"I'm bringing her around, Feyodor. We'll hit those bastards chasing us!"

As he spoke another shot kicked off from the second ship, and he felt a shudder as the ball crashed into the stern of the *Flying Cloud*. It emerged an instant later from the front, fragments of the wood frame and fabric punching out with it.

"Hydrogen could be leaking from the front and rear bags into the heat chamber!" Feyodor cried. "One spark and we'll burn!"

"Get your bombs ready!"

Jack pushed the rudder to the right, swinging the ship around through the eye of the wind. He looked over his shoulder. The enemy ships were starting to turn as well to avoid the ground fire from the Rus, but his maneuver had caught them. The range closed rapidly.

"Feyodor, get ready!"

Feyodor nervously looked up through the heat-exhaust hole as he pulled out a jar of benzene.

"Now!"

Feyodor lit the taper and dropped it onto the nose of the enemy ship a hundred feet below. The jar hit the air bag and rolled slowly down the side, tumbling off and plummeting to the ground.

"God damn it, there's got to be a better way!" Jack screamed. In frustration he unholstered one of the revolvers and pumped six rounds straight into the enemy ship.

Feyodor aimed the blunderbuss down and fired into the ship, peppering it with dozens of holes.

He pulled out two more jars and lit them. Leaning far over, he hurled them down. One bounced off as if it hit a loose blanket. The second one cracked open but the fuse sputtered out, and the ship was astern.

Jack screamed every imprecation he could imagine, as the enemy ship moved forward while they continued to drift astern.

"Half-power!"

He started to turn, the second ship drifting by

fifty yards to his right and low, the Merki under-neath unable to shoot up. The third ship was nearly up to his level, nose-high. The two Merki in the cabin were working to reload their small cannon.

They were back over Vyzima, drifting north with the wind. The hangers were off to his right. A mile away the *Yankee Clipper* and the three enemy ships were running in a circle, like lumbering giants unable to strike each other.

Jack was mad with frustration.

The enemy ship drifted by to his left, the Merki abandoning their cannon. One of them lifted up a bow and sent arrow after arrow toward him. He pulled out another revolver and blazed away, while Feyodor, cursing foully, pointed the second blunder-buss and let fly, without results.

"Full power, Feyodor! Pour it on!"

Jack pointed the nose up again, sensing that they were slowly starting to lose a little lift, then pushed over to an easterly course, running straight toward the melee with the *Yankee Clipper*. The enemy ships were still turning behind him.

He looked back to the south. The enemy bomb-ships were still waiting out of range. There was no way he could catch them with the wind in their favor, so he pressed in to the east. If the enemy damaged the hangers now, there'd be no possible hope of landing and getting repaired in time to escape to Kev.

One of the Merki ships engaged with *Yankee Clip-per* swung in alongside the ship, firing its light can-non straight in at the cabin. Jack cursed bitterly as he saw the engineer slump forward in his chair, the ship continue blindly on. The assistant engineer unstrapped himself from his rear chair and, climb-ing over to grab the controls, pushed the aero-steamer straight east.

A second Merki ship was now above *Yankee Clipper*, moving to drop down and fire from astern.

"You better hang on, Feyodor."

"What the hell are you going to do?"

"Ram the son of a bitch!"

Jack grabbed hold of the controls and eased out a little hot air, then dropped the nose slightly. The enemy ship, intent on its prey, continued to turn in, its tail swinging around.

Jack nosed over, their speed increasing.

"You're mad!" Feyodor cried, wide-eyed and looking over Jack's shoulder.

"Shut up and grab hold!"

He pointed the nose straight in at the enemy's tail. The range closed to fifty yards and then twenty, the enemy ship moving slowly to line up a shot.

The nose of the *Flying Cloud* slammed into the rear of the Merki ship, and the gas bag undulated and quivered. Jack felt the forward spars of his own ship cracking as he pulled up at the last second and drove a glancing blow in, raking across the top of the enemy ship. The shattered forward spar sliced into the enemy vessel.

He pushed the nose hard up, shouting with glee as he looked down on the jagged hole in the enemy vessel.

"Bomb the bastard now!

"We'll burn!"

"Bomb it!"

Feyodor pulled out another five-gallon jar, stuck the wick into the furnace, and quickly pulled the flaming taper back out. They passed above the jagged tear, not thirty feet below.

"Drop it!" Jack shouted.

The jar tumbled down, striking near the hole. The jar didn't break, and the container seemed to balance atop the enemy aerosteamer, the wick still flickering brightly. A nearly invisible fringe of blue flame ignited around the hole, spreading outward. The jar tumbled into the flaming gap and disappeared, blue flame surging up. Within seconds it seemed as if the entire top of the ship had been ripped open by a blue razor of fire.

The *Flying Cloud* surged up on the column of heat, shreds of burning fabric flaring up around them.

The enemy ship collapsed, and started its death-plummet.

"Get us down!" Feyodor screamed.

Jack looked back to the tail. A section of flaming silk, a dozen feet across, was pressed up against his ship, burning fiercely.

Jack yanked the exhaust vent open even as he turned to run with the wind.

It was like a nightmare: the flaming silk from the enemy ship pressed up against his own vessel, burning, with him watching it and unable to do anything.

The vent was full open, and, nose-down, he went into a dive. Off to his right he saw the Merki ship impact in a fireball of flame, and he remembered the body tumbling out of the last ship he had destroyed.

"I think she's catching!" Feyodor screamed.

Jack looked back over his shoulder. A thin section of fabric was fraying back, revealing a wooden spar underneath.

"Hydrogen rises! If it was on top, we'd be gone already!" Jack shouted, even as he watched the flames lick out, fringed in blue. Chuck had told him that you could strike a match inside a ship and it wouldn't burn, because it needed to have air mixed in. But that was small consolation now, for some of the gas had to be leaking out. The fabric continued to burn.

In a flash, the flame started to race up the side.

He looked down. It was still a long way. Behind

him the enemy ships were pressing in, while off to his right the *Yankee Clipper* was running east, getting out of the fight and heading toward Kev. At least he had saved that ship.

What the hell am I doing? he wondered. It's *my* ass that's about to get burned, the devil with the other ship! I'm going to burn!

He started to scream, even as he guided the *Flying Cloud* into a steeper and yet steeper dive. Feyodor was openly calling on the Saints, reciting his sins and begging for forgiveness.

"What the hell do you mean, you slept with Svetlana?" Jack suddenly shouted. "I thought she wanted *me*!"

"I'm sorry!" Feyodor wailed. "Oh Kesus, it's burning."

"You'll burn, god damn it!" Jack cried. He felt a shudder run through the vessel as the lift dropped away and the ground came up faster. The flame was racing toward the tail and over the top of the ship, but the forward bag was still intact. The ground was racing up, trees scattered through an upland pasture rising up like spears to impale the dying beast.

Jack pushed the rudder hard up. For a brief second he thought they would drive straight in, but then the controls responded and the nose began to rise.

But they were coming down fast, far too fast, as he raised the nose higher and yet higher.

The shadow of the ship moved rapidly across the ground. Yet more trees were just ahead.

Jack felt heat licking around him, heard Feyodor screaming.

He pulled back hard, and the ground leaped up to meet him.

*   *   *

Pat stood on the hill, cursing silently as the fireball of flame rose up from the distant woods.

"It was one of ours," somebody whispered.

Pat nodded.

"At least he took a bastard with him," another sighed.

"They can afford it, we can't."

The other six aerosteamers now started in, swooping down out of the sky, engines humming. Along the open stretch of rail back in the town, thousands of troops raised their weapons, volley fire slashing out. The first bombs dropped away, and seconds later explosions rippled through the station area and marched on into the city.

A second ship and a third dropped in. The third lined up slightly south of the track and came in low, only several hundred feet off the ground.

Up forward, a locomotive exploded up into the air, a direct hit. Pat groaned and looked away.

The ship that hit it continued on, rising up lazily and drifting off to the north. It rose slowly, turned through a circle, then turned yet again.

"Must have killed the crew!" someone shouted.

The rest of the ships swooped, staying far higher, their bombs far wide of their targets.

The enemy ships made their slow, ponderous turns, then headed off to the east. Far off in the distance the lone Rus ship struggled to climb, still pursued by its tormentors, while the Merki vessel with the dead crew slowly continued to turn, drifting farther and farther away with the wind.

"A hell of a mess, gentlemen," Pat snarled. "We'll be lucky to get out of here now."

"What do you mean, the country is empty?" Jubadi snarled.

On either side of him columns were racing down

the road, heading south at a gallop. He looked back to the river. Two of the Yankee iron ships were anchored just below the crossing, and they were spraying the river with shot, forcing the umens to go farther upstream. Even then they had to time their crossing to get between the shots of the heavy enemy pieces.

A message dropped from one of the cloud-flyers heading to the spot where the Yankee army was boarding their iron-riders had revealed the news. Suzdal was empty, the countryside around it empty. They were gone. Jubadi had not believed it. Now the messenger had come with confirmed word.

He looked down the river road, where a column of warriors was riding fast. A scythe of canister swept out from a ship anchored farther down the river, dropping dozens. The warriors pushed through the tangle and galloped on.

"Find some trails further back from the road!" Jubadi shouted. "We can't advance to Suzdal and be shot at like this!"

"There are no other trails," Muzta announced quietly.

Jubadi turned to look at him angrily.

"Then by the ancestors, we'll cut a damned trail! Bring up the Cartha prisoners, get a umen to work on it. We're moving too slow."

"What will the umen cut with?" Muzta said, a trace of bemusement in his voice.

"With their swords, if need be!" Jubadi snarled.

He looked back at Tamuka and Hulagar.

"What kind of people are these?" he roared. "They know they're beaten. We offered them terms, a return to the old ways. Isn't that enough? Now they run, all of them, leaving their land. I thought land was life to these cattle."

"Obviously not," Tamuka said quietly.

"As I already learned," Muzta said.

"Yet we've beaten them in every battle. I thought we'd take Suzdal and it would be over."

"Why?" Vuka snapped, dropping his usual veil of disdain and looking over at Tamuka.

"They want the death of all of us and nothing less," Tamuka said sharply.

Jubadi looked at him with cold rage, and then back at the messenger.

"You saw the city?"

"I entered it. It is empty, my Qarth. The last of their cannon crews were pulling out and moving south, down toward the sea."

"Empty," Jubadi hissed.

He had thought of the moment of triumph, his host arrayed, charging in through the breach for the kill. Or, overawed, the enemy would show their obeisance and surrender, to their own humiliation and that of Muzta. Now neither scene was likely to occur.

He looked back up the road. Hundreds of his best were dead all along it, riddled by the iron ships that had harassed them all day as they rode south.

"Damn them all!" Jubadi roared. He kicked his horse around, lashing it into a gallop. He pushed through his staff and set off for the south.

The pass was cleared and he rode on, oblivious to the iron ships, which ignored him in his ride. They were aiming at the heavy clusters of troops further back.

"Come on, the hell with the guns, run for it!" Pat shouted.

The city of Vyzima was in flames behind him, illuminating the nightmarish scene.

The long line of trains was finally ready to move, the wreckage cleared, the track repaired farther up the line where several Merki had been dropped off from an aerosteamer in a vain attempt to cut the rail.

Behind him twenty guns were drawn up in a arc across the tracks, Merki cavalry moving in on all sides. A mile farther out a column was racing parallel to the line.

The gunners fired all their pieces at once and the crews turned, running frantically.

Pat stood atop the armored car positioned at the rear of the last train. The gunners ran past him, the guns beneath him firing their sprays of canister over the retreating men.

Shots were echoing out from all sides, bullets hissing past, arrows streaking in.

"Go, go, go!" Pat screamed, running down the length of the car, waving a lantern.

The engine forward cut loose with a high shriek. As he leaped from the last armored car to the next one, the train lurched forward so that he almost lost his footing. He continued to run down the length of the car. Gaining the far side he leaped down to the flatcar, crowded with men, who were reaching over the side to pull up the last of the fleeing gunners.

"Out there!" somebody shouted.

Pat looked up to see two men coming out of the lengthening shadows, one dragging the other.

"Jack, come on!"

Petracci picked up his pace, limping hard, and Feyodor moved along beside him. Both were struggling to hold the other up.

Pat looked up forward, but there was no way to signal the train to stop.

"Let's go!" he shouted, leaping down from the train, stumbling, and getting up to run.

"God damn it, general, we can't lose you too!" somebody shouted.

"Then help me, you bloody fools!"

Several more men leaped off, running down the grading. They grabbed hold of Feyodor, while Pat came in and nearly lifted the diminutive engineer right off the ground. He ran hard up the embankment, slipping on the loose ballasts.

The train was slowly picking up speed.

"Run, damn it, run!" It was like a chant, shouted by the hundreds who were leaning out of the boxcars and standing on the flatcars to watch the drama, oblivious to the Merki cavalry who were starting to range in from the other side.

Pat felt his breath coming short, his stomach knotting from the effort. Hands reached out and grabbed Jack, pulling him up. More hands grabbed Pat, lifting him. His heavy body dragged dangerously close to the wheels, but then he was back up on the flatcar, gasping for breath.

"I told you we shouldn't throw the firebomb," Feyodor gasped, looking over angrily at Jack.

"Well, I should have left you out there!" he roared back. "You were doing Svetlana behind my back!"

"She wanted it!" Feyodor snarled. "And I'll be damned to fly with you again—you almost killed me with that damned ramming."

Pat started to laugh between his gasps for breath.

"Anybody got a drink?" Jack asked, too weary to argue anymore.

Half a dozen men pressed forward, offering canteens of vodka.

Jack smiled and looked around at his admirers, word already racing through the train that the aerosteamer engineers were on board.

"A hell of a show," Pat said, coming to squat by Jack and take the canteen. He belted back a drink.

"Thanks for saving me. Thought we'd never make it."

"Was worth it," Pat replied.

Jack offered the canteen to Feyodor, who, though still grimacing, nodded his thanks and patted Jack on the shoulder.

"Thanks for pulling me out of the wreck," he sighed.

"Couldn't leave you behind—it'd look bad," Jack replied, gingerly taking the canteen back and cupping it between blistered hands.

"Emil will get you two patched up, and you'll be back up in no time," Pat said, the men around him nodding and grinning.

Jack looked around at his admirers, and swallowed hard. Back up there? he thought. Not on your life, not for anything. He lay back on the rumbling car and tried to block out the terror of falling, falling in the flames of Hell. Try as he might, the shaking would not go away.

Pat touched him lightly on the shoulder and stood back up to look off to the west.

They'd gotten out, just barely. The last train out of Vyzima, and he felt sick at the thought of it. The bastards had taken all the country for barely nothing—a fraction of the casualties suffered by the Tugars—and over fifteen thousand of their own army dead, missing, or wounded.

The troops on board were talking excitedly about their escape, breathing easy again after the last tense hours of holding till the line had been cleared. Pat knew that once the excitement of the escape had worn off, the colder reality would settle in.

They were now an entire race in exile.

As the train moved through a gentle curve, Pat looked forward. All the way to the horizon, moving off into the evening, was train after train, showering sparks. Nearly thirty thousand men riding east, escaping at least temporarily the death closing in around them. The men around him, lightened by Jack's presence, were behaving almost as if they had somehow pulled off a victory.

If this is victory, Pat thought quietly, looking back to the west, I sure as hell would hate to see defeat.

Jubadi Qar Qarth reined in his mount, his heart pounding with superstitious dread.

The goal was before him. The home of the Yankees, the center of their power, all that threatened his people and all the races of the Everlasting Ride. It was before him. But they had left something else. How had they known?

A rider came galloping out of the city, the gold pennant of a Qar Qarth rider fluttering from a pole behind his back. Those on the wooden footbridge over the Vina cleared the way as he lashed his mount on.

He pressed up the slope, the silver bells tied to his saddle ringing out a warning, the long column of the advance guard parting.

He reined in hard and bowed low in the saddle, the dirt-encrusted pennant dipping down over his head.

"Empty, my Qar Qarth. Entirely empty, as first reported."

Jubadi looked away.

They were gone.

How could cattle do this? It was foreordained that cattle were to be *qufa ga huth*, those in one place—only the Chosen were to ride forever. Had an entire land of them become like the accursed wanderers?

"Hulagar!"

"My Qarth."

The mud-spattered shield-bearer drew up beside him.

"It's empty! They're gone, they're truly gone!"

Hulagar nodded without comment.

He paused for a moment, looking off to his left at the thick trees pressing down on the road. Something prickled his senses. Some vague foreboding, the *tu* sight whispering.

Look, look outward, do it now.

Hulagar looked back at the huge banner fluttering before the bridge, and his thoughts focused on it instead.

Before the city of Suzdal, set between two poles, floated the mourning banner, the black flag with the red eye of Bugghaal, the banner flown only when a Qar Qarth was dead.

"How did they know?" Jubadi whispered, trying not to show his fear. All around him were shouts of alarm, as the warriors came out of the pass and saw the banner for the first time.

Jubadi knew he must not show fear, yet his heart was pounding in his throat.

"How did they know?"

"Pets know these things," Hulagar whispered, suspicions boiling over. Again there was that vague sense, and he looked back toward the woods.

"And they are gone," Jubadi whispered.

What now? He had thought this would be the climax, that it would be decided here. He had thought that at this moment he would ride into the buildings in which their miracles had been made and claim them for his own.

"The factory buildings?"

"Empty of everything," the messenger said, his voice trembling. "Everything is gone—their machines, the machines that made machines—everything gone except for the empty buildings."

"They're gone, aren't they?"

Jubadi looked over his shoulder and saw Tamuka edging up, Vuka beside him.

Somehow the sight of Tamuka filled him with a cold rage. He struggled to control it. The shield-bearer had been right, his *tu* had told him. Jubadi felt a trembling inside. If Tamuka said the wrong thing now, his head would be in the mud.

"I am sorry, my Qar Qarth," Tamuka said, no trace of emotion in his voice.

"The cowardly bastards!" Vuka snarled. "To abandon their yurts without a fight! They are beneath contempt."

"Remember you are fighting cattle," Tamuka replied.

Muzta, followed by his son and half a dozen staff, came up to join the group.

He reined in and looked at the high hills of the pass rising up to his left.

"They fought hard for this position—it's where we almost cornered them. A good fighting withdraw on Keane's part."

"It sounds as if you almost admire this cattle!" Vuka snapped.

"In a way I do," Muzta replied. "He beat me, and now it appears as if he's escaped you."

"Not for long!" Vuka roared, looking back at Muzta.

There was a cold moment of tension between the two.

"You'd like to kill me, wouldn't you?" Muzta said quietly.

"Do not taunt me now, Tugar," Vuka said coldly.

"And if I do?"

Hulagar edged his mount between the two.

"The enemy is over there!" Hulagar snapped, pointing toward the east.

"But of course," Muzta replied with a smile.

Throughout the exchange Jubadi had sat in silence, looking at the banner floating lazily between the two poles, fluttering in the early evening breeze. He took off his lacquered helmet for a moment to wipe his brow.

How could they possibly know? He thanked his ancestors that Sarg was not here. The old shaman most likely would have fallen to the ground in convulsions, a bad thing for morale.

He realized that the group around him was silent, waiting.

"They cannot run forever," Jubadi finally announced. "They are not like the wanderers. Their machines burden them down, they are tied to their roads of iron."

He looked over at Muzta.

"Where did they run to?"

Muzta leaned over to one of his chant-singers, who marked the Path of the Everlasting Ride and spoke in whispered tones. Then he looked back at Muzta.

"The land is flat, fertile, the soil black from here for thirty days' march by yurt. The land between is narrow, only ten yurt marches across between the forest and the sea. The land of the Rus ends in a ridge of hills, drawn as if in a line, moving from the forest to the sea. Two yurt marches is the distance there."

"Thirty days, six for an umen," Hulagar said.

"If they've stripped everything," Tamuka ventured, "four or five umens might advance, but all of them . . . ? And what of the Horde itself, what will they eat?"

"Not another word!" Jubadi snapped, looking back at Tamuka, the threat in his voice all too evident.

Hulagar moved away from his Qarth and drew up alongside of Tamuka.

"If you value your life at this moment," he whispered, "turn away."

Tamuka looked over coldly at Jubadi and, bowing, he backed up his mount and moved to the side of the road, Hulagar following.

"I tried to warn him," Tamuka hissed when they were no longer in hearing of the Qar Qarth.

"You are a shield-bearer, not a Qarth or a war advisor," Hulagar retorted, grabbing Tamuka by the shoulder. "Your responsibility is to be the *tu* for Vuka. You overstepped yourself when you spoke before the Qarths and he suffered you to speak, for at that moment it was better coming from you than from him. But by all the ancestors, Tamuka, he is still my Qar Qarth, and yours. You have lost sight of your place."

"It is a new world," Tamuka replied. "He does not see that. Down deep he is still too confident, he still feels that this is no great threat. I know better."

"Would you be Qar Qarth?" Hulagar asked sarcastically.

"Yes!" Tamuka hissed.

Hulagar drew back in horror.

"I did not hear those words," Hulagar whispered. "By all rights I should strike you down."

Tamuka looked at him defiantly.

"He knows that the heir murdered his own brother. He does not see the hidden threat of these cattle. He is not ruling, Hulagar, and I say that under the protection of my office."

"You would use that to hide behind," Hulagar retorted. "He is my Qar Qarth and my friend, and he has done well."

"That is your problem, Hulagar Shield-Bearer, you have allowed your charge to become your friend."

Hulagar said nothing, for there was no sense in denying what was true.

"Yet still he rules well."

Tamuka said nothing.

Hulagar looked back over his shoulder toward Jubadi, who was waiting.

"You shall be removed as shield-bearer to the Zan Qarth," he said coldly.

Tamuka chuckled softly.

"And who shall ride by Vuka to protect him from himself?"

"There is always another."

Tamuka cursed inwardly at his impetuousness. So it was finished. Without comment he fell in behind Vuka, who looked over at him. Though he had not heard the confrontation between the two shield-bearers, he could sense that Tamuka had lost something in it, and he smiled at his discomfort.

"We throw ten umens forward at once. The rest will follow within three days," Jubadi said. "We will still have our supper of Rus flesh. The cloud-flyers will sail eastward, to find out where they hide and mark them for our advance. We will leave the Cartha cattle here, to scour the fields, to work the land behind us and bring forth something by the time our yurts come up. They have run from us, but we will strike them yet."

He looked back at the banner still fluttering in the breeze. Again he was filled with foreboding, and looked over to Hulagar as if seeking advice.

"The new Qar Qarth is the one who burns the banner of mourning," Hulagar whispered.

Jubadi spared a quick look at Vuka, who gazed upon the banner with a curious mix of fear and desire, as if it already marked his ascension to power.

"I must do it myself," Jubadi announced.

Hulagar nodded in agreement.

Jubadi drew a deep breath and spurred his mount to a slow canter.

He gazed off to his left. As the last of the trees marking the edge of the pass dropped away, Hulagar looked as well, again feeling that vague sense. Uneasy, he shifted his bronze shield.

Júbadi continued down the gentle slope to where the river flowed, several hundred yards away. A Yankee ironclad, masked by the low bluffs, was barely visible, marked by the single plume of smoke and the top of a mast bearing the banner of Rus.

"Let *them* see us go into their city," Jubadi sniffed, and the staff chuckled at his words.

The silent ones ranged out around him, forming a circle, watching intently, nothing escaping their notice. Alongside the road several horses laid dead, their riders stretched out beside them, capes over their mangled forms.

"To kill by placing exploding shells in the road— it is cowardly," Jubadi growled.

"It kills nevertheless," Muzta replied.

Muzta looked past him, toward the hills east of town, the barrows golden in the late afternoon sun.

"That is where my glory rests," Muzta said quietly.

Jubadi nodded, saying nothing.

He leaned back in his saddle tired and disappointed, and yet the moment had a pleasure to it. They were across the river and into the heart of the Rus. Losses were not too bad, considering what they had faced. The Yankees had suffered two defeats in less than a double moon, and their morale surely must be dropping away.

He could feel that his mount was tiring—it had been a long ride from the ford. He hadn't bothered to name this horse. It was a vanity, given how quickly they died. Cattle were cattle, but a horse was the companion of life, the saying went. If he had allowed himself to feel for all the mounts he had lost, his heart would have emptied long ago.

He looked over at Hulagar, who rode as always at his right side, shield on his arm. Jubadi remembered how, when he had thought himself alone, his shield-bearer-to-be had wept over the killing of his own first horse. He smiled.

"A warm day, is it not?" Jubadi said, looking up toward the deep blue sky.

"I thought the rains would never end," Hulagar replied.

"The weather had to change," Jubadi said absently.

Coming down the slope, he looked off to his left. Through the turn of the river valley he saw the vast buildings of the Yankees several miles upstream. Even from this distance they looked large. They filled him with an uneasiness. He had hoped to capture them with their mysteries inside. Now they were hollow shells, like corpses that had rotted on the inside, the useless skin and bones all that was left.

The iron-road bridge was still intact. It was a disturbing sight as well. How it had been made was beyond his understanding. He realized that all of it was beyond his understanding. The iron road, the steam-breathers that rode them, the guns, the cloud-flyers, the ships of iron that floated. All of it a mystery.

He looked back for a moment at Tamuka, who rode behind him and to the left of Vuka, shield up as well.

Was the young shield-bearer right, after all? Should all the cattle of this entire world now be slain?

How would that change us? he wondered. Who would be our food? Who would make all the other food we devour with such relish? Who would fashion our bows, our saddles, our yurts, the iron hooves for our horses, the armor we wear, the arrows that fly, the adornments that give us delight?

Jubadi looked up toward the city. His warriors were already sweeping the walls. From high windows he could see his warriors in the buildings. Atop the stone building of cattle worship the standard of the Merki was already flying, warriors beside it.

There was no one in the entire city. A strange moment this. He had expected either to enter it in flames, or to ride in as he had all the other cattle cities of the last two and a half circlings—the beasts lying on the ground, faces pressed to the dirt in obeisance. Never had he seen this.

He looked over at Hulagar.

"Tomorrow, first light, I want us to move hard. We must not give them time to regroup. They are on the edge of being beaten, and they know it, I know it. We can run them down. It is impossible for their steam machines to take every last cattle all the way to Roum in the little time they have had. They must have stopped only partway, at those hills Muzta spoke of. There we will finish them."

Hulagar nodded an agreement.

"They must not be given a moment's time. If we move swiftly enough, panic will strike them, perhaps then they will surrender. If not, we will drive them, and then surely the Roum will give up as well."

He looked back at his cavalcade.

"This is but a temporary setback. The foxes have run, but their legs are short, while ours are long. We will have them in our circle before half a moon is past."

The group nodded, the beginnings of smiles lighting their worried features.

The gentle slope past, he rode out onto the river plain, toward the wooden bridge over the Vina. On the low banks of the opposite side were the outer works of the city. He rode onto the bridge, the hooves of his horse sounding hollow on the boards. Hulagar looked nervously over toward the Neiper River. Strange, there was no Yankee iron-ship in sight. This would have been an ideal place for them to have a ship ready with canister, to sweep any who crossed.

Directly ahead were the outer bastions. Halfway up the side the banner fluttered darkly. Hulagar looked up at it nervously. Jubadi sat for a long moment, then swung down from his mount.

"A torch," he said quietly.

"A moment, my Qarth," Hulagar interjected. With a motion of his hand the silent ones went up the slope, stamping the ground as they moved forward in a line.

The line had reached a spot just below the banner when there was a sharp snap of light, a thunderclap explosion. Hulagar leaped in front of Jubadi, who recoiled, crouching down.

The smoke cleared. Though they could not speak, still they could scream. The torn remains of a silent one lay to one side. Another was down, holding the stump of his leg, a high keening shriek escaping his lips.

One of his companions knelt down beside him and, waving his hands, silently spoke. The wounded one, shaking in agony, raised his hands and moved them in reply. The companion stood back up and drew his scimitar. There was a flash of steel, and the keening stopped.

Hulagar exhaled slowly and looked over at Jubadi, who had watched the scene without emotion.

"They knew this would draw you," Hulagar said. "Somehow they knew. It was a trap."

Jubadi looked over at him.

"Well, now it is sprung, let's burn the damn thing. I'm tired and hungry. Bring up a cattle. We'll eat well tonight, and forget about this."

A silent one came up bearing a torch.

Hulagar could see the barely suppressed fear in Jubadi's eyes as he looked back up at the black banner.

"How did they know about this?" Jubadi whispered.

He started up the slope, Hulagar following behind him.

He looked around closely. The wall was lined with his warriors. The river was empty. How could they have known?

Jubadi reached the banner.

"This is but the sacrilege of cattle!" he shouted, his voice carrying across the field and reaching the thousands of warriors who had paused as they spread out across the plains. "I, Jubadi, take the yurts of the cattle as my own. I, Jubadi, still live as Qar Qarth, and spit on the roasted bones of our enemy the cattle."

He touched the torch to the bottom of the banner, holding it there for long seconds until it had started to flare into flame. He stepped back.

Hulagar looked back out across the field.

How?

The insight came of a sudden: the cattle Yuri.

His gaze shot over to Tamuka, who was watching the ceremony, a thin smile lighting his features.

*   *   *

Yuri pushed the gray piece of canvas aside and peered out. Several Merki had ridden right over him, the first wave spreading out. One of their horses had fallen as it clambered over the slippery boulders, the rider cursing so hard that he had almost laughed at the Merki's discomfort. They had ridden on, leaving him alone and never seeing his concealed position.

Yes, it was now.

He crawled up out of the small cave dug in between the boulders and barely peered up over the edge, looking out between the trees. He tried to suppress the shivering, not sure if it was from lying hidden in the damp cave all day or from fear.

He raised the telescope and extended it to full length, pushing it out through the canvas curtain to scan the column riding down the road. He had no trouble in spotting him. The broad shoulders, that manner of riding. It was not a double, something he had been known to use in battle. No, it was definitely him.

That knowledge alone had been the key to the argument with Keane. He alone could easily spot Jubadi. There were Cartha who had seen him before, but usually only for a brief moment. Only one person could do this. He had ridden behind him for twenty years, pet to his son's shield-bearer. He alone could pick out Jubadi no matter where he was, whether in full ceremonial armor and with standards about him, or as he was now, in battle armor and as undistinguished as his silent ones.

There was Hulagar, and Yuri felt a twinge of regret. The shield-bearer paused to turn his mount and look over his shoulder.

Was the *tu* calling? Yuri froze, his breath coming shallow. He shifted the telescope away so as not to be looking straight at him, fearing that the inner spirit was calling the warning.

He could almost sense the probing, the looking outward. He had seen far too many examples of the sensing not to believe in its power. He could feel the hair at the back of his neck prickling.

He waited.

Hulagar turned his mount and continued on, crossing the bridge behind Jubadi Qar Qarth.

Moving slowly, Yuri reached down and brought up the long leather case. He untied the drawstring and brought it out, the long brass tube barely visible in the darkness of the narrow dank cave. The tiny hovel was filled with the scent of oil, metal, and polished wood.

He calmed his breathing. There was still a little time.

The same place for five heartbeats, Andrew had told him.

He peeked out from the curtain once again. The sky was a dark blue, going into early evening.

It would be warm farther south. The horde yurts already going into their clan circles. The sun-watchers preparing to call out the songs of evening prayer.

"Vu Bac Nov domicak gloriang, nobis cu [Hear, ancestors, ride now the night sky]."

He whispered the words, smiling.

Keane was right. He had become them far more than he was now human, cattle. He had taken pride in his master, shield-bearer to Zan Qarth. And yes, he had eaten of their meals.

And he had grown to like it.

Andrew had sensed that. That is why Andrew had never allowed him to hold his child.

His child. My children.

There was my child, Olga. Her mother. He

smiled. A girl of the Chin, soft, delicate, oval-faced, almost a child herself.

Beaten to death for spilling fermented milk on her mistress, first wife of Jubadi, and then cut up for the pits. Olga, my only child. It was better that I smothered you with my own hands than for you to be thrown into the pits.

"How long?" he whispered.

After Barkth Nom, at the place where the three rivers join into the salted sea. Fourteen seasons.

Season after season he had nursed his memory, his hatred, his self-loathing for doing nothing. For squatting over the bones that were tossed out of the yurt for the pets.

Endless seasons of the ride—at least in that there had been life. He had seen the whole world. Mountains that pierced the heavens, seas so thick with salt that one bobbed upon their surface. He had seen the twisting storms and the heavens alight with fire, and had laughed inwardly while his masters cowered. He had seen battles, standing atop a high hill— the beauty of the umens moving through a high sea of grass, their blocks of ten thousand moving as if guided by a single hand, filling the heavens with their thunder.

He had seen twenty races of cattle—the Chin of his beloved, the dark Ubi, the Toltec, the Constan, yet more Rus upon the far side of the world. He had seen their cities gleaming, their people bowing. He had heard their lamentations, and the horror of it all had frozen his soul so that he had become as unfeeling as the earth.

At least he thought he had.

And then there was Sophi. A pet taken from Constan.

Where was she?

Most likely with the yurt of Hulagar even now,

and with her, yet another child. There was a warming of his heart, which he had thought beyond caring.

So *that* had been the promise of Tamuka. Kill Keane and they would go free, fail and they go to the feast—even the child, who would witness the death of her mother first.

"Don't think about it," he whispered to himself.

It would have been so easy, he realized, and he looked down at the ring on his finger. He pushed against the side of it with his thumbnail, striking the tiny stub. The poisoned needle snicked out, invisible in the dark.

Why not?

Because I am a coward? he wondered. He shook his head. Fear had been burned out of him long ago—a pet finally lost all fear in a world without hope. A free man feared death because he would lose the pleasure of life, but for a slave death was a release.

Why not?

The night he had first met him he was ready. Was it the brief sight of the child?

It was the simple humanity of it, brought by Keane. The simple decent humanity of a family living without fear, a humanity that could be annihilated for the innocent sin of spilling a cup of milk.

They thought he had forgotten.

For after all, he was only a cattle, a soulless cattle.

Now they would know. He could only pray that Sophi would in the end understand, that the child at least would never know the horror of living in a world ruled by the Merki. Because if he had killed Keane, they would truly have won.

So Keane had turned him back upon them. Yuri knew he was being used, that Keane did not care what happened to him now, only that he succeeded.

He smiled sadly, allowing the emotion of self-pity to form for the first time in years.

He peeked back out, watching the silent ones moving up the slope. There was a flash of light. Four heartbeats, five . . . The *boom* washed past him.

Keane had said it was just over one thousand yards away. The measure was meaningless to him.

Yuri saw him again, starting up the slope.

He reached down and brought the Whitworth sniper rifle up. He pulled the tampon out of the muzzle, then looked carefully at the six-sided bore to make sure no fragment of wood or speck of dirt was in the bore.

He had been practicing with this terrible device daily, ever since Keane had first suggested that this was the only way to save all of them. Andrew had considered numerous other plans. Traps in the city, a sniper in town, exploding shells hidden away, fire from the iron ships. Yuri had laughed at all the suggestions, pointing out the methods of the Merki. It was only when Keane had shown him the Whitworth that he had known that here was the means.

With the first hundred practice shots, he had slowly worked his distance further back. The second hundred, he had sharpened his skill. The third hundred, he had polished his craft, shooting on a hidden range set up near the mines above Fort Lincoln, where the slope of the ground matched that where he now was.

He watched the small pennant fluttering atop the poles that held the banner aloft. The wind was coming out of the west, slightly gusty.

If the wind had been too hard, if it had rained, if Jubadi had come this way too late in the day, if the riders who had passed by had looked just a bit more closely . . . There were so many "ifs" that had played out into his hands.

He brought the heavy Whitworth up, checking the percussion cap on the nipple. He slid the gun forward and rested it in the groove carved into the rock. The weapon fit into the hard, stone trough, chiseled to match it.

He moved his shoulder into the curved stock that had been recarved to fit him perfectly. He pressed his eye up to the long brass scope mounted down the length of the barrel.

He moved the weapon slightly to the left, then pulled a thin sliver of lead out from a pouch. He tilted the weapon up slightly, put the lead under the barrel, and then looked through the scope again.

Just a bit low. With almost imperceptible pressure he raised the rear of the weapon up not much more than a fraction of an inch.

The cross hairs were set for this range and this range only. The gun was tuned for this one shot and no other.

With his right thumb, he clicked the hammer back.

Jubadi was moving up the slope. Yuri moved the gun ever so slightly, tracking him.

Five heartbeats in one place, that's how long it would take the bullet to travel to its target.

The smoke from the torch in Jubadi's hand was curling from right to left.

Difficult.

The sights were set for the range—all he had to do was place them on the mark. The wind. The smoke shifted, curling straight up.

Hold it there.

Jubadi leaned forward, running the torch along the bottom of the banner.

It caught.

The Qar Qarth of the Merki Horde stepped back, dropping the torch.

Yuri touched his finger against the first trigger and pulled. He felt the tumbler click. It was now on a hair setting, a mere touch to the second trigger would finish it.

Jubadi stood still, watching the banner flare up.

Yuri took a final breath in, let half of it out.

The smoke curled slightly to the left.

He moved the cross hairs just to the right, almost onto Jubadi's arm.

He brushed the second trigger with his finger.

The hammer slammed down with a click.

"Sir, the line up ahead is clear. The Merki are across the northern rail line and through Vyzima. They'll be across our tracks in a couple of hours, maybe sooner. Why are we waiting?"

Andrew looked down at the telegrapher, who stood anxiously by the side of the train.

"In a moment," he whispered, and turned to look back to the west.

Hulagar turned. There was something. He knew it. He looked over at Tamuka, who was gazing straight at him, an uneasy look in his eyes.

Hulagar brought his shield around, moving up toward Jubadi. Ritual be damned.

Yuri hissed out a curse, cold sweat beading on his forehead.

He yanked the hammer back. The unexploded percussion cap was wedged on the nipple. He pushed against it with his fingernail, struggling to free it. His fingernail split. He ignored the pain. With an audible pop the cap flipped off.

He fumbled with the cap box at his waist, spilling most of them out. Taking hold of a fresh small copper cap he slipped it onto the nipple, then cocked the hammer full back.

He leaned back down and pressed his eye to the sight, anxiously moving the Whitworth back and forth.

There.

Calm, he cautioned himself. There's only this one chance.

Don't think of anything else, just this. Not of her, not of the smothered baby limp in your arms, not of Sophi, not of the pits, the blood on your own hands. Nothing, think of nothing but this. Think of twenty years of waiting for redemption. Redemption now, with the flick of a finger.

He drew in his breath, his finger touching the first trigger.

He saw Hulagar moving toward his target, Tamuka moving behind him. Tamuka. There was a flashing moment of understanding, as the shield-bearer of the Zan Qarth seemed to look straight at him. Could it be that after all . . . ?

He pushed the thought aside.

He touched the second trigger.

"My Qarth, leave this place now!" Hulagar hissed.

Jubadi looked back at him, the banner kicking and swirling as flames raced up its silken folds.

"There is something terrible about this place," Jubadi said softly. "I miss the steppes of home."

Hulagar looked away from him, and from the corner of his eye he saw something.

What?

A thin puff of smoke. A gunshot? Why? It was so far away.

Hulagar felt his heart tighten, as if it had frozen. And then it thumped hard. Once, twice.

"Jubadi!"

Hulagar turned. The world was going impossibly slowly. He stepped forward, moving up behind Jubadi. Rushing to raise the shield up behind his Qar Qarth.

He felt as if his heart were about to explode, as it thumped again and then once more.

Jubadi was looking straight into his eyes, a curious look, the slightest of quizzical smiles ... the eyes suddenly went wide with astonishment.

"No!"

Even as Hulagar reached out, raising the shield up across Jubadi's back, he saw the hole, ever so small, appear in the middle of his friend's back. A ghostly shower of blood exploded out of Jubadi's chest, spraying into the still burning banner.

"No!"

Jubadi started to turn. His features were strange, as if already going into dust and darkness. The eyes held on him.

"Hulagar?" It was a drawn-out whisper.

The shield fell, as if drawn into the earth. It struck the ground and rolled slowly down the slope. Hulagar reached out, grabbing his friend who refused to fall.

He felt the blood pulsing out of Jubadi, each contraction of the heart spraying out its dying, diminishing stream.

Hulagar pulled him in tight, arms around him.

"I just burned the banner of my own funeral," Jubadi whispered, as if he were the victim of a paradox beyond his understanding.

"My Qarth."

"The dream," Jubadi sighed.

"Wait for me, my Qarth."

A thin smile crossed his features.

"These cattle, they are ..."

A shudder passed through him. With a sigh,

Jubadi's head cradled on Hulagar's shoulder. The shield-bearer raised his face to the everlasting sky and stood in silence.

Jubadi va Griska, Qar Qarth of the Merki Horde, was dead.

Hulagar stood alone, holding the body, feeling the last pulse of the heart slip away, the legs go limp, the final breath whispering on his cheek.

There was a moment of silence, as if the world had ended, as if Bugglaah had drawn her curtain across all present.

A single cry rose up, a high ululation of mourning, joined in an instant by another and another, until the cries of thousands thundered across the land.

Vuka came up, Tamuka behind him with his shield raised, the silent ones crowding round.

Hulagar looked into Vuka's eyes and saw the terror, the dread, the anxious gaze, as if another such bolt would appear to strike him down as well.

"Vuka va Jubadi, know that Bugglaah has gathered thy father," Hulagar said, his voice choked. "When the moon of mourning has passed, you shall be proclaimed Qar Qarth of the Merki Horde."

Vuka nodded, saying nothing.

"Tamuka Shield-Bearer, fulfill your duty. Get him to safety until we find the murderer."

Tamuka motioned for the silent ones to close in around the heir and lead him away. Vuka did not look back, nor even reach out to touch the body of his father. He was led away.

"There can be no time for mourning," Tamuka said, looking straight at Hulagar.

"There will be the moon of mourning!" Hulagar cried. "I rule until the heir is anointed, and the law is to be obeyed. The Horde will cease to move until then."

"That is why they did this!" Tamuka shouted, his voice barely heard above the wild screams of lamentation.

"When the mourning is done your Qar Qarth will have his vengeance, but not before. Now leave me."

Tamuka hesitated.

"I am sorry, my old friend," he whispered. Reaching out, he touched Hulagar on the shoulder.

"For me, or for the Merki?"

"For you," Tamuka replied.

Hulagar looked into his eyes, and there was a moment of wondering. Already he knew in his heart who had done this. But what of Tamuka?

The shield-bearer of the new Qar Qarth turned and walked away, barely noticing Muzta of the Tugars, who stood to one side, saying nothing.

Lifting up the body of his Qarth and cradling him in his arms, Hulagar turned and watched as the last of the flaming banner flickered away, the smoke curling to the everlasting sky.

The guard pulled back the canvas screen. The small chamber stank of powder, and also of death.

"We found it!"

He reached in, grabbing Yuri's body by the hands and pulling it out.

He felt a slight flicker of pain, as if stung by a thorn.

The cattle looked up at him with lifeless eyes, his features fixed in a curious smile. The warrior suddenly felt weak, light-headed. He sat down and looked over at the body again.

There was a ring on Yuri's finger, a thin needle projecting out of it.

The Merki started to scream, knowing what he had just done to himself.

The screams did not last for long.

*   *   *

"Raise the signal flag," Bullfinch said, looking over at the boy crouched alongside him in the pilothouse of the ironclad *Fredericksburg*.

He looked back down at the sealed orders that he had opened, as ordered, when the insane, blood-curdling screams had started on shore.

"Mr. Turgeyev."

"Aye, sir."

Bullfinch looked through the hatch down to the gun deck below, and broke into a smile.

"Pass the word to the crew. The ruler of the Merki is dead. Now let's start tossing some shells into their caterwauling hides."

Looking forward, he saw the three red pennants break out atop the *Novrod*, which was anchored several miles below Suzdal. The word would be flashed down the river, to a spot where the signal tower positioned above the mines could pick it up.

The sky was darkening, the red sun turning the scattering of clouds into scarlet plumes of light.

The only sound was the soft puffing of the engine up forward as it vented off some steam. He could sense their tension, their wondering why he had waited here, thirty miles beyond Novrod.

He heard the clattering of the telegraph key and felt his heart tighten up. He waited.

The door to the telegraphers' room opened and he heard the boy moving down the length of the car, the door opening behind him. The boy handed him a slip of paper.

He opened it.

He stood looking at the paper for a long moment, then folded it up. He stepped back into the car.

They had been waiting patiently, none knowing why he had asked that the train stop here.

"I just got a signal from Bullfinch's ships on the Neiper," Andrew said quietly.

He looked back down at the paper again.

"Three red flgs flying from the *Fredericksburg*."

He looked back up and saw their quizzical gazes.

"Jubadi, Qar Qarth of the Merki, has been killed by a sniper before the gates of Suzdal."

There was an uneasy stirring.

"It means," Andrew said, his voice sharp and filled with a cold power, "that for the next thirty days all offensive operations of the Merki will cease until their mourning is finished. We will have the time to get the line at Kev ready, we will have the time to prepare."

"Glory hallelujah," Kal sighed.

Andrew nodded, unable to say more.

Casmar stood up.

"Yuri did it?"

"It was Yuri."

"And?"

"He is most likely dead. He told me what he would do. There was no hope for him of escaping, he knew that when he volunteered." Andrew paused. "When I volunteered him for it."

"May he find rest," Casmar said, making the sign of blessing.

"The outcast saved us," Kal said, shaking his head ruefully. Coming to his feet, he walked over to Andrew and took his hand.

"*You* saved us, as well."

"No, I just gave us a little more time," Andrew replied softly. "No, it was Hans, all those boys that we lost, our own people, those yet to die. They are the ones who saved us, who will save us."

He hesitated.

"And Yuri . . . he found some peace, and gave us one final chance."

He looked around at the group.

"Tell the engineer to get us going," he said.

He wanted to say more, to tell them what was coming. That they had thirty days now, but that when the Merki came on again it would be for vengeance as well. He thought of Yuri's letter, laying out his reasons, his advice, and what to expect. Vuka would be unpredictable, but then again Vuka most likely would be the least of their worries.

"Excuse me," he whispered, and turned to step back out onto the platform. He didn't even hear the excited cries, or notice the instant lifting of their spirits, the return of their belief that they might somehow survive after all. Their euphoria was like that of a drowning man who finds a raft in the middle of the ocean. There is the moment of rejoicing, until the reality sinks in that one has most likely traded the swift death of drowning for the slow one of starvation. But for the moment, their spirits had returned.

Andrew wanted to say more, yet the words would not come. How could he also say that he had deliberately set out to kill someone? War had always been impersonal, killing in the heat of battle, that is how it had always been. But this was different.

Since the moment he had first met Yuri the plan had started to form, coming into clear light the morning he had heard of Hans's death. Even as the evacuation plan, which had always lingered in the back of his mind, had formed into reality, he knew there would not be enough time. It had always been time, ever since the day they had first decided to stand against the Tugars. There was never enough time for all that needed to be done.

He had worked all of it out in such detail, sitting with Yuri and learning how they thought, planning the murder out in every detail.

And it had worked.

Andrew looked down at the letter from Yuri.

I know I have been used by all sides, especially by you to save my own people who would kill me. In doing this, I guarantee the death of the only two I still love within this heart of stone. I know I am used by Tamuka as well, for in either course I suspect I am merely his tool.

Yet I forgive you, Andrew Lawrence Keane.

Andrew crumpled the letter up and put it back into his pocket.

He had committed a cold, calculated killing of his rival. It mattered not that Jubadi had planned the same for him. Yuri had never confessed to that but Andrew knew, having realized it in the story about a pet who had killed a Qarth to save his family.

There should be no remorse, no tinge of guilt now. It was a war of survival for both races. If he had not done this, if Yuri had not sacrificed himself for a people who despised him, in ten days the Merki would have been through the White Hills, slaughtering the refugees by the hundreds of thousands.

Yuri had saved the Rus, all the people, by this one assassination.

But Andrew did not have to like it.

The train lurched beneath him, and he grabbed hold of the railing.

Last train out of Rus.

Behind him the land was empty, a ghostly vista, an entire people gone into exile.

Will we ever come back, he wondered, or is this the beginning of an exodus that will take us around the entire world? It was hard to imagine that they could ever fight their way back.

Damn it, they *had* to come back. This was their land, their dream, their homes. Suzdal was theirs. If it took an entire generation, they would be back. He might die, they all might die in the months to come, but somehow some of them would survive and return until they had finally won.

The train started to pick up speed as it crested over the low hill. The tiny station was behind them now, the building and a pile of hay alongside of it burning brightly to match the colors of the evening sky. As the car reached the crest, Andrew had a brief, final view: the low hills lining the Neiper standing out on the distant horizon, the lush fertile fields silent, the villages silent, the church bells, which had for so long toiled the ending of the day, silent.

"Somehow, we'll come back."

He looked over at Kathleen as she came out the door and leaned against the railing, Maddie resting against her shoulder fast asleep. Together, they watched their land as it seemed to drift away.

"You did what you had to do." Her free hand slipped around his waist.

"It doesn't mean I have to like it."

"I wouldn't love you if you did."

He looked down at her, and for the first time since he had lost Hans, a smile lit his face.

The engineer played out a sad, melodious song on the whistle, as if calling a final farewell, and the last train out of Rus continued down the slope, racing eastward into the gathering night.

ABOUT THE AUTHOR

William Forstchen, born in 1950, was raised in New Jersey but has spent most of his life in Maine. Having worked for more than a decade as a history teacher, an education consultant on creative writing, and a Living History reenactor of the Civil War period, Bill is now a graduate student in military history at Purdue University in Indiana. *Rally Cry* the first volume in The Lost Regiment series, was published by ROC Books in 1990.

When not writing or studying, Bill devotes his time to the promotion of the peaceful exploration of space or to one of his numerous hobbies, which include iceboating (a challenge in Indiana), scuba diving (an even greater challenge in Indiana), and pinball machines.

If you and/or a friend would like to receive the *ROC Advance*, a bimonthly newsletter featuring all the newest and hottest ROC books and authors, on a complimentary basis, please fill out this form and return it to:

ROC Books/Penguin USA
375 Hudson Street
New York, NY 10014

Your Address
Name _____
Street _____ Apt. # _____
City _____ State _____ Zip _____

Friend's Address
Name _____
Street _____ Apt. # _____
City _____ State _____ Zip _____